Song

A Novel of Tarzan and La

Jim Malachowski

BY

Jim Malachowski

Seti Press
Sarasota, Florida

Jim Malachowski/Seti Press
songofopar@gmail.com

Song of Opar/Jim Malachowski — First Edition May 2018
First Printing Limited to 100 copies

ISBN 978-1-387-64363-9

Book Design by Jim Malachowski

Cover Design by Jim Malachowski

Interior Photography and Design by Jim Malachowski

Interior Costume Design by Jim Malachowski

*This book is dedicated to the following ladies
in my life —*

*My sister, Rosemary, who bought me countless
comic books —*

*My sister, Teresa, who bought me my first
ERB novel —*

*My wonderful wife Doro, who has
indulged me with a fine collection
of ERB novels —*

Author's Note

I had much assistance in writing this novel. I thank my wonderful wife Doro, for enduring the early drafts of my work. She offered an endless amount of advice during the development of the story.

Thanks to Jim Sullos, President of Edgar Rice Burroughs, Inc., for granting me permission to write and publish this novel.

Special thanks to Gary A. Buckingham for his expert editing. And excellent advice.

Thanks to Judy Krenkle and Dr. James V. Swanson who spent countless hours reading and critiquing.

Thanks to all the long-suffering models who put up with me in the photographic sessions for this novel. All the images were shot in GW Burns' studio in Sarasota. The costumes, sets, image conversion and artwork are of my imagination and design.

Thank you again, Ladies and Gentlemen:

Maria as La

Renee as Mery and Nedjam

Amy as Ayesha

Shana as Kiya

Helen as Oah

Caroline as May-at

GW as a Sacrifice

Morris as Waziri

CHAPTER INDEX

Illustrations

A – Temple
B – La's Private Pool
C – Private Temple
D – Agricultural Area
E – Livestock Area
F – Huts of Neteru
G – Dormatories

H – Wealthy Homes
I – Wall Opening
Note:Map not Proportional
Opar Area – 1/4 X 1 mile
Temple Area – 300' x 60'

Song of Opar

BY

Jim Malachowski

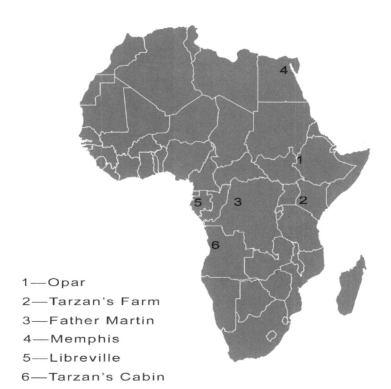

1—Opar
2—Tarzan's Farm
3—Father Martin
4—Memphis
5—Libreville
6—Tarzan's Cabin

"Words have a magical power. They can either bring the greatest happiness or the deepest despair."
Sigmund Freud

CHAPTER ONE — THE NILE

As every schoolboy knows, the Nile River is the second longest river on our planet – second only to the Amazon and then only by a hundred miles or so. It is also known that the Nile flows from south to north and eventually ends up, after branching several times in the Delta of Northern Egypt, into the Mediterranean Sea.

What is not known is precisely where the river begins, and the question has been asked for centuries why it flows North. The answer as to why is quite simple — the great Rift Valley is higher in elevation than land on the way to the Mediterranean.

John Hanning Speke came close to identifying the source of the Nile as Lake Victoria in 1858.

Hapi was the god of the Nile in ancient Egyptian religion. Hapi was typically depicted as a unisex being with a large belly and pendulous breasts, which represented the rich harvest the Nile's inundation provided. He was painted wearing a loincloth and ceremonial false beard of a pharaoh and god and was shown with green or blue skin, representing the Nile water.

The ancient Egyptians believed that Hapi controlled the creation and the rise and fall of the Nile. He was believed to live in a cavern beneath the cataracts of the Nile near Aswan. The water around the cataracts was very rough and dangerous to boats, as it boiled and flowed around the huge boulders in the river.

The cult of Hapi was mainly located at the First Cataract on Elephantine Island. His priests were involved in rituals to ensure the steady levels of flow required for the annual flood. On Elephantine Island, the official nilometer would carefully measure the level of the Nile to predict the amount of water for crops. Egypt's farmers were taxed using a projection of potential crop size based upon water levels measured at the nilometer.

The White Nile originated deep in the Nyungwe Forest of Rwanda rather than Lake Victoria, as the river's original explorer John Hanning Speke declared in 1858. However, Lake Victoria officially remains a principal source of water for the Nile. When the White Nile reaches Khartoum in the Sudan, it joins the Blue Nile, which originates in the Ethiopian mountains.

The flooding of the Nile, known as the inundation, was caused by torrential rain in the Simien Mountains of Ethiopia. It carried millions of tons of rich topsoil which it gradually deposited along the journey to the Mediterranean. This annual event took place between June and September. In some places, the water would rise thirty feet. When the present Aswan Dam was constructed in the 1960's, the inundation no longer happened.

This topsoil allowed the farmers of Egypt to have the most bountiful harvests in the Middle East. The vegetables and a seemingly endless supply of protein, in the form of fish from the Nile, enabled people to develop their mental capacity earlier than many contemporaries in most other countries. A good example was while Egypt was engineering and building the pyramids, the inhabitants of Europe still were chasing rabbits with sticks.

The Sudd is located in southern Sudan. Sudd is an Arabic word which means barrier. It is the world's largest swamp averaging twelve thousand square miles. During the rainy season, it may extend to over fifty thousand square miles. The White Nile carries topsoil and dumps it into the Sudd. The Sudd acts as an immense retention pond: silt, in the form of topsoil, is carried from the Simien Mountains and is layered six miles deep in the Sudd.

For thousands of years, the Sudd was an impenetrable barrier to navigation along the Nile. It contained a seemingly endless amount of vegetation, including probably the largest number of papyrus plants in Africa. From the time the Sudd was first discovered through today, it has been a natural habitat for mosquitoes, with their ability to carry and inflict malaria in humans. The mosquitoes caused untold suffering to all those who tried to cross the Sudd, to either explore Africa or to search for the source of the Nile.

In 61 CE, the Roman Emperor Nero sent a party of soldiers to explore the interior of Africa. This was the first recorded attempt to cross the Sudd. The military party was not able to get beyond the Sudd and marked the limit of Roman penetration into equatorial Africa. For the same reasons, in later times, the search for the source of the Nile was particularly difficult. It eventually involved overland expeditions from the central African coast, thus avoiding travel through the Sudd.

The Nile was the great highway which connected cities in the long country of Kmt, as Egypt was called by the ancient Egyptians. River navigation was easy. The current always ran from south to north, and the prevailing wind was the opposite coming off the Mediterranean, which the Egyptians called the Great Green. The river was wide and except for the time of the inundation, a relatively easy way to travel. If you were traveling south to north, the current would power your journey. If you were traveling north to south, a sail was used to push the boat.

Vast stands of papyrus hugged the shore and provided a home for the many and varied species of birds, snakes, and mammals of all sizes. The Nile River was also home to the feared Nile Crocodile which effortlessly killed many people daily, along with an innumerable amount of domestic animals. The Nile Crocodile was a fearsome creature, up to 18 feet in length and fifteen hundred pounds. The crocodile grabbed his unfortunate victims by a leg or arm and dragged them to the bottom of the river. The victims would be drowned and stored for later consumption in the roots of the vegetation. The only natural enemy of the crocodile was the hippopotamus. The hippopotamus was a serious threat to any boat. If trying to defend her young, the female hippopotamus would attack or overturn boats with relative ease. The bite of a hippopotamus was strong enough to tear even the largest crocodile in half.

3

Jim Malachowski

The hippopotamus was a favorite hunting target of the Egyptian nobles, even Pharaohs. They hunted with spears and bows in the reeds and papyrus groves. Legend has it that a First Dynasty Pharaoh was killed by a hippopotamus during a hunt.

CHAPTER TWO — TRAVELS TO MEMPHIS

The sacred white Ibis gracefully lifted from the Nile. Barely disturbing the still water, as it rose spreading its great wings. As Menkhaf watched, he smiled believing it was a good omen, since the bird crossed the river in front of the dhow signifying good luck. The sun had just made its appearance in the cobalt blue sky. Most of the people who lived near the river were still sleeping, and the only sound was the occasional soft moo of a cow. The trip would be effortless. It was a matter of navigating away from sandbars, letting the current carry the boat northward to Memphis, capital of Kmt. The two men who crewed the boat were more than enough for the easy trip.

Menkhaf, his mistress, Melit and the crew would sail the dhow north from Aswan to Memphis, boarding an hour after the sun had risen. The light breeze was still cool, as Melit was boarding the boat and complained, "Menkhaf, why do we have to start so early? It is still cold, and I am not used to getting up at this hour." Menkhaf just smiled in answer to her comments and bade her sit down on two piles of cushions. One of the men delivered a basket which Menkhaf's mother had prepared by the kitchen staff. It consisted of containers of beer and bread, which had just been baked that morning along with some choice pieces of roast goose wrapped in lettuce.

After the morning meal had been enjoyed, Melit began asking the same questions she had been asking since Menkhaf had told her she would be accompanying him to Memphis. She was one of Menkhaf's six concubines, and although he did not want her to know, she was his favorite.

For all her bold talk, Melit was insecure. Menkhaf had had enough concubines over the years, that he recognized the common thread of insecurity which he had seen in many other women. Melit began by asking, "Do I have enough clothes and sandals? Do I even have the right clothes? Will your friend Henenu and his wife like me? You are not going to leave me by myself while you are in a lot of silly meetings, are you?"

After this barrage of questions, Melit returned to her favorite topic asking, "Are you sure we will have enough time for shopping? Some of the other ladies in the harem have told me the bazaars of the capital are large and wonderful. Please make sure we have enough time for me to shop properly."

Menkhaf was enjoying the quiet and the cool breezes on the second morning of the three-day journey to Memphis to meet with Pharaoh. Melit was still indulging in the comfort of their bed, and he appreciated a break from her seemingly endless chatter.

The previous evening, the crew had brought the dhow to shore for a dinner which they prepared. One of the men brought a cast net and was able to catch eight or ten tender Nile perch, which they cooked on a small fire. The rest of the meal was lettuce and vegetables which had been brought with them. The meal was followed by a peaceful night's sleep on the boat. The crew however preferred to sleep on the shore near the fire. The men took turns staying awake, guarding the boat.

They made excellent time, covering about one-third of the trip's distance the first day, despite leaving after sunrise. They planned to reach Memphis the following day in late afternoon, just in time to refresh themselves, before being honored guests for dinner.

Menkhaf was the eldest son of four children. He was a tall and slender man who was living his 22nd summer. He was enjoying this break from his many varied and demanding duties in the service of his father. Upon his father's death, Menkhaf would be the fifth generation to rule Kmt's southernmost Nome (region or state) — Aswan. Under the present Pharaoh, the forty-two Nomarchs had been steadily and quietly usurping the authority that a strong Pharaoh would never have allowed. The usual quibbling between nomarchs had given way to open hostilities and had yet to be addressed by Pharaoh Pepi II, nor would it ever be during his long reign.

For the second time since leaving Aswan, Menkhaf speculated on why Pharaoh had summoned him. There did not seem to be any threats to Kmt especially coming from the south. The Kushites, who shared Kmt's southern border were always a reason for concern, but not from a military standpoint. They were the source of Kmt's gold which they grudgingly paid to Pharaoh as a thinly veiled form of blackmail. The gold kept Pharaoh from invading and taking over Kush[1]. Periodically when the annual tribute was late, or the Kushites seemed to have forgotten, Pharaoh would send in several hundred troops to remind the Kushites of their obligations to him.

The Kushites were considered the best archers in the region and their skill in producing bows and arrows was unsurpassed. Unfortunately for them, they were not an equal adversary to Kmt. They were made up of many squabbling tribes, and it would be centuries before they would unite into a country and throw off the yoke of Pharaoh's demands. Fifteen hundred years later, Kmt would be ruled by Kushites.

Menkhaf dismissed the Kushites as not being the reason for the meeting because his father had spies among the Kush rulers and received reports on a regular basis. His father used this internal division to his advantage in negotiations and business dealings with the Kushites.

Menkhaf was looking forward to seeing his father's friend, Henenu. He had been informed in a letter that Henenu had also been invited to the meeting with Pharaoh. Menkhaf had written back to Henenu and arranged a dinner with him the night before the meeting. Henenu and his wife

---

[1] This is Biblical Kush, roughly modern Sudan. Hindu Kush Mountains of Asia are unrelated.

Ikhernofret had extended the hospitality of their waterfront house for the duration of Menkhaf and Melit's stay in Memphis. It would be good to see his father's friend again, and they would enjoy lavish rooms and meals in his Memphis home. Perhaps they would be given some insight into the reason for the audience. It would also be good to hear all the court intrigue and gossip. As a second mission, his father had given him detailed instructions on what information he should try to ferret out in the capital about Pharaoh's current governing policies or anything else he could use to his advantage.

Memphis was the primary city in Aneb-Hetch, the first Nome of Lower Egypt, and was the capital. It was located about 15 miles south of modern Cairo and was a thriving port and trading town which served ships from all locations on the Mediterranean. Memphis remained the most significant city in Lower Egypt until the rise of Alexandria centuries later.

As Henenu looked out at the Nile, he was refreshed by the cool breeze that came from the water helping to cool the palace. Henenu was a deputy of the Vizier, the most important man in the country after Pharaoh. He was the person who saw that Pharaoh's orders and wishes were carried out, plus he was Pharaoh's confidant. While he was not personally enthusiastic about how Pepi II ran or failed to run the country, he also knew when to keep his thoughts to himself.

A servant announced the arrival of Menkhaf and Melit. Henenu was more curious about Melit than seeing Menkhaf again. He had a somewhat roving eye toward the ladies, and he was clearly more interested in Melit. She was a tall and slender woman of about nineteen, dressed in a modest linen sheath with elegant gold trimmed sandals. Henenu's interest in Melit faded a bit when his wife joined the group. She was a portly woman in her forties. Despite the expensive, lovely dress and makeup, she still gave off a distinctly frumpy appearance. Henenu's marriage had been a marriage of convenience. His wife's family were wealthy merchants and owned extensive amounts of property. Much of their holdings were in the commercial port area. They had enough connections in Pharaoh's court allowing an ambitious young man the opportunities he would otherwise not have had.

Menkhaf and Melit talked about the rigors of the trip north and their brief tour of the area around the harbor of Memphis. They had been escorted by guides, and security Henenu had provided.

After dinner Henenu and Menkhaf retired to the balcony to enjoy a private conversation and the cool night air. The fine wine from dinner had done its job, and both men spoke at great length of what was on their minds about the meeting with Pharaoh. Henenu shocked Menkhaf when he openly speculated about what "the old fool" wanted this time. Menkhaf was about to get a lesson in capital politics, meaning there were two schools of thought on Pharaoh. One opinion was he was letting Egypt slide into ruin with his lack of action and absence of interest in the good of the country. The other view being he was a great leader and did not deserve the criticism he was being given.

Henenu stated his fear that Pepi II wanted another trade expedition into the continent's interior. They were expensive, a logistic nightmare, costing many lives and were not worth the effort.

"Plus," he continued, "I cannot understand Pepi's fascination with those damned pygmies. He has had them brought back since he was a child. The only thing that they do is amuse Pharaoh. They are messy creatures that have to be cleaned up after and are hated by Pharaoh's household staff. Also, they are very hard to capture." Henenu's final thoughts on this subject were delivered with somewhat of a smirk, "There is something strange about a grown man's fascination with small men."

"I had hoped," said Henenu, "that Pepi II would finally do something about those crazy sun worshipers in Heliopolis. For centuries, we have been worshiping the same gods, and they have been good to us. But these Sun Priests are too ambitious for my liking. I would not be surprised if they were to set up their own King and compete with the rightful Pharaoh. There are also rumors they are killing members of their sect and vocal outsiders who dare to speak against them. Next thing you know, they will be bringing back human sacrifice, as it was practiced by our ancient ancestors. Pepi II should send in a few hundred soldiers and wipe out these dangerous people and their crazy ideas."

This was the first time Menkhaf had heard about the sun worshipers. Their temples and influence were concentrated in the capital and the delta area of Kmt. It was disquieting, the idea of another competing religion rising in the country. The priests of the temples of Ptah were openly hostile toward these new sun worshipers. The Ptah priests were major landowners and in possession of much political power, especially with Pharaoh.

After hours of conversation and endless speculation, it was decided to wait until their meeting to find out what Pharaoh wanted. It would seem that Pharaoh was keeping his thoughts to himself until morning. With any luck, if the ideas were too outlandish, hopefully, Henenu would be able to change Pharaoh's mind.

Chapter Three — Meeting with Pharaoh

Both Henenu and Menkhaf hoped it was going to be a short meeting. The sun had already risen over the horizon several hours ago, and Pharaoh had still not joined the two men. He was known for being late and ill-prepared for meetings. Fortunately, the room was located deep enough in the palace that the morning sun had not made it unbearably hot yet.

Three scribes entered and stood behind the chairs which had been set up in the meeting room. Their function was to write down every word uttered. The various conversations would later be combined by a master scribe into one document. Several copies would be carefully written on papyrus and stored under different categories in the palace archives.

Pepi II was the fifth of six pharaohs making up the Sixth Dynasty of ancient Egypt. The Sixth Dynasty began in 2282 BCE and ended in 2117 BCE.

Pharaoh entered the room silently as his linen shoes did not betray his presence. He was a short heavy man who had a slight wobble when he walked. His snowy white hair spoke of his age and emphasized his longevity. Pepi II was 74 years old and in his 68th year of rule. Despite this fact, he would rule for another twenty-six years. Most Pharaohs would reign for an average of fifteen to twenty years.

Pepi II told the men to be seated, and he began. "I do not have time for a long meeting with a lot of explanations, so here are my wishes and as much background information as you need to know." He looked at Menkhaf and said, "Your father and grandfather helped Kmt, and me, with exploration and trade missions into the mysterious jungles many days march from the southern border of Kmt. It is time for you to earn your generous salary, only this time with a different agenda."

"What is the agenda?" Pharaoh continued, "The agenda is gold," Pepi II answered his own question emphatically. "Our trade relationship with Kush is becoming unstable. Each year they are producing less and less of the yellow metal for tribute. Our trade partners around the shores of the Great Green (the Mediterranean) are demanding the precious metal for payment since their crops have been sufficient to feed their people. Consequently, they do not want our grain and produce. They want gold."

"You men are to establish a colony outside of Kmt to find and process gold and transport it back to the treasury here in Memphis twice a year. You will determine how many mining towns there will be and with the aid of some traitors from Kush you will explore locations for those colonies. These settlements are not to be public knowledge. They are to be secured with our troops. You are to be extremely careful that these damnable sun worshipers are excluded from knowledge of my plans. It is bad enough that we have to put up with them in Heliopolis and Memphis. I do not want them establishing a foothold for their crazy religion in the south of Kmt."

Pepi II continued, "You are to plan this project for me and present details in seven days. Do not fail! I am giving you a free hand in how this is done, but I want this mining operation and the production of gold to be accomplished as soon as possible. You will come back to me with both plans and a timetable for the first shipment of gold next week. If I have made everything clear, and there are no questions, you are dismissed. Scribes will leave the room now." As the three young men silently gathered their pens, ink and papyrus rolls and left, Pharaoh signaled with his eyes for the two men to remain.

"I did not want the scribes recording my deep concern for this project and the need for the gold. Projections for the amount of gold needed next year will be more than the Kushites will produce. I will say again: this mining operation must be functioning and productive within a year."

As soon as he voiced the question, Menkhaf knew he had exposed his inexperience when he asked, "Does Pharaoh have any names in mind for these cities?" Pharaoh snapped back with, "I want them called complete and productive — understood?" Menkhaf felt his face redden and he dared not look at Henenu, afraid of what he would see.

Pepi II stood, turned on his heel and exited the room without another word.

CHAPTER FOUR — THE PLAN

S even days later, Pharaoh entered the room and glanced about the long glistening table. With his eyes, he made contact with all five people whom he saw standing before him. "Sit down, and we can get started this morning." Henenu and Menkhaf shared a brief glance and both thought of the two hours they had been waiting for Pharaoh to arrive for the meeting, and how the room was beginning to become uncomfortably warm.

The other invited members were Piye a military general, and close confidant in Pharaoh's inner circle, and Apries, the chief architect for the court highly trusted by Pharaoh. Lastly, Thuthy, First Prophet of Ptah and Overseer of the Treasury, so that Pepi II could guarantee the God's blessing.

After a brief pause, Pepi II said, "I have reviewed everyone's thoughts and proposals on their responsibilities for this undertaking." Again, Pepi II looked at all the attendees and gave the message, "The responsibility for success rests with you five men."

"We will begin with Thuthy for his plan." Thr priest was a polished speaker and spoke eloquently about his intercessional role in guaranteeing

15

the success of the project. What he failed to mention was that in return for Ptah's blessing, the temples in the country would receive ten percent of the treasure generated by the expedition – every year. The lion's share of the tithing would end up in Thuthy's purse and some of the lesser leaders of the Temple. Thuthy added one more item saying, "We will, of course, provide priests for the expedition. They will stay in the new cities as long as they are needed to look after the spiritual well-being of the people."

The ancient Egyptians were resurrectionists. Their ideology centered on the tenet that at death, and 'beautification,' the embalmed body would rise again in the afterlife. It was for this reason, during its long history, Kmt never had colonies outside its borders. The fear was if a person died outside Kmt, his body could not be brought back in time for beautification, as mummification was called. He would have no chance of rising again in the afterlife. This one simple statement would have ramifications into the distant future. It would bend and shape the inhabitants of the new cities into people that no one in Egypt would recognize.

In private discussions with Pepi II several days ago, Thuthy had told Pharaoh about his religious concerns about an established colony outside the country's border. Pepi II had cast a steely-eyed gaze upon him, and said, "Make it happen. I am donating a large amount of the gold to the temple." His gaze deepened, and he whispered, "Some of which I feel certain will find its way into your treasury." With a face quickly reddening, Pharaoh continued, "Find a loop-hole, a dispensation, find something. And find it now!" Thuthy's face had turned an ashen-white when Pepi II had leaned close and whispered the threat. It was a weak and stuttering voice, that answered, "Rest assured Majesty, I will find a religious exception that will allow this to happen as you wish." Pepi II smiled and stated very clearly, "Nothing will stop this plan!"

One of the people who came on the trip south, unnoticed, was an older woman named Soma. The vast majority of members of the expedition had no idea who she was or what she did. Soma and Henenu both preferred her to be just another female worker on the ship. Thuthy and his son, Neith, knew of Soma and her disciples. He was quietly elated she would be on the voyage. Her skills would be needed when the new religion was introduced, hopefully during the lifetime of Neith.

Henenu knew Soma from her work in the temple, and her work with the sick and injured. She was what we would call today a shaman, a medicine woman, a healer, an interpreter of dreams. She and her students were the emergency doctors and pharmacists of ancient Kmt. She liked the gold the rich gave her for pleasing them.

Soma's experience would be invaluable to the colonies. She could set broken bones, stop bleeding and suture deep wounds from work accidents or animal attacks. She knew remedies for common ailments and could function as a midwife.

Soma had been a member of one of Pepi's expeditions into the interior of Africa when his main objective had been finding male pygmies. Others had loftier goals and sought wood for incense, medicinal trees and shrubs that could be brought back and planted locally. Temple priests were interested in hallucinogenic drugs used to enhance religious thought and worship. The rich were looking for and would pay heavily for recreational drugs such as khat and psychedelic iboga. Iboga was a shrub native to West-Central Africa whose alkaloid containing root bark was chewed or brewed into a tea. It induced hallucinations in large concentrated doses.

An iboga experience could take several directions. Larger amounts led to vivid hallucinogenic visual effects, a dream-like state that occurred during total consciousness, and possibly last several hours. As the effects dissipated, there followed an experience where memories and past traumas were lived again as an out of body perspective.

Soma saw herself as a healer. She derived great satisfaction from helping the sick and injured. Her pharmacy knowledge and expertise were always given free. Her skills in assisting in a difficult birth or a broken limb were always given likewise at no charge.

Soma had trained many women and a few men as healers, so she felt comfortable in joining the expedition. She looked forward to being able to use her skills full time and to be able to explore the jungles of central Africa for new medicines and drugs.

The Daughters of Soma would exist and prosper well into the twentieth century. The women who carried on this service were almost always named Soma and would serve the rich for gold and everyone else as a service.

After Thuthy had concluded his remarks, Pepi II thanked him and assured him that the temples would be generously rewarded for Ptah's love and protection.

Pharaoh motioned to Piye and told the group, "I am very pleased with Piye's well-thought-out plans for his part of the expedition." Piye would be in charge of the soldiers who would provide security, and since boats that would be used for transport were within the military jurisdiction, he would provide them as well. Men to work the sails (for the trip south) and rowers (for the return trip) would also be secured. Piye would buy slaves from Kush, who would begin the work of mining and provide labor for whatever building was needed for the safety of the workers and administrators.

Since many large ships would be constructed for the transport of troops, workers, building material and food, much wood was needed from Kush. The ships were constructed of planks and were "sewn" together by ropes inserted in drilled holes – as iron nails were unknown. Water would cause the ropes and wood to swell, and they would become watertight. Also, a ship could be taken apart if portage was needed, such as to avoid dangerous rocks and currents. The design of large wooden ships was the same as papyrus boats. They had a flat bottom and no keel. In many cases, the single mast and sail were located and fastened in the gunwale.

Piye provided guidelines for the type of boats needed to transport gold back to Memphis. The army would provide scouts who had some experience with the jungles found in the southern environs of Kush. Kushites would help select sites for the mines. Pepi II was pleased with the plans as presented by Piye and next turned his attention to the presentation of Apries.

Apries was by far the oldest and most learned of the group. He was a superb administrator and had great skills in higher math and technical writing. Because of his age, he was not expected to join the expedition but would select one of his advanced apprentices for the building tasks.

"Majesty" he began, "there are many more variables that we do not know about the site location and the kind of buildings we will need. It will be determined how much protection the workers and administrators will require. The answers to these and many more questions will not be apparent until we see where we are going to locate the new cities. I, therefore, offer the services of my oldest son Nebre, who is my most experienced and skilled architect. He has the training and understanding to know the problems the expedition will be facing, and how best to provide safe habitat and work structures. Nebre will be carrying my plans for basic structures which he can easily adapt as needed. He will use slaves for mining and all other work. He has some experience with metallurgy and will see to the task of getting the gold from the cities back to Memphis."

Menkhaf would be responsible for getting the expedition from Memphis to the province of his father – a distance of almost two hundred leagues (almost 700 miles). He would be in charge of food, including fresh vegetables, acquiring the tools and materials they would need, locating rest areas and nightly sleeping locations. He would also be responsible for getting relief workers for the boats.

Menkhaf was pleased. His father's role would be extracting from the Kushites whatever else would be needed. Menkhaf's father had already bribed the right people into providing preliminary mining locations and the men to begin the mining work as soon as the expeditions arrived. Menkhaf thought he would help his father get the expedition moving through Kush. He had thought the provisioning of men and ships, as an aide to his father, would end his duties with this expedition.

Pepi II looked at Menkhaf and said "Menkhaf, I am choosing to appoint you as the Nomarch of the Nome which will encompass all the gold mining cities. You will be in charge of finding mine sites and providing safety and security to the administrators and workers. You will be in total charge. This effort will be the most exacting and time-consuming task that anyone at this table will have because it will be ongoing. The fate of the expedition and probably the fate of Kmt will rest in your hands."

Menkhaf felt the same cold feeling in his stomach he had experienced during the end of the first meeting with Pharaoh, as he felt the weight and gravity of his part in the expedition become a reality.

At this point, waiters began to appear carrying large containers of food to be enjoyed. The air was filled with the steam that rose from the bowls, and the fragrance of the different dishes was a great treat. Servants in a steady stream carried trays of freshly baked bread, lettuce and onions with olive oil, lentils cooked in broth, grilled onions and the main course of a roast of beef. For dessert, the servers presented small date cakes covered with honey and beer made from barley. The choice of beef for the main course showed Pharaoh's pleasure with the work of the committee. Beef cattle were not plentiful in Egypt and their meat only occasionally enjoyed by the very wealthy.

The meal signified the beginning of the end of the formal meeting. Pharaoh said. "I am pleased that everyone has presented good plans for my dream. I am sure we will be successful. As the weeks go by I will be speaking with you individually about additional details that I require."

Everyone at the table eyed the wonderful and tasty dishes that had been prepared and were being served, all except for Menkhaf, who had lost his appetite.

Pharaoh made one last statement, "You will all notice there was only one scribe in this meeting and he is my personal scribe. Everything to do with this plan and this meeting is a state secret. Revealing this plan will bring a death sentence. There will be no speaking of this to anyone. The only records of this expedition will be kept by my scribe. There will be no other public records of this project." Heads nodded in acceptance of the grave consequences that no one wanted.

The season of Shemu was chosen for the expedition to leave Memphis for central Africa. Shemu was known as the season of harvesting of crops. It corresponded to February to May, when the Nile was at its lowest and the current the slowest. Also, of great importance, was any large boulders or other navigational obstructions would be visible.

As evening descended, Pharaoh Pepi II visited the temple of Ptah. His visits were becoming more and more frequent as his inability to govern increased. His litter was met at the entrance by two senior priests. There was a private entrance into a large hypostyle hall, dimly lit by long narrow windows, known as clerestories. These openings were located very high on the walls and provided hazy light.

As Pharaoh and his companions walked deep into the temple, the rooms became progressively darker. Finally, they reached the last room – the holy of holies. The priests left Pharaoh at the entrance to the sacred room and took up positions outside.

The Egyptians believed that Ptah lived in the holy of holies. Pepi II began by asking Ptah for his blessing for the expedition to the south. He reminded Ptah that for his blessing and support, the temple would be greatly rewarded with a large share of the gold.

He then asked for assistance with the coming inundation of the Nile. He had been making this same request daily, for the last several years. If the inundation did not return to its previous level, there was the strong possibility that Kmt would cease to exist.

For several years, inundations had been only half of what was needed for crop irrigation. Many of the planners in the government had expressed concern that without a return to usual levels of flooding, there would not be enough crops to feed the people and animals. If the water level of the Nile kept dropping, the population of fish the common people relied upon for protein would be greatly reduced, and many would go hungry and thirsty. And die.

Pepy's tone of voice addressing the god indicated his inner desperation.

Pepi II had not told the men during the meal that for the past several years the Nile had not risen high enough to produce the bumper crops of the past. Hence, there was not an excess of vegetables and grain to trade around the Mediterranean. The truth was, there were barely enough crops being grown to feed the people and animals of Kmt in the north.

Pepi II was inwardly worried because the vegetables served at the luncheon had not been grown in the area. They had been transported by boat from Waset, several hundred miles to the south, where the drought was a bit less severe.

Pepi II also did not tell the meeting attendees that several of the nomarchs were being compensated by him quietly, for their loyalty to him and to maintain peace between rival nomes. This bribery was beginning to become public knowledge, and the nomarchs were demanding larger amounts each year. Appeasement was a problem that Pepi II seemed powerless to control due to his nature of avoiding controversy within his government.

Pharaoh Pepi II had unknowingly sown the seeds of the false religion, the worship of the sun, into his plans. By his choice of which priest to send, he would exclude the worship of Ptah and promote sun worship in the colonies but not even the kind of sun worship that Thuthy would recognize.

Once away from the view of Pepi II and his spies, Thuthy would begin the slow and careful conversion of the people from the worship of Ptah to the worship of the Sun Disk known as the Aten. This conversion could take centuries.

In the records of the very earliest dynasties, there were mentions of human sacrifice, always in a way to please the gods. Servants of a dead king, including animals, had been buried alive with him. There were also scant records of human sacrifices to please the gods in times of turmoil. This practice has been discontinued in the years of Dynasty One.

Thuthy believed it was time to bring back that practice. The old fool Pepi II did not realize that human sacrifice would have ended the drought.

CHAPTER FIVE — ESTABLISHMENT

The expedition sailed south from Memphis and was able to reach Waset (today's city of Luxor) in two weeks, where they stopped to rest and regroup before continuing. Traveling south took longer against the river's current. The next part of the journey would include negotiating cataracts which began south of Waset at Aswan.

Whitewater rapids made up cataracts in the Nile River, between Aswan and Khartoum. There were six cataracts constituting a great hazard to boat traffic in either direction. The expedition was fortunate the water of the Nile was quite low so that the boulders and other obstructions were visible. There were two locations where the boats were emptied, removing the supplies, provisions and crew. A few men were left on board to aid with navigation. All other men were guiding the boats with ropes from the shore. Navigating the cataracts was extremely heavy work made worse by the temperatures reaching one hundred twenty degrees. It was so hot that one of these portages was performed at night, thanks to a full moon.

At Khartoum, the Nile divided into the White Nile and the Blue Nile. The journey continued sailing west on the White Nile for another two weeks.

The expedition consisted of one hundred soldiers, two hundred women who would do light work, and two hundred additional men who would be in charge of construction and beginning the mining operations. Many of the men and women performed multiple duties, such as scribes and artists.

Travel was south on the Nile. The ships changed course onto a feeder river heading east before they reached the Sudd. Their initial destination was the western side of Ethiopia's mountain ranges. Hopefully, they could quickly find indications of gold, and establish the three towns.

As the boats navigated, workers were instructed to create markers consisting of stacks of rocks on the shore, so that in a year or so, they would be able to find their way back to the main trunk of the Nile.

Kush had agreed to provide guides and mining expertise to the colonists, on the condition that any new mines would be a week's march from the Kushite gold fields. The Kush guides led the expedition into extremely mountainous terrain containing heavy jungle. The goal was to build three cities in the form of a triangle, about one day's march apart. In case any of the cities were overrun, there would still be a functioning mining operation. The cities were also located within one hundred miles of the Nile's main body. There would need to be a stream that would provide easy access from the main city's port to the Nile.

The weary travelers finally arrived at a spot the Kush guides had chosen for establishing a semi-permanent base camp. Here they could relax after the long and grueling river voyage. From here several teams were sent out to scout for locations of the three cities.

Scouting parties consisting of Kushites, Egyptian architects, and a small squad of soldiers. They were under orders to only identify promising locations. They were instructed to return to the central camp when the scouting was completed. The scouts remembered Pharaoh's words: "… Egypt could never have too much gold."

The Kushite's expertise would come in handy during the excavations of tunnels in the search for veins of the precious metal. It would be the most labor-intensive portion of the operation. Many shafts would probably need to be dug before a vein was found. Luck and the blessings of Ptah would be necessary to find enough gold for the first shipment to Pharaoh.

The Kushites taught the Egyptians how to build sluices to capture alluvial gold. The streams contained gold flakes or nuggets that were carried downstream by a moving body of water. The grains and nuggets of gold could then be extracted from the silt in the sluices. Some of the younger and agiler women would perform these lighter mining duties.

Careful planning would be necessary to ensure the safety of the precious shipments. The Nile had to be a sufficient volume so portage of the boats would not be necessary. Since transportation of the gold would only occur twice a year, it was critical that the ships were in place at the right time for the important transfer of wealth. The colony carpenters would be charged with building smaller boats that could swiftly travel the Nile, with small heavy cargo.

When all the scouting parties were back in camp, the expedition leaders sought to celebrate with a grand meal of antelope and wild hog roasted on great spits. Several men had made enough beer so all could indulge. Menkhaf, in his role as expedition leader and nomarch of the three provinces, addressed the group, thanking them for their hard work. He assured them that Pharaoh Pepi II and the god Ptah would rain down blessings and reward their efforts.

After dinner, Menkhaf announced: "Three locations for the cities have been found, and according to reports, each meets or exceeds the requirements for gold mining establishments. Perhaps we will meet Pharaoh's expectations of having ingots delivered to him within six months."

Menkhaf chose one location and had all energy brought to bear on getting that city built and starting the hard work of mining for gold. The Kushites had promised one hundred slaves would be delivered to each city, when built, for construction and mining operations. Once the last of the slaves had been delivered, it would effectively end Kush's role and their support for the colonies. Pharaoh Pepi's dream of an endless supply of gold for Egypt would succeed or fail solely on the people of the colonies.

The first city was named Akh which means "the body and the soul" and referred to relatives who had left this life. The ancient Egyptians worshiped their ancestors and sought their aid in this life.

The land surrounding the three colonies was inhabited by Bushmen and Pygmies. These tribes were hunter-gathers. The tropical forests of central Africa were occupied by Pygmies, who had an average height of less than four feet. Also, living here were Khoisan (known as Bushmen) and the Khoikhoi, who were the Hottentots. The Africans who would eventually dominate central and southern Africa were tribes who spoke variations of the Bantu language. These tribes were not hunter-gathers but fierce warriors who would move south from their origins. They were cousins of the great Zulu Nation which fought the invading army of Great Britain to a stand-still for most of a century.

The city of Akh was completed in three months, offering meager protection from wild animals and potential unfriendly natives. A stockade was built to protect the workers, and the people slept on the ground or in makeshift huts. More permanent buildings were later constructed in the traditional Egyptian manner of mud bricks, which had been baked in the sun.

Akh was near the mines and close to the small river which provided drinking water. It was built in an opening in the jungle that had been cleared. The stockade gates faced the river, and the back of the city ended at the small hills. This city, as were the other two, was meant to house about three hundred people, of whom one hundred and fifty were miners. The remainder consisted of supporting roles of security, farming, hunting, and cooking. There were several men and women who were well versed in Egyptian medicine. Their services were often needed as injuries sometimes happened due to mine wall collapses, and encounters with the local animals.

The second city to be constructed was Opar, located nearest the navigable water since it was to be the residence of the nomarch, Menkhaf, so better construction methods were utilized. Menkhaf had the foresight to begin making mud bricks from the time construction on Akh had begun. Therefore, when the construction workers began building Opar, there were a large number of mud bricks for a nomarch's house and private quarters.

The workers were slow to adjust to the humidity and great heat of the jungle. The temperature in the north of Egypt was just as high, but here the humidity drained the workers after short periods of heavy work. When two workers had died from heat exhaustion, schedules were revised to exclude any exertion in the middle of the day, and more tasks were scheduled for early morning and late afternoon.

Unbeknownst to the Egyptian settlers, there was a large change in climate and rain patterns in the region east of the colonies. Instead of day-long rains at this time of year, there were periods of no rain at all. The level of the river had been slowly and steadily dropping. The torrential rainfall in the mountains of Ethiopia was the source of the great rise of the Nile in July. This lack of rain was to have catastrophic consequences for not only the inhabitants of the three cities, but would be a significant cause of the collapse of the greatest civilization in the world.

CHAPTER SIX — THE NETERU

Conventional thinking today holds that if you were on a subway or bus and sitting next to another person, you would be unable to distinguish between Neanderthals and Homo Sapiens.

Appearance wise, Neanderthals' bodies looked similar to ours except they could be very hairy. They tended to be shorter and somewhat stockier (which would help the body retain heat during the European ice ages). The Neanderthal heads had prominent brow ridges, wide noses, and highly angled cheekbones. Neanderthals learned to control fire and lived in caves which sheltered them from the ice and snow. The caves were plentiful in the areas their remains have been found.

Neanderthals had a large brain which made speech a possibility. They were known to have made and used complex stone tools.

It is not known if Neanderthals and Homo Sapiens interbred. Some theories believe they did not occupy Europe at the same time. Other theories are the genes were different enough to make live births of mixed parents difficult but not impossible.

The commonly held scientific thought today is that Homo Sapiens and the Neanderthal people both originated in Africa. Through several migrations, they made their way north following the Nile, then headed west for the land route into Europe. The popular theory is that the Neanderthals left Africa, in several migrations, before Homo Sapiens. Fossil evidence shows that Neanderthals migrated as far east as Asia, much before Homo Sapiens.

As with all migrations, the best and brightest usually had the idea to leave, for whatever reason, and search for new territory. It could not have been for overcrowding, for there were probably less than one million people on the earth.

Homo Sapiens and Neanderthals lived in proximity, but what their exact relationships were no one knows. Surely there were times of war and conflict, and there were times that the two peoples co-existed in peace. It would seem to be so, since in some eastern European people there are still Neanderthal indicators in their DNA makeup.

The Neanderthals, at least in Europe, vanished about thirty thousand years ago. No one knows why; perhaps they didn't adapt to the European weather changes that occurred once the Ice Ages ended. Homo Sapiens seemed to have adapted to these changes much better.

There were never a tremendous number of Neanderthals alive at one time, so there could have been many reasons for this somewhat fragile group of people to die out. In a small group, the most common belief is a number of either men or women died in a relatively short time. Then, the birth rate would drop and would not replace those members who died. So, the Neanderthal people would slowly cease to exist within a few generations.

In central Africa, Neanderthals still existed until the mid-twentieth century. They lived a secluded existence, similar to the mountain gorilla which was not known to exist until 1902. All the Neanderthal groups lived in a hundred mile radius in the mountains of East Africa. Altogether, there were less than a few hundred Neanderthals left in the world.

It is not known how these men were referred to in Africa.

Some are known to have been referred to by the Egyptian word Neteru.

Jim Malachowski

Chapter Seven — Settling In

After six months, the city of Akh was producing a below-goal amount of gold from the several mines which had been started. The city of Opar was complete and the last several months had seen the excavation of mines and the search for gold. The third city named Ra-mat was under construction, and preliminary tunneling for gold had begun.

Menkhaf was aware that he had only a few months to extract gold from the ground, cast it into ingots and ship it to Memphis. Luckily the trip north would be with the current, so several smaller boats should be able to make the trip fairly quickly. The ships would be flying the blue and white colors of Pharaoh and would be considered under his protection. No one would dare interfere with their mission or question what they were doing so far south. Menkhaf was planning for the first gold shipment after the inundation had subsided, which would be about October – four months after the flooding and high water in the Nile began.

Gradually over the past five years, the inundation reaching Memphis and the rest of northern Egypt had been steadily declining. This year there would be no inundation at all. This would be the first time there would be almost no crops. Cattle and livestock began to die from lack of food and water. The ramifications of this drought would be felt the most in northern Egypt, although it would subside somewhat farther south. The city and nomes around Waset (modern Luxor) would see a lesser effect from the drought. Due to a large amount of water contained in the Sudd, the effects of little rain would not be felt as much south of Kmt's border.

There was a growing dissatisfaction with Pharaoh Pepi II. It was the pharaoh's job to ensure the gods provide water which the land desperately needed. Pepi II had been praying to Ptah and every other deity he could think of, to no avail. He had been demanding an answer to Kmt's problem from the priests of the temple of Ptah, and likewise, they could not provide a reason for the gods' apparent abandonment.

The nomarchs of the forty-two nomes of Kmt were constantly meeting with Pharaoh, demanding that something be done. They were all feeling pressure from their citizens about the lack of food and the fact that everything around them seemed to be falling apart.

Pharaoh began to stop accepting audiences from his nomarchs, and he took to secluding himself in the deepest depths of the palace.

He had received no answers to these growing problems.

CHAPTER EIGHT — FIRST GOLD SHIPMENT

Pharaoh Pepi II's nomarch in the new cities, Menkhaf, looked with pleasure on the three traditional boats, known as feluccas, which the carpenters were finishing. In a few days, the sails would be completed and attached, and the boats would be ready for the first gold shipment to be made to Pharaoh.

This first shipment consisted of about three hundred pounds of gold in four ingots of seventy-five pounds each. Pharaoh had insisted that there be a gold delivery as soon as the cities were functioning. Menkhaf was hopeful that this amount of gold would be pleasing to Pharaoh. He was happy the first shipment would almost fulfill Pharaoh's expectations.

Two of the feluccas would be used to transport the gold shipment. The other boat would be for soldiers dressed in peasant clothing, so as not to draw attention to their journey north. Menkhaf thought it would take the boats twenty to thirty days to make the nearly thirteen hundred mile journey with the current. The Nile should be flowing heavily with the beginning of the inundation, and the current taking them north would push the boats along swiftly with little need for oars, just the steering rudder.

Ten days later, Nomarch Menkhaf and a few dignitaries including the High Priest of Ptah, stood on the river bank, which would lead their gold carriers to the Nile. They watched as the three boats and twenty men sailed to the east with their precious cargo. The High Priest concluded his prayers, for the safety of the men and cargo, and the ceremony ended.

Against his better judgment, Menkhaf went home to his wife, Melit. Melit had been all for becoming his wife and moving with him to the new cities. She had heard it was a great adventure, and she believed it. The great adventure died when they had their first baby a few months ago, and there was no wet nurse for the child. Melit had complained incessantly, about her figure being damaged from the birth and now her breasts would be likewise ruined. This conversation was carried out many times and always ended with her angrily throwing objects and barricading herself in one of the bedrooms.

Menkhaf had other matters on his mind. He had nightmares some tragic event would happen to the gold-carrying feluccas. He had constant worries that Pepi II would be displeased with the quantity of gold that had been extracted. Pharaoh had to understand they were just beginning their mining operations, didn't he?

It would be a long several months before the three ships sailed back to the dock at Opar. Hopefully, there would be enough administrative duties to keep his fears under control, until they had proven groundless.

Three weeks later, one of the boats and four of the men returned unexpectedly. Menkhaf was summoned at his administrative office to come to the dock immediately.

All the men appeared to be suffering greatly from exposure and hunger. Menkhaf looked at the terrible condition of the men, and he asked the scribe to see that the men were cared for and given rest for two days. They were to meet with him on the third day in the nomarch's palace.

On that day, the men were shown into a meeting room and invited to sit on the cushions on the floor. One of the men who survived was Moas, the expedition leader, and he was the first to speak. Moas was a man nearing forty years old. Having been a military officer, he had been chosen for the expedition south not only because of his background but because he had much experience with boats and navigation.

"The four of us thank Nomarch Menkhaf for allowing us to rest from our journey. All of us are feeling better and are grateful for the kindnesses we have been shown."

Menkhaf spoke in an even tone that said he was holding his temper until he had heard the men's stories. "We are anxious to hear the story of your voyage, and want to know what went wrong."

Again, Moas spoke, and answered with a single sentence saying, "The Nile is gone." The eyes of the eight men in the room went wide in disbelief – what Moas told them was inconceivable, and bore greater ramification for Kmt than the loss of the gold. The survivors nodded in assent that this was what they had found. A stunned Menkhaf asked the men what they meant, and he asked for a more detailed explanation.

Moas spoke saying, "Nomarch, we sailed the river wast to where we knew our river was the closest to the Nile. The twenty men then portaged the boats and the gold overland for several miles to where we should have found the Nile. As you remember from our youth, the Nile is a mighty river in some places a quarter of a mile wide. When we made our establishment voyage, the water was low, lower than anyone could remember. We found the markers we left that established the Nile that would lead us home. Instead, we found the Nile to be only half as wide as when we came here. The water and the riverbed had dropped 25 feet, and we could walk on the river bank. The Nile was only one hundred feet wide and very shallow."

Moas continued, "The current in the Nile was very weak and barely moved the boats. We were forced to find some trees with which we could make poles to move the ships forward. We worked hard, propelling the boats in this manner for ten days getting close to Aswan. Low water would mean the cataracts were more pronounced. We stopped many times, and the sights on land were the same, there were almost no crops growing. The shadoofs used to bring Nile water into the irrigation ditches were dry. There was so little water that the farmers were carrying it from the Nile and were using cups to water each plant. Everyone in the small villages was being used to carry water. Transport of water was a back-breaking job, but the people were afraid of no crops, or highly reduced harvests which would result in starvation."

Menkhaf asked, "So how far did you get?" Moas answered that the boats had been abandoned about twenty miles from where the cataracts had ended at Aswan. The Nile was continuing to get more shallow, and it was useless to go further. Three men were sent on foot toward Waset to check on the river conditions, only one of whom returned. The lone survivor stated that his companions had died of exposure and hunger and the Nile did not have enough water for the boats. Two other men were dispatched to Memphis, carrying a message of the plight of the expedition. They were never heard from again.

Moas continued "We lost more of our members who had remained with the boats. We had no luck finding crops or catching fish. The sails were raised and the wind moved us fairly quickly back to the connecting river. We did not stop anywhere to rest. We returned immediately to the docks of Opar to tell of our tragic voyage."

Menkhaf could not believe what he had just heard. The loss of men and ships of gold was hard to accept, but he knew that if what the men were saying was true, conditions down river around the capital would be much worse. Also if this were so, the Kmt they had left would be no more. These thoughts he kept to himself, and he tried to say something of a positive nature.

All the heads at the meeting nodded in ascent. They wanted to believe the problem with the Nile was only temporary. Menkhaf decided they would send out another scouting expedition in six months to see if boats could reach the capital with gold shipments and return safely.

Menkhaf ended the meeting by saying, "We appreciate your efforts and are sorry for the bad outcome. We will make more attempts, but not very soon."

CHAPTER NINE — REALIZATION

Menkhaf was recovering from a bout of malaria. The illness had lasted two weeks. His face reflected the effects of many bouts with malaria, showing a man much older than his true age.

His scribe came into his office and stood quietly until his presence was acknowledged. Menkhaf inquired who was asking for him, and his scribe answered, "The leader of the river party, Nomarch."

Menkhaf had mixed feelings about speaking with this man. Emotions ranged from hoping they had found the Nile navigable, to the knowledge that sat on his chest like a cold rock. His worst fear was the Nile was gone. With it came the dread that the colonies were truly on their own. There would be no assistance from Pharaoh. They could never go home. He would not see his parents even though they were relatively close (if they were still alive). Travel to them would be impossible to imagine. They would have to walk and carry food and water for the several-week trip. He put these thoughts out of his mind and spoke to the man who stood in front of him.

"Well, what is the answer?" The man replied, "It is not good news. The Nile is even lower than last year when we made this same attempt. This time we went inland and looked for people along the river, but there were none. We located several villages and found them deserted. We discontinued the search for people after a week of making a circle of about twenty miles. As you know, Excellency, the vast majority of people in Kmt live within a mile of the Nile."

The interview lasted another half hour. Menkhaf asked the same questions over the previous five years and received the same answers. This was the latest of the annual failed gold delivery voyages. However, this time he asked about the man's thoughts. The answers somewhat surprised Menkhaf. When asked "What do you think is going on?", The man answered, "I am not one of the superstitious fools who seek all their answers in the Gods. I believe something has changed. Wherever the water comes from for the Nile, it is no longer available. We should count ourselves lucky that we are living here in the forest. Yes, we have lots of rain, but we also have plenty of water to drink. We have all the food we can grow, and in general, I believe most people are happy here."

Menkhaf asked what he thought was going on in Memphis. The man thought for a minute and said, "I fear the worst. I believe the people are suffering as never before. They are enduring starvation and lack of water. As you remember, Nomarch, the Nile had been gradually dropping for several years before we were sent on this mission. So, this is at least ten years of diminishing water from the inundation. I fear that the worst may still be ahead and the consequences will be catastrophic for Kmt."

Menkhaf slowly nodded his head to acknowledge that he had heard his worst fears said out loud. He said in the strongest terms that none of the information in this meeting would be shared with the people. He told the man to convey this command back to the other members of the search party. The man acknowledged his wish and left the room. The meeting was over.

Menkhaf slouched in his chair, letting the meeting settle into his mind. It was imperative that the common people not know how serious the situation at home appeared to be. It would cause panic and a general disruption for the colonists.

Menkhaf did not know what to do next, but the problem would be solved for him. He died several months later of a massive attack of malaria. Since there was no clear line of succession, the High Priest of Ptah assumed the nomarch's leadership role.

CHAPTER TEN — FALL OF THE OLD KINGDOM

Pepi II was living the last years of his ninety-four-year reign. It was about the year 2119 BCE, and Egypt was facing the total collapse of civilization. Pharaoh Pepi II had simply reigned for too many years. In the last twenty years, his mental capacity had been seriously impaired, as he drifted in and out of reality.

His grandson had been propping Pepi II up, in hopes that he would be the heir to the throne, and be named Pharaoh when Pepi II died. He had held this belief for twenty years now, and he had become an old man also. The Nomarchs of the regions supported Pepi II, but only because he allowed them to do whatever they wanted. He was always like that, an ineffective ruler making incredibly bad decisions.

For the last several years, there had been almost no inundation of the Nile, and the people were dying in great numbers because there was little grain and other crops, no drinkable water, and few fish. The central government had collapsed, and the country was in chaos. The rule of the day was lawlessness and every man for himself.

In the area around Waset, jealous warlords were taking turns at overthrowing Pepi II. The Egyptian historian and priest, Manetho, was quoted as describing this period as having:

"….. seventy kings who ruled for seventy days."

The meaning of his statement has come to be interpreted as: The seventh dynasty only lasted a few months and had seventy "would be pharaohs." None of the aspiring rulers had enough support to endure. This situation would not stabilize for more than a hundred years. The Old Kingdom of Ancient Egypt had totally collapsed.

Chaos was running supreme in Kmt. All the pyramids were broken into, robbed and the bodies of the ancients burned. This happened to most graves of any person of importance. The thieves were looking for gold and jewels that were buried with the deceased. Foreigners were entering Egypt's unguarded borders and were sacking graves and cities.

In a document written about this period, two hundred years later, the following comments were made:

"Poor men have become men of wealth. He who could not afford sandals owns riches. The robber owns riches, the noble is a thief. Gold, Lapis Lazuli, Silver and Turquoise, Carnelian, Amethyst are strung on the necks of slave girls, while noblewomen roam the land hungry….."

Pepi II was considered the last major ruler of the Sixth Dynasty. Although the period of chaos lasted more than one hundred years before the return of centralized government, it would not be until the Eleventh Dynasty, several hundred years later, when Kmt would have a Pharaoh strong enough to unify and rule the entire country.

Upon the death of Pepi II, the records of the foundation of Opar died also. There was not even a hint that a colony outside Kmt existed. During the sacking of Pepi II's palace, all documents public and his private correspondence, including the ones concerning Opar were burned by the furious mobs of Egyptians who blamed Pepi II for the demise of Kmt.

CHAPTER ELEVEN — ON THEIR OWN

Thuty, the High Priest of Ptah back in the temple in Memphis years ago, had chosen his son, Neith, to be part of the expedition to establish the gold mining towns. There was a reason he was chosen, besides being Thuthy's son. Neith was fiercely loyal and would never betray his father, plus he was willing to travel outside of Egypt. Not many people were willing to do that for fear of dying away from home, not being interred in Egyptian sand with the guarantee of resurrection and life everlasting.

Neith was a tall man by Egyptian standards, almost six feet and slender. He had been a priest in his father's temple for fifteen years and was anxious to be approved for promotion, even if it meant leaving the soft living of the temple with the many female acolytes.

He like his father was a follower of Ptah in name only. Their true allegiances were to Ra the Sun God. The plan was, after the colonies were established, to introduce the worship of the Sun God, just as Thuthy would do in Memphis, once the old fool Pepi II was dead.

Upon the death of Menkhaf, Neith assumed the role of nomarch of the colony and moved into the nomarch's quarters, which were slightly less

41

Spartan than his own. He cared little about Menkhaf's wife and child, considering her to be an expendable person and having too much of an aristocratic air. He was glad to see her dropped a few levels in importance.

Neith relished the idea of having a dual title of High Priest of Ptah and Nomarch of the Colonies of Opar. He did not, however, consider the responsibility for the several hundred people who fell under his care. He was a lazy person. He chose people and put them in charge of the areas they knew best. As it turned out, his was a better way of governance than Menkhaf had employed. Menkhaf waited until he heard that something had gone wrong before he acted, and that was usually to castigate someone where the problem had occurred, even if they were blameless.

One of the first decisions Neith made was to stop the yearly attempts to find and navigate the Nile back to Memphis. His logic was to let nature correct the problem of no water and prevent upsetting the citizens of Opar even further. Neith was trying to keep morale up and avoid the feeling of abandonment.

Ten years into his reign there came a problem no one could have predicted. The Oparians had kept to themselves and had not reached out to any of the indigenous people who lived close to them. Security had been lax. The main source of danger had been the great cats which would occasionally wander into the camps at night looking for an easy meal. A branch of fire was usually enough to drive them off without any casualties or injuries. The people always warned their children not to stray too far into the forest for fear of leopards hiding in the trees. Every year one or two children wandered into the jungle and were killed by the stealthy cats.

Muvo, the superintendent of mines, came to the nomarch's reception area and said it was of great importance that he speak with him. He was admitted to the office, and Neith spoke to him and asked what was so important.

Muvo began, "Nomarch Neith, I was traveling to the colony of Akh for my inspection of the mines to check progress on gold production. Akh has always been a bit short of their mining quota of gold, and we had agreed that it was important that we keep an eye on their mining operations. When my party got close to Akh, we noticed the area was quiet with hardly any sounds. There was no one to greet us, and our guard immediately went up. We looked in the village, and there was no sign of people, the same with the mines – no sign of activity. When we walked to the river, we found the remains of several men. They appeared to have put up a struggle but were killed by either arrows or spears. Whatever had happened had occurred several days ago, judging by the condition of the bodies. We went back to the mine and found where the miners had stored the gold, it was still present, and we recovered it. Missing was the food from the village and the crops in the fields. All had been taken."

Muvo had been a military man in the Pharaoh's army, and he was prepared for the next question from Neith. "What do you think happened to the people? You are telling me that men, women, children, and the provisions had disappeared. What do you think happened?"

"I think 'men who hunt men' raided them. I don't know where they came from or who they were. The Kushites warned us about the people who lived in the land south and west of Kush years ago. They said we should be careful of those people. It would seem the men who hunt men are aware of our presence and operations in Akh and thought it would be easy to wipe out the settlement and enslave our people. We found, in their cook fires, the leg and arm bones of humans. This tells me they were cannibals as well as slavers."

After a moment's thought, Neith asked, "Is there anything we can do to get our people back? Should we risk sending men on a rescue mission?" Muvo's eyes dropped to his lap as he answered, "We can always send some soldiers to try to trace where the 'men who hunt men' came from, but we would need a better-armed force than we have now to get our people back. I do not think we can risk an encounter with a large number of warriors. We would lose many of our men – old and young. As always, Nomarch, this is your decision, but if you are asking me, I would not recommend a confrontation with these people. Near the river, there were tracks of many men in addition to our people. It is obvious they probably put our people into boats of some kind and are very far away by now. They have several days of lead on us. Even if we put together a search and rescue party, we are already a week or ten days behind the "men who hunt men.'"

Neith dismissed Muvo and sank back into his chair contemplating his next move. He could attempt to follow the 'men who hunt men' and risk a confrontation. Or, he could attempt to enlist the aid of the Kushites.

He discarded the idea of the Kushites. It had been many years since the two peoples had spoken. He did not want to lose more soldiers chasing after a war party, risking many more men's lives. He had no idea of the number of their opponents or their armaments.

Neith reached a solution that would increase the colonists' security and give him the excuse to introduce the Sun God – Ra, as a better protector of the colonies of Opar.

CHAPTER TWELVE — A NEW DIRECTION

Neith called his head of security and ordered a three-member group of soldiers dispatched to try to find the raiders who had enslaved the colonists in Akh. His orders were to try to locate where these savages came from and if there would be any way to free any of the colonists. He told them quite emphatically "You are on a mission to help the colonists who were enslaved – not to add three more captives to their haul. If we can establish where they are being held, we can perhaps develop a plan to free them. It is important to find where the raiders call home so that we can at least keep an eye on them."

Nebre, the son of Apries, whose father had been the architect of the development of the three cities that made up the province of Opar, had made the perilous journey from Memphis and was an invaluable member of the colony.

Neith and Nebre had enjoyed an evening meal, and Neith was anxious about the subject for discussion after the dinner meeting. Neith started by saying "Since the attack on Akh, we need to rethink the security of the remaining two cities. I depend on you Nebre to give me the answers that are in your heart. I know you have thoughts and ideas that can make us more secure in our mining operations." Neith continued, "The attack upon Akh is a shock to all of us. The Kushites had assured us that there were no unfriendly tribes of savages living in the area. Obviously, some like the cannibals are traveling through, or have relocated here."

Nebre usually had little contact with Neith since he assumed the governorship of the Opar colony, and he was not yet comfortable opening up and saying what was on his mind.

Neith must have sensed this, and he sought to assure him by saying, "There is no reason for you to withhold your thoughts and fears from me. I may not agree with you on everything you say, but if I do not agree with you, I will not criticize you. Please tell me what is on your mind."

Nebre drew a deep breath and blurted out this thought "Neith, we must relocate the cities of Opar and Ra-mat. Right now the inhabitants cannot be assured of safety. I think we must scout the surrounding area for a location, and consolidate the two remaining cities into a new Opar. Then we can be defended by a small number of soldiers, and we can be safe."

Neith thought for a moment and asked "What of the mines, and the gold that we are supposed to send Pharaoh each year?" Nebre answered with a half smile on his face and said, "How can dead men mine gold or anything else?" Neith smiled weakly back.

Amose and Ako were leading a hunting party to find warthog and gazelle that would feed the nobles of Opar and Ra-mat at for a few days. The second day north of Opar they came upon gazelles in a field of waist-high grass. They had crept on their hands and knees, keeping the breeze blowing in their faces, to get within spear throwing distance of the animals. They had been crawling to approach the herd for several hours. It was now almost sundown. They wanted to have killed their prey, dressed them and be under cover of trees before dark, avoiding nocturnal predators

Ako was the impatient one and had been making a sign to 'hurry up' to his brother for the past hour. Amose signaled for them to separate a bit, and to get closer to the prey. He did not want a half day's stalking to be in vain.

Finally, Amose made the signal to stand, select a target and throw his heavy spear. The brothers stood, and fifteen feet from them was the herd of gazelles. Both men launched their spears, and both pierced their targets behind the front legs. The animals went a few yards and dropped. Ako noticed movement to the brothers' left and saw three more hunters fifty yards away who also had been stalking the herd. Two had managed to slay the antelopes, and the five men all looked at each other with surprise.

Also watching the tableau that had played out in front of her, was Sabor the lioness. She was interested in feeding her cubs that night on antelope. Her two babies had recently been weaned and were anxious for a dinner of raw and tender meat. Sabor looked with extreme displeasure first at the herd of antelopes that was now scattering and running in every direction. She then turned her attention to the smell of blood that had traveled in the air to her sensitive nostrils. She was quite hungry, and the odor of blood was making her more daring. Ako was the first to see the lioness and sounded an alarm to his brother. Neither man had another weapon, as their spears were ten yards away buried in the chest of the antelopes. The only thing the two brothers could think of was to run toward the other hunters and hope they could make it to the trees that lay just beyond. One of the other hunters saw what was going to happen. The lioness would have one of the two men before they both could make the trees. He ran toward the charging lioness, and with all his strength he threw his heavy flint-tipped spear. It struck the lioness in the side just below the ribcage, a serious wound that would eventually kill the great cat.

All five men had turned and run from the wounded lioness, who had leaped in the air in an attempt to dislodge the spear. She had fallen heavily, and the butt of the spear had caught on the ground. The lioness' weight had driven the blade up into her chest puncturing one of her lungs. The fight was leaving her body quickly. She hoped in her motherly way that her cubs would survive her death.

Within an easy climbing distance of the trees, the five men had a chance to examine each other closely. There were some looks among all of them that asked — 'do I trust these males?' 'Are they friends or enemies?' Ako had been the closest to being caught by the lioness, and he smiled at the other three hunters. It seemed tension was broken by that simple gesture.

The three men looked very different from the Opar hunters. The Opar brothers were about five feet six and slender of build. Their hair was black, complexion was olive, and they wore clothing of linen. They bore a similarity to a Greyhound, slender and built for speed. The three other hunters were about four inches shorter and probably forty pounds heavier. Their faces were round, and they were extremely hairy on body and face. Their clothing consisted of animal skins which were tied about their bodies. They were similar to a bulldog — short bowed legs, wide bodies and not the most attractive faces.

One of the three hunters pointed toward the sky and made a motion that the sun was going down signifying they should be leaving with their food. Quickly they cut straight tree limbs with stone hatchets, making poles, to carry the antelopes to safety. The three carcasses were rapidly gutted, bled and placed on the poles. They were carried by the brothers and two of the other hunters. The largest hunter picked up the smallest antelope and slung it around his neck and started walking as though it weighed a few pounds. The three hairy men motioned for the Oparians to follow them – where they did not know.

Several months had gone by since the raid on Akh. The three-man recon team had just returned from trying to find the captured colonists, and the news was not good. They had paddled feverishly for two weeks trying to catch up with the raiders. The fear was the raiders had gotten out of their boats and cut inland, leaving the Opar men to follow the wrong path. The team did not speak during their journey but communicated by hand signals. Every ear was tuned to hear the faintest sound.

Toward evening the men heard sounds of talking in the distance. They waited until dark, and one of them quietly moved toward the conversation. From a distance, he saw a large number of ebony men. A quick count told him there were about a hundred warriors. They were very tall, extremely muscular and highly decorated with tattoos and piercings of bone. In the center of the black men were the colonists – a count of them revealed there to be about seventy men, women, and children. The captives were bound at the wrists with grass rope and were heavily guarded by armed men with short spears.

Upon closer examination, there on the logs of the cook fire were what appeared to be animal parts that were roasting for the evening meal. The man looked with shock and realized what he was seeing was two butchered humans being cooked. His blood ran cold.

The man returned to his other two companions and relayed the bad news. The colonists were not captured for slaves. They were going to be used for food. Probably some of the women and children would be spared, or saved until they got back to their village.

The men did not wait for the sunrise. There was a full moon, and they navigated slowly back to a place where it was safe to talk in low tones. The braver man said sadly, "There is nothing we can do for our friends. There are too many warriors. I think we should leave now so we can be assured of not being captured. It does not matter where they came from – we do not have enough men to give them a good fight should they come back and find Opar. I believe it is most important for us to get back alive and tell what we have seen, so plans can be made to defend our home."

CHAPTER THIRTEEN — ALLIANCE

Four months passed very quickly for Amose and Ako. Returning to Opar with the slain animals was very far from their minds. They were busy enjoying the cool mountains that were home to their new friends. Try as they did, the brothers were unable to learn what the strange people called themselves, so they decided to call them Neteru, which means guard in the Egyptian language. Both men were surprised with one thing about the Neteru. They had white skin. It was covered with a generous amount of hair and dirt, as personal hygiene was not very high on their agenda.

Over the years, hunters from Opar had encountered others who had always been people of dark skin. The brothers thought it strange to find people in this part of the world with light skin. Since they had white skin, they felt a kinship with them, more so than with the Kushites. Little did they realize their new friends were an entirely different race of people.

The mountain retreat was cool and very secluded, thanks to the close-growing trees, bushes and vines. Caves in the sides of the mountain provided both security and safety as well as permanent housing for the two hundred members of the Neteru. They used an area at the bottom of the mountainside for community cooking and gatherings. As night approached, primitive ladders were used to gain access to the caves.

The brothers had made some progress learning the language of the Neteru and teaching them the Kmt language of the Oparians. They were having a much easier time learning the Neteru language. The Neteru were not gifted with the highest intelligence, and a new language was very difficult for them.

The Oparians could not learn where the Neteru had come from, or how long they had lived there. The Neteru had no concept of time and had no words to measure time concepts. They seemed to enjoy the day very much and made no plans for anything except for hunting and fishing in the nearby river. Given the fertile soil and more than adequate rain, their simple vegetables were easy to grow.

The brothers were fascinated by the flint spear points. Seeing the possibilities of improving their arrows with flint points. Flint was unknown to the Oparians but was found in abundance in the Neteru country. One day while they were walking in the mountains, near a stream, a glint caught their eyes. In the water was a gold nugget, a small, but significant find. Amose showed the nugget to his companion, and the man wrinkled his nose and said the word 'soft.' Amose interpreted this to mean it was too soft to make a good spear point. Amose smiled and put the nugget in his pouch.

After the brothers had retired for the night, Amose brought up a subject which had also been on Ako's mind. Memories of the cannibal attack on Akh had upset both men. Ako said, "I wish the Neteru lived closer to Opar, as it would be beneficial to both of our people if we lived closer together." Amose agreed and asked, "Why would the Neteru want to relocate and come and live with us near Opar?"

"We should be heading for Opar soon. Our people are probably worried about our safety, and I am sure they are getting very hungry for some roasted steaks." With this, a large smile appeared on his face, and Ako caught the joke and began to laugh.

"I think the best idea at this point is to invite one of the Neteru whom we first met and the chief's son to come back to Opar for a visit," suggested Amose. "Perhaps they will get the idea."

The next day the brothers and their new friend began the journey home. Ako had a female companion in Opar and was anxious to return to see her. Amose was hoping Neith and the other leaders of the colony would see the Neteru as becoming partners in survival in this dangerous world.

Neith spoke to the assembled residents while they were eating their evening meal. "I want to make it clear to all of you that each idea is being considered to ensure the safety of everyone here. As we speak, Nebre and several of his assistants are scouting for a new location for the city of Opar. As plans become clear I will keep you all informed."

Neith continued, "I have been praying to our God Ptah, and asking why this terrible event was visited upon us. I am disappointed to say that I have not received anything that can be viewed as an answer." Neith added, "Perhaps Ptah cannot hear us from where we now live."

This information about Ptah was as shocking to the assembled people as was the cannibal attack. Ptah had been the people's main God for their entire lives. The majority of the people had private adoration areas in their homes, complete with a statue of Ptah.

"Lastly," Neith stated, "we have lost many of the people in this colony to the cannibals, and we need for all the women here to do their very best to bring a new life into the colony by next year at this time." Neith smiled at the lovely female faces seated before him and thought to himself, "I will surely be giving this project my best effort."

When Amose and Ako came walking back into Opar, they were greeted quite boisterously. Their friends and family assumed they had been killed and added them to the tragic casualties of the cannibal attack. The residents of Opar were very interested in their traveling companions and wanted to know all about them. Amose introduced them as one of the Neteru men who had saved their lives and the son of the Neteru chief.

Word reached Neith, and he invited the brothers and their companions to eat with him that evening. Amose described their adventure and rescue while hunting for meat. Amose said, "Ako and I owe our lives to this man, and thank the chief's son for his hospitality." Ako translated the parts the Neteru did not quite understand. The Neteru plainly appreciated being in the center of attention. Amose thought this was as good a time as any to reveal his thoughts to Neith. "Nomarch Neith," he began, "my brother and I both think that an alliance with the Neteru people would be of mutual benefit. We think the Neteru and the people of Opar would learn from each other and would be a stronger colony than if we were on our own."

The nomarch smiled, saying, "Yes, I believe you are correct, Amose. I have been enjoying this fine dinner and thinking of the ways that the two peoples could benefit from an alliance. While you were gone hunting," he said with a smile, "we have decided to relocate Opar to a more secure location. I am sure the Neteru could be of great help in finding a different site for the New Opar. Amose, would you be so kind as to translate our wishes and plans to the Neteru guests, and ask them if they would like to join us in building and living in a safer city?"

A few days later the Neteru men announced they were going back to their mountain, and they would speak to the chief and council of elders about the offer of joining forces. The chief's son said that he thought it was a good idea to live close to each other.

Upon their return to the mountain caves, the chief's son reminded his father that the tribe had had skirmishes with the cannibal warriors. The chief agreed and said that alone or together, they would probably have to deal with them again. The consensus was it was better to fight the cannibals with the Oparians than by themselves. The agreement was reached to relocate near Opar.

Six months later the Neteru had completed the move to Opar. Everyone thought the integration of the Neteru would be a benefit to both people but no one thought their assistance would come as quickly as it did.

The military men of Opar taught the Neteru how to use bow and arrow and the short spear. The bow and arrow were particularly useful when dealing with men who were at a distance; the short spear was very useful in hand to hand combat.

Three days ago scouts had spotted war canoes in the river five miles from the ruins of Akh. Ten sentries, several of which were Neteru, had been deployed at different locations which could provide access to the city of Opar. The plan had worked, and now the scouts had to get back to Opar immediately and get the people ready for the next step.

As soon as the alarm had risen in Opar, all able-bodied men – including the Neteru – grabbed their weapons and raced to the spot where the Oparians had planned to initiate contact with the invaders.

There was a spot on the trail between Akh and Opar that had extensive rising mounds on either side. The hillocks were elevated about ten feet above the trail. The men carefully spaced themselves so they could manage their bows without interfering with the warriors on either side of them. The thirty men, fifteen on each side, stuck their arrows in the soft earth in front of them so that they could fire again as quickly as possible.

The cannibals walked confidently in a large group laughing and joking as they went. They were suspecting no resistance since all the other raids had offered none.

The cannibal warriors were forced by the terrain to move in a somewhat single file. They detected nothing until thirty men rose in unison and fired their arrows almost simultaneously. The first volley all found targets. The men at the head and tail of the lines of archers had the job of making sure that no one escaped by running ahead, or retreating backward. The second, third and fourth volley of the deadly shafts all found targets, so a fifth volley was not necessary. The tips of the arrows had all been dipped in the venom of the Black Mamba snake. The Black Mamba was known as a two-step snake – once bitten a man had about two steps to walk before he died from the venom. Of course, because the venom had dried on the arrow points some of the cannibals were able to make more than the normal two steps. The men of Opar and Neteru walked among the downed enemies and cut the throats of any survivors. The count of cannibals who would not be returning from this trip varied from seventy-eight to eighty-one. No one cared whose count was correct. The important thing was that the people of Opar would probably never be troubled by these cannibals again.

CHAPTER FOURTEEN — THE MARCH OF TIME

During the nine months following the ambush of the cannibals, there was a more relaxed feeling among the colonists of Opar. The ever-present feeling of dread had been replaced with a feeling of optimism. Perhaps it was the births of thirty-five babies in the colony that helped people forget about the horrible events that had taken almost a hundred and fifty lives.[2]

Neith was addressing the men and women who were responsible for the establishment of the New Opar. Over the years since he assumed the leadership of the colony, he had become increasing verbose.

Neith continued his progress report by saying "I am happy to announce that Nebre, our architect and planner, is beginning his third attempt to find a site for the New Opar. Unfortunately, his first two expeditions were not successful in finding a site which meets our minimum requirements."

---

[2] Five hundred was the initial number of settlers. About one hundred fifty were killed in the destruction of Akh.

"Perhaps with the addition to his party of several Neteru, he will be able to have some success. He will concentrate his search on the territory to the north of our current location It is the old home of the Neteru, and I am sure their familiarity with that territory will come in handy."

Neith was silent for a few minutes, and his opinion of the Neteru flashed in his mind. While he valued and approved of them joining the colony, he wondered how they would contribute. Their language was very limited, and their ability to learn Egyptian only worked for a few of the Neteru. He did not think they were very bright people.

Perhaps he was too critical. They had learned to become proficient in the use of bow and arrow. They had made a big contribution in the rout of the cannibals. Neith knew there was going to be a large amount of heavy labor in building the new Opar, so they would come in handy.

Neith resumed his address, "I want to thank the women for their fine efforts in adding over thirty new citizens to Opar. We are hoping there will be at least that number of babies born in the coming year." Neith was responsible for at least three of these 'new citizens.' He added a phrase that was received with mixed reaction, despite how they felt inside they all smiled – "Thanks be to the Flaming God." So, it was starting.

Neith returning to his main topic of discussion, said, "For our safety in the time we have left to live in this area, we have posted men and women as scouts. The sentries will work in a rotation, watching for groups of people entering the area near Opar."

"Also, we have sent a small number of people back to Akh, with orders to obliterate any signs people ever lived there. All the huts and buildings are to be burned. Any plants that can be salvaged for Opar will be a priority. The mines which were being worked were camouflaged. We see this as being a fall back should the mines around Opar and Ra-mat fail."

Three months later, an exhausted Nebre and his men returned to Opar and were immediately summoned by Neith to a briefing on their scouting for a new home. Neith folded his arms against his chest, in a somewhat defensive stance, and expecting bad news he asked, "Well, how did the exploration go this time?" To this point, Nebre had shown almost no emotion, but he could contain his excitement no longer. "I believe we have found our site for the new Opar."

Neith let out a sigh of relief, and a tentative smile crossed his face. He did not want to be too enthusiastic until he had heard the details. Neith motioned to one of the ladies who served him and asked that food and refreshments be brought to the four explorers.

"So," Neith said, "please tell me about the location."

Nebre, showing his enthusiasm, spoke rather quickly and did not want to be interrupted "It is about one hundred miles north of the former Neteru village. It is high in the jungle, surrounded by much taller and steeper mountains on three sides. The peaks around the location will be ideal for the Neteru, as they contain caves, some quite large. Another wonderful thing about this place is that all the time we were there, the mountains and valleys were covered with heavy fog. Not only does this help to conceal our presence, but the fog helps to moderate the temperature. I cannot say that it will be somewhat cool all year, but I am sure the heat will never be as great as in our present location. The land that I have calculated for the buildings, temple, living quarters, gardens and livestock area will only take up one-third of the valley surrounded by the mountains.

"In front of the mountain opening was a long desolate valley, with a small river. Any approaching person or party can be seen by the sentries at a long distance. Beyond the valley is a tall escarpment, appearing to be very difficult to climb. Both of these features will enhance our security."

"The location for the city is somewhat elevated above the valley, but the plateau is made up of both limestone and granite both of which we will use to create a beautiful and strong city. It will not be a flimsy makeshift temporary facility like the present Opar, but a city that will last for all eternity." Nebre concurred the location was the best possible.

Neith asked "Any indication of gold in the area?" "We did some preliminary scouting and found there is some gold flake in the mountain streams, so I would say there is a good chance. Speaking of water," Neith added, "while there is no water that goes across the plateau, there are several large streams and a river that should intersect the Nile — if it is still there — should we want to attempt to make the trip north to Memphis."

The smile on Neith's face broadened. "I believe you have found our new home. I would like to travel there, after you have rested, for a first-hand look at the site." A great sense of peace came over the group starting with Neith and Nebre and extending to all the other people in the room.

One month later a weary group of ten men and women returned to Opar, and all were satisfied that the location would be the best possible choice for the new city. Neith began the return feast with a prayer to the Flaming God. Again, a mild sense of 'what is that about' spread through the room, but no one questioned the meaning, and everybody looked forward to a relaxed evening. It appeared that building a new city was about to begin.

The weary travelers had looked forward to home and being filled with beer and a fine meal. Neith took Nebre aside, and told him, "I want to work with you on the design of the new Opar. Please meet with me every morning to go over my ideas for the new city." In his heart, Neith could not have cared less about the city in general. He was most interested in the design of the Temple to the Flaming God.

The next morning Neith and Nebre met early before the heat of the day began. Neith confided the following, "Nebre, how soon can we move the city to the new location?" Neith had on the trip given Nebre permission to address him by his name and not one of his titles; a show of confidence and friendship that Nebre appreciated very much.

Nebre answered "Neith, I believe that it is in our best interest to move as soon as possible. The only consideration is that I do not know your thoughts on is the mining operation." Neith answered, "The mining operation was interrupted when the cannibals attacked us and have not resumed in Opar or Ra-Mat."

"If I may, I want to confide a vision the Flaming God revealed to me. The old fool Pepi II is dead, Kmt and Memphis that we knew and loved are no more. So, there is little use to try to mine gold and build a strong new Opar at the same time." Nebre shifted uncomfortably in his chair and said, "I have thought and wondered the same for many months now, I just don't see how our beloved country could survive without the Nile."

Neith continued, "I have never heard of anyone living as long as Pepi. I thought he might be immortal. The vision made it clear he was not immortal, and he was no God."

"That decided the issue for me, my friend," said Neith. "We will have our most trusted people plan the move and begin the journey to the new Opar. In a few weeks, you and I will have the plans drawn for the city. Since both Amose and Ako are trained stonemasons, do you agree they should be in charge of construction, training new masons, and teaching the Neteru to do the heavy work?"

Nebre's thoughts were already on the layout of the city, and he absently nodded his agreement.

CHAPTER FIFTEEN — THE NEW OPAR

The brothers Amose and Ako were thrilled with their new titles as the chiefs of construction of the new city. Their father had been a stone mason in Memphis until he was seriously injured and was not able to work again. Men with one leg were not in great demand. He was able to stay working in the construction of tombs and temples, but never again was he a man of importance. He was just another light-duty laborer. The thoughts of how their family and father had suffered after the accident was very much on their minds and they vowed inwardly to work more carefully to avoid serious injury.

The ten-day trip to the new Opar was made many times by the nearly three hundred and fifty colonists and by the additional one hundred Neteru. The most important item was just getting all the peoples' belongings to the new site.

Once this was accomplished, the women were left in charge of building temporary shelters which would house their family and livestock. Great care was taken in moving crops. Many of the vegetables had been brought from Kmt and were not native to this area. Guards were posted to prevent any intruders during the build-up of the new encampment.

Once the family goods were moved, the men began to transfer records from the government buildings. The mining equipment was moved next. Lastly, all signs of the two remaining cities were obliterated. Buildings were demolished and burned, and any remaining crops pulled up. The mine entrances were filled in with rubble, and locations carefully recorded, just in case they would be needed in the future.

Neith and Nebre, his architect, had labored for several weeks on plans for the new Opar. They had worked in great harmony despite Neith's emphasis on building the main temple to the Flaming God. Nebre was somewhat at a loss why a mining town like Opar would need such a flamboyant and huge temple. However, he accepted Neith's ideas and visions and incorporated the design into the city plan.

Nebre sometimes wondered if the city would be completed in his lifetime. He estimated that the buildings would take fifteen to twenty years given the small workforce. Only time would tell.

The opening on the valley floor between the mountains that would bookend the new Opar was about one thousand feet. This gap would be later closed with a high wall and small entrance. The project was not six months old, and already there were several courses of stone that made the wall about four feet high.

Amose had taken on responsibility for construction of the wall. Ako took it upon himself to be in charge of the quarrying of stone. Quarrying the stone for the wall was going to be the most time-consuming task, so many more men and women were assigned to cutting, shaping and polishing the large stones. The Neteru men would provide the heavy work of moving the stones from the quarry area, to the base of the wall and lift them where they were needed.

Neith was on one of his weekly inspection tours of the wall's progress. He said, "Amose, you are doing a really good job of getting the wall started. I can only hope we do not run into some problem that will cause a delay." Amose thanked him for the compliment and said: "I will pass your praise onto Ako and his people. They like Ako and are willing to work very hard for him." He continued, "When we get this wall up to fifteen feet, perhaps we can surprise the workers with a week off. I know Ako, and I would love to go with you. It seems as if it has been a year since we have been hunting and we both miss it." Neith smiled and nodded his approval and said, "Yes, that will be a great reward, I know everyone would like to have some time with nothing to do."

Neith spoke to Amose of a project that he wanted very much. "Amose, this is important, not only to me but for all the people who have worked in making Opar a splendid city for Kmt. I have spoken with Nebre, and he is already working on a special project design.

Amose listened intently, and asked, "Neith, what do you have in mind?"

Neith continued, "It is important for the future generation of Oparians to know where they came from, and who we were. I have commissioned Nebre to design four large plaques that will tell of our history in starting the colony. They will tell of our sacrifices and the bravery and skill of the people who created this wonderful and beautiful city. I want you, Amose, and your brother Ako, to know that your names and titles will be carved in these tablets in a place of great honor and prestige. A few of the stonemasons remembered the language to carve.

"Amos was quite taken aback that he and his brother were looked upon in such great favor by Nomarch Neith. Amose said, "My brother Ako and I thank you for this great honor. We are very pleased that our names will forever be linked with the building of Opar."

Neith added one more item, "Amose, this is the best way I know of to ensure our immortality."

Both Neith and Amose knew this was going to be a very long project. They remembered Nebre's thoughts expressed to them about hoping that he would live to see the city completely built. It seemed appropriate to them that they were now having the same thoughts.

Time progressed with the building project foremost in everyone's mind. Once the wall neared the point of being three-quarters complete, Neith insisted that workers should be diverted to the construction of the Temple of the Flaming God.

After ten years, the wall was completed. A good start was made with the temple. The gold tablets were being cast, engraved, and would be mounted in the main walkway within the next year. There was enough gold left over from the several years of mining to make the dreams of Neith a reality.

Perhaps in a few years, the effort would be made to re-start mining operations, and the search for the route north to Memphis. Neith was apprehensive if Pepi II had truly died there would be another pharaoh who would want the gold and would find about Opar when he went through Pepi's records.

Little did Neith know that Pepi II had not recorded, at least in public notices, any information about the reason he had established the colony of Opar and where it was located. The information Pepi II had written was in his private files, with instructions to his faithful scribe and his son that upon his death all his private papyrus records were to be destroyed. He did not want any of these private Opar matters to be used to judge him in the matter of his legacy. Even though he was in his final years a beaten man, hated and blamed for the downfall of Kmt, he still wanted his legacy to be respected for eternity.

CHAPTER SIXTEEN — CHANGES

It is always remarkable to look back and see the changes that have occurred in a thousand years. However, it is sometimes even more amazing to see the changes that occur in one hundred years.

If we had traveled back in time to the colonization of the New World, beginning in roughly 1470, we would find some startling differences. We probably would not understand the fifteenth century English language, and those people would not understand the twentieth-century English language. They would not be able to comprehend that in roughly five hundred years we would have walked on the moon. We would not be able to comprehend what those folks believed, what they feared, and how they conducted their lives.

For the colony of Opar, the changes came quickly – happening in the first four generations after the founding.

Then almost no change at all …..

Within the one hundred years after the city of Opar was completed, there came a relaxation among the people. They felt they were secure and protected by the mountains and walls they had built.

The first hint of a problem came when the chief scribe asked one of his assistants to find him a roll of papyrus with information he wanted. The man came back and said, "I do not know what has happened, but all the papyrus scrolls in storage have been destroyed. The scrolls fell apart, and they are covered with a black coating that has made them unreadable."

The chief scribe asked, "How long has it been since the scrolls were checked?" He knew the answer that this question. After the new city had been built, the scrolls had been moved to one of the caves which dotted the mountains ringing the city. The new location of Opar was much moister than was Memphis. It seemed to rain here almost every day, and it never rained but perhaps one day a year in northern Kmt. The chief scribe knew what had happened, but he was powerless to recover the information lost.

Literacy in Kmt was never very high. Estimates are that no more than five percent of Kmt's people were literate. Lack of literacy was acceptable in a country of hundreds of thousands of people. In a small group of a few hundred people who lived in Opar, it would mean that within a few generations, there would be no one who could read the gold tablets or inscriptions that graced the walls. There were no schools or teachers who knew what was important to teach children.

Although there was no thought given to it at the time, the majority of people of Opar who could read had died out by the end of the second generation. Some people who thought reading and writing important had schooled their children. Unfortunately, by the end of the third generation, less than one percent of the population was literate. By the end of the fourth generation, almost no one in Opar could read or write.

Mining operations around Opar had been started up again late, in the rule of Neith, the second nomarch of Opar. It became apparent during the casting of the gold tablets for the Temple of the Flaming God that there was not enough gold to make the tablets according to plan, thus the necessary resumption of mining.

It was during one of the exploratory mining trips that precious stones were found – diamonds, rubies, and sapphires. At that time, the roughly shaped stones were considered an oddity – 'pretty colored stones' and of value only to the ladies who were lucky enough to receive them as gifts made into jewelry. One of the miner's wives had become quite adept at cutting precious gems, to show their colors to their best advantage and make them desirable to some of the upper-class ladies.

There were eight to ten attempts to find if the Nile was navigable to Memphis. Both Neith and all his successors had left oral orders that searches were to be made every few years to see if the Nile had risen enough to be able to transport gold back to Memphis.

Several of these expeditions had not been attempted. The men had little interest in the perils of a journey they knew was doomed from the start. So, they had a three-week vacation where they enjoyed hunting and visits from their wives or girlfriends, in a pre-arranged location miles from Opar.

The High Priest made the decision there would be no more efforts to navigate the Nile back to Memphis. They would try again in ten years. That ten-year expedition never took place, and further attempts to find the condition of the Nile were forgotten.

With the loss of literacy and all written records, the language began to change. Egyptian names were becoming less frequently used. Many new one or two syllable names were given to children—names that were easier than the ancient names of their forbearers. The Neteru language, much simpler than Egyptian, was becoming more accepted by the colonists. As the generations passed, there was a general blending of the two languages into one. This was aided by another factor – the male population was beginning to dwindle and become out of proportion with the female population. The cause for this was the number of men killed while hunting and construction of the new city.

The Neteru men began to be seen by many of the women, who had lost their significant other or were looking for a first relationship, as acceptable male companions. This was especially true of the less comely females. Oparian women and Neteru male relations were less likely to bear children. Conception happened, but miscarriages were almost the rule.

Live births were only about five out of one hundred pregnancies. This fact was causing a very gradual decrease in the overall population in Opar.

The walled city and main buildings were completed in roughly one hundred years – almost four generations. It was a costly project with probably thirty males and fifteen females killed in the construction. Many were killed by falling stones or falls from collapsed scaffolding. Broken limbs were common. Many men and women were lamed by improperly set bones or died from infections. The emphasis by Neith had kept the people's focus on construction, to the exclusion of other crafts. Many other skills were lost for this reason.

One of the wings of the Temple butted into one of the escarpments that surrounded seventy-five percent of Opar. The nomarch at the time was still very conscious of security for his little kingdom. He said there needed to be storage for the gold and precious stones that were being mined. He meant several floors of storage below the temple floor needed to be constructed.

To keep the population busy, it was decided by the nomarch and ruling council that the excavations would continue for the foreseeable future. Levels of floors would be created and secured for not only wealth storage but for residences and private apartments for the High Priest and the ruling council.

Eventually, long stairways were excavated that led to concealed exits to the outside world. One of these opened near a large flowing stream. All the exits were carefully concealed and camouflaged.

There were several factors that created changes in the east and central lands of Africa. Beginning somewhere in the seventh century CE, the countries of the middle east began to send expeditions into Africa seeking slaves. Yemen and the other Arabian countries began seeking female slaves for household duties and male slaves for heavier work. The clans inside Ethiopia were a chief supplier of black slaves who were captured in the interior and relocated for sale in the port cities of Massawa and Tajourah.

These Ethiopian cities were a short distance from the Port of Aden on the Arabian Peninsula. Thousands of slaves were removed from Africa, often sold by their black brothers, and were enslaved in the countries of the Middle East. As a result of the slavers, the more peaceful tribes in Africa were the first to be captured and sent north. The tribes that were hostile resisted the slavers and were left alone.

Christianity arrived in Africa during the first or second century and was centered primarily on the Northern Egyptian coast. Christianity spread slowly and eventually came into conflict with the advances of Islamic people starting in the seventh century CE.

The Christian churches during the 14th century began to spread into the interior of Africa. Christian missionaries, in later centuries, worked for the end of slavery, education of the native people and the hope of betterment.

Unfortunately, both the slavers and the missionaries brought with them diseases which the Africans had never seen and had no natural defenses against in their bodies. Imported sicknesses would attack and kill countless native people and even ravage the colony of Opar in the centuries to come.

CHAPTER SEVENTEEN — CITY OF BLOOD

Almost four thousand years had passed since the expeditions initiated by Pepi II left Memphis to establish gold mining operations. The city of Opar was located far south and east of Kmt's southern border, in the high and rugged mountains.

The gold mining had been the only constant in the long parade of years, interrupted during the building of the new Opar. Additional storage for gold was built in the subterranean rooms beneath the Temple of the Flaming God. There had been a steady accumulation of solid gold ingots, which now filled three large storerooms. Many of the gold workers over the centuries asked, "Why do we keep mining the yellow metal and pretty stones?" The High Priest knew the people needed a purpose to exist. The answer to the question was always the same, "One day the gods who sent us here will come back and demand their gold."

The population of Opar had risen in the last few hundred years to almost five hundred people. The Neteru had shrunk in numbers to about fifty men and thirty women. Mating between the women of Opar and the Neteru had produced very few children. The children resulting from these couplings seemed to be incapable of fathering children with either population of women. Centuries ago there was a shortage of men, and some women tried to establish relationships with Neteru men, for either children or companionship. The relationships did not last because the two races were just so different in base personalities and genetics. Over the centuries, the High Priest or Priestess had chosen the Neteru to be their bodyguards and guardians of the temple.

The Neteru people who had survived to this point had become withdrawn and unfriendly, choosing not to interact with other Neteru men or women. They were subject to extreme personality swings, from quiet and restrained to physically violent. The change seemed to occur in a few heartbeats. When this occurred, men would get out of the violent man's way, and the women would hurry to find their children and keep them from harm. There had been several occasions where the Neteru male would strike out at whoever was nearest to him, with whatever weapon he had in his hand. Innocent people had lost their lives in this way. The person affected by this blinding rage would eventually calm down and return to normal – as though nothing had happened.

The desire for the city of Opar to be hidden from the world was helped by nature. The almost constant fog and mist which occurred were a very effective camouflage. The sometimes low-hanging cloud phenomenon had been noted during the scouting expeditions which sought to find a site for the new Opar. It was one of the reasons the city was built in this lofty terrain. The other consideration was the high and steep mountains which surrounded the site on three sides. The people of Opar were still paranoid about outsiders and did everything to hide information about the city and its inhabitants.

The worship of the sun disk, known in ancient Egypt as the Aten, had been a part of the Egyptian pantheon of gods since the very beginning dynasties when the country was in its infancy. The Great Hymn to the Aten was composed in the 14th century BCE by the Pharaoh Akhenaten. He made worship of the Aten the state religion of Egypt, and he declared the Aten to be the only god to be worshiped.

The following words from that poem attribute the creation of the world, and its maintenance to the Aten:

O sole god, like whom there is no other!

Thou didst create the world according to thy desire,

Whilst thou wert alone: All men, cattle, and wild beasts,

Whatever is on earth, going upon its feet,

And what is on high, flying with its wings.

There were no mentions of human sacrifice that have come down to us from the ancient religions of Egypt. Both the worship of the Aten and the worship of Ptah and Amun seemed to have been peaceful in dogma and practice. In the First Dynasty, there is evidence that servants were buried, presumably alive, when a king died and was interred. In several tombs, the number that accompanied the dead king was in the hundreds. That practice seemed to have ended with the First Dynasty.

So, where did the association and linkage of human sacrifice in the colony of Opar originate?

There was nothing in the early records left by the builders of the Temple of the Flaming God, so it would seem the passion for human sacrifice must have appeared well after the completion of the temple tablets. These were the only written history of Opar that had survived to the modern times.

The ancient Egyptians always had a fascination with gold and considered it to be the blood of the gods. For many centuries the precious metal was only allowed to be owned and worn by the pharaohs and his closest circle of the aristocracy. The Egyptians believed it was one of the keys to eternal life. That is why most of the Pharaoh's coffins were made from solid gold. Some of the rich upper class tried to follow the pharaoh's lead by covering their coffins with gold leaf.

As the permanent city of Opar was being built, it would have been vulnerable to attacks by almost anyone who happened upon the location. Since there were no records from this period, we must surmise there were no attacks, and the priesthood was seeking ways to thank the Flaming God for protecting them.

Or, the priesthood sought to ensure the protection of Opar by the Flaming God by giving him the blood and sacrifice of human lives.

It was believed that gold was both a gift from and the blood of the gods. This belief explained why it was so coveted and pursued with such great enthusiasm. The priesthood would have wanted to give back to the Flaming God a gift in kind. The blood of a person was invaluable, so if he could be convinced to give up his blood, and his heart – the Flaming God would be very pleased with the magnitude of the offering. The priests believed the blood of enemies was the greatest sacrifice that could be made. The fact that the inner circle of the High Priest would be allowed to drink the blood of victims proved their devotion and made them partners in the sacrifice.

Over the years more than one traveler had come to the walls of Opar, where he was greeted, brought into the Temple of the Flaming God and killed by having his heart cut from his living body. The High Priest or Priestess would drain the blood from the body and would invite their inner circle to drink the blood. The High Priest had told his inner circle that drinking the blood of invaders would not only strengthen them but also please the Flaming God. They were told the Flaming God had guided the unfortunate men or women to Opar, and the High Priest would please the Flaming God by sacrificing them. The Flaming God would consider this to be a sign of obedience by the people of Opar, and the Flaming God would be so pleased by the sacrifice that more blessings would follow.

There had been many human sacrifices over the years. The people thought the Flaming God would inform the High Priest that he needed reassurance that the people still loved and worshiped him. The sending of visitors to the gate was the Flaming God's way of asking for this reassurance. The High Priest would also put together a party of Neteru, and they would search for a potential victim who would be brought back to the city of Opar for sacrifice.

The heart removal process had evolved over the centuries until it was an art. The High Priest would have the victim restrained by either hands or ropes to the altar in the Temple of the Flaming God. The sun would flood into the sacred altar room as the victim was made secure to the altar. The High Priest would approach from the victim's left. After dedicating the victim to the Flaming God, he would cut through the flesh of the diaphragm located below the rib cage, with a sacrificial knife made from obsidian. Experience would have taught the priests, that even an obsidian knife (that could rival the sharpness of a modern surgical scalpel) could not cut through the rib cage. So, the process would begin with a deep incision directly below the rib cage. The High Priest or Priestess would force a hand into the gaping wound and locate the heart. Since it is the only beating object in the chest cavity, it was easy to find and grasp. The heart, when seized and yanked by the High Priest's hand, would release from all attachments without further cutting.

The muscle is roughly the size of a small grapefruit, and would easily fit into a High Priest or Priestess' hand. It would continue to beat for ten to fifteen seconds after it had been removed. The priest would show the still beating heart to the victim who would be losing consciousness at this point. He would then lift the living heart over his head as a presentation to the Flaming God and to the attending worshippers. Grooves and depressions in the sacrificial altar would catch the victim's blood, which would be shared in golden goblets. The serving of sacrificial blood was accomplished by female temple acolytes. The body would then be removed and fed to the farm animals of the city.

As did many ancient people, the Oparians watched the day sky for changes in the Flaming God. Sometimes they watched, particularly toward evening, as it changed from gold to a shade of crimson, and disappeared below the western horizon. Possibly the changes were interpreted by the High Priestess or Priest as the Flaming God was demanding a sacrifice of blood.

CHAPTER EIGHTEEN — THE STORY OF WAZIRI

The Waziri people were one of many different tribes that sprung from the ancient Bantu people. All these tribes used a derivation of the Bantu language. They dominated the middle of Africa from the east coast to the west coast. The feared Zulu tribe of the nineteenth century was also a branch of the Bantu and still live in the area around Natal.

The Waziri people had been forced to migrate south to escape Arab slavers who captured their women and children and killed many warriors. At the time of the relocation, the Chief of the Waziri was called Chowambi, and he was still remembered by his tribe for saving their existence. Despite being fierce warriors, the Waziri were no match for the flintlock muskets of the Arabs, and they lost many men in skirmishes with the invaders. Chowambi made the correct decision moving his people south where the jungles were heavier, and his men could better defend their families.

Normally the chief of the Waziri was named Waziri also. Chowambi was an exception to this convention. However, the reason is not known. His son was named Waziri, and as he was Chowambi's only son, he was assured to be chief one day.

Waziri was in his 25th year of life. It was the year 1840 CE.

Waziri, like many of his fellow male warriors, was a tall man, several inches over six feet. He weighed about one hundred ninety pounds, all of which was muscle. He was a graceful man who moved with a light step and always seemed to be on alert. He was a man of great strength despite the fact that he did not have huge bulging muscles. Waziri was always the first fighter into battle and the first to risk himself in struggles with wild animals.

Waziri was a great favorite of the ladies of the village. The older women cast their eyes upon him in the hope he might find interest in them. The younger girls were always trying to find some way to attract his attention.

As the chief's son and heir, Waziri was entitled to as many wives as he wanted. His latest, a fourteen-year-old beauty, had been captured during a raid fifty miles to the north. She joined his other two wives, who looked at her with disdain and envy. Waziri had just spent his first night with her and was deeply disappointed. She did not have any wifely skills and did not seem interested in learning any. Waziri knew he had made a mistake and was ready to turn her loose to see if she could find her way home, and be rid of her. He thought better of the idea and decided to throw her to the wolves — his other wives.

After such a disappointing experience, Waziri needed something exciting to occupy his mind. His thoughts returned to the gold bracelet his older cousin had found years ago. Chowambi had sent his cousin several times to search for a more secure location for the tribe. The search ended when no better location could be found after several long attempts. Waziri's fantasy was that he would go back to where the golden bauble had been found, and find more; enough to make him the richest man in the village. All he had to do was to get his cousin to reveal the location, a detail his companion had been unwilling to reveal in the many tellings of this story.

He decided to visit his cousin and ask him to repeat the story. The story had been told to him several times before, but Waziri always hoped there would be some new nugget of information remembered. There never was.

His cousin told the tale again, "Five of my warriors and I were on a scouting expedition far to the east, almost two month's journey. We were searching for any evidence of the intrusion of the hated slavers and a more secure location for the tribe."

"We had been following a river through the jungle and were confronted by high mountains and a sheer cliff that seemed to go to the left and right as far as could be seen."

"It was late in the afternoon, and we were foraging for greens and berries for dinner. I decided the men needed a good meal and a night's rest before we scaled the cliff. I did not want anyone falling during the difficult climb because we were pushing ourselves too hard."

"One of the men motioned for me to come over to him. We were in silent mode as this was strange territory for us, and we knew nothing of the people who may live here. As I approached, I could see part of a skull and a few bones the jackals had not dragged away. As I knelt and looked closer, I saw why my companion had called me. There, mostly buried, was a glint of gold that had been revealed by a ray of sunlight. I acknowledged the warrior's find and asked him to move back a bit. I, with trembling hands, gingerly dug around the object. It soon became apparent this was not a wrist bracelet, but a much larger ornament meant to be worn around the neck. The weight was considerable. It had no markings or engraved designs. My feelings were that it was obviously owned by an important man. I lifted the bauble and wiped the dirt off, giving me my first complete look at the treasure. My heart was pounding as I examined the find. As expedition leader, the trinket was mine, but I needed to remember to reward the sharp eyes of the young warrior. I placed the necklace around my neck and enjoyed the evening meal very much."

"The next morning after we had our morning herb tea, the group discussed what we should do next. We collectively agreed we should try to find more gold, and perhaps the village of the dead stranger."

"My thoughts went to why the man had ended up here, at the foot of the cliff. We had no idea how long he had been dead. Perhaps he had fallen from the cliff. I thought it a good idea we climb and investigate further."

"It took us all of the following morning to scale the cliff, and fortunately, we reached the top with no falls or serious injuries. The climb was long and difficult and exhausted the men, so we rested for the remainder of the day. The next morning we began our search in a very cautious manner."

"We agreed we would search the area for seven risings of the sun. Upon reaching the plateau, we saw an impressive ring of mountains covered by fog. The morning was quite cold, so much so the men could see their breath. The fog caused concern some wondering if they had entered some lair of evil spirits. As the men rested, the fog and mist began to fade away, and a large walled city began to reveal itself. Emerging from the mist was the rounded top of a building located behind a great wall. The city looked very large and foreboding even from this distance. Leading up to the wall was two miles of relatively flat and desolate land, consisting of large boulders and stunted and gnarled trees. I began to think perhaps the men were right about this being the lair of an evil spirit."

"Again, we planned our next move, and I decided we would observe and conceal ourselves until we found if the inhabitants were friendly. I was anxious to see what we would find."

"Four days later our patience was rewarded as we saw several heavily armed men walk from the wall and head in a southerly direction. As they passed us, at a distance of one hundred yards, several facts became evident. The men were white, shorter than we, and were dressed in some garments that were not animal skins. They appeared to be at ease and moved confidently forward — as though they had done this before. One other detail noticed was the small monkeys that three of the men had perched on their shoulders, and without restraints. Also noted was the fact that one of the men had a gold collar around his neck, much like mine."

"I sent several men to scale the mountains that were behind the walled city. I wanted to know what was behind the wall, and what could be learned about the people who lived there. The rest of us fanned out and at a safe distance followed the men who had exited the city. We were careful to be sure to mark our trail so our climbing warriors could find and follow us."

"After several days of following the men, we determined they were hunters and not marauders. They had killed several antelopes and one zebra. We watched with great hunger as they gutted and bled out the game. Another curious event then unfolded for us. Two of the men called to the monkeys, who were busy eating fruit in a nearby tree. The monkeys immediately dropped their fruit and scurried to the ground and climbed up to the men's shoulders. A small piece of cloth was tied to each of the monkey's wrists; they were given some command in a language that was strange to us, and the monkeys immediately scurried off toward the city in the clouds."

"The next day several older men and women carrying baskets appeared through the mist, seemingly led by the monkeys. The men and women began to skin the animals and cut the carcasses into rough quarters. With this completed, the older men built fires and smoked the meat slowly. After smoking, the people began to carry the meat back to the city. From our hiding place, we were not only able to observe what was happening but were able to smell the cooking meat as well. The smell was pure torture," my cousin added with a laugh.

"We silently withdrew and backtracked for several miles. We were all eager to discuss what we had seen. Our scouts who had climbed the mountain rejoined our party, and we were once again at full strength. The climbers were anxious to tell what they had observed. That night we again had a meal of edible greens and berries, for we did not want to risk a fire that would betray our position."

"Moabi was the leader I had assigned to observe from the mountains surrounding the walled city. Moabi began, "First, I have reason to believe that we were observed by the inhabitants of the walled city. It is a feeling, nothing I can be sure of but .... We were a great distance above the city; there was no place where we could get closer without positively being seen."

"Here is what we observed. There appear to be several hundred people living behind the wall. They seemed to be two different races of men. The main, larger number of people were white. These white men looked to be in charge. They spoke a strange language, and I was not able to understand any of the words I heard used. I have never seen white people before except for the slavers. At first, I mistook the others for some form of a gorilla, but I was wrong. The others were very hairy and as ugly as any monkey. They had short, squat legs and their torsos were quite large, and they appeared to be powerful and well armed. My guess is they are the protectors of the white race. There were several guard stations on top of the wall and I thought it would be impossible to enter without being seen, and having an alarm given. An attempt to enter the city from the mountains would also be ill-advised. The mountains were quite steep, and we believe it impossible to make a surprise entrance into the city that way." This concluded Moabi's observations.

"I remember asking Moabi why he felt he was being observed." He had a look on his face that he did not want to utter what his thoughts were, but he did continue.

"All the time we were on the mountain, I had the feeling we were being watched, by someone quite near to us. I know I sound like an old woman because there was no one there, just us warriors and some small monkeys that were scurrying around the sparse shrubbery that grows on the mountain."

"Moabi had not been present during our observation of the hunt and the use of the small monkeys. That level of animal training I had never thought possible, using monkeys as messengers and as sentries. After much discussion lasting until almost dawn, we decided not to make contact with the people behind the wall. It would be impossible to contact them without going into the city, and that did not seem like a smart idea. No amount of gold would be worth our lives."

So, my cousin concluded by saying, "A couple of the men were afraid the people were spirits, and the rest of us had other reservations about going into the city of the clouds. Thus we rested for a few days and began our long journey home."

This time, as my cousin told the story, a new ending had been added, the part about the monkeys, and leaving with no contact. As my cousin poured more beer into my bowl, I thanked him for telling me the tale again. He smiled and poured himself some more beer.

I said to him "Too bad cousin that you do not remember the way back to the walled city." He lifted his bowl to his mouth and said "Oh, but I do. I have a map and detailed directions recorded. If you are interested, perhaps we could work out an arrangement."

Quizzically I asked, "What sort of an arrangement?" I had an idea where this conversation was going.

"What if we could trade the map and directions to the cloud city for something of great value that you have?"

I could not be this lucky, could I? "What is it you would like to trade for this valuable information, my cousin?"

He looked me in the eye and said, "Do you know that new wife you captured in the raid, a few weeks ago?"

"Yes," I said, somehow managing to keep a smile off my face.

Jim Malachowski

CHAPTER NINETEEN — MERY AND NEDJAM

Mery was the first High Priestess whose name has come down to us. She was born somewhere near to 1820 and became High Priestess about 1837, upon the death of her mother. She was the first ruler, male or female for whom historical information has become available. Even by today's standards Mery would be considered an attractive woman. She was about five feet four and weighed one hundred pounds. She had an outgoing personality, and everyone who came into contact with her liked her almost immediately.

Mery had been named by her mother as her successor to the position of High Priestess. There had been no opposition from the male aristocracy of Opar. As a contingency, her mother had made arrangements with some of the military men, and they agreed to enforce her wishes. That contingency never happened.

Mery ascended to the title, without any assistance from a regent. Her mother's handmaiden had helped her in the first few years of rule, but that quickly ended when she died suddenly.

Mery had grown up with several young girls who were being screened as potential attendants to the High Priestess. The girl who stood out from the others was Nedjam. She was ten years younger than Mery, and they had known each other since they were small children. The relationship between them evolved and grew from childhood friends to one young woman who ruled and the other who supported the High Priestess.

Nedjam was an inch or two taller than Mery. She possessed a slender figure and had a quiet demeanor. Nedjam was fiercely loyal to Mery. The other female attendants came to realize how close Nedjam and Mery were and were very careful what they said about Mery when Nedjam was within hearing distance.

Both young women shared something else in common, the lack of eligible young men. They would talk for hours about the imagined strong and weak points of men, and more than once concluded they would both die as virgins having never found a man that suited them.

Life for a young High Priestess was very undemanding. The biggest item on her agenda was what clothing to wear, or what makeup to have applied to her face. There had not been a sacrifice to the Flaming God for almost a year, and Mery was just as glad. Her mother had taught the mechanics of what to do, and she had learned the ceremonial chants and dances that preceded a sacrifice. Mery was probably remiss in watching the skies for a signal from the Flaming God that he demanded a sacrifice. She was somewhat of an agnostic about the religion of Opar, not nearly as bloodthirsty as many of her predecessors.

Yesterday, two hunters came back with a strange story and had requested an audience with the High Priestess. Nedjam found one of the hunters attractive, and she convinced Mery to give them some of her time. During the discussion, Nedjam sat on a chair off to a side, and listened to the conversation – and admired one of the men.

The more senior hunter, Tur by name, narrated the happening. Tur and three other hunters were looking for zebra or antelope on the grassy plains thirty miles south of Opar. They were watching a small herd of antelope and were deciding on how to approach when one of the sharp-eyed men spotted movement close to a tree far to the left of the animals. It was a man who was dressed only in a loincloth of what had been once white material. The man was somewhat slender and had a dark complexion and a heavy black beard and mustache.

The hunters decided to see what the man was doing. They were also curious to see if there were any more men hunting with him. Obviously, he seemed to be hunting, but he was not sneaking closer to the antelope, and he did not seem to have a spear or bow and arrow. They watched as the stranger raised a device made of metal and wood, pointed it in the direction of the beast. There was a flash of light, much smoke and a second later a very loud explosion like thunder. The hunters were startled by what they had just witnessed and were frozen in their crouched positions. They watched silently as the man walked to where the herd had been and saw him kneel in the tall grass and cut the throat of a badly wounded antelope.

As the men watched, they noticed movement in the grass and saw a straw-colored lioness slinking through the perfect camouflage. The hunter had his back to the lioness, and neither heard or sensed her approach – until it was too late. The lioness lept upon the crouched man. Her mighty jaws clamped on the back of his head, and she crushed his skull like it was an eggshell. The antelope was hers now. The lioness raised her blood-smeared face and smelled the hunters from the breeze that had shifted and was now delivering their identity to her. She gave a low, breathy growl warning the men not to approach. When she saw no movement coming through the knee-high grass, she grabbed the antelope by the neck, threw the hundred pound carcass over her back and walked quickly out of the field and back to her six-week-old cubs.

The hunters from Opar were momentarily stunned by the events that had just happened in front of them. The entire incident had taken less than ninety seconds. The stalkers cautiously went to the spot where the dead man lay and examined his body. Up close he was a stocky man in his mid-twenties with a swarthy appearance with much hair on his head and body. He appeared to be well fed and was probably part of a larger force of men.

Tur and the others were more curious about the man's weapon than the dead man. It lay beside his body and Tur picked it up. It was heavier than a spear. The metal was shaped like a hollow reed only much larger and still smelled of the cloud of smoke. There appeared to be some moving parts near where the wooden parts became attached. Tur did not show his apprehension as he handled the muzzleloader gingerly to examine it.

Tur, as the leader, decided they should backtrack on the hunter, to determine where any companions might be located. The men spread out and began to follow the trail through the grass. Near a tree fifty yards back they found a crude backpack and a long dress-like garment. He had obviously taken it off to stalk the antelope herd. They removed the contents of the bag and found some fruit, a small container of water, a pouch of dry powder and ten metal balls that were quite heavy. The perplexed men put the contents in the pack and continued on their backtracking.

After a day of walking, they had found nothing to indicate either the man's origins or any companions. They decided to discontinue the search and get back to the task of hunting meat for the city. After three days of success, they returned to Opar and requested a meeting with the High Priestess.

Mery had listened with more interest than she felt in her mind. When the hunter finished the narration of the story, Mery leaned slightly toward him and asked, "Tur, what do you believe is the significance of what you witnessed?"

"Majesty," Tur began, "I believe there is some danger for the people of Opar from men equipped with such weapons. I am not sure how the weapon kills, but it does it at a greater distance than an arrow can be shot. I wish we had been able to examine the antelope as it may have given us some clue of how the device works. It is hard for me to believe that the sound and smoke it creates kills." Mery waited for more conversation from Tur, when none came she continued, "Tur, you did well to bring this information to our attention, and also bringing back the device with the man's supplies. Perhaps one of the temple priests or learned men can get some more information." Tur bowed deeply and backed out of the room.

Mery called one of the Neteru bodyguards and had him remove the muzzleloader, and the man's pack from the room, with instructions to have the weapon stored and studied. Mery informed the Priest who had come in with the guard, "I want to know how this device works and find out if we can make more of them."

She dismissed all but Nedjam, and they went back to their private quarters. Mery bade Nedjam be seated at a table which contained fruit and beer. Mery looked at Nedjam and asked, "What did you make of that discussion?" Nedjam thought for a minute and said, "I don't see why Tur thought that device was so important. Dead is dead. What is the difference, killed with a knife or killed by that device?"

Mery agreed, and the matter of the muzzleloader was soon forgotten. It was also forgotten by the priests, and it was put in some obscure storage place where it remained for many years.

CHAPTER TWENTY — WAZIRI'S JOURNEY PART 1

Waziri had left his village several days after the gold discussion and trade with his cousin. He needed time to think about making the trip to the city in the clouds his relative had described to him. It was impossible for Waziri to keep his thoughts on the upcoming trip. His home contained so many distractions. His wives were always arguing and fighting among themselves and with their neighbors. His cousin had begun to complain about the foreign wife he had wanted so badly a short time ago. His father, the chief, always had some errand for him.

Finally, Waziri had enough, and he told his father he was going on a hunting trip and would be gone for a week or more. Hunting was the furthest thing on Waziri's mind. He had to decide if he wanted to make the long and dangerous trip to the east. He knew of a quiet area twenty miles from his village where he could take one or two companions, and get his wish for solitude. Both companions he had invited to accompany him were very stoic and solemn men. Both were excellent hunters and just the kind of men he needed to be around now.

Foremost in Waziri's mind was the lure of riches. The thought of being the wealthiest man in the village, as well as being chief one day was very important to him. Secondly, was how to get the gold away from the people in the cloud city, as he was sure they would not just give it to him. A fight with a well-armed force of men was probably not worth the loss of life that would surely happen. He knew that his father would not allow a large number of warriors to accompany him. The number of healthy warriors was not enough to defend the village, let alone to leave the village undefended for several months.

Perhaps there was another way ....

The trip had been good to clear Waziri's head and help him make a sound decision with a mind free of other distractions. Upon his return, he sat down with his father and told him his plans. He told his father of his desire to bring back the gold metal. His father listened to Waziri's words about the people who inhabited the cloud city, saying, "You are right to be cautious about the people in that city. We believe they have lived in that area for many centuries. They guard their privacy very strictly, and there were tales that these people are more fierce than a casual encounter would disclose. They worship very different gods than we and do not hold much value for human life. Rumors have come to me of them having taken men and using them in mines that produce their yellow metal. Waziri, I understand your curiosity and desire for riches, but should anything happen to you, our warriors would not be able to come to your aid. Think carefully about your decision. Also, given the number of men in our village, I do not want you to take any more than three of them with you."

Waziri listened carefully and replied, "My father and chief I thank you for your thoughts and concerns, but I will be going — and I will be respecting your wishes, by only taking a few warriors with me. I ask your blessing and your sacrifices to keep me safe and return successfully to you."

Several days later, Waziri and his two friends Murvo and Dingane left the village very early in the morning before anyone else was awake. They had all been born in the same year as Waziri and resembled his body stature and character. They had been friends since childhood and had faced many trials during the migration and growing up in a new home in a hostile land. All three men had killed an Arab slaver in years past.

The men traveled light and intended to live off the land as much as possible. They only carried their bows and arrows, spears and a large shield. Implements to make fire were stored at the bottom of their arrow quiver.

The three young men were able to sustain for the first ten days a rapid pace, which was twenty miles a day in the grassland and a slower pace of fifteen miles in the jungle and hilly terrain.

Every evening Waziri and his companions pored over the map and the instructions before retiring for the night. Waziri had promised his two friends that they would share in any yellow metal they would find and bring back. The need for adventure was high in all three men, and Murvo and Dingane would have come on the adventure even without the promise of gold.

After almost six weeks of travel, the three men stood at the base of the escarpment. They knew that their search had been successful and the city in the clouds was little more than a hard days climb away. They were very excited to be this close to their prize. Murvo laughingly said to Waziri, "You should be ashamed of the terrible things you said about your cousin. His map and directions were true, and here we are about to become rich men." Waziri and Dingane laughed at the joke. All three men were apprehensive about what the following days would bring.

The next morning was cool, but they welcomed the brisk weather for the strenuous climb that lay ahead of them. Breakfast was eaten quickly and quietly, each man keeping his own thoughts.

Late afternoon brought them to the summit of the escarpment. Despite some near-harrowing accidents, the worst any of the men suffered were scrapes, bruises and strained muscles. They only wanted to rest and begin the balance of their adventure the next day.

The following morning brought even colder weather. The fog and mist were only a few feet off the ground. The men waited until the sun made a bright spot in the fog, so they could then orient themselves with the map. The fog was so heavy that if one of them became disoriented, it would be easy to walk over the edge of the escarpment and fall to his death.

The men talked quietly among themselves and made a decision they would try to find a cave where they would be more comfortable and have some shelter from the night's chill. The plan they had developed during the long trek was to find a good vantage point and watch for anyone exiting the city who appeared to be a laborer, following them until they had located the mines. They knew about the hunters who must make lots of hunting trips, and they dismissed the need to follow them.

After a week of the fruitless vigil, Dingane had thoughts that seemed to jeopardize the entire expedition. "Waziri, we have watched for many days, and have seen no activity, other than three sets of hunters leaving the city. What if there is no more gold to mine, or they just don't mine for gold anymore? Or maybe they do not come out the front gate. Perhaps they have paths or a trail into the mountains from the rear of the city." Waziri had been thinking the same thing and was embarrassed that someone else had verbalized concerns. The creeping doubt in his leadership was beginning to set in. He answered, "Dingane, you may be right, I have had the same thoughts. I believe we should climb the mountains in the rear of the city and observe from that direction. We will begin this new strategy tomorrow."

Three days later, the change appeared to have been a smart move. The morning, while cold, did not have the heavy fog. The uncomfortable warriors discovered several men in the far distance making their way through a pass in the mountains. Waziri whispered to his companions, "Mark in your mind where you believe the men are coming from and where we think they are going. Let's move now to where we think they are traveling."

After another relocation and several arguments about where they were, the men's diligence was rewarded as several people had walked within a hundred yards of them. Waziri motioned for his men to follow, hoping the mines were nearby. Waziri silently recited a prayer to his totem, asking for success and guidance.

Waziri's party allowed the men from the city in the clouds to get far ahead of them. They did not want any sign given to the workers they were being followed. After a two-hour trek, they came to the destination of the men's journey. The work crew was made up of two heavily armed gorilla-like men – the Neteru. This was the warrior's first close-up look at the Neteru with their stocky bodies and short bowed legs. They were heavily armed with bows and arrows, and heavy clubs called a cudgel. The other members of the work party were black men, but different from the Waziri warriors. The black slaves were shorter and somewhat more muscular. Their noses were less aquiline, and they just looked different. The Waziri warriors were all glad the slaves were not from their family of tribes.

The three men melted into the jungle where their presence and observation was less likely to be seen. They watched the comings and goings for several days. On the fifth day, the watchers observed two of the black men, at the end of the day, carrying heavy baskets. They were having a difficult time and required frequent rest to get the baskets of ore over the steep mountain pass.

After the men had left, Waziri let his excitement show saying, "This is the secret that will make us all rich. The rocks the slaves are carrying back to the cloud city contain the yellow metal. Tomorrow after they leave we will go into the hole in the mountain and see what the men do there to get the yellow metal. Perhaps we can just take some of the yellow metal out of the ground without anyone noticing."

The next evening when the laborers had finished for the day, Waziri and his two companions walked to the mine with torches they had made during the day of soft dry wood and tinder. They lit them at the entrance and walked into the mine. The three men had to duck their heads when they entered, being several inches taller than the workers. They were amazed how dark and deep the mine went into the earth. After thirty minutes of walking on a downward slanting path, they came to the end of the mine shaft and were amazed to see rocks embedded in the wall with streaks of gold gleaming in the torchlight. All three men's eyes opened wide, and they tried to break out the gold-bearing rock from the wall. They had little success as they had underestimated how hard it was to find and obtain the precious metal.

The torches were beginning to burn down, and Waziri said, "We should leave this tomb, and discuss how we want to get the gold quickly before we exhaust our torches."

As the men approached the mine entrance, their eyes were not used to brighter light and even at this late hour, they were having difficulty seeing. As they stepped out of the mine, and their eyes became adjusted to the light, they were startled to find seven men all with arrows pointed at them. Waziri's blood ran cold when he realized they had been discovered. He immediately began to blame himself, as the group leader, for being stupid enough to be captured. He did not want even to think about what was to happen to them next. His father's words about no help coming rang loudly in his mind.

Chapter Twenty-One — Waziri's Journey Part 2

Several of the gorilla-men put down their bows and began to tie the three men's hands behind their backs. Out of the corner of his eye, Waziri saw Dingane shove the man who was trussing him, and he grabbed the knife that was hanging at the gorilla man's side. From behind him, another gorilla-man slammed the back of his head with a heavy cudgel. Waziri was shocked how quickly this event had taken place. His heart sank for as the blow was delivered, he saw the light in Dingane's eyes go out. He was sure his friend had been killed.

With heavy hearts, they were led back through the hills and toward the cloud city. After a short walk over the coarser terrain, their heads were covered by a thick and foul-smelling piece of animal hide, and they were led through the mountains along a well-worn trail. Both Waziri and Murvo were in a state of shock and were in no mood to communicate, so they were both quiet. The only sound they heard was their breathing under the hood.

They could tell they had arrived in the city, for they could hear the sounds of people in the distance, farm animals and the laughter of children playing. They were led up several steps and into a building which was several degrees cooler. Next, they were taken down two flights of stairs, and they heard the sound of a wooden door opening and the protest of its leather hinges.

Waziri and Murvo were roughly shoved into a room and someone grabbed their head covers. Their hands were still bound securely behind their backs and it seemed no one was going to remove their restraints. The door closed behind them and they were again in absolute quiet and total darkness for the second time in the last three hours.

Waziri endlessly paced the floor and mentally berated himself for being a terrible leader, allowing them to be captured, and he blamed himself for Dingane's death. The room appeared to have been hewn from stone and seemed to be empty. No sound came, nor was there any light – just total and complete darkness. No food or water was available, nor was any brought to the two prisoners.

Sometime later, it could have been hours, or it could have been days, the door opened, and two of the gorilla-men strode into the room, grabbing Murvo by the arms dragging him from the room. This happened so quickly that Waziri did not even have time to speak anything to his friend.

Waziri became quite unnerved in the gloom, now that he was alone. He missed his friends and missed their conversations. The room had not seemed so frightening when Murvo was present. It was quite another thing to be alone in the total darkness.

After another long passage of time, the door opened again, and Waziri was manhandled into a hall and up two flights of stairs. He then came to a large hallway with doors on either side of the corridor. He was guided through a large circular room with a round roof opening which let him see the sky and the sun entering the chamber. It also illuminated a stone altar which contained dark brown stains.

With one gorilla-man on either side of him, he stood before two empty chairs, and a closed door slightly behind them. Waziri's heart was racing. He had a feeling that his fate was going to be determined by the two people who were going to sit in front of him. The door opened, and a white man and woman walked slowly toward the chairs, their eyes were glued to his face. The man appeared to be a few years older than Waziri and was rumpled and overweight. His walk told Waziri that the woman was in charge, the man was ruled by her. The woman appeared to be a few years younger and was extremely beautiful. Waziri tried very hard not to assess her body too much, especially her bare breasts. He forced his gaze to the woman's face.

Mery, the High Priestess of Opar, spoke to him in words that had no meaning to Waziri. He shook his head slowly to acknowledge he had heard but did not understand. The man turned to the woman and spoke in a strangely feminine voice, "Mery, I do not know why you are bothering speaking to this thief. We questioned the other one for several hours, all for nothing. If he had known anything, he would have said so before he was sacrificed to the Flaming God."

Mery, with a look of exasperation, answered, "Yes Set, I know. It was highly unlikely he was going to understand our words. But I thought it worth a try anyway. I am curious about these black people. He appears much different from the blacks that we use for mine workers. His face is strange and look at his body." Set felt a sting of jealousy in him from Mery's last words, and he thought it better not to respond to her comment.

Set tried to change the subject, "Are you thinking about trying to educate another savage? That did not work well with the two filthy bearded men who wore those white dresses. Neither was bright enough to realize that their lives depended on learning to speak with us. Do you want to try again to educate another savage?"

Mery looked at him and smiled patronizingly, "You know me, always willing to try another approach. Remember, you were in charge of trying to educate those two surly beasts. Besides, he may have some knowledge of the fire tubes. The gods know you have never made any progress in learning how they work. If I were you, I would not speak of stupid savages. It would seem as if we have more than our share of those. What do you think?"

Set ignored the sting of comments from Mery; after all, she was the High Priestess. He quietly said, "Correct as usual, Mery."

The thoughts again came back to Mery, as to why had she allowed Set to be Opar's High Priest. He was fat and lazy and had more interest in the low-class prostitutes than he did in her. Mery thought she should have a man appear by her side, and a poor excuse for a man was better than no man at all. Her caustic banter toward Set was her disgust of him manifesting itself.

Mery turned to him and said in a stinging manner of speech, "You would not mind if we tried to educate one more savage, would you Set? There are so many things about the outside world about which I am curious. This time we will try a different approach – a woman's approach not with that fool of a teacher you tried last time. Women have ways of getting information out of the dumbest savages." Set laughed slightly, and he shook his head in agreement, but added, "Just don't forget this man is a warrior if ever I have seen one. He is a killer and will do anything to get out of the city. Don't endanger anyone's life." Mery listened and smiled demurely.

Nedjam, the chief handmaiden for Mery, was a few years younger than she and was her favorite. Nedjam had been secretly watching and listening to the proceedings in the throne room with great interest. Even though the black man was younger than she, Nedjam found him very compelling and extremely handsome. She had never seen a man of any color that was so tall. He probably was at least six to eight inches taller than she.

After Nedjam had listened to the conversation, she felt her heart begin beating fast in the hope she was going to be involved somehow with this wonderfully handsome savage.

When Waziri returned to his cell, he noticed several things had changed. Most obvious was a lit candle and a supply of candles and flints. There was a bowl of water and some dried meat and fruit on a small table. Also, new was a low stool. The biggest surprise was that his guard had removed his restraints. It was great to begin to have feeling and the use of his hands.

Waziri was physically and mentally exhausted, as he slumped onto the stool. He could not even begin to assess what had gone on in the throne room. Obviously, there had been some disagreement between the man and the woman on what to do with him. He looked about at the food and drink and was cautiously optimistic about his prospects. Clearly, the woman wanted something from him, but he could not even imagine what it might be. Just when he began to think about the future, his thoughts went back to his two friends. He wondered if perhaps Murvo was still alive. Too exhausted to eat, Waziri lay on the stone floor and fell into a deep sleep.

Later that evening, as Nedjam was helping Mery prepare for bed, she spoke, "May I ask a question? I know it is not my concern, but what are your plans for the black stranger?"

Mery had her back turned, and with a smile, she answered, "Why does this concern you? Do I detect a bit of caring in your question?"

Nedjam blushed slightly and answered, "He is very handsome and quite different from the other men in Opar."

Mery turned and looked Nedjam in the eyes and said, "I am now speaking to you as the High Priestess, not your friend. I know where you are going with this line of questions. I must caution you; this is a savage warrior who would do anything to gain his freedom and go back to his fifty smelly wives." Mery allowed her face to change into a soft smile.

Nedjam smiled also and said, "I understand your concern, Majesty." Nedjam was amazed how transparent her inner thoughts were to Mery. But then, Nedjam had been with Mery for many years now.

Mery turned and walked toward her sleeping couch, "We will talk more about my plans for him in the next several days."

Several days later Mery called Nedjam and asked her to be seated in Mery's private quarters. She was speaking as the High Priestess, and not Nedjam's close friend. "Nedjam, as you know, we have tried in the past to get some information from captives, and we have failed miserably. Set, in the past, has insisted that we use one of his friends to try to teach them our language. I want to try something different this time. I would like you to attempt to either teach this black warrior our language, or you may need to learn his language."

"There is some great personal danger in this for you, and we will have guards present at all times when you two are together. I want you to think about the consequences of my request, and give me your decision when you have made up your mind."

"Majesty," Nedjam began, "I believe I have made up my mind. I could not help but hear your conversation with Set in the throne room. I am curious also about this man. There is something about him that I find mysterious and compelling. I would like to know more about him, and quite honestly about the world beyond our wall."

Nedjam continued, "And as you know, I am attracted to him like a woman."

Mery replied, "Nedjam, I knew you would be attracted to him. Again I say, be careful of your female interest in him; he could use your feelings against you, not to mention putting you in great danger. Again I say, beware."

Nedjam answered, "Majesty, I understand the perils and possible rewards. I am ready to serve you and my city."

The next morning Waziri was awakened by two burly guards, who ushered him out of the temple to a group of middle-aged women congregated around a large pot of hot soapy water. One of the women ordered the guards to strip the prisoner, which they did. As his dirty clothes fell away, the women's eyes scanned the prisoner's body from head to toe, and he received some appreciative looks. Waziri pretended he did not notice, although he was smiling inside. The women fell upon him with wet soapy linen cloths and began to bath him, and dried him when they were finished.

Two of the women wrapped a short kilt around his waist, which was the garment men wore. One whispered to the other, "I hope this skirt is long enough," to which both women, and most of the others, fell into raucous laughter.

To Waziri, who felt like this indignation would never end, it was a relief when he was taken back to the temple and the small room. The two guards who had accompanied him gestured to sit down and stood beside him. The other chair in front of him was empty. Waziri had no idea what was expected of him.

A slender woman, dressed in a white linen sheath dress, entered the room from a doorway behind the vacant chair and sat down in front of him. Nedjam was shaking inside both from being this close to the warrior, and from having no idea how to accomplish the teaching task. She was in no hurry to start speaking to someone who could not understand her.

Nedjam and Waziri quietly surveyed each other. He believed this woman would be someone who could influence his fate.

Nedjam pointed her finger at her chest and said her name. To her amazement, Waziri pointed his finger at his chest and said, "Waziri." Nedjam had gotten her point across. Waziri realized this session was to learn to communicate with each other. Nedjam was delighted, and Waziri gave a cautious smile. He breathed an inward sigh of relief. If they wanted to learn to communicate, they did not wish to kill him — at least not yet.

The sessions went on every day for a month, and it became evident that Waziri was an intelligent man. It soon became apparent to Nedjam that she needed to learn his language as well. The Oparians language had a limited vocabulary because of Opar's closed and isolated society. The educational dialog was going to be a long process, with lots of frustration on both sides.

At the end of a month, Mery called Nedjam in for a progress report. Mery was delighted to hear that there was some common ground and that there was some rudimentary understanding between the black warrior and Nedjam. Mery asked, "Is there any way to speed this up?" Nedjam answered, "The only way I can see to do that is to lengthen the sessions, and perhaps move out of that little room. There need to be more objects for us to learn their names. Time, Mistress, is what this will take. In the last few days, we have been able to talk with each other in simple short sentences." Mery answered, "Go back to your work, you are doing well. If you wish to go outside, just be sure to take the guards with you. Make the warrior understand if he tries to escape he will be killed."

Two months later Mery gave Nedjam a list of things she wished to know from the warrior. Nedjam came back the next day with answers to most questions. Mery was pleased with the answers, and with the progress that had been made.

Another month and Waziri and Nedjam were able to communicate abstract ideas. Waziri was a fast learner and was able to learn Nedjam's mother tongue rather quickly. Nedjam was able to learn the Waziri language rapidly also. Without knowing it, they were able to communicate using words from both languages when the need arose. This process had become automatic.

As the months of study progressed, it became evident to Nedjam that her attraction to Waziri was becoming stronger. Sometimes he was hard to read. He had a dignified personality and did not like to show his emotions, but Nedjam thought he also had feelings for her.

One afternoon Mery said she wanted to have a session with the prisoner in the throne room. Nedjam informed Waziri, telling him not to be nervous, that she would help him with questions he did not understand. She would translate his answers to Mery.

Waziri did his best to answer the questions in his new language. He did quite well, needing little assistance from Nedjam.

About an hour into the discussion, Mery motioned to a guard who was standing at the door to enter. To his amazement, Waziri saw the guard carrying one of the flintlock muskets used by the Arabs. He was apprehensive about where the conversation was going.

Mery spoke, "Waziri, do you know how to make this death tube work?"

He answered, "Majesty if you have all the parts, I believe I can make it work. The evil men who carry these have slaughtered many of our people. We have killed a number of them and have harvested the weapons from their dead. We learned how they work."

To which Mery responded, "You will gain great favor with me if you can make this device function."

Jim Malachowski

CHAPTER TWENTY-TWO — WAZIRI'S JOURNEY PART 3

Waziri viewed the leather purse which held the black mixture; there was not much available. He asked if there were other supplies of this powder. The answer was no. Waziri continued, "My people were able to discover the makeup of this substance. I can probably make it work if there is a cave nearby where bats live. This material is the most difficult to find; the others are easy." [3]

A demonstration was scheduled the next morning to see if Waziri could get the weapon to function. With little fuss, Waziri was able to get the gun to fire, reload and fire again. There were several military men in attendance, all of whom were very curious about the muzzleloader. Only two or three scouts had ever seen one of these weapons fired. Several soldiers were busy trying to dig the musket ball out of the tree that had been the target. The soldiers were very interested in hearing if Waziri could teach some of his men to manage the weapon and assist them in finding the raw materials to make black powder. He agreed to help with all

---

[3] Saltpeter. Found in bat droppings. Harvested by soaking the guano in water, then collecting the crystals.

concerns. Nedjam was as proud of Waziri as was possible. She had made her mistress grow in stature to the military and had made Set look more incompetent. It was a win/win for everyone except Set.

Mery had been present when the muzzleloader was fired and was clearly frightened by the loud explosion and the great billow of smoke produced. Mery had told Nedjam that there was another matter from the past that she wanted help with from Waziri. But even before the demonstration was over, Mery had retreated to her private quarters. The noise and smoke from the weapon had clearly unnerved her.

Later in the afternoon, Nedjam spoke privately with Waziri expressing that Mery was pleased with them being able to understand each other, and also for the assistance concerning the death tube. Nedjam told Waziri she was going to try to convince Mery to let him have more privileges.

Waziri asked Nedjam, "From where did your people come? Were your people driven here to escape the white slavers?" Nedjam answered, "No one can remember where we came from, but there are legends that are passed down from people whose job it is to remember. Who can say how many of the memories are accurate." She continued, "One day I will take you to the yellow tablets. Perhaps you can read what they say. No one here in Opar can understand them."

Waziri was content to spend some time here, as there was always the lure of the gold. He was also becoming romantically attracted to Nedjam because of all the attention she showed him. These feelings he did not want to show her. Utmost in his mind was going home and seeing his father again. The gold had lost some of its importance.

Several days later as Nedjam was assisting her mistress in dressing, she asked Mery if she could talk to her as a friend. Mery nodded her permission and waved her hand toward a chair, inviting Nedjam to sit. Nedjam was nervous and blurted out, "Majesty, I believe I am falling in love with Waziri."

Mery sat back in her chair, a smile appeared on her face, and she said, "I am shocked." This smile released the tension that Nedjam felt, and she poured out her feelings. Mery listened carefully, then spoke, "Nedjam, I have repeatedly advised you to get close to this man cautiously. At first, I feared for you being physically injured, now I fear for your heart. You know as well as I do that he would give anything to get back to his people. He cannot possibly be happy with being a prisoner here in Opar. I am sure he can read your heart, and probably will use your feelings against you."

Nedjam listened carefully. There was nothing said that she had not heard from the voice in her heart. It was good for Nedjam to hear another woman confirm her greatest fears. "Majesty, I know you are right, but I desperately want a male companion and children. There is no man here in Opar that even appeals to me. I have known them all since we were children, and I find them all dull and uninteresting." Nedjam continued, "Would it be so wrong to be in a relationship with this man? I believe he is good. He speaks of his father and mother all the time and is concerned with their well-being. He is bright and has experiences and skills that no man here possesses. Also, he is big and the most handsome man I have ever seen. Plus Majesty, I think he has feelings for me."

"Nedjam," Mery began, after a brief pause for deliberation, "I will take your request under consideration as the High Priestess, but I hear and understand your words about the current crop of men in Opar. I heard the same complaints from my mother and grandmother. I have heard myself saying those same words," she said with a small laugh.

"Nedjam, I am glad you told me your inner thoughts and I would advise you when I decide what I will allow you to do." Nedjam knew the conversation was over, and she rose and thanked Mery for her advice, and assured her she would be patient.

Several weeks later, Mery announced to Nedjam that she was lifting some of the restrictions on Waziri. He would still be watched but from a greater distance. She reiterated he would be killed if he attempted to leave the city. Mery made an exception and would allow Waziri to go on short hunting outings with experienced hunters.

Mery also told Nedjam in private, that she was leaning toward allowing a relationship with Waziri. Down deep Mery knew it would be good to have some children fathered by a strong man.

Waziri was ecstatic about the new freedom and promised Nedjam he would not try to leave Opar. He played dumb about a possible relationship with her, although everything in her words and actions spoke volumes about her feelings toward him.

After three months, Mery gave her blessing to a relationship between Nedjam and Waziri. Within a few months, Nedjam was pregnant with the first of three children she would quickly bear with him. Both Waziri and Nedjam were pleased to have their relationship sanctioned by the High Priestess, and they were very much in love.

One day the guards spotted a man wandering not far from the wall. The standing order was to capture and bring strangers into the city. The most frequent outcome for foreigners was that they became new sacrifices to the Flaming God.

The man appeared to be exhausted and offered no resistance to being brought into the city. Forty-eight hours later, the man had developed the classic signs of smallpox. He had been ill, wandering for many days, and the disease became active when he came into the city. Almost two weeks later, a week after the man had been sacrificed to the Flaming God, other residents began to exhibit symptoms of the disease.

Mery brought Waziri and Nedjam into her private quarters. She had a worried expression on her face, and she said, "Five more people have come down with signs of the illness. Waziri, do you know anything about this sickness?"

Waziri answered, "Yes, majesty. This disease visited our village when I was a child. A person from far away brought it somehow; it killed many of the people in our village."

To which Mery replied, "What should we do?"

Waziri answered, "Anyone who has touched the sick man will probably become ill. It would be advisable for your Majesty to depart the city, and stay away until this curse ends. It could take a moon to leave. The illness will kill some, and will only scar others. There is no way to predict who will live and who will die."

Waziri continued, "Majesty, take a few hunters for protection, and whoever else you want to save and leave the city."

Mery thought for a moment and said, "Nedjam, you and Waziri get your child and wait for me by the city entrance. On the way get two hunters, ones who just came back from a week's absence this morning, and have them join us. There is no need to tell anyone what Waziri has told us."

The party left the city and headed north into the mountains, and hopefully to safety. The two hunters moved a bit ahead of Nedjam, Waziri, their infant child, Mery and Set, to be sure there was no danger. The hunters were able to find a large cave that would accommodate all of them. They were busy for a day clearing out debris and making the cave somewhat livable. The next few weeks were spent watching each other for signs of the disease, but luckily no one had been infected.

There was much time and little to do while the small group was in exile from Opar. Mery announced to Nedjam that she thought would be a good idea for her to learn to speak the Waziri language. Mery continued, "There are so many times I wanted to speak to you in private. We should begin speaking Waziri's language. Since we are all gathered here with not much to do, I think it is a good idea to start now." Set, as was his practice, was either drunk or sleeping, and was not included in the language plans.

One day when they were alone, Mery said to Nedjam, "Nedjam, you are my closest friend, and I trust you more than anyone. Someday, I want to have children with or without Set, and I am charging you with teaching them the Waziri language. And I am asking for something else, should I die before my children can be on their own. I want you to be responsible for making them ready to rule Opar. Set is not aware of this arrangement, so I will make this secret known to some of my closest military confidants, in case you need to have my wishes forced on Set." Mery continued with a serious look on her face, "Nedjam, I would be pleased to have you as a surrogate mother for my children."

It would be almost five years before Mery would bear a daughter and no sons. Set always thought he was the father, a confirmation that Mery would never make. Perhaps military assistance had come at a cost.

In all the fear and disruption caused by the spotted-illness, further death tube demonstrations and the search for materials to make gunpowder were forgotten. When the ruling party returned to the city, there were further distractions that prevented anyone from learning how these mysterious objects were related and how they worked.

Mery sent one of the hunters back with strict orders not to enter the city, but to ask guards if the illness had run its course.

The man returned and said no one new had become ill, no one had died for a week, and all bodies of the dead had been burned. Mery decided to wait another week to be sure the curse had run its course and had gone.

When the party did return, they found that thirty people had died from the spotted curse. Mery was extremely depressed. The deceased represented a large portion of the city's population, most of whom were younger people. This was going to ensure that the birth rate would not replace the dead for many years.

Mery called Nedjam into the throne room and spoke to her, not as a friend, but as High Priestess. "Nedjam, I am going to make what seems a strange request to you and Waziri. We need as many babies as the women of Opar can produce. We must produce thirty new babies in the next two years. The number of births in Opar has been declining over the past years, and we must reverse that trend immediately."

"I am going to ask Waziri to impregnate as many women of Opar as he possibly can. The child you and he made, appears to be bright and strong. We need a man who can help Opar survive." Nedjam tried not to show the hurt and anger she was feeling. Mery continued, "I can see this is not to your liking, and I can't say I blame you. We have to do whatever we need to do to survive as a people."

Mery asked softly, "Do you want to tell Waziri, or do I?" With eyes full of tears, Nedjam answered, "I will tell him your orders."

Waziri listened to a hysterical mate, who told him the High Priestess's command. He nodded and told Nedjam they would talk again after she had regained her composure. Waziri thought, first, the slavers killed many of my people and we were lucky to survive. Now something similar was happening to my adopted people.

In the next two years, Waziri's help had produced at least twenty-five new babies, plus two new children with Nedjam. There was a change in the relationship between Waziri and Nedjam. They seemed to be drifting further apart as he was spending more and more time with other women.

Nedjam seemed content letting her children fill the emotional void. These facts did not go unnoticed by Mery.

Finally, two and a half years after the spotted curse, Mery called Waziri and Nedjam into the throne room. Mery invited them to be seated and began by saying, "Both of you, my friends, have made sacrifices that I could only ask from you by being the High Priestess. I believe you have weakened your relationship to save Opar. I at this moment release Waziri from his obligation to stay here. He may stay as a citizen and noble, or he may return to his people with my blessing." There was not much to say at the meeting, and Mery dismissed Nedjam and Waziri politely. They would have much to decide, but only each other's ears should hear the discussion.

Both Waziri and Nedjam knew their relationship had been changed and probably damaged beyond repair. They agreed to think about what they should do and talk again in a few days. They did not share a sleeping couch that evening, as they had not for almost a year.

When they talked again, they agreed to part company. Waziri told Nedjam, "I have had dreams that my father is calling me, and I need to see him before he dies." Nedjam, with tears in her eyes, thanked Waziri for the three wonderful children, and she would only speak highly of him when they grew and asked of him.

Waziri had a very short audience with Mery, where she thanked him again for his sacrifice. She motioned to a large leather bag by his chair and said it was a gift of fifty pounds of gold, as thanks from a grateful people. Mery apologized for destroying both his and Nedjam's happiness, and she was sorry to see him leave. And lastly, Mery asked, "Please tell no one of us. I beg you. We are so afraid of being destroyed by some enemy. Please never come back." Waziri gave his word and quietly left the throne room.

A quarter mile down the road to the escarpment, Waziri turned for one last look at Opar and saw two women standing near one of the guard stations atop the wall. Their eyes met for a moment, and Waziri turned his face to the west — and home.

CHAPTER TWENTY-THREE — THE REIGN OF AYESHA

It was the year 1874, one of the major events of the year was the arrival of the body of the famous African explorer David Livingston. He had died in Africa the previous year. His body arrived in Southhampton on April 16, and he was interred in Westminster Abbey two days later.

In Opar, the current High Priestess was Ayesha; she was the daughter of Mery who had died too young. She had been ruling Opar for the last two years. There was a High Priest, Set, but he was a figurehead and was concerned mostly with the young female temple acolytes, eating and drinking beer. He was a man of about fifty, greatly overweight, prone to long afternoon naps. He had been the significant other to Ayesha's Mother. When his physical strength permitted, he attempted to have a relationship with Ayesha. Ayesha hated him, not only for the way he treated her mother but for the amorous and unwanted advances upon her.

The name Set was a common name for the High Priests of Opar. Set, in ancient Egyptian mythology, was the man who killed Osiris. Osiris was one of the founders of the ancient Egyptian pantheon.

For the past several centuries, Opar had been ruled by women. The inhabitants of Opar could now be divided into several categories. The ruling class consisted of the High Priestess, her handmaidens, the High Priest and a few of their supporters. The middle class consisted of about seventy-five men and women who had been smart enough to rise above the remaining population. The other three hundred and fifty people were miners, farmers, hunters – and the people who did all the thankless menial jobs around the city. The last fifty were the members of the Neteru, who served as temple guards and protectors of the High Priest and Priestess.

The women had seized and retained power over the years simply because the men had lost all interest in ruling Opar. For the last several centuries the isolation and privacy had become complete. The Neteru had not been called to protect the city. Occasionally they would accompany hunters into the jungle. Most male members of the middle class spent their days eating and drinking beer with their friends and could not care less about doing anything beyond their pleasure.

Ayesha had taken a romantic interest in one of the hunters who was about her age. She wanted some male companionship, children and someone who would get rid of Set's constant attention and unwanted advances. Ayesha was a bit taller than most of the other women of Opar. She had dark hair and blue eyes – which was rather unusual. She was quite a handsome figure of a woman with a walk denoting her status, and authority, over the city.

Ayesha was a very cautious woman, who kept her thoughts and fears to herself and did not confide in her handmaidens, even though several of them were her best friends. She worried about taking Ware for her companion, afraid of what Set would possibly do to him or even to her.

Set had already threatened her, "Beware Ayesha, I will be very angry if you do not choose me as your mate, allowing me to father children with you. I have seen the way you look at that lowly hunter. He is so far beneath you. I cannot believe you have any interest in him."

Ayesha let her anger get the best of her, and she screamed her answer to Set saying, "Get out of here you old fool! I would rather rut with one of the dogs in the street than allow you to touch me. And, have a child with you, I would rather try to mate with your ugliest Neteru."

Nedjam, perhaps the handmaiden she was closest to, was working in the High Priestess' reception room. She had been High Priestess Mery's confidant, and she continued those duties for Ayesha. Nedjam could hear Ayesha and Set speaking, even though she could see them. She smiled to herself and could not wait until Set left the room in a fit of rage. She did not have long to wait.

Ayesha screamed at Set, "Mind your own business and leave me alone. I am the High Priestess, and I will do as I please. I do not want or need your advice or permission." Set turned on his heel and walked rapidly out of the High Priestess' reception room.

Nedjam entered the room, and Ayesha asked, "Well, Nedjam, did you hear all of that? The old son of a dog has a lot of nerve talking to me that way."

Nedjam laughed again and smiled at her friend. "Ayesha, I never knew what your mother ever could have seen about him as a mate. I know because she told me she regretted ever getting involved with him. The only good thing that came from their mating was you, Ayesha."

Ayesha looked at her friend and gave a bit of an embarrassed smile and said "You knew my mother well. Did she feel that way about me?"

"Yes," Nedjam answered "sometimes your mother was harsh with you because she knew that you would be the High Priestess, and she wanted you to be prepared. I think your mother knew that she did not have much time left when you were born. Shortly after your birth, she confided that she believed she did not have enough time to prepare you. Thank the Flaming God that she lived until you were fifteen, and were able to be named High Priestess before she died. I know the last several years of her life were filled with pain, and she was greatly weakened. Who knows what might have happened if she had not prepared you for her position, and Set had usurped your power?" Ayesha had indeed thought of the consequences of her mother dying any earlier than she did, and her skin crawled with the thoughts of Set touching her.

Ayesha gestured for Nedjam to sit on the divan with her. She was still shaken by the encounter and argument with Set, and she needed some council from her chief handmaiden. "Nedjam, I am tired of having to fend off advances from that old dog, and I have just about made up my mind to take Ware for my mate."

Nedjam had counted her words before she offered her thoughts, "Ayesha, there are not a great number of eligible young men in Opar. There are plenty of men who would make your life miserable, probably even worse than Set. I think Ware would be a good choice. He seems to have a kind heart and believe me, that is very important in a long-term relationship. I hope you accept my thoughts; they are coming from my heart." Ayesha smiled and gave her a look that told Nedjam that these words were what she wanted to hear.

Jim Malachowski

CHAPTER TWENTY-FOUR — AYESHA AND WARE

Ayesha climbed the stone stairs that hundreds of her predecessors, both High Priestesses and High Priests, had climbed to reach the ground floor of the temple. The main temple floor was forty feet from wall to wall and was two hundred fifty feet in length. There were perhaps ten doors which led to offices, meeting rooms and stairs and of course, the round room which housed the Altar of the Flaming God. The circular altar room was about fifty-five feet across. This sacrifice room was large enough to accommodate seventy-five spectators taking part in the ceremony. There was a balcony above the ground floor which would accommodate another fifty spectators. The temple roof had a circular opening which allowed the Flaming God to view the sacrifice which was taking place on the altar. The circular centric room was twice the height of the main temple.

One level below the temple were apartments for the High Priestess or High Priest, their handmaidens, temple offices, meeting rooms, and storage. The next two levels down were the treasure vaults of Opar. All underground access doors were heavy wood planks reinforced with metal bars lockable both from the inside and outside. There were also stone

118

doors inside the wooden ones that were sturdier and cleverly mounted so they could be easily closed and locked only from the inside. Within the stairway, theses stone doors were well concealed making it hard to tell they were not just a wall. The only illumination in the staircase was from torches placed in sconces on the wall

The Temple of the Flaming God had been an ongoing project for almost four thousand years. The renovations and modifications to the temple had been slow, but there was not much else to keep the laborers and stonemasons busy.

The quarrying operation during which the great exterior wall had been built left huge pits over sixty feet deep and ran roughly in a north to south direction. At the lowest level of the excavation, the stonemasons were instructed to begin the creation of three interconnected passageways, one atop the other, that would eventually parallel the floor of the temple. The initial purpose for these tunnels was for the storage of gold, and secure apartments for the High Priests and Priestesses. All three passageways could be locked from both the inside as well as the outside.

The gold which had been recovered from the mines and streams was brought near to this second-level tunnel entrance, where it was smelted and poured into ingots. After the gold was cooled in the molds, it was brought into another tunnel for storage in rooms that led off the sides of the channel. As the centuries passed and more space for gold was needed, the third level down also began to be used for storage. The outside access was changed to lead to the third level down.

During the early construction of Opar, Nebre, the son of Apries, had been the architect. Under the leadership of Neith, a small temple, about fifty feet long and twelve feet wide had been built at the north edge of the city. The temple was located in a small oasis area, which became the private bathing area of the High Priestess. Nebre had kept insisting a larger temple be built, and that temple was constructed on the stone quarry site.

During the quarrying operations employed to build the wall, an extreme amount of stone had been required and had been removed from this location. It was here that the architects began construction of the Temple of the Flaming God.

The walls of the main corridor were covered with hieroglyphics telling the story of the founding of Opar. The focus of honor was several large gold tablets telling the lives of the first several High Priests and the men who had overseen the construction of the city and the temple.

Since storage in the second level was full, the latest project Ayesha and Ware ordered was the completion of the third level of storage. There was an access point to this level from inside the hill behind the south end of the temple wall. There was a cave about five feet in height and five feet wide. It was used to bring ore to the temple area for refinement. The entrance to the cave was hidden by shrubs and foliage, and there was a gate that was secured from inside the cave, which kept the uninvited out.

There was another danger in this lowest tunnel that was not apparent. There was a wide gap in the floor, which invaders could not see so they would fall to their deaths in an underground river flowing beneath Opar. Even if invaders did hear running water or see the gap, there was no way for them to get over to the other side. When workers needed to travel across this trap, planks of wood were laid across the chasm allowing free access. These boards were only in place when workers were present. In the case of a siege, the corridor could hide some of the inhabitants of Opar, and the river access would provide water. Several of the side rooms were used for cool storage of smoked meats and other foods.

The third level staircase was located on one side of the tunnels only – the side opposite of the water trap. These stone steps led to the two underground levels above. There was another short set of stairs, in the mid area of the first level tunnel, which provided access to the circular room containing the Sacrificial Altar. This access was used exclusively during a sacrifice to the Flaming God, which allowed the celebrant to appear without going through the crowd.

Tonight was one of those nights that Ayesha just could not sleep. Her mate Ware was resting quietly, not disturbing her. Even before Ware became her mate, she often had nights where she could not sleep. The private chambers of the High Priestess were located below the floor of the temple and were cool despite the fact that it was mid-summer. Her bedroom was not the problem.

Ayesha quietly slipped out of the silks that adorned her couch, looked and smiled at the slumbering Ware, and in her bare feet made very little sound as she walked up the stairs that led to the main floor of the temple. Ayesha had made this walk many times when her mother was alive. She loved to climb even more, the steps that would reach the top wall of the temple and the cool damp mountain air. There were no trees close to the wall, so she was safe from leopards and other climbing predators. It seemed to her that she could relax here and solve whatever problems her thoughts brought to her.

Ayesha sat on a block of stone, took a deep breath of the cool air and started to feel better. She was still concerned about Set. While he had not bothered her with unwanted advances, he still gazed at her with a look of hatred, and she just did not trust him. Ware realized that Set was an annoyance, but he was not aware of how deeply Ayesha feared and hated him.

Ayesha's thoughts went back to Ware and when she had first met him. He and several hunters had been presented to her in her reception room because of a large amount of game they had killed on their just completed hunting trip. Their eyes had met several times while he was standing before the High Priestess who was seated on her couch. She thought now: we were attracted from the first time we saw each other.

Ware was one year older than Ayesha and about three inches taller than she. He carried himself with an air of confidence. He was the son of a hunter who supplied meat to the city and had learned his trade well from his father and grandfather. Ware was gone from Opar for weeks at a time, and this made Ayesha nervous and fearful both for his safety and her own. Ware was deeply in love with Ayesha. He was very attentive to her needs and would always do whatever she asked of him. A few times he had awakened and climbed the stairs to be with her under the night sky.

Tonight, Ayesha's thoughts went back to her mother, Mery. She missed her very much. Beginning when Ayesha was nine or ten years old, her mother had not only begun to teach her how to rule Opar as High Priestess for the good of the majority of the people but also how to strengthen her hold on the holy office. Mery had declared that Ayesha was to be her successor, both to her handmaidens and to a small number of the aristocracy. Mery's chief handmaiden, Nedjam, who had been her mother's closest advisor, was given the duty of seeing that she would be sure Ayesha held the title and power of High Priestess, just as she had done for Mery. Nedjam was in her early forties and was a quiet woman who had an incredibly sharp mind. She also could read into the hearts of those to whom she was speaking. She was able to see instantly where their allegiances lay.

Upon hearing the declaration that Ayesha was to rule, Set flew into a rage. He and his few followers had been counting on him being named ruler of Opar, as well as High Priest. Set and most of Opar realized that the title of High Priest was merely a figurehead title as the real power in Opar rested with the High Priestess. He was lucky to have that much. Mery had confided in her handmaidens that she had accepted Set as her consort only because there was no one else available. Set had wondered many times if he was the father of Ayesha as he thought, "She is about as much like me as a monkey." As this idea had been going thru his mind for years, he began to imagine the identity of Ayesha's father. He kept these feelings to himself until Mery had declared Ayesha to be her successor as High Priestess. This idea became another reason for Set to fuel his paranoia and anger, not only toward Mery, but also Ayesha. Now, these feelings included her consort, Ware.

Ayesha wondered what her mother, Mery, would think of Ware as her choice of consort. Ware was a man of many skills, as well as being a great hunter. He was a great leader of men. He was liked by almost all the men of Opar and he led most of the food-hunting expeditions. He was pleased when he perceived one of the eligible women of Opar looking at him in a way that was very flattering to a young man. He was always faithful to Ayesha and despite his seeming indifference to the politics of the city, he always had a friend or two, however, watching over Ayesha during his absences.

Ayesha was concerned when Ware took his men and ventured into the jungle and grasslands around Opar. Their favorite game to hunt was either zebra or antelope. Both of these animals could be found in abundance to the south. When sufficient game had been killed, Ware's men would send messenger monkeys back to Opar requesting additional assistance with smoking and carrying the meat back. Ayesha was always relieved to hear that one of these messages had been received. It meant that Ware and his men had been successful and would be coming home soon.

Not everyone living in Opar was anxious to live out their lives in a rut of sameness. Over the centuries, many men, and usually their families, packed up some meager belongings and struck out to get away from Opar. There must be some memory buried deep in people's genes because they always tried to travel north from whence their ancestors had come. Once these people traveled out of the mountains surrounding Opar, they were immediately in the heavy jungles, with all the dangers that lie there. The unfortunate ones that traveled east to get around the great Sudd usually were captured by the fierce tribes that inhabited what is now known as Ethiopia. Most of these adventurers never made it as far as Ethiopia. Many succumbed to disorientation and were lost in the dense forest. Others could not find water or would be attacked by animals that were common in that part of the jungle.

On this particular trip, Ware and his hunters had found their game early, so their hunting was over sooner than expected. Once the meat had been transported by the laborers back to Opar, they decided to do some exploring.

Cha was Ware's best friend, and the two men were like brothers. Both had a strong helping of wanderlust and a natural curiosity about their surroundings. They had decided to ask three of the other hunters to join them for several weeks of exploring. This was not the first time they had set out on their own, and they were looking forward to something different. Ware and Cha had decided to travel west just to see what was there. All of the men had developed a good knowledge of woodcraft and were confident in their ability not to get lost and to be able to live off the land. They had traveled about two days when they began to encounter evidence of people living in the area. Immediately they went on high alert, all talking ceased and hand signals were the order of the day.

Upon cresting a hill, they saw in the valley below, about a half mile away, a large force of about two hundred heavily armed black warriors who had created a temporary kraal. Cha whispered to Ware, "These men appear to be headed in our same direction. It probably would be a good idea to let them go ahead, and not give way our presence." Ware agreed and whispered, "After we have watched them today, we need to go back to Opar. We are no match for even a small party of these men." The five hunters agreed and hid and observed for the rest of the day. They began their trip back at dusk and were careful to have one of their hunters drop back to be sure they were not being followed.

In the morning, they were exhausted after marching for many hours in the last two days. The five men sat around a small fire roasting their supper and discussing the events of yesterday. Ware was saying "Those were very impressive warriors that we came across yesterday. They were accompanied by no women or children; it was a war party. When we get back, we need to warn Ayesha about a possible threat to Opar. I don't know where they were coming from, but it was from near Opar."

Cha answered back by saying, "Ware, I have an idea. We should try to pick up the warrior's trail and backtrack to see where they came from, and discover their purpose here." Ware agreed that they would start out the next morning.

The next day after a cold breakfast of bird eggs and berries they started out in search of the warrior's trail. It did not take long since two hundred men created quite a disturbance. The broad trail was easy to follow. The black warriors obviously had not seen any reason for stealth. Three days into the backtrack the five hunters came upon the purpose of the warrior's trip. They reached the remains of a fairly large village which was still smoldering.

The hunters carefully and quietly circumnavigated the area at various distances. After many hours of reconnaissance, the five joined back up and agreed they had seen no human activity within a five-mile distance of the village. They then decided to go into the kraal to investigate.

There had been thirty huts for eating and sleeping. There was a large community center in the middle with lots of acreage being used to grow crops. Obviously, this was not a village of warriors, but rather farmers. As the men searched, they saw that a large number of people had been killed. The scavengers had done their job of sanitizing the village. However, there was enough information in the skulls and bones to tell an interesting story. They did not quite understand why so many of the dead were babies and old people. There were a few adults killed by the short thrusting spears of the warriors. There did not seem to have been any of the invading warriors killed in whatever skirmish there had been. And curiously, none of the crops in the fields had been taken.

The men decided to continue with the backtrack to see where it would lead. The hunters' curiosity quickened their steps as they tried to catch up to whatever people were making the trail they were following. One fact caught their eyes. Some of the prints were the size and shape of a zebra's. The hunters had tracked enough of these beasts to recognize their spoor.

After four more days, they came upon the answers to their questions. In the distance, they saw dust rising from a large group of people walking along the edge of the great forest. The terrain had changed from heavy jungle to low grassland, and it was easy to see a long distance. Ware and his men stayed hidden in the jungle while continuing to observe the trekkers until they were only a few hundred yards away.

The first thing they saw were about a hundred men, women and walking children all shackled together by metal chains around their ankles or necks. The next observation shocked the five warriors. They saw twenty men astride beasts that were brown or white in color, larger than a zebra. They were obviously being controlled by the men who were riding them. Those on the creatures' backs were dressed in long flowing garments. Their heads were covered by a heavy cloth held in place by a piece of rope circling their foreheads. The skin of the men that they could see was not as black as their captives but was similar in color to Ware and his men. The riders were obviously in charge and were whipping the chained people to keep them moving. The captives were being directed to the north and east, a fact that meant nothing to the hunters. They were headed for the Red Sea, which was another long march, where the Arabs would herd them into ships for a short trip across to Arabia and slavery.

One of the female slaves had gotten free of her foot restraint and was trying to get to freedom by running back into the jungle with its cover of trees and low shrubs. It was not to be, as one of the men removed a pipe-like device from his back and pointed it at the woman as she ran. There was a loud explosion and a copious amount of smoke. The woman threw her arms up and collapsed on her face and did not move. There was a ragged hole in the center of her back that was oozing a great deal of blood.

The five hunters were somewhat perplexed by what they were witnessing. They had been children, or not yet born when Waziri demonstrated the old flintlock. They probably had an idea that the people were being transported for slaves. What they did not know, was who the mounted men were, and why the black warriors had helped them.

The five hunters remained unmoving in their hiding places and stayed there until the caravan had moved completely out of sight. Both Ware and Cha were interested in examining the female who had been killed at such a long distance.

Cha was the first to arrive and said, "She is dead. There has to be a connection to the pipe the man pointed at her and her death. It happened so quickly that I did not see anything come out of the pipe. If it did it must be much faster than an arrow."

Ware took out his knife and enlarged the wound in the woman's back. "Look, Cha, there is a piece of rock of some sort. Odd, it is smooth and perfectly round. No one was seen throwing anything at her, so it must have come from the pipe." Ware wiped the projectile with a leaf and put in his quiver.

The five men looked at each other, and all were thinking: "We don't know who these men are, but they are to be feared. They have a weapon that is unknown to us, and other undreamed of advantages. Plus, those beasts they rode, are surely better than walking into battle." The biggest supremacy was not openly spoken of, but was on all their minds – they had an alliance with a fierce tribe of black warriors who appeared to live nearby.

They decided now it was imperative to get back, safely and quickly, to Opar and discuss these curious events with Ayesha and the High Priest.

CHAPTER TWENTY-FIVE — THE WAR COUNCIL

Ten days of hard travel had brought the five hunters back to Opar. They walked down the desolate valley, with its large boulders and gnarled trees. They approached the high wall to get into the city. The entrance was built to be a small and winding passageway. It had been designed to allow a few persons in at a time. Upon entering, one had to make a 90-degree turn, ascend several steps, and then another 90-degree turn in the opposite direction. There were two watchtowers located near the narrow entrance on top of the high wall.

Ware motioned to the other hunters by pointing at the top of the wall near the entrance. There were no guards above. He glanced up and remarked, "That will have to change immediately." The other four men knew what he meant, and nodded their agreement.

The next morning Ayesha called a meeting in the throne room. There were two hunters, Set, the High Priest, and the five members of what could loosely be called the ruling council. Set was annoyed at being disturbed so early in the morning when he asked his friends, "Does anyone know what this is about, and why it is so important for us to have to meet at this time of day?" There was no answer. The two hunters Ware and Cha entered the room and stood with the other men, waiting for Ayesha to appear.

Ayesha looked into the throne room from a small hole in the wall and spoke quietly to Nedjam saying, "I think I will let them stand there for a bit longer." A smirk was on her face as she looked at Nedjam.

Nedjam smiled back and thought, "You are learning…." She took Ayesha by the shoulders and said, "You will be making a powerful enemy shortly and you must deal with that antagonist quickly and decisively." Ayesha took her arms and said, "Yes, very rapidly."

Ayesha walked swiftly through the connecting hall which ran from her private quarters to the throne room. She ascended the four steps and sat looking down at each face. Providing no seats had been Nedjam's idea. The meeting was not a social occasion. The seriousness of the meeting was apparent, plus Ayesha wanted no doubt as to who was in charge.

Ayesha began with a false smile at Set and asked, "Set, are you not in charge of security for the city of Opar?" Ware lightly nudged Cha in the ribs. The annoyance was gone from Set's face, and he quizzically responded, "Yes."

He was not sure but, it would seem that he was about to be embarrassed. Set was right. Ayesha smiled and leaned in a bit closer to him and asked, "Why were there no sentries on duty yesterday during the day, and, as I know, none on duty last night?"

Several of the council members took a short step away from Set. They did not want any of the spill-over from this to hit them. "Perhaps by the end of the meeting, Set, you will have changed your mind about sentries, and how lax you and your security troops have become."

Ayesha was in control. She had started the meeting by making Set and the councilors feel ill at ease. Now she had made it more uncomfortable for the council, especially Set, making him responsible, and negligent.

"As you all know, Ware and Cha were leaders of a hunting expedition for meat for the city. They came back to Opar yesterday with some interesting information they learned on the trip," said Ayesha.

She had already heard the account of the black mercenaries and the slavers, but wanted the council and Set to hear the whole story. Ayesha looked at Ware, and said, "Ware, would you please tell us about your expedition. Do not bother with details of the hunt. Please tell us what you saw as you were returning to Opar."

Ware, with some assistance from Cha, related their experiences. Careful attention was drawn to describing the black raiders with their tube that killed the farmers.

After Ware's presentation, Set answered by saying, "I do not understand what this could have to do with us. I don't see any reason for concern."

Ayesha's face turned crimson, and she glared at Set and said "You old fool, what if those black mercenaries or the men in the long white clothing had found their way to our front gate? They would have found no sentries, no resistance, and they would have taken everyone in Opar to wherever they took those poor black farmers. Now, do you follow? I don't know about you, but I don't want to end up in a pleasure palace of some foreign power. You would be too old for a soft job and would probably be killed on the road to wherever."

Set had been given the death tube by Mery, with instructions to find out how the device worked. It was to be his first priority and he was to question any new prisoners on the off chance they may know something. Set had forgotten those instructions long before Mery's death and he was amazed that Mery had told Ayesha of his task. Ayesha remembered her mother's concerns about the old flintlock, and that she had charged Set with investigating its operation. Of course, when asked, he was forced to say he had made no progress over the years. The old gun by now was covered with rust from neglect.

Set's face contorted with rage and he found himself with no answer to the charges. Ayesha continued, "Effective immediately, Ware will be in charge of security for Opar and the Neteru will all fall under his leadership. Cha will be the lead hunter. Set, you will immediately vacate living in the palace of the Flaming God, and I will see that you have a hut built in the rear of the farming area. You are forbidden to enter any public building in Opar. Ware, you and a couple of Neteru will accompany Set to his living quarters and see that he removes only his items. Nothing is to be taken that belongs to the Flaming God or has any connections to anyone who lives or governs from this temple."

Ayesha glared at him again and said, "One more transgression like this and you will find yourself on the Altar of the Flaming God."

Ayesha watched as the guards ushered the shaken Set to his quarters. She motioned to Cha and said in a low voice, "On the next hunting expedition take that old fool with you, and see that he does not return. You know — a terrible hunting accident." Ayesha smiled to Cha and gave him a wink of her eye. Cha just grinned and said in a whisper, "A pleasure, Majesty."

Ayesha motioned to the three security guards who were standing near the door, and she gave the following commands, "Bring in chairs and refreshments for the committee and Cha. Ware already knows my wishes for him and the contents of this meeting." A look of gratitude came from several of the committee members, who appeared to be on the brink of collapse after the unexpected turn of events in the meeting.

After the chairs had been arranged, the handmaidens of the High Priestess brought out chilled beer, wine and some light refreshments. Ayesha looked at the committee and said, "Any comments on Set's removal from office, or his dereliction of duty in endangering everyone in Opar?" Ayesha looked from face to face and waited for a response from each man. No one had a word to say and seemed to be relieved that the meeting was going in a different direction. "Good," Ayesha said, "because we have several topics to discuss. The main topic is the security of Opar and a replacement for the High Priest."

Ayesha took a gold goblet, sipped the wine and found it suited her taste. Inwardly, she was congratulating herself on how well she had handled the first part of the meeting. She smiled to herself on how she had humiliated her mother's hated husband.

Lost in her thoughts, she missed the first part of the question. She asked for the question to be repeated. One of the councilmen asked, "What do you think is the right path in handling the black intruders and the men with the death tubes?"

She replied, "The first thing we need to do is strengthen our sentry activities and come up with a plan to keep any invaders out of the city. Opar is very self-sufficient. We could withstand invaders attempts for months, even years. I propose we give Ware a week to acquaint himself with defending the city and have him give us his thoughts."

Another council member asked, "Should we not try to apprehend one of the men who carry the death tube? We could force him to explain how it is made and how it works." Ayesha answered, "We risk too much trying to catch one of these men. What if he were to evade capture? We would have announced there are people here to be enslaved." She continued, "Even if we capture a man with death tube, how do we communicate with him? I do not believe we have the knowledge to build one of his death tubes. I would rather we hold this idea until we know a bit more about these strange people."

At this time Ware rejoined the meeting and was obviously pleased with himself. Another council member, an obvious friend of former high priest, asked: "What will become of Set?" "Right now, I do not know," answered Ayesha. "He will be confined and kept away from everyone, probably in one of the locked rooms under the temple." Again, his friend Jub asked, "Will he be offered to the Flaming God as a penance?" Ayesha thought for a moment and replied, "No, I do not think the Flaming God would be pleased with Set as an offering."

Ware took the opportunity to define his ideas about tightening security for Opar. "Many years ago, our ancestors who created Opar built sentry posts on the outside wall. These will be manned every hour of the day and night. I have already told the Neteru security leader that if a sentry is caught sleeping on duty, he will be severely punished." Ware continued "I heard a legend from one of the old men a few months ago, about how the builders of Opar used water to slide the blocks for the walls and temple. There was a tale that someone found a black liquid that was slipperier than water for moving the block. The story goes that care had to be given during its use because if it got too near a fire, it would begin to burn, and it was nearly impossible to extinguish the flame. I am going to see if anyone among the common people remembers anything about this liquid that burns."

Ayesha turned toward Ware with a look of bewilderment and said, "Please don't spend too much time on the mythical liquid. Anyway, I don't see how this could help us." Ayesha pressed on.

"Do any of you have thoughts for a new High Priest?"

CHAPTER TWENTY-SIX — THE STORY OF JUB

J ub left the meeting somewhat shaken. He was terrified that his friend, Set, would be killed. Jub and Set had been friends since boyhood. They had both discussed how they hated the way Ayesha was running the city of Opar. Set had told Jub Ayesha was too much like her mother. Ayesha's mother, Mery, had betrayed him and relegated him to a figurehead of a High Priest, and Set believed he was the laughing-stock of the city. No one cared for him. But the reality was that most people thought Set was a joke who did not deserve a wife as wonderful as Mery.

Mery had died of tuberculosis when Ayesha was a child. The symptoms and the onset of the disease began about two years before her death. The illness advanced quickly, and within a year Mery was bedridden and had relinquished her daily duties to Nedjam. Mery expired very early in the morning. Nedjam had been checking on her condition for weeks quite frequently. Nedjam knew that Mery's end was near, as she was sweating profusely, almost delirious, and unable to breathe except in short gasps. She held her while the life left her and cried for the rest of the night for the loss of her friend. Nedjam made the announcement the next day and said that Ayesha would be taking over as High Priestess, but was in mourning and would not be available to see anyone for the near future.

Set, of course, was nowhere to be found during the last weeks of Mery's life. Nedjam assumed he was drinking with his friends or carousing with some of the prostitutes from the poorer sections of the city. His only care was that he would be assuming leadership of Opar, having forgotten that Mery had named Ayesha as her successor with Nedjam as her regent.

Jub's ancestors had always been a part of the aristocracy of Opar. What made them so special was lost in the past. Jub was not a particularly intelligent or attractive man. His rapidly receding hair was as white as the snow that lay on the mountain tops. Jub's wife was a corpulent woman with a loud voice, and usually had nothing good to say about anyone — especially Jub. Consequently, Jub was in the company of his beloved as little as possible.

One of the good things that could have been said of Jub was that he was loyal to his friends, although he did not have many. Jub spent a few days thinking how he might help Set. He was driven by the idea that Set may be rotting and starving in the locked room beneath the temple, or that Ayesha would have Set killed before he could rescue him. But, help exactly how — Jub did not know.

Jub had been talking with one of the servants who tended the garbage and clean-up of public areas around the temple. His name was Ho, and he was a Neteru. He was perhaps five feet two inches tall and two hundred and twenty-five pounds. Ho had the strength of an ox, and the breath and body odor of one also. He was not very bright, but he had a natural gift with woodcraft and was very comfortable roaming the jungles around Opar.

Jub had been looking for Ho all morning and finally located him sitting in the shade of a tree. Jub nodded to Ho, saying hello. There was a bit of small talk concerning the weather. Jub could tell he did not have Ho's complete attention. He got Ho's attention by asking, "Ho, have you ever received any gold rings or coins for your hard work?"

Ho's head dropped then slowly he turned his grimy face and said, "No one appreciates me here. People barely speak to me, and most of the time I feel like I am not seen. One day that is going to change and they will be sorry when I am gone."

Jub asked, "Ho, where would you go and what would you do?"

Ho answered, "Don't worry about me, I have a place to go, and I can get all the food I would ever want." Jub's ears perked up when he heard Ho's last statement.

Jub let the conversation lag for a few moments and came back with, "Ho, do you remember my friend the High Priest Set? Well, he has been falsely accused of a crime and is being imprisoned in the temple." Jub gave his most sincere look and said, "Can I rely on you to keep a secret?"

Ho nodded. "I would like to help my friend Set to escape this terrible mistake, and perhaps leave Opar. Would you be willing to help us?"

Ho thought for a minute, remembering the mention of gold from before, and he asked "Why should I do this for you? It seems like you don't like me very much either and you avoid me – like everyone else."

Jub strongly disagreed and with much back-patting, and smiling seemed to be winning Ho's approval. "Ho, I want you to think of my first question. Remember, I have gold coins and gold rings. If we can come up with an arrangement, you could have a few of the coins." Please keep what we have been talking about our secret, and let me know if you want to discuss helping Set again." Without looking back, Jub rose from the hard ground under the tree and left Ho smiling.

Jub walked to his house. It had been built for his family centuries ago, and it was one of the structures made of stone. It had several small rooms and an outside kitchen which kept the rest of the house cooler. Jub's wife was there and in a foul mood. She started with her usual rant. She needed another domestic worker for meal preparation and laundry. Jub thought, "Someone else to scream at …" He went out the front door to a bench and sat in the shade of the tree in his yard. "That settles it …" Job thought, "I have put up with all I want to from that ill-tempered bitch."

With Ho's assistance, and his decision to get away from his wife, Jub was pretty much fixed on the idea of trying to get Set out of imprisonment and Opar. It would take some careful planning. If anything were to go bad, it would show Ayesha where his loyalties lay, and he would doubtlessly lose his position on the council.

Two weeks later, Jub was ready to put his plan into effect. He had visited twice with Set speaking to him through the locked door. Jub shared his escape plans with Set, who approved of the idea. Jub had told him the name of the Neteru guard with whom he was friendly and who was willing to help. Jub had convinced the Neteru to aid in getting Set out of confinement. The guard knew where the keys were hidden and agreed to assist in exchange for a generous amount of gold.

A word about currency — gold coins were legal tender, and they were accepted for goods and services. The coins came in two denominations with the smaller being worth about one-quarter of the larger. Cheating and stealing were dealt with very severely, by the removal of the right hand, a very obvious sign that the person was a thief. As with all countries that use a currency, the wealthy usually were smarter than the average citizen. The aristocracy was able to accumulate and hoard money. The citizens were not allowed to own gold that was not in the form of coins or collars.

Three hours after midnight found Jub and his guard friend feeling their way along the main corridor of the temple. They came to the stairs that led down to where Set was being held. The guard had the key to the door. Now that they were beneath the main floor of the temple, Jub decided to take a chance and lit a candle. The door was unlocked and opened with a grateful Set squinting against the light. Set was all smiles and embraced his friend Jub. Jub made a sign to be sure Set was quiet, and they began their flight by climbing the stairs to the main temple floor. The guard left them and went back to sleep, but with a small sack of gold coins for his trouble.

Jub and Set made their way in the stygian darkness that was Opar on a moonless night. They went down the street from the temple entrance and along the wall until they came to the exit that would lead them to the valley outside. It was here that they joined Ho, who possessed a bow and quiver of arrows, his heavy spear and a sack of provisions. Jub picked up the sack of his belongings that Ho had brought for him. They passed through the small entrance maze and stood outside of Opar for the first time in their lives.

Ayesha and Ware were reclining on their stomachs head to head, looking down from the top of the main exterior wall. Ware whispered to Ayesha, "There go two real thorns in our sides and that stupid clod of a

Neteru as a bonus. I am just glad that we will not have their blood on our hands. We will let the gods deal with them in the jungle."

"Clever," said Ayesha, "and we have the guard to thank for coming forward with the tip that they were going to release Set and leave the city. Please be sure you reward him handsomely." Ware and Ayesha waited until the darkness had swallowed the three men below them. They rose, dusted themselves off and went back to their quarters for some well-deserved sleep.

The next morning found two extremely exhausted middle-aged men, begging Ho to stop and take another break in their flight from Opar. With Ho in the lead, the three men had traveled probably seven or eight miles in a northerly direction where the mountains became steeper. There it would afford them the protection of being able to hide.

Sheeta, the leopard, snapped open her eyes at the sound of a branch being broken. She was lying on a forked tree limb thirty feet above the ground. Her last kill had happened the previous evening when an unsuspecting antelope had stopped at a nearby stream for a drink. Sheeta had made short work of the antelope, ending its life with a quick wrenching bite to the neck puncturing the jugular, for a merciful death. The leopard carried the kill up a tree, lodging it securely in the branches. Later this great cat would feed herself and her two cubs. The offspring were almost ready to be on their own, just requiring some more coaching on hunting techniques.

Three men approached Sheeta rather casually and continued on their way toward the northern boundary of the cat's territory. Sheeta had flattened herself on a sturdy limb and observed them with fascination as they passed almost directly beneath her. She watched them noisily disappear into the mist of the jungle at first light. They would be easy to find again, as they had a smell of weakness about them.

Chapter Twenty-Seven — Search For Information

Within a year, the residents of Opar had almost forgotten the frightening information that Ware had brought back from the hunting trip. The people of Opar had always thought of themselves as being the only people that existed in this part of the mountains and jungle. Nothing, however, could be further from the truth. Within a hundred-mile radius of the city, there lived many tribes of indigenous people, eking out an existence in small groups. Most of them were just as happy, as the people of Opar, to fade into the jungle and never be seen. Many were farmers, who lived their lives growing crops for their families and their village. There were no war-like tribes that lived in this area. The hostile tribes were located many miles east of Opar, nearer the coast of Africa.

Security in and around Opar had never been higher. There was a newly renewed sense of safety with Ayesha and Ware, and most of the ruling council. Ayesha and Ware periodically sent small groups of heavily armed men into the jungle, just to look for anyone moving through the area, and any new people who may have migrated and settled nearby.

One of the scouting forces found the hiding place of Set, Jub and Ho. They watched for several days and were able to see one old man. The Neteru Ho was nowhere to be seen, and they assumed he had either abandoned his companions or was no longer alive. The scouts were not able to ascertain the identity of the remaining man. He appeared to be confused, listless and not able to take care of himself. His hair and beard were quite long and snow color. The man was skinny, very dirty and was wearing ill-fitting pieces of animal hide. He looked quite desperate, but the scouts were under strict orders, if the men were ever found there was to be no contact with them, and no assistance. After three days the scouts quietly withdrew leaving no trace.

Another scouting party traveled very far to the south. All had been warned never to come in contact with people who lived there as they were believed to be cannibals. If they were not cannibals, they were an extremely formidable tribe of warriors, known as the Mursi. The Mursi were tall and told the story of their war-like behavior by creating scars on their shoulders that showed how many men they had killed. They would drink a type of beer that would make them very aggressive. Most of the women and a few men had pierced their lips and inserted wooden disks, some of which were eight inches across.

While the advance party was traveling through Mursi country, they happened to see a group of men on horses wearing heavy cotton garments that had never been seen before. Their robes came close to the ground, and their head coverings were secured in place by strands of light rope. The scouts kept their distance and observed the men. Finally, one of the men left the group and began to walk into the jungle, probably to relieve himself after breakfast. He was nearly a hundred yards from his companions, and they did not seem to be concerned about his actions.

The item that made the man interesting to the Opar scouts was the death tube that was strapped to his back. In charge of the group was Sabi, who was young and aggressive, and looking for a way to distinguish himself to Ware. "We are going to capture this man and learn the secrets of his weapon," Sabi told his companions. "We are going to accomplish this quietly, and carry him out of here before his companions realize he is missing." The lookouts hid behind trees on the path the man would follow to rejoin his companions. He passed the tree where Sabi was hiding, and as he did, Sabi stepped out behind him and struck him in the head with a stone. The man fell unconscious and the scouts of Opar picked him up immediately and carried him away.

When they had gone about a mile, they put their captive on the ground, cut strips of cloth from his burnoose, and bound and gagged him. They inserted a stout branch behind his elbows to keep his arms immobilized so they could force him to walk the way they wanted him to go. The leather strap on the death tube had been cut, and the mysterious weapon was being carried very gingerly, by one of the lookouts. The bleeding from the head blow had slowed. The man appeared to be quite woozy and was easy to guide. It was a long two-week journey back to Opar. The captive had to be assisted the first several days, as he had a real problem walking. He seemed disoriented and could only go for short distances without rest. The prisoner said nothing to his captors. The scouts spoke very little, but at night they would sit around the campfire and talk in low tones with frequent glances over at the prisoner who was bound securely to a tree.

As they neared Opar, which was not yet in sight, they cut more cloth from the prisoner's burnoose and blindfolded him. The prisoner was aware that he had been taken on a circuitous route to enter a walled city. He heard only people talking in a strange tongue and at a distance. No one near him was making a sound. He found himself being led down a long flight of stairs into a cool room. His blindfold was removed, and he was seated on a wooden bench and watched as the men disappeared through a doorway. The entrance was closed and locked.

The next day, the prisoner was removed from his confinement and was taken outside by four of the burliest Neteru. His clothing was removed, and he was scrubbed by several giggling women. His hands were again tied behind his back, and he was led down the cool central aisle of the Temple of the Flaming God. The Neteru guided him into the reception room where Ayesha would first see the captive.

Ware and Ayesha walked through the doorway that connected to their private quarters. Ayesha ascended the three steps to the platform where her divan was located. She sat down and let her eyes take in the naked and obviously frightened man in front of her. Ayesha turned to Ware who was standing beside her, and she said, "This man does not look all that dangerous to me. Where is the death tube?"

Ware answered, "No, he is not impressive. However, the death tube makes him a formidable enemy."

Ayesha looked bored, asking, "So what are we going to do with him now? Do we think he can learn to communicate with us? There must be some reason to keep him alive."

"I agree," said Ware "we can try, but I do not have much faith in his ability to learn our language. He is valuable because he knows how to use the death tube. We could eventually figure some of it out, I am sure, but having him show us would save a lot of time. I think he is useful to us, and we should give teaching him a chance."

Ayesha looked at Ware and in a very serious tone said, "Ware, my instinct tells me that this enemy is more of a liability than an asset. His escape could be the end of Opar. Now, is this information and risk worth keeping him alive?"

Ware nodded and said, "I believe it is worth the risk. We will keep double guards on him at all times."

One of the elders of Opar began the tutelage of the prisoner. There were no formal school or teachers in Opar; nor had there been for thousands of years.

One of the first pieces of knowledge the elder discovered was the Arab's name was Ali. It was a slow and painstaking process. After two months the elder, Ptah, was called by Ware for a report. "Well Ptah, what is the level of progress?" asked Ware.

Ptah answered, with a sigh and downcast eyes, "Ware, I have made few strides with Ali. He seems to have no interest in learning our language. I know he has some knowledge of our words, but he fakes that he does not understand. I am sorry that I have failed in the task you assigned. Will my life be forfeited?"

Ware smiled and shook his head saying, "Of course not Ptah; I think the captive needs a bit of encouragement to apply himself a little better to the task at hand. Have the man brought, by the guards, an hour before sunset to the sacrificial altar."

Two weeks ago, another Arab had been captured twenty-five miles from Opar. Obviously, the Arabs were still looking for Ali. The three scouts from Opar followed him silently through the jungle, and toward dusk, he made camp for the night. The men waited until he was asleep and fell upon him and quickly made him their captive. Next, to him, they found his death tube and a bag of his belongings, which they gathered up. Then they began a speedy trip to Opar leaving one of the scouts behind, with the task of checking if there were any more Arabs looking for Ali.

Late in the day, the preparations for the schooling of Ali were completed. Ayesha chose one of her handmaidens and gave her the authority to carry out the religious sacrifice. As the time approached Ayesha stepped up on the raised dais and sat in her chair, with Ware at her side. Out of sight in the hallway, Ali was placed in a small cart, and his hands were bound to the sides. When he was secured, the servants of the High Priestess were allowed to come into the circular chamber.

It had been hot as most mid-summer days were, and the color of the sun was turning from white to a golden yellow. The chosen priestess ran into the chamber, and all were watching her. Her eyes were wide with religious fervor, and she began a sing-song chant calling upon the Flaming God to accept their sacrifice and continue to bring prosperity and security to Opar. The other attendees in the chamber answered the celebrant at the appropriate places in the chant. The long incantation finally finished. The other handmaidens passed through the crowd and distributed golden goblets.

As the incantation concluded, the captive was wheeled into the chamber and for the first-time Ali saw his friend tied to a stone altar in the middle of the room. The new prisoner's eyes met Ali's, and he shouted in Arabic, "Oh Ali, my friend and brother, please save me. I fear I am going to be killed."

Ali was numbed by the tableau before him, especially the sight of his friend lying helpless on the cold stone altar. "My friend, I am a prisoner here also, I can do nothing to help you, except pray to Allah for your soul."

One of Ali's guards stepped up into the cart and grabbed Ali by the hair forcing him to watch what was going to happen next.

Ayesha turned and whispered to Ware. "I hope I did not waste a morning's worth of instructions on Meye. It is her first time performing a sacrifice. I do not want to risk the wrath of the Flaming God." Ware nodded seriously.

Meye walked slowly to the naked man tied to the altar. The crowd of spectators had been driven to a fever pitch by Meye's dance and the spoken incantations to the Flaming God. Their faces were contorted with expectancy as they held their cups high and pushed ever closer to the altar.

Ali's eyes were wide, and he could not believe what was happening. Despite his best efforts, he could not look away from the scene at the altar which was unfolding before him.

The obsidian knife in Meye's hand moved slowly, as she began chanting another prayer to the Flaming God. The descending blade rested briefly beneath the prisoner's ribs. With a wicked grin, Meye made a deep incision from one side of his torso to the other. For a second, there was no blood, and everyone thought she had missed the cut. Then the victim's blood gushed in copious amounts. It ran down his sides and into the holding depressions of the altar. The Arab had immediately gone into shock and barely felt Meye's hand force its way under his ribs and into his chest. Meye immediately grasped his heart and with a strong yank, pulled the beating muscle from the prisoner. Meye first showed it to the victim and raised the still-beating heart, with blood streaming down her arms, up into the sun's light as it weakly fell thru the opening in the temple roof. The audience could not be held back further, and they surged forward, filling their gold goblets with the warm blood, drinking it greedily. The prisoner's eyes glazed over and he was spared watching any more of the ceremony.

Ali had a feeling he was floating and was detached from what he had just witnessed. His eyes rolled back into his head, and he slumped to the filthy floor of the cart. He awakened minutes later to an empty chamber with no sunlight coming through the roof. Ware, Ptah and Ayesha stepped out of the shadows. Ware grabbed him by the hair and lifted him to his feet snarling into his face, "I know you understand me. Unless you want to join your friend on the altar, you had better learn to speak to us. We have many questions for you." Ware and Ayesha continued past Ali and walked back to their chamber.

Ayesha said proudly, "I thought Meye did an excellent job with the sacrifice. What do you think?"

Jim Malachowski

CHAPTER TWENTY-EIGHT — THE BIRTH OF A CHILD

The famous African explorer, Richard Francis Burton, died in 1890. He along with John Hanning Speke had sought to find the source of the Nile River in the mid-1850's.

Ayesha arose from her couch and the soft sleeping silks, walking silently over to Ware's bed where she stood and looked at him in the near darkness of their quarters. Their rooms were located one story below the main floor of the Temple of the Flaming God. This year marked the fifteenth year of their union and Ayesha was more in love with Ware than ever before. He had thrown off the covers and was lying on his back sleeping in the nude. Ayesha felt a warm feeling begin to spread in her chest and stomach, and for a passing moment considered waking him. But no, Ayesha admired his fine physique and compared it to when they first became lovers. She was sure his body had only gotten better to behold. His shoulder length hair was framing his tanned and handsome face. There was some gray at his temples, and a few streaks were beginning to show through his full black hair. Ayesha wanted to run her fingers through it but again thought better. She smiled to herself and thought, "I'd better wait until morning."

144

Ayesha was somewhat of a night person. Many evenings she would rise and either walk the empty main corridor or climb the steps to the roof of the temple. In the times of the year when it was very hot day and night, the residents of Opar would either sleep on the flat roofs of their homes, or they would rest on mats thrown on the soft ground outside.

Due to the total darkness that surrounded the city of Opar, the night sky was ablaze with stars. There were many more stars visible than today, even in the darkest of civilized environs. All the constellations the priest-astronomers relied upon for counsel and information were so clear, they seemed to be close enough to touch. The other prominent feature was the great river in the sky known as the Milky Way. To the Oparians the Milky Way was the great place where beloved ancestors resided.

On some nights Ayesha would go to the temple roof and look for the star she had designated to be her mother. She would speak to her for hours. Tonight she confided in her mother; she believed she was pregnant. She asked her mother for assistance to make sure the child would be a boy. These long conversations and the emotions they aroused, tired Ayesha, and she would return to her sleeping silks for a dreamless rest. But not tonight; she was still awake and wanted to see the great gold tablets. She descended the stairs to the main temple floor.

Ayesha lit the small candle she had brought with her and held it high, watching the circle of yellow light it produced on the gold tablets. The pattern of candlelight gave the illusion that the symbols were alive and moving. Ayesha was always drawn to the tablets because she believed they represented the distant past. Somehow, she imagined, they told the story of the people who founded Opar. She wished she knew what the strange carvings meant. She had questioned everyone, since she was a little girl, for any information. There was no one alive in Opar who knew anything of the strange characters, so all their meanings were left to her imagination.

Many miles to the west of Opar, very near the Atlantic Ocean in a country that would be called Angola in the future, there lived a couple. They had been abandoned, thrown off a ship onto a desolate and unfriendly shore. They were now trying to survive in the jungle somewhat away from the beach. Life was hard for them. Their trip to Africa had been for the man to take over a post in the British Foreign Service.

John Clayton and his wife, Alice, had done their best to create a safe shelter from the fierce beasts which seemed to be everywhere. One day there was an encounter with a large great ape. John had been unprepared having only an ax, and not his rifle. The ape attacked John and had it not been for his wife; he would have been quickly killed. She seized the rifle and shot the ape in the back. The wounded anthropoid turned to see his tormentor, left John, and proceeded to attack Alice. In its struggle to kill Alice, the bullet had done its work, and the ape died beside the unconscious woman.

Alice never recovered from the shock of the ape's attack. She threw her energies into her son who had been born shortly after; a son whose parents would not live to see grow into a man.

The year was of their stranding was 1888.

Ayesha walked out the main temple entrance onto the cobblestone street in front of the temple. The road was about twenty-five feet wide, and the wall that protected Opar was on the other side. She looked to her left and could barely make out the maze-like entrance. Ayesha looked up and saw the sentry on duty walking his beat on the top of the wall. He noticed movement below him and nodded his head to acknowledge her presence, signaling he would guard her nocturnal wanderings.

Ayesha turned and strolled back toward the temple. As she did, she looked curiously at the two statues that resided on either side of the great door. They were taller than she. The bird was obviously a falcon, but she did not know what was on the head. The other figure was a strange creature – the body of a man and the head of a beast that she had never seen. This statue frightened her deeply, as it always had, and she made a quick protecting sign with her fingers, dropped her gaze and entered the temple again. She walked to the staircase which would lead her back to her sleeping quarters.

This moon was the third time she had not gotten her monthlies. She was so excited thinking about a son who would be High Priest and take over for her to lead the people of Opar. She was too nervous to confide in her favorite handmaiden, Nedjam.

Nedjam was also the most mature of all her handmaidens. Most of the other girls were younger and were still, to varying degree, in the giggle stage of young womanhood. When it came time for the birth, Nedjam would be the only one Ayesha would allow to assist her.

The more Ayesha thought about the prospect of having a child and heir, the more excited she became; and the more apprehensive she was about Ware's reaction. She was afraid Ware would not be pleased with the idea of having a son for whom he would be responsible. Ayesha need not have worried. In the morning when he heard the news Ware was ecstatic, kissing and hugging Ayesha.

Nedjam was the first handmaiden to learn the good news. She and Ayesha were like best girlfriends as they shared their happiness. Their joyful screams were heard from one end of the temple to the other.

After all the celebration, Nedjam put her hands on Ayesha's shoulders, drew her face close and whispered solemnly and gently, "I will be with you between the stones." Ayesha sighed and whispered back, "You are the only person I want there with me."

In the ancient world, the matter of birthing a child was accomplished differently from today. The mother squatted nude, her back against a wall, with her feet on two stones about eight inches off the ground. This technique gave gravity an opportunity to aid in the birth. The midwife, in this case, Nedjam, would be between the stones waiting for the baby to emerge and drop into her hands.

The birth happened after almost twelve hours of labor and had left Ayesha exhausted. Ware had been ordered imperiously from the room, and guards had been posted to be sure of Ayesha and Nedjam's privacy.

Ayesha collapsed after the birth from exhaustion and was assisted to her couch by two of the most mature handmaidens. She watched through bleary eyes as Nedjam approached her with a child wrapped in clean white linen. Nedjam placed the crying infant in Ayesha's arms and whispered in her ear, "You had better start thinking about girl's names."

Both Nedjam and Ayesha smiled. Ayesha chose the name La for her new daughter.

Jim Malachowski

CHAPTER TWENTY-NINE — WAZIRI'S JOURNEY ENDS

Tarzan was the name he used in Africa. In Britain, he was known as John Clayton, Lord Greystoke, a member of the British House of Lords. He was currently about twenty years old and coming into his physical prime. He was several inches over six feet tall, a bit taller than his late father. His gray colored eyes, for the most part did not reveal his innermost thoughts and feelings. His thick, jet black hair hung to his shoulders. He was a bit more muscular than his friends, the Waziri.

Tarzan had recently lost an encounter with his European arch-enemies, Paulvich and Rokoff. They had grabbed his legs and thrown him off a ship that was close to the west coast of Africa. He was able to make it to shore — and familiar surroundings, as it turned out. He recognized the area containing the cabin, built by his father, where he had been born.

He decided to forage in an easterly direction, and after many days of leisurely travel he came upon an ebony warrior. He had never traveled this far east before and was in unfamiliar territory. The warrior was Busuli, who would become a great friend of his for many years. He saved Busuli from Numa the lion and was taken back to Busuli's village as a gesture of thanks.

Tarzan remained with the Waziri, and after a few weeks began to learn their language and converse with his new friends. He loved the hunting expeditions with the men of the tribe.

As Tarzan's grasp of the Waziri language strengthened, Busuli told him their history and legends. In the north, the tribe's traditional home, they were a strong and influential people. That is until the Arab slave traders encountered them. They enslaved many of the people and killed numerous warriors. The primitive weapons of the Waziri were no match for the muskets of the slavers. The tribe had been so reduced in size and strength that Chowambi, their chief, made the decision to leave their homeland and migrate south to their current location.

Many years later, the Arabs and their confederates, the Manyuema, stumbled upon their new location. The Waziri were able to kill all the scouting party to the man, so their new village remained a secret.

Chowambi gave Tarzan his first hints of the cloud city of Opar. The information came from Tarzan's inquiry about the number of gold ornaments he saw on the people. Chowambi told Tarzan, "You should talk with Waziri. He was one of the men who traveled to Opar when he was a young man." Waziri was an old man at this point, perhaps too old to effectively rule and lead his people.

Tarzan did have several talks with Waziri and learned all he could about his experiences in the cloud city. Waziri was grateful that he had found someone who was interested in his stories. Most of the tribe knew of his journey and the fact that he returned, several years later, with a large amount of gold. But very few knew all the details of his experiences which he had related to Tarzan.

Days later, a large group of the men of the tribe gathered for an elephant hunt. While they were several miles away from the village, a wide-eyed messenger found them and stated that the village was under attack from the Arabs and their henchmen, the Manyuemas.

When the hunting party returned, they found the invaders had taken over the palisade and were set to defend themselves from within the Waziri village.

Rage and hatred had overwhelmed Waziri, and he and a group of warriors stormed the entrance to the village. They were all cut down by musket fire. Tarzan was able to free some of the enslaved people and lead the warriors to a victory over their hated enemies. At dinner that night to celebrate their victory, they named Tarzan the new chief of the tribe.

Tomorrow they would begin to mourn and take care of the dead, including their former chief Waziri.

A few days later the members of the tribe gathered around the massive funeral pyre in honor of Waziri and the other fallen warriors. His children and grandchildren spoke briefly about how he had taken care of the tribe and how all loved him. Despite the five year absence, Waziri had been remembered as a great leader, and there were not many dry eyes around the fire which had reached fifty feet into the air.

As Tarzan watched the funeral pyre burn away, his thoughts went to the words of Waziri concerning the people in the cloud city of Opar and his experiences there. Did they even still exist? Did they still have as much gold as Waziri had mentioned? Would any of Waziri's offspring there still know of him? He made up his mind to travel there to satisfy his curiosity.

He wondered, and hoped, his desire for gold would not end up the same way for him as it had for Waziri.

Tarzan stood on a branch a hundred feet away, observing the celebration of his friend's life and thought of all the wondrous things Waziri had told him. He would have many pleasant memories of his friend.

He speculated about the journey that Waziri was on now, and wished him well.

CHAPTER THIRTY — THE FIRST GOODBYE

Ware loved his daughter, La very much. He was very protective of her and was proud of almost everything she said and did. He was never critical of La's words or actions. To celebrate her seventh birthday, La had convinced Ware to take her on a meat gathering trip with him. (Ware brought several extra hunters to guard La at all costs.) He had always told La of his exploits, and she was fascinated by the tales of the animals. She had begged him to take her for months, so Ware decided to take her on a short expedition. This was the first time La had ever been outside the walls of Opar, and she had a thousand questions.

The small party had left Opar at first light and traveled out of the mountains and into the broad knee-high brown savannah of grass. La paused upon seeing the vast stretches of low mountains covered in green and the lush flatlands with every shade of brown and green. She wanted to absorb the beautiful vistas that lay before her. They walked for several hours, then in the early afternoon, Ware called for a rest for lunch. The baskets the hunters had been carrying were opened, and lunch was laid out. Grilled goose was served with vegetables, then fruit for dessert.

Ware and La sat away from the other men. Cha was Ware's best friend and constant hunting companion. He was always on guard duty, slowly walking around the resting group. Ten minutes later another hunter would take his place. Several of the men carried the small messenger-monkeys who could be dispatched back to Opar for aid in less than a minute.

Ware broke the silence and asked La, "Are you enjoying your gift today?"

"Oh yes," she answered, "this country is so beautiful, so much better than that ugly old pile of rocks we live in."

"We live where we do because it is safe and secure. Our people are not many, and we need somewhere we can keep our enemies out. We have never had to defend our selves against a large army, and I hope that never happens. Why do you think we kill every stranger that gets close to Opar?"

La nodded, "You are probably right. I never thought about that."

La was quiet for a few moments and said, "Are there people who live over those mountains that are all around us?" Ware did not answer but rather waited for her to continue. "Someday I want to see what is beyond our wall. Not all the people who live there should be feared. Am I right? Ware (this was the first time she had addressed him by his first name), I don't think I want to spend my life ruling Opar. Even now I am bored to death. I don't believe anything has changed in Opar in a thousand years. Has it?"

He answered, "Not much."

La continued, "I am not sure I believe totally in the Flaming God. I know you are shocked. Please don't tell my mother." Ware continued his silence and smiled inwardly. "Why can't you and I and mother just leave, and explore the beautiful land where we could live?"

Ware stepped in at this point saying, "La, this is the only life your mother and I have ever known. Our curiosity is not as strong as yours. Would you have us abandon our people? They probably would not survive without our leadership. We must rule Opar and provide a good life for them. This is our job and our responsibility. The gods, whether the Flaming God or some other, would not look favorably upon us for abandoning our responsibilities to our subjects."

"You must think I am terrible," La said dropping her head. Ware responded quickly saying, "No, I don't think you are terrible. You are a young person and think differently from your mother and I. You can believe whatever you want. It is your actions on which people and the gods will judge you."

"We have been enjoying lunch long enough. We have a long walk home so we can get there before dark." He looked at one of his fellow hunters, and the man smiled and nodded his head. "However," Ware said, "there is one more thing I want you to see."

"La, I want you to stay close to me, in observing this wonder. There is also great danger." The party, led by the nodding man, crossed over a small hill and walked down to a large stand of trees that were spaced closely together. Ware gave La a hand sign not to talk or make any noise. They crept out of the warmth of the sun and into the shadowy gloom of the trees. Fifteen minutes went by, and the scout raised his hand for the group to stop. One other man went to the left and one to the right, walking silently.

Presently one of them returned and motioned the group to follow him. Ten minutes later they came upon denser forest and a small waterhole perhaps twenty feet across. The water was brown and not very inviting. As they skirted the pond, they began to hear branches breaking and the sound of very deep rumbling from several different sources.

The lead hunter crumbled some dry leaves in his hands and let them fall. They fell back toward the man. A gentle breeze was blowing toward them. Slowly advancing, they came to a small clearing, and everyone stopped. The man next to La pointed to the shadows in the trees, and her eyes saw a gigantic creature that had been standing there but seemed to materialize before her eyes.

La gasped, and her mouth fell open when she saw the creature. "It is so close, how could I not have seen it?" she asked herself. More leaves and branches were being ripped and shoved into the large mouth. An eye the size of a ripe melon seemed to be looking right at them, then looked away. The great elephant's stomach began making louder sounds. Suddenly there appeared a slightly smaller female and a very small baby. La marveled, how can these huge creatures move through the forest without making a sound?

The hunter in front turned and motioned with his head that the group should leave the forest before the adult elephants became agitated by their presence. Everyone quietly backed out. Reluctantly La had to be coaxed by Ware to leave. When they were a hundred yards away, Ware spoke to La, "I am glad we were able to find elephants and show them to you. If man is not threatening to them, they can be very docile. If they are angry, you cannot believe how fast they can run and be upon you before you can defend yourself. They are beautiful beasts, but they can be some of the most dangerous animals in the forest."

La hung on every word from Ware and was speechless from the encounter. Later she peppered Ware with questions about the jungle and the elephants. This had been a wonderful day for La, as well as for Ware.

They made good time walking home and were able to go through the entrance to the city before the Flaming God disappeared. It had been a day La would remember for the rest of her life.

Ware's love and respect for La had grown greatly over the past two years. He felt she had matured greatly, and she would make a wonderful High Priestess. Ware sometimes felt a tinge of sadness that he and Ayesha did not have a son to look after them in their later years. The sadness always left quickly because of what he saw in La's makeup. He was able to see parts of La that came from him; and traits and mannerisms that came from Ayesha.

Six months after the trip into the jungle Ware, and his best friend and constant companion Cha, were leading a small party of hunters on their weekly search for meat. The men had found a small herd of antelope and had killed three of the animals. Two of the men stayed with the kill and began to dress the animals for transport back to Opar. Ware wanted one more kill which would make this trip the usual success.

Once the antelope had settled down, the stalkers were able to begin advancing again. They advanced slowly toward the herd on their hands and knees in the waist high grass. The wind was blowing toward the hunters and was not betraying their presence to the animals. When they were within twenty-five feet of the herd, Ware selected a young buck, then stood and shot him with a well-placed arrow. The arrow pierced the chest behind the foreleg and Ware was sure the animal was dead when it went down immediately.

Ware and his companion ran toward the fallen antelope and wanted to begin the skinning process. This particular creature, called an Oryx, possessed straight horns about eighteen inches long. Ware quickly advanced toward the rump of the fallen antelope and walked a few quick steps to get close to the throat, which he would cut. The animal's head was down close to his front legs, and Ware knelt and reached over to grab the ear to bring the head up and expose the jugular vein in the neck. He gave a grunt when he felt Ware touch him, and he quickly reared his head back toward Ware.

The Oryx's long straight horn penetrated Ware's chest and his heart. He was dead in seconds. Cha was about to remind Ware of the horn danger but had not been quick enough. The man raced to Ware's side, and pulled him away from the Oryx and looked at the wound. It was clear the wound had been fatal. The man eased Ware onto his back and ran screaming back to his companions.

Three hours later the group approached the gates of the city with Ware lying on a makeshift stretcher. The journey back had been dead silent. Each man had loved and respected Ware, and each relived their private moments with him. The same men had been hunting together for over fifteen years, and all had enjoyed a very close bond.

Two of the men stayed outside the city entrance with Ware's body, while Cha went into the temple to find Ayesha. He was led by a guard into a small room to await Ayesha. She entered the room with a frightened look on her face as if she already was aware of the news.

"Majesty," Cha began, "there has been a terrible accident, and I have to tell you Ware is dead."

Ayesha' scream was loud enough that it was heard by almost everyone who was in the temple of the Flaming God. Ayesha collapsed and had to be carried by Cha to her sleeping couch, where Nedjam and the other handmaidens rapidly gathered to find out what had happened.

CHAPTER THIRTY-ONE — MORE CHANGES

Five months had passed since the death of Ware. Ayesha was in labor again, with her second child. Nedjam was the sole handmaiden present assisting with the birth and providing support. Ayesha said between spasms of pain, "Even though I have done this before, I am still afraid, Nedjam. You remember all your promises to me if I do not survive this ordeal." Nedjam gave a supportive smile and nodded her head.

Three hours later, Ayesha and her newborn daughter were resting comfortably when Nedjam brought a wide-eyed La the room. La, as usual, was full of questions and had little idea of the ordeal her mother had just undergone.

La asked, "Can I hold him yet?"

"La, the baby is a girl, not a boy."

"Why, Mother, Ware and I all wanted a boy, so why is it a girl?" La commented wrinkling her nose. Ayesha's heart ached when La mentioned her father's name.

Nedjam said "No one can control that. We should all be grateful the baby is healthy, and your mother came through the birth with no problems."

The answer seemed to satisfy La, and the two exited the room quietly to let Ayesha rest. As they exited, Ayesha opened her eyes and could not control a smile; she was so proud of La. That and the fact that Nedjam was one of the few people who could control La.

La was quite headstrong and opinionated even at this age. She seemed bored by the lessons Nedjam, and a tutor tried to teach her.

The tutor told Nedjam, "This is a sign of the child being very smart, and she is ready for more advanced challenges." There was another side to La that not many people had seen. La could be as cold as the top of the mountains in winter. These two factors invariably led to the emergence of the personality in La that Nedjam most feared. Nedjam dreaded La becoming a cold-hearted, vengeful woman, inclined to punish anyone who disrespected her. May the Flaming God have mercy on those that put her in that mood.

La, in this state of mind, did not think clearly, or seemingly at all. She cared not for her words or deeds and took no thoughts about possible consequences. Nedjam hoped that La would grow out of this area of her personality.

La was lukewarm on learning the sacrificial ritual chants and incantations to the Flaming God. That year Ayesha would allow her to be present, properly guarded of course, during a sacrifice to the Flaming God. Those present sometimes got caught up in a frenzy, and people were injured and could be killed.

It is amazing what a child will accept as normal; for example, the taking of life in a most grizzly and brutal manner. Through all the generations, the need for human sacrifices to the Flaming God had been explained as a way to worship him and to ensure his blessings and favors on his chosen people.

A month ago a suitable victim was found by the hunters and he had been welcomed into the city. The captive had been fed and locked in a cell adjacent to the circular altar room. The day of the sacrifice was designated by one of the priests, whose job it was to interpret the colors, and other nuances, of the Flaming God. From that message, he would set the hour and day for the sacrifice.

Ayesha was still grieving the loss of Ware and just wanted to be near him one more time. She had experience with the nectar made by Soma. After the last sacrifice, Ayesha had seen and talked with her mother Mery and had been comforted by that experience. That old fool Set had tried to come to her when she had last drunk the Nectar; she had screamed for him to go "back to the hell you deserve." Ayesha had planned to take a larger than usual dose of the Nectar to assure a visit from Ware. She wiped tears from her eyes as her desire to see Ware faded and the reality of the ceremony took charge.

La had been with Ayesha during her preparations for the ceremony. Ayesha had placed the more elaborate headpiece on her head. She inspected the female temple acolytes. Upon approval, she invited the Daughters of Soma into the room. Soma brought two assistants with her, and each carried an ornate pitcher. Ayesha touched one of the pitchers and asked, "Is this the pitcher for me and the temple acolytes?" Soma answered, "Yes, Majesty. Twice the strength as that for the guests." With La at her side, Ayesha motioned for one of the female acolytes to bring forth the tray of gold goblets. Ayesha watched as Soma and her assistants filled the goblets. The larger of the goblets was for the use of the High Priestess. It held twice the amount of all the other goblets.

La whispered to her mother, "What is that?"

Ayesha answered, "It is the Nectar of the Flaming God. It brings me into contact with him during the ceremony and for the next day. If you have any more questions, you will need to hold them until I can answer them without the presence of the Flaming God."

La's eyes opened wide, and she decided she had better not ask any more questions right now.

Ayesha spoke to the acolytes and the assistants of Soma, "Please serve the invited the other nectar and remember the Neteru are not to be served any drink. They will try to drink some if a guest sits down a cup. I am relying on you servers not to let that happen."

As the Daughters filled small goblets in the circular altar room, Ayesha raised her goblet, which invited the other acolytes, minor priests, and minor priestesses, to raise their goblets. In one voice, they chanted a prayer inviting the Flaming God to be in the altar room with them and to bless the people of Opar for their efforts. All drained their goblets, and the service began.

After watching Ayesha drink the Nectar, La had been taken by guards up the stairs to the balcony. From there she watched the remaining service surrounded by guards. The invited nobles and the Neteru guardians of the temple had chanted the incantation to the Flaming God. The Neteru then brought the prisoner into the oval sacrifice room in the center of the temple. They hoisted the captive onto the sacrificial altar and secured his hands and feet to iron rings on the ends of the altar.

The altar was built in such a way that beneath the shoulder blades of the victim there was a mound that thrust the heart area of the victim higher than any part of his body. Right on cue, a handmaiden of the High Priestess had in a mock skirmish established the High Priestess's authority over the prisoner by driving the Neteru away from the prisoner and from the altar. She then disappeared, and Ayesha entered from one of the arched entrances, the sacrificial knife held high over her head. She began another chant to the Flaming God, which everyone in the room took up. Slowly and deliberately Ayesha began to move around the altar to face the crowd, and toward the terrified and struggling victim tied to the altar.

With glazed-over eyes, Ayesha turned her head toward the crowd, an almost unworldly look upon her face. The crowd saw Ayesha's eyes roll back into her head and with lightning speed the knife descended, pierced, and ripped open the man's chest. In the blink of an eye, Ayesha was holding a still-beating heart above her head. The blood was running down her arms to her rapidly rising and falling breast. The guests upon seeing the heart, let out in one-voice a scream of release, and they rushed the altar attempting to find any drops of the blood to put into their cups. The crowd was tightly packed around Ayesha and the altar. The people were anxiously trying to force their way to the acolytes who were dispensing small amounts of blood.

The next morning Nedjam was still tending to Ayesha who had to be helped to her quarters from the sacrificial altar. Ayesha was just beginning to be able to formulate some semi-understandable speech. She had been sitting all night speaking with the Flaming God, and toward morning let out a shriek that awakened most everyone in the complex. She had screamed her mother's name, and the tears were coursing down her cheeks.

The look on her contorted countenance appeared more painful from the makeup which had been so carefully applied the day before. It came cascading down mingled with sweat upon her once-white sleeping gown.

La had been standing wide-eyed in the doorway. She came in, stared at Nedjam and asked, "Is my mother alright? She looks like she is going to die. Nedjam, I am afraid for her."

Nedjam looked at La and said, "La, you were told not to bother your mother today, she is still recovering from the visit of the Flaming God. She will be alright, I am sure. You need to leave now and not come back until tomorrow. If your mother sees you, she will get even more upset."

Nedjam had hidden her fear for Ayesha very well. La had no idea that she was just as worried. Ayesha had taken a very strong dose of the Flaming God's nectar and was now paying the price.

Nedjam had watched a similar reaction play out when Mery was alive and High Priestess: an emotional conversation with the Flaming God, followed by many hours of sleep. Ayesha obviously was still stinging over the loss of her mother and Ware, and had received a visit from Mery, or thought she had.

At an appropriate time, Nedjam would advise Ayesha to drink less of the nectar. She would not say that she feared for Ayesha's life, just that it would be better not to be a negative example to La.

Nedjam walked down the corridor to La's room and found her sitting on her sleeping couch. Nedjam sat down beside her and asked, "So La, what is on your mind?"

La, after a brief pause, "Is my mother better? I almost did not know her; she looked so bad."

"Your mother and every other High Priestess have had to endure this pain during the sacrifice to the Flaming God. This is the cost of talking to the god. When you are older, and you are High Priestess, you will have to endure this pain also."

La's eyes opened wide as she thought about this. Nedjam continued, "Remember, when you are older, your outlook on the world will change greatly. La, this is not something you should concern yourself with now. In a few hours, you visit your mother, and you will see everything is fine."

"La, I have not slept all night, I am going to my room for a rest." Nedjam tried to hide her pain from La, and everyone else. The knot in her chest was bad again, and the numbness in her left arm had returned. She had exerted herself greatly yesterday afternoon and evening, not to mention being up with Ayesha all night. Thankfully Ayesha had fallen asleep before Nedjam left the chamber to look in on La.

As she lay on her couch waiting for sleep, Nedjam thought about La. At this age, La was as tall as all of the women and some of the men of Opar. She could be one of the tallest people in Opar when she reached maturity.

La's personality revealed a strong inner self. She always believed that her decisions were correct. She was not one to take advice readily and was headstrong about doing things and seeking advice later. She did not seem, at least now, to be aware of the ramifications of her words and actions. She, even at this age, was trying to control both Nedjam and her mother. Nedjam believed, despite these issues, La had a kind heart, which she showed in holding and playing with her baby sister Kiya.

Nedjam had not drunk any of the Flaming God nectar, and so her head was clear. She did want to talk with the Flaming God and ask him to grant her more years with La and to be able to transition her into the role of High Priestess. Nedjam desperately wanted to be known as the handmaiden who had served three High Priestesses.

After a sleep of several hours, Nedjam walked slowly back to Ayesha's sleeping quarter. As she walked in, she saw that Ayesha was awake and was staring at the ceiling. She rolled her head so that she was looking at Nedjam. Nedjam did not like what she saw in Ayesha's face; she looked worn and haggard as if she had not slept. Finally, she spoke in a low and raspy voice. "You know I talked with my mother and Ware last night. I knew I would be able. It was so good seeing them together. They seemed happy, and Mother told me she was pleased with my governing of Opar. Ware told me he loved me very much and was so sorry we were not together."

Nedjam could not hold her tongue, "Ayesha, you know I am not a believer in the Flaming God. La came in the room when you were brought back from the sacrifice, and she was horrified by your appearance. I had to spend several hours getting her calmed down."

Ayesha turned her face from Nedjam and whispered "I'm sorry. I did not want her to see me after the sacrifice."

Nedjam continued, "You must never again drink so much of the Flaming God's nectar. You know, of course, that people here in Opar have died after drinking that vile potion. I was very afraid you would not wake up this morning. I was so upset and worried about you."

Ayesha gave a weak smile and said, "Sorry I upset you so badly. I will not do that again." A cloud passed over Ayesha's face, and she began crying again. Nedjam asked what was on her mind.

"Last night, when mother and Ware were finished talking with me, they turned and began to walk away. After a few steps, they both looked back to me and said: "Prepare yourself Ayesha, your daughter will die the most horrible death imaginable." Then they vanished.

Nedjam went cold inside and tried not to show Ayesha her feelings. "I hate to say this, but I believe the leaves that make the potion made that thought in your heart."

"So you don't believe that will happen? I am so fearful for La."

"No, Ayesha I do not. Please get up now, and let the handmaidens bathe and dress you, and I will get you some breakfast."

Nedjam turned quickly and exited the room. The look of horror came and the feeling of cold-fear in her chest intensified. "Oh, please do not let this vision be true. I must make a plan to protect La even more. This just cannot happen." Nedjam found herself nearly running to the kitchen area of the quarters.

Jim Malachowski

CHAPTER THIRTY-TWO — FATHER MARTIN

D'Arnot had insisted that Tarzan stay with him in his very well appointed apartment in Paris. He had invited Tarzan to visit him, after their harrowing adventures in Africa. D'Arnot felt much gratitude toward Tarzan for rescuing him from Mbonga's tribe of cannibals.

D'Arnot had been trying seemingly unsuccessfully to prevent Tarzan from renouncing his title and holdings as the rightful Lord Greystoke. Tarzan had even gone so far as to have business cards created with his name as *M. Jean C. Tarzan.*

D'Arnot had received a message earlier in the day from an old friend of his, Martin Ober, saying he was going to be in Paris for a few days and would love to see D'Arnot, as this will probably his last trip to the city for the foreseeable future. D'Arnot gave Tarzan a little bit of background on Martin Ober and the history of his friendship with him. Tarzan accepted the invitation to come for a cup of coffee and some conversation and to meet someone who had been a very close friend to D'Arnot. His relationship with D'Arnot had been somewhat of a non-personal one. This would be Tarzan's first glance into D'Arnot's past.

The afternoon was pleasantly warm after a rather cool morning in late spring. D'Arnot and Tarzan arrived at the cafe and were waiting for Martin's arrival. D'Arnot recognized his friend Martin as he walked casually down the street toward the cafe. Martin was a tall man about six feet and slightly overweight, and he had recently celebrated his twenty-third birthday. Martin was sporting a mustache, which he had grown to make himself look a bit older. D'Arnot introduced Tarzan as Monsieur Jean Tarzan, for this is how Tarzan wished to be known.

After the introductions, D'Arnot said, "Martin, it is so good to see you. I have lost track of you; are you still attending seminary?" Martin replied with a nice smile on his face saying, "I have completed my studies, and have been ordained, so I am a true Jesuit priest. In the next few weeks, I will be assigned to a parish probably in the countryside." What Martin had not said was that he was able to complete the eight-year training program in just six years.

"Monsieur Tarzan, I understand from D'Arnot that you were raised in Africa. This first visit to the continent must be quite a change for you. Hope you are enjoying yourself." Martin added with a sly smile "D'Arnot will know all the right restaurants and the other places of male entertainment in Paris. I do envy you somewhat you know." All three men enjoyed a laugh at Martin's humor, and the afternoon passed quickly. After a several hour visit, Martin excused himself saying he had to visit his parents where he would be enjoying his mother's cooking.

It would be four years before Tarzan would see his new friend Martin Ober again, and then in an unexpected locale.

CHAPTER THIRTY-THREE — LOOKING BACK

In the world outside of Opar it was several years into the twentieth century. The calendar as such was unknown to the people of Opar. They still reckoned time by the number of years that the High Priestess or Priest has been on the throne.

The years have passed quickly, Nedjam thought as she looked at herself in the polished bronze sheet of metal that passed for a mirror. She did not like the vision of the woman who looked back at her from the mirror. She saw an old woman looking back, but Nedjam did not feel inside like this woman looked. She knew she was slowing down and did not have as much energy as before, but she still had the ambition to keep serving.

Nedjam thought back to her children, something which she had been doing more and more lately. Her three children fathered by Waziri had long ago left her everyday care and now had families of their own. Her oldest, a son who was the image of his father, ramrod straight even now, one of the most skilled hunters in Opar. He would still occasionally join in the hunt, but rarely did his diminishing skills allow him to participate fully. He was closing in on his sixtieth year and was becoming more dependent upon his children and grandchildren.

Nedjam's youngest daughter had died in her teens when sickness made its way through Opar.

Her middle child, a daughter, had two older children. Later in her life, she gave birth to a daughter that was the same age as Kiya. Her name was Oah. She was strong-willed and had a mysterious air about her. Nedjam could see in her eyes that she was thinking or even plotting about something, but she always kept her thoughts to herself. Frequently Nedjam brought Oah into the temple area where she and Kiya would play.

For the past several years since she was ten, Ayesha had requested La become more involved with the governance of Opar. At first, La resisted and took very little interest, wanting to go back and play with her friends. After three years of sitting next to her mother, and being a part of the leadership of Opar, La began to enjoy the experience, especially when she saw her mother wield the power of her position.

Nedjam saw her role as Ayesha's closest advisor begin to change. In her heart, she welcomed the lessening of her responsibilities. She began to spend more hours with La, and the subjects of their discussions were becoming increasingly adult, especially with the awakening of La's interest in the young men of the city.

Some of the early discussions of men came in this area, "Nedjam when I am High Priestess, do I need to have a man seated next to me?"

Nedjam answered emphatically, "There is a big difference between want and need. Your mother has filled the role of High Priestess very well since Ware's death – without the council, or companionship of another man. You take a man to be your mate because you want him, not because you need him. You have many years to choose the right mate."

Nedjam could see the interest in men, and La's curiosity. She wisely knew that La could meet a young man and fall hopelessly in love with him. Nedjam just hoped it happened in her lifetime, so she could temper La's passion and guide her judgment and actions.

Late one summer evening, Ayesha called for Nedjam. When Nedjam arrived in the sleeping room, she found an extremely ill Ayesha. Over the years Ayesha had had several bouts with malaria, but this was the worst episode Nedjam had seen. She sent one of the younger handmaidens to bring Soma immediately.

When Soma the healer arrived, she found an unconscious Ayesha. One look and she knew this malaria attack was extremely deadly. Ayesha was perspiring heavily, and breathing was becoming more labored. Nedjam sent the handmaiden to bring La.

La was upset and crying uncontrollably at the sight of her mother. Nedjam gave her a comforting pat on the shoulder and sat next to her. Soma broke the silence, "There is no remedy I can give her that will ease this illness. I am afraid you should expect the worst."

Near dawn, Ayesha breathed her last, and La became High Priestess of Opar.

CHAPTER THIRTY-FOUR — THE REIGN OF LA BEGINS

The temple was quiet as a tomb as the news of the death of Ayesha circulated throughout the city. Nedjam canceled all scheduled appointments and issued an order that La would be assuming the position of High Priestess, but would be in mourning for the next few weeks.

Nedjam spent most of her waking time with La, trying to convince her that she was ready to rule. "La, you must soon ascend to the High Priestess' chair. When you are ready, I will schedule a few matters of little importance for you to resolve. Remember the council will be watching you closely, and you must impress upon them your ability to rule. We do not want them even to bring forth the idea of wanting a High Priest to serve with you. There is some talk that a few of them believe you are too young to rule alone."

"Nedjam, I will be ready, but I will need you to be with me for support."

"I will be right there for you, La."

The morning of the first meeting of the council was one month after the death of Ayesha. All the members at the beginning of their remarks expressed once again their sorrow at Ayesha's death, even the ones who hated her.

Nedjam had coached La on what would come up and how to respond. The first was a progress report on the extension of the corridor on the third level tunnel under the temple. Nedjam had advised her to say, "Keep me informed on the progress." The next item was to be more meat for the common people — a low-level item. "I will speak with the hunters," was the advised answer. The third item involved a land dispute between two friends of council members. Nedjam advised, "Settle this among yourselves. If I get involved neither of you will like my resolution." The meeting progressed quickly, for everyone except La, and all seemed pleased with her handling of the situation.

La gained much confidence from this meeting, and rarely needed Nedjam's council and coaching again. La's conversation with Nedjam revolved around missing her mother, missing Ware, and her desire for male companionship. The first two were easy for Nedjam; the third were feelings she had remembered from her past when she was La's age. She tried to give her the same hollow advice she had been given — when the right man comes along, you will know.

After some blunders in the first year of her rule, the second year was going along smoothly. La's confidence was at an all-time high, and she was enjoying her role as High Priestess.

Then came the first sacrifice to the Flaming God in which she was the principal celebrant. The man was almost certainly an Arab scout who was looking for potential slaves for the Manyuema to capture. He had made the mistake of approaching Opar when hunters were returning from a successful meat-seeking expedition. He became curious when the lack of clouds and mist that day allowed Opar to be seen. The men were able to easily capture him because he had injured his leg and was unable to elude their pursuit. He was taken into a holding cell just off the circular sacrifice room. One of the hunters ran to La's office and informed Nedjam there was a candidate for sacrifice.

Nedjam gave the man a verbal reward, with the promise of a more tangible one to come. She then went to La and informed her of the capture, and told her she thought it would be an easy sacrifice for La's first time. From the look on La's face, Nedjam could tell this news was uneasily received.

La had not drunk any of the Flaming God's nectar, so she was more aware of the boisterous activity from the guests and the other viewers crammed in the balcony. The Arab began to scream and plead for his life in a voice that was foreign to the ears of anyone close enough to hear. As the ceremony progressed, the more hysterical he became, flailing about the altar. When it came time for La to remove his heart, he was thrashing like a fish out of water. La grabbed him by the throat to hold him down, but he was stronger than she and was able to break her hold. While this was happening, La made a rapid lunge with the sacrificial knife. It missed the area below the ribs, and instead entered his stomach on the right side.

La looked at Nedjam, confidence obviously shaken, who was standing in the front row, and she mouthed a command to her. "Quickly, La. Open him up now! Get this done!" La again raised the knife and swiftly brought it down and opened the Arab from right to left under the ribs. She rapidly forced her hand through his diaphragm and grabbed the heart and with a mighty pull, brought it out of his body.

The crowd had gotten back into the sacrifice, with yelling by some of the men and swooning by some women. The shouts of the prayers were deafening inside the round chamber. The crescendo reached an even higher volume when La held the beating heart above her head while screaming the final prayer of acceptance to the Flaming God.

La was feeling a sense of accomplishment as she looked at the hysterical men and women who were watching the still beating heart she held over her head. La could feel the warm blood running down her arms and onto her heaving breast. She got a feeling in her chest that she never thought would be possible under these circumstances.

La dropped the heart next to the corpse on the altar and backed away as the invited fought to get a few drops of the sacrificial blood into their golden goblets. She was seeking Nedjam as she was proud of herself and her ability to overcome a shaky start. She also wanted to retire to her private quarters and to clean herself of the blood.

La and Nedjam wove through the boisterous crowd not saying much of anything to each other. When they reached La's sleeping quarters, Nedjam summoned two handmaidens and ordered them to bath La and make her ready to retire.

As La looked at Nedjam, a tinge of sorrow entered her mind. The woman who stood before her was not a young woman anymore, or even a woman of middle years. Nedjam had become an old woman, and La had been so engrossed in herself that she had failed to notice.

Nedjam smiled at La and said, "You did well tonight, the next ones will be easier. Try to drink a swallow of the nectar; it will help you focus on what needs to be accomplished."

CHAPTER THIRTY-FIVE — FINAL INSTRUCTIONS

Eight months after the botched sacrifice, La and Nedjam had just finished a strategy meeting concerning the ongoing problems of the city. The last item on the agenda was Nedjam's recommendation that La dispatch another expedition to find the elusive, slippery black substance. The ancients had used it to move large stones that became the city wall and the buildings of Opar. Nedjam had recalled that the Waziri people used the black liquid to create bright torches for use during night travel and exploring dark places. Nedjam stated, "Your hunters need to be told again how important this substance is for the defense of Opar. Try offering a reward to any man who finds a source of this material." La nodded in agreement.

For the last several months the conversations between Nedjam and La had taken on a more urgent nature. Nedjam had seemed like she was trying to cram information into La's mind.

While Nedjam was talking, La looked at her over the luncheon meal, which Nedjam had not touched. She seemed to be fading away before La's eyes. She wanted to hug her and hold her close. La knew better as that would signify she was upset when looking at Nedjam.

Nedjam seemed to be shrinking in stature, and her skin had taken on a distinctly yellow pallor. However, her voice was the biggest change. It was no longer full of command and power but was weaker and lower in volume. There had been times during ceremonies and meetings that she thought Nedjam was napping. La noted to herself that she had to get Nedjam to rest more and gain some strength back.

A cold feeling went through La's body. What if Nedjam knew she did not have much time left, and she was trying to give La all the information she held in her mind? La felt tears welling up in her eyes, and she rose and got a goblet of water from a pitcher on a sideboard in the room. She had to fight these tears away, she thought.

When she went back to her chair, she asked Nedjam, "Are you feeling well? You seem tired today, is there anything I can get for you." Nedjam thought for a moment and smiled saying, "No La, there is nothing you can do, because there is nothing wrong."

Nedjam went to her quarters after her meeting with La and was seated in her favorite chair. She was smiling to herself, as though she had completed her task. She thought about her goal from several years ago that was she wanted to be remembered as the handmaiden who had served three High Priestesses. Maybe she was pleased this goal had been accomplished, or she felt she had prepared La to be alone as High Priestess of Opar.

Ten days later the celebration of Nedjam's life had taken place in the back part of the city's enclosure, near the wooded pond that had been a favorite place of Nedjam and all the High Priestesses she had served. The tears flowed freely down La's face as she concluded her thoughts on what Nedjam had meant to her and her contributions to Opar.

At the conclusion of La's talk, the funeral pyre was lit, and everyone stood silently until the logs which held Nedjams body had collapsed into ashes. By then the crowd had left the funeral, leaving La alone by the fire.

CHAPTER THIRTY-SIX — THE NEW CHIEF HANDMAIDEN

A s the fires of Nedjam's funeral pyre died down, having burned all the wood, La turned to walk back to her suite in the temple. She saw a man looking at her across the fire. Finally, he spoke, "La, it is Cadj. I am a temple priest. I became a priest when my father died a few months ago, and I inherited his post."

La nodded, the last thing she wanted was to talk with one of the temple priests. "What is it, Cadj?" she asked impatiently.

"I know it is too early for you to think about a new chief handmaiden, but I have been asked to bring a name to your attention. Her name is Oah. She is the granddaughter of Nedjam and a man who visited Opar many years ago."

La thought yes, now I do remember, Oah used to play as children with Kiya, my younger sister. I believe they are the same age. La responded to Cadj, "Yes, I do remember, Nedjam loved her very much."

"Oah asked if you had made a decision on your choice for Nedjam's replacement. She and I both feel you should at least consider her." Cadj, without waiting for an answer, turned on his heel and walked back to the temple.

In the evenings, the black liquid, which had been found after much effort, was put into small pots and a cloth wick was lit. The oil gave off a lot of smoke but was good to light major walkways in the city, and entrances to the temple.

La smiled at the light produced by the black liquid. It was one of the last subjects Nedjam had brought up to her, as needing La's attention. Now it was used, for the first time, to light Nedjam's exit from this world.

La thought the conversation strange and promised to investigate Oah a bit further. As she was walking down the dimly lit main corridor in the Temple of the Flaming God, she came across one of her younger handmaidens. She signaled the girl to stop and asked her, "What is your name?" "May-at," the girl answered. La said, "May-at, come into my sitting room, I wish to speak with you."

The color dropped from May-at's face, and La thought she was going to faint. "Have I done something wrong or said something to offend you?"

La smiled at the girl and said, "No, not at all. Come and sit with me."

May-at came and sat nervously on the edge of one of the chairs. La said in a strict tone, "If you wish to be in my favor, you will never repeat anything I say to you, or that you hear in my rooms. Do you understand?"

May-at's eyes were wide, and she nodded her head yes.

"Good," continued La, "I will need a handmaiden to assist me. I want to give you a chance to earn the job by your work in the next several months." La had decided she needed someone in the job until she could make up her mind. Her first choice was Kiya, her younger sister, but like Oah she was young, too young.

La returned her attention to May-at and asked, "Are you interested?"

"Oh, yes," was the enthusiastic reply.

"How old are you, May-at?" Sixteen was the answer. "Tell me about yourself and what you have been doing here, before tonight." The nervousness was mostly gone, and May-at spoke quickly. She was obviously a clever young lady, and La began to like her. She would keep her close, even after Kiya was named Chief Handmaiden in a few years.

La began fishing, "Tell me of the other young handmaidens." La then sat back and listened until May-at came to Oah. La pretended to have no more interest in Oah than in any of the other girls. She would have plenty of time to get more information about Oah as time went on.

La told May-at she would continue to reside in the handmaiden residence, but she would spend most of her time in the company of La. May-at beamed a wide smile. La again admonished her, "You may tell your friends you will be working with me, but nothing else. Understood?"

May-at became a bit more serious and assured La of her obedience and loyalty.

CHAPTER THIRTY-SEVEN — THE VISITORS

Saba, captain of the sentries, came running into the reception room of La's quarters. He spoke quickly to May-at who happened to be in the room. "Please tell the High Priestess there is a large group of armed men approaching."

May-at knew the importance of this message and ran to find La. When she heard the news, she told May-at to bring the sentry into her reception room and provide him a chair. When La entered the room, she saw Saba had been seated, and given a goblet of water.

La looked at the sentinel. It was nearly midday when she had been notified. "Tell me about these men — are they few? We should be able to send some soldiers out and capture them, correct?"

The sentry answered, "Mistress, they are still very far away at the other side of the valley. I saw them by the amount of dust their feet were making as they walked toward Opar.

"When do you think they will be close to the city?" La asked.

"This afternoon, if Opar is their destination. Let's hope they do not see the city and change their travel direction."

"How many men do you believe there to be?" La asked.

"I would guess more than twenty of them, your Highness. At present we do not know for sure the number, or how they are armed. We do not even know if Opar is their destination."

"Come and accompany me to the wall when the Flaming God is nearly touching the mountains behind Opar. We should know more by that time. Now go and get some rest until then." The man bowed and walked out of the room. Before he made the door, La said, "Have Commander Mitry come here right away."

Shortly after Saba left, the Commander of the Guard was announced and ushered into the reception room. This was La's first crisis, and she hoped her face did not betray the fear she felt inside. She remembered what Nedjam had advised her should this ever happen, "Let the military take care of any attempt to invade the city. Protect yourself by hiding in the lower levels."

"Mitry, what do you advise?" La asked. The Commander replied, "To the best of my knowledge, this is the first attempt of an armed group of men to approach the city. It has always been just some lost wanderer. I think we should wait until they get closer and just observe for now. We do not know if they intend to invade, or just investigate us. If they continue to come directly toward the city, I would believe they know who we are and that we have gold. Perhaps later we should try to frighten them away. I am going to inform the Neteru guards and the archers to prepare for a fight. But for right now, I believe we should keep all signs of life hidden. I am ordering all fires and cooking extinguished before they get close enough to know we are here. Perhaps they will think this is an abandoned city and move on. If they send scouts in, we will attempt to capture them. The Flaming God has not had an offering in a few weeks now."

La breathed a sigh of relief and said, "That sounds like a good plan. I have told the Chief Sentry, Saba, I want to observe the men that are approaching later today. Would you accompany us?"

"Yes," was his answer. And he added, "We must be careful so that no one sees us. The Flaming God will be behind us at that time and I believe it will be difficult for them to see us on top of the wall. However, we need to be careful that no one sees us." La thanked him and said she was looking forward to his company later.

A short time after La was climbing the steps that reached the top of the wall. The sun was close to setting. She turned her attention to the party that was advancing on Opar. One of the most sharp-eyed sentries, named Horus, believed he counted fifty black warriors and one white man out in front. The party was still a distance away. Horus estimated they would be near the wall in one or two hours, just about the time the Flaming God would fall below the mountains beyond Opar.

La decided to return later when the men would be very close to the wall.

La looked down at the party that was now a few hundred yards away. She was watching the heavily armed black warriors and was impressed. Then the white man became visible as he moved to a position of leadership at the front of the party. La's eyes went wide and her heart started racing like never before. The man leading was as big as the biggest black warrior. He wore a leopard skin loincloth, a rope slung over one shoulder, a large knife hung at his side, and bow and quiver of arrows slung over his other shoulder. His long black hair was moving in perfect unison with his gait. La was astounded at the man's physique. He was the finest figure of a man she had ever seen. He was still too far away for La to make out his complete face and his age. She could not stop watching him as he walked with authority toward the wall. Mitry had warned La three times now to crouch down, lest the party see her. His face showed a flicker of a smile when he saw how La was looking at the leader.

La took the commander by the arm and very clearly told him, "If the Neteru guards capture the white leader, they are not to harm him. Make that very clear to all of them. If they kill him, they all will forfeit their lives."

Tarzan and the Waziri had had a difficult day, and even Tarzan was tired. They had climbed the escarpment and trekked across the barren rocky valley, stopping only for water. The climb up the sheer rock face had taken more time than Tarzan anticipated but, no one had been injured.

Tarzan knew the men were very tired so he instructed them to make a quick camp, and prepare to enter the city tomorrow.

From where La was watching, she could almost make out what the white warrior was saying. La had the feeling she could understand some of his words; then dismissed the thought. That could not be so.

His warriors reclined and ate the smoked meat they had been carrying for their evening meal. Tarzan ate a few nuts and a piece of fruit he had been given by one of the warriors. Darkness had completely fallen, but Tarzan was still restless to get into the seemingly deserted city. A few of his more curious warriors came with him.

The military commander, Mitry, had his men check to see there were no fires or cooking taking place. The street and the temple were deserted, and everyone who lived or worked in the temple had been advised to leave. Mitry signaled one of the women he had chosen to howl like a hound from hell. The commander looked down and saw it had the desired effect on a lot of the men. They had risen, looking about and seemingly had lost their nerve for being this close. The white man glanced up and dismissed the howl as though it were nothing. He began to walk along the wall, seeking entrance. When the commander saw the white man might attempt to enter the city he signaled to the Neteru to follow in the shadows and if the opportunity presented itself, capture the intruder.

The ape-man did find an entry point. It was less than two feet wide and, after a left turn, led to a set of stone steps. The steps ended, and a right turn was necessary to pass through the entrance and onto a wide flat paved walkway. On the other side of this was a large temple. Tarzan's excellent night vision was able to discern the detail in the stone, and the pair of strange creature statues in front of what looked like an entrance. As he walked slowly and looked around, he felt as though he were being watched. Once or twice he thought he saw movement out of the corner of his eye.

Tarzan entered the temple, and he could make out in the dim light, there were rooms off the main hall. But what caught the ape-man's eye were the large gold plaques mounted on the walls. They were covered with strange engravings; birds, waves, feet, heads, and bodies. Tarzan could not make them all out, but there was something in the back of his mind that told him he had seen these symbols before.

There was another of the mournful screams. Tarzan continued and entered through a doorway to a room off the main temple corridor. He looked around as best he could in the stygian darkness. He relied more on his nose than his eyes. He could smell men had been kept in this room. Strange men, who were not the people who lived here. Tarzan sensed there were other people in the room with him, and he was right.

As if on a signal, several very strong arms grabbed him and wrestled him to the floor. One of the arms held a cudgel and it came crashing down on Tarzan's head. Tarzan lost consciousness, and the next time he opened his eyes, he was lying in the room he had been exploring, bound with heavy ropes.

Jim Malachowski

CHAPTER THIRTY-EIGHT — THE SACRIFICE

L a awakened a bit later than usual. She called for her maid but there was no response. Nude, La arose from her sleeping silks and went to find someone to assist her. There seemed to be nobody in the servant quarters. La grabbed a sheet, stepped into the hallway and saw May-at walking away from her. La shouted her name, and she came running back. "Where is everyone, and where were you going?" she asked.

May-at turned and answered, "We are all going to the sacrifice to the Flaming God."

"Who is being sacrificed?" La asked with a curious look on her face.

"The man who invaded the city last night, don't you remember?" was May-at's answer.

"By whose order?" La asked, her face becoming crimson and her eyes wide with rage.

"Why, Cadj, the High Priest" was the response. La's temper exploded as she looked at May-at. The anger subsided when she remembered

Nedjam's advice, "Keep your anger to yourself, always control your thoughts no matter how upset you are."

"Get my ornaments and some clothing. Meet me at the place where I enter the sacrificial ceremonies and be quick about it!" Without looking back at May-at, La turned and ran down the hall.

La remembered the military commander, Mitry, had spoken to her late the previous night, saying the man had been captured after a massive fight and was held, heavily bound, in a retaining room for her interrogation. La asked if he had been injured and the man answered: "No he has not, but he killed two Neteru and broke the arms of three of my soldiers." La smiled and said, "I will reward them, don't worry." She had then gone to her sleeping couch, retiring for the night.

La glanced about as she reached her destination. Catching the attention of one of the Daughters of Soma she motioned for her to come immediately. The girl came to La with a tray of Flaming God nectar in two goblets. The server thought it was unusual for the High Priestess to be nude for the sacrifice, but said nothing. La grabbed the two goblets from the girl's tray and emptied one into the other. She instructed the girl, "Give this to Tha, the big Neteru, standing right over there." The server nodded to acknowledge she had understood, and she moved to where Tha was standing. La watched as the Neteru smiled when he grabbed the offered drink. La knew what effect the drink would have.

The server knew better than to question the High Priestess about serving a Neteru, and she did as she was instructed. She served the Neteru and watched as he drank the brew in one or two swallows. Tha was a hulk with so much hair he looked more like a gorilla than a man. He had the cruel eyes of someone who was a problem even sober.

May-at had found La, after running from La's dressing room with her ceremonial knife and accouterments. La quickly dressed, for the ceremony had already begun, and Cadj was ending the long incantation to the Flaming God. A minor priestess had entered the room with a cudgel and was going through the crowd, as part of the ceremony, acting as though she were driving them back from the victim on the altar.

La saw Mitry and motioned for him to come over. She instructed him, "Whoever is in the portal over there, dressed in the High Priestess' headdress," she pointed, "arrest her, and keep her under your guard until I come for you. Do not fail me." Mitry's face drained of color, as he hurried across the room and dragged Oah from her place in the ceremony entry.

Tarzan lay on the sacrificial altar. He had been forced to drink a goblet of drugged water by the Daughters of Soma. The drug was wearing off, and La could see he was straining at his bindings in an attempt to break them.

The jungle lord, on his back; his head turned to watch the beautiful young woman who had just entered the room by one of the arched doorways. The other priestess was being physically dragged from the room. This was his first look at La, High Priestess of Opar. The woman he saw entering was tall, probably five feet and ten inches with a slender, well-proportioned figure. Her hair fell below her shoulders. It was dark in color with a hint of red. She wore a short wrap skirt and no other clothing that was not ornamental jewelry. She was dressed in a more ornate way than the woman who had begun the ceremony. La had an aura about her, a commanding presence; her very entrance into the room caused the crowd to quiet down. The invited watched her every move and gesture as she gracefully made her way to the altar.

Tarzan saw her look at one of the incredibly ugly men, and then turn her gaze upon him. He looked into the face of a woman a few years younger than he. The face was classically beautiful with dark brown eyes and full red-painted lips. This woman looked at him as though she had seen him before; there was a sense of recognition on her face. While she was clearly in charge of the ceremony, there was also a faint sense of hesitation in her slow movements toward him. There was a look coming from her that told Tarzan she was having second thoughts about sacrificing him — at least he hoped so.

Tarzan returned to the more pressing issue he faced. He struggled mightily against his bonds. Lying on his back, he raised his feet as much as the restraints allowed. This position gave him as much leverage as possible to loosen his bound arms. He felt the ropes around his right arm begin to yield, then the restraint on his left arm also. Another minute of putting every ounce of his mighty strength into freeing himself might allow him to extricate himself. He listened to the words coming from the newly arrived priestess and hoped it would be a long prayer. He would need more time to get free.

The priestess moved slowly and gracefully toward him until she was a few feet from the sacrificial altar. She looked into his eyes, and Tarzan could swear he saw the ghost of a smile on her lips.

What happened next would haunt Tarzan for sixty years. The round sacrificial room became absolutely silent. All movement by the people ceased. The altar room, which had been lit by a weak ray of sunlight coming through the opening in the roof suddenly became bright, almost painfully so. Tarzan had lost all feeling of urgency with his bonds, as he felt a sense of calm wash over him. He slowly turned his head and watched as the priestess raised herself on her tip-toes, stretching her body to it's fullest height. Her motion seemed odd, as though he was viewing a motion picture slowly – one frame at a time.

Tarzan watched her hair as it fell free when she tilted her head back as far as it would go. Facing the opening in the temple roof, she lifted her arms slowly, holding the long wicked looking knife in her left hand.

He could see her eye closest to him opening wide, and in a whisper, he heard her utter four words.

Tarzan was puzzled by the meaning of what she had just said. He thought the words were part of the ritual. They were not.

As this was happening, Tarzan glanced away from the woman. His gaze moved to the round opening, in the temple ceiling, far above his head. It appeared as though the entire roof was fading away and was replaced by a surface of shimmering liquid. It was as if he were looking up from the bottom of a well.

This hallucination lasted for a few seconds and was gone. Tarzan attributed what had just happened to the drink that had been forced upon him.

He shook it off and returned to the task at hand — his restraints.

La's anger had left her mind as she entered the room. She had watched as Oah had been physically removed from the sacrifice a few minutes ago. She glanced at the attendees and noted to her elation, that no one seemed to care Oah had been replaced as chief celebrant. The potion of Soma had done its job. As she watched that happen, her confidence returned. La watched as one of the minor priestesses was finishing the chant, (her part of the ceremony).

La looked at the drunken Neteru and said a prayer to the Flaming God that the nectar would act soon. As if on cue, the hulk of a man was bumped heavily by another Neteru. He whirled around with his cudgel raised and swinging. Unfortunately, his first victim was the luckless Daughter of Soma who had served him. She fell, her skull crushed by a heavy blow. The bloodlust in the Neteru erupted, and he began whirling and hitting anyone within striking distance. He killed at least two and badly injured several other ceremony attendees. Instantly the room turned into chaos, with many fleeing to get away from the crazed Neteru.

La, quietly and quickly, moved to Tarzan still on the altar. Leaning close, so no one else heard, she spoke to him in a low voice, "Be still I will free you." Tarzan looked at her, not understanding her words. He tried speaking to her in English and French with no response. In desperation, he spoke in Waziri, "Free me, and I will save you."

La's eyes went wide with the understanding of his words, and she worked faster cutting the ropes until they finished parting. She could not help but notice the man had been very close to freeing himself. She was impressed with his strength. No one before had ever been able to escape from the ropes on the altar. Tarzan quickly rubbed his wrists trying to get feeling back in his hands. He slid from the altar in time to see the last guests running for their lives out of the sacrificial chamber.

Tha saw the ape-man in front of La in a challenging stance. Tarzan glanced over his shoulder and said to La, in Waziri, "Give me your knife, and move out of the way." La did as requested, and she was horrified as Tarzan began to advance upon the Neteru.

The crazed man emitted a piercing scream, lifted the cudgel high over his head and charged at Tarzan. Tarzan sidestepped the Neteru, and as the man passed him, he thrust the sacrificial knife into Tha's stomach and ripped. Tha barely seemed to notice. Tarzan began circling the drunken Neteru, seeing an opening and quick as a cat, leaped upon the Neteru, circled his left arm around his neck. He pulled the man's head back. In an instant, Tarzan slit the Neteru's throat from one side to the other. Tarzan knew the wound would be fatal, and he dropped off the man, out of harm's way, and began to lead the staggering Neteru away from La. Tha was gushing blood in great amounts, from his throat and stomach wounds, with each step he took. Tarzan watched his eyes, and he began to see the life fading out of them. After a few more haltingly clumsy steps, Tha fell face first onto the stone floor – dead.

Tarzan went back to La, grabbed her arm and said, "We need to go somewhere private before all your people come back looking for me." La turned motioning toward a door, and they went down two levels of roughly hewn stone steps, into the bowels of the temple.

CHAPTER THIRTY-NINE — TWO CONVERSATIONS

L a and Tarzan descended the two staircases noiselessly and without speaking. It was important for them to be as far from the sacrificial room in the temple above, and as quickly as possible.

After a short walk, in total darkness, La opened a heavy wooden door and entered. Tarzan stopped inside the door and heard La move into the room. There were scraping sounds and fire was applied to a candle on a small stand. She moved to the door, closed and locked it. There was a low ceiling, and the size of the space was approximately ten by fifteen feet. There were two chairs and wooden containers that were sealed and stacked against the far walls. The room smelled like it had not been opened for many years.

The lord of the jungle broke the silence, "What is this place?"

La answered, "This is the private storage of the High Priestesses of Opar. I know of ten queens who have used this room. No one is allowed in here. You are probably the first man to enter since its construction."

Tarzan had meant that more about the city than the room and began again, "Tell me of the city."

La answered, "I am La, the High Priestess of the city of Opar. We are a peaceful people who only want to be left alone."

Tarzan continued by introducing himself, "I am Tarzan. I have traveled many days walks to visit this city." He continued with a smile on his face, "Given my welcome in the ceremony today, you do not seem like peaceful people."

"You came here like a thief in the night, and I was not responsible for the ceremony that almost took your life. I had given strict orders you were to be captured and interviewed by me. Those orders were not carried out."

"You obviously have someone here who does not think you are in charge."

La's face colored and she hissed, "Cadj. He and his consort will pay for this insult." La's face was so contorted by anger that Tarzan was quiet for a few moments until her rage settled.

As La regained her composure, Tarzan asked, "Tell me how you know the language that you and I are speaking now."

La answered with a smile, "I am so glad we can understand each other. My grandmother and her handmaiden learned the language, and it is now spoken by the High Priestess and a few of her confidants. It is used to keep information from prying ears." She continued, "How do you know this way of speaking?"

"It is the language of the black warriors who accompanied me to Opar. One of their ancestors lived here for a few years many years ago."

La's eyes and face dropped, and Tarzan could barely hear her response, "My grandmother, my mother, and I all were served by the same Chief Handmaiden. Her name was Nedjam, and she died a few months ago. She was the mate of that black warrior who lived here."

"Some of the warriors who accompanied me here are descendants of that man. He was a great leader of his people. I met him a few weeks before he died, and he told me of your city and the love he still had for Nedjam."

The turn in the conversation relaxed La, so she settled back in the chair and became less tense and defensive. La studied the man seated across from her. Her heart began to beat so fast she was afraid Tarzan would be able to hear it. La had always dreamed of men and her standards for what she wanted. The men of Opar had fallen so short of her expectations that she would not even consider a relationship with any of them. The man across from her was so close to her dream-man that she was frightened of the feeling rising within her.

Tarzan began the conversation again, "La, tell me the story of your people. When I entered the temple last night, I saw gold tablets on the walls and they contained symbols that mean information. Do you know what they say?"

"During the last years of my mother Ayesha's reign, I was part of all the inner secrets of Opar. There were a few times my mother brought up the subject to my tutors about what they called 'history.' I remember hearing that our ancestors, many generations ago, came here from a mighty river that no longer exists. The old men believed we were sent here to find gold, which we did. We have so much of the metal stored on this level that there is no space left. We still go through the motions of looking for gold, but …" La's voice trailed off. She continued, "Who knows if anything those men said was the truth, or just imagined events?"

La began again, "As you know, we worship the Flaming God. Our religious beliefs dictate that we offer him gifts of sacrifice — human sacrifice. It is also a way of preventing strangers who come close to Opar from finding us and telling our location to enemies. We know the gold has value to many people, and if it were known we had much, we could be inviting invasion."

"There are legends that the ancients made their thoughts known through the symbols, like the ones on the gold plaques. But the ability to do that has been lost for a very long time," La continued.

"Other than some children the black warrior fathered, there had been no new people in Opar as far back as anyone can remember. We all keep mating with people who are closely related to us. My mother thought this was a bad thing. She said that is why so many children born who seem to have no intelligence. One day, Tarzan, I am afraid there will be no one left here in Opar." Again, La seemed to be depressed by what she had told Tarzan.

She quickly changed the subject, "Tarzan, I know you must be hungry. Let me go back to my quarters to get us some food and drink. I would like to continue talking with you; plus we need to decide what your future will be in Opar."

La rose, went to the door, and told Tarzan to lock it after she left. Tarzan called after her, "Find my hunting knife; it was my father's." Tarzan thought to himself, "What did she mean, future in Opar? I have no future in Opar."

La swiftly climbed the stairs that led to the main floor of the temple. Upon entering she hurried to her quarters and summoned May-at. "May-at send a message to commander Mitry and tell him I need to see him immediately." May-at nodded and started to leave. "Stop, May-at. I need you to go to the kitchen and have them prepare a basket of food and drink. I need this as soon as possible. Have them bring it to me here. Then go and find Mitry."

A short time later, Mitry appeared at her reception area. La finished dressing, took him to a table and put her head close to his and asked, "Where is Oah?"

"She is in custody, as you requested. That new priest Cadj has been trying to find her, and asked me to look for her."

"If you need to, take her outside the walls of the city. I want you to question her about who told her to dress as the High Priestess for the ceremony. I suspect treason and I do not want Cadj and Oah to speak with one another. Someone disregarded my command and ordered the stranger to be sacrificed. I want to know who gave that order. Once again Mitry, I am relying on you."

Mitry's answer was, "And you will have my loyalty always, Majesty."

La picked up the basket of food and drink and began to walk to the staircase. Waiting for her was May-at with a very worried look on her face.

"Mistress, is something wrong? The other handmaidens have said that Oah is missing and they fear the worst. The invader has disappeared, and everyone is terrified for their lives." Looking at the basket, May-at asked, "Is there anything you need from me."

"No" was the answer. "May-at, I need you not to say you saw me. I have everything under control. But I need your trust."

"As always, Mistress," said May-at bowing, but the worried look on her face was still present.

The ape-man had not locked the door as La had requested. He knew he could handle anyone who opened the door. La slowly descended the stairs, with her mind whirling. She was feeling the pressure of having to deal with Cadj and Oah. Somehow she needed to tell Tarzan of her feeling for him and convince him to remain in Opar.

Tarzan could see the strain on La's face when she entered the room. She and Tarzan seated themselves, and La put the basket of food between them. She bade Tarzan to help himself.

The silence was becoming deafening to La. She blurted out a question and was sorry almost as quickly as it was out of her mouth. "Tarzan, do you have a woman?"

"Yes, there is someone," was his answer. La felt the crush of that one word. She had prayed to the Flaming God that Tarzan would find her as attractive as she found him.

Tarzan thought back to the Countess de Coude, and her fascination with him and the trouble it had caused. Tarzan's mind was working rapidly, trying to think of a way to placate La. He did not want to remain a prisoner in this city as Waziri had been. Beyond the Countess, Tarzan did not have much experience with women. D'Arnot had introduced him to many society females, and many beautiful young ladies who were singers or actresses. But beyond casual relations, Tarzan's real feelings were for Jane Porter.

La spoke again, "Tarzan, I need a man like you who will help me rule Opar. You will want for nothing. I will give you all the riches of Opar if you return my affection."

"La," Tarzan began, "I have all my life lived free in the forest. My friends are the animals that are part of the jungle. I cannot give all that up. I would not be happy, even with a woman as beautiful as you. All the riches of the city of Opar are not enough to make me stay. Look at Waziri, as much as he loved your handmaiden, Nedjam, he longed for freedom and wanted to be able to visit his family so far away. Under the laws of Opar, he was not even allowed to go outside the gates without the fear of forfeiting his life."

Tarzan concluded, "La, I would rather die than be confined in Opar. No one knows the future, and perhaps one-day things between us could be different. Who can say?"

"So La, it is up to you. You can call your soldiers and have me returned to the sacrificial altar and murdered if that is what you want. I notice you did not bring my father's knife as I asked you. That must mean you do not trust me and do not want me armed."

"That is not true, Tarzan," returned La, "I do trust you. I have many things on my mind, and I just forgot. I will have my handmaiden find the knife and return it to you."

"Will you at least stay for a few days, as my friend? I may have use of your great strength and wisdom. There is a big storm brewing in Opar"

Tarzan smiled and said, "Yes, I will stay for a few days, and provide you whatever advice or support you need."

La rose and walked to the door and said, "I will have more food brought to you and move you to a room that is more comfortable than this storage area."

La went back up the stairs to her room and gave May-at orders she was not to be disturbed. La was very upset and angry that she had not gotten her way. But she was aware that Tarzan was right about not being happy to be confined – sometimes she felt the same way. After many hours of alternating tears and sleep, La's mind began to address the problem of Cadj.

The next morning La again swore May-at to secrecy and sent her to find Tarzan's knife. May-at was to take it and food and drink to Tarzan. This took a bit of convincing, but May-at obeyed reluctantly.

La sent a messenger to have members of council meet in her public room as soon as possible. An hour later three of the members reluctantly appeared. La explained what had happened with Cadj and the botched sacrifice and asked for their advice. Better to have them on her side, than be kept in the dark.

La vented all her rage and frustration at the meeting. Most of the attendees had never seen this side of her. Finally, after some discussion, one of the members told La, "Your mother designated you High Priestess. It is clear Cadj and Oah have disrespected you, and the position you hold. The council will agree and enforce any decision you make about their fate." The meeting adjourned quickly, and La sent for Mitry.

Mitry arrived shortly and was seated in La's private sitting room. "Well Mitry," asked La, "what have you learned from Oah?"

Mitry began, "She is a very strong woman; I would be careful of her. She has ambitions well beyond her means. She blames Cadj for talking her into disobeying your orders. I do not believe she is telling the whole truth; I think she helped plan this treason. I would advise killing them both."

La dismissed his advice, fearing she would regret it in the future. She let her love for Nedjam keep her from killing Oah. It followed in her mind, that if she spared Oah, she should spare Cadj also.

She ordered Mitry to arrest Cadj and bring both him and Oah into the main throne room. La also ordered the senior priest, her chief Neteru guard, and two of Mitry's chief lieutenants be brought there as well.

La had May-at watch the attendees assemble, and had them seated. Cadj and Oah stood bound and stripped naked for the meeting with La. She let them stand for most of an hour to emphasize their unimportance to her. She slowly made her way to the throne, after telling May-at not to accompany her.

La sat on the throne with her head down looking at her feet for several minutes, as if deep in thought. Quickly she raised her head and glared at Cadj then at Oah. La's face was scarlet with rage. She put her hands on her knees, leaned forward, and glared even more hatefully at the pair before her.

"Cadj, you son of a hyena, and you Oah, you traitorous bitch, you do not deserve to live. I should have you both killed for disobeying my direct orders. I will not suffer traitors. My advisors on the council warned me to have you both killed as an example, and I may still do that. However, I am sentencing you to work in the mines for one year. There you will be the slaves of the slaves. You will do the dirtiest and heaviest work until your bodies are broken, and you are cured of your treachery."

Cadj opened his mouth to say something. La screamed at him, "Shut up you arrogant fool; you have nothing to say that I want to hear. If you have any brains in your head, you will not speak for the next year. At the end of the year, I will then determine if you are to live or die."

"Get these traitors out of my sight. If they cause any problems in their mine work, kill them immediately."

La left the throne without a further glance at either Cadj or Oah. She went to her apartment to decide what was important—how to deal with Tarzan.

CHAPTER FORTY — THE JOURNEY HOME

Tarzan spent the next three weeks in Opar. He had been concerned about his Waziri companions, so La sent two of the hunters out to search for them. The hunters found them, on their way back to Opar, much ashamed for deserting Tarzan. They delivered Tarzan's message that he would meet up with his friends before the next new moon and they should camp about a mile away from the walls of Opar.

The jungle lord thought that La's attitude toward him had mellowed. He hoped she had given up the idea of his staying in Opar (and becoming her mate). Once the problem with Cadj and Oah had been resolved, La seemed more relaxed and less apt to fly into a fit of rage.

Tarzan had met May-at and liked her very much. She was a very level-headed woman and was a good voice of reason for La. The city had calmed down after Tarzan's botched sacrifice. The people had been told by the rumor mill that somehow the intruder had escaped under cover of darkness. Little did they know that Tarzan was staying in a room one floor down in the Temple of the Flaming God.

La had emptied her private area of anyone who might see Tarzan and brought him into her sitting room, where they could have long talks. La was extremely curious about Tarzan. She asked, "Would you tell me about your life?" Tarzan told La of his parents, what little he knew, about his adopted mother Kala and the great apes he lived with as a child and adult. La had never seen an ape, and her eyes were wide when he described them to her.

Tarzan did not speak of anything that was beyond her comprehension. La had almost no understanding of where she lived on the earth. She did not know there were nations of men everywhere; there was different weather, various ways to travel, other religions, and not all men were her enemies.

Tarzan noticed something about her words in Waziri. Sometimes she interchanged words from her native language into the Waziri language. Her pronunciation and meaning of words were different from the Waziri people. Tarzan thought this unusual that in fifty or so years the Waziri language had changed within Opar from a few women's use.

La hinted that she would like to visit other parts of the jungle, just to see who and what was there. From this, he thought La was not as attached to Opar as had been her female predecessors. Tarzan also thought that La's emotional feelings toward him had just been shoved down. He felt she was still romantically attracted to him, and he thought it would be best to leave Opar soon.

He agreed with La that in exchange for some gold he would be available should she ever need him. La should send a message via one of the monkeys. The message would take about one moon to reach him.

Tarzan had La bring in two of the younger hunters and May-at for directions on how to find the Waziri kraal to the west. He believed that if three people knew the way, someone would be able to find the Waziri village. May-at and the hunters were bright and seemed to understand Tarzan's directions. One of them asked if he could accompany Tarzan and the Waziri back to their village. Tarzan replied, "Ask your High Priestess, but remember it is a long and difficult journey."

A few days later Tarzan bade farewell to La and began the long trek west to rejoin his beloved Waziri. La had asked him to leave by the main city entrance but well after dark, so he would not draw any attention. La had told him the gold he wanted had been taken to the Waziri encampment.

La tried very hard not to shed tears as she said goodbye. Neither La nor Tarzan had any idea if they would ever meet again. La wanted so much to throw her arms around him, and kiss Tarzan's lips, but she settled for a quick peck on his cheek.

In a wavering voice, she whispered, "Come back to me."

Father Martin threw his English Oval cigarette into the fire, promising himself it would be the final one of the evening. There probably would be several more. This was a time when Martin was thinking about his life in Paris, and how he came to be living in French Equatorial Africa. Martin was very homesick; he missed his parents, especially his mother. Once the task of getting his meager belongings was settled, the remorse and memories of the recent past began to return to his consciousness.

Martin's problems had begun about a year ago at his parish in the countryside of France. It started as simply counseling a young woman who had lost her husband in a work-related accident. Martin had let this get out of hand until it became a physical relationship with the woman.

Some of her neighbors had noticed his frequent visits, complaining to the pastor of his church. He had asked Martin quite frankly what his relationship was with the woman. Martin had admitted it had been a mistake on his part. He was sorry, and he would break off the relationship immediately. The pastor was not impressed with either Marton's candor or his promises, and he said he would get back to him with a decision on what his punishment would be for the affair with the young woman.

Martin had thought he would be reassigned to another parish, probably far away on the other side of France. However, this was not to be the case. His pastor called him into his office and told Martin he was being sent to a parish in central Africa. The superiors felt it would be best if Martin were moved out of France, into an area where he could make a difference in the lives of the people he served. He was young enough to be able to withstand the rigors of an African parish. The Church would have him out of sight, and hopefully, the embarrassment he had caused would fade away.

Martin had been put aboard a ship with basically his belongings and enough money to get to his end destination. He had not been given any instructions, other than he would be in charge of a small rural church, hospital and school. Martin was replacing a priest who had died there several months ago. His only staff would be two nuns who served as teachers and nurses to the native people.

Martin's two-week tramp steamer trip began in Brest, France, in steerage accommodations. The ship landed in Libreville in what is now Angola on the west coast of Africa. The long train trip inland was very difficult, even for a young man like Martin. It was rainy, humid and just generally unpleasant. Martin's new posting station was near the town of Improndo, fifty miles north and west of the Ubangi River.

He was met at the train station by his two charges. The nuns led him along a path through the jungle leading to where their church, school and hospital were located. Martin and the nuns would be the staff who served the native people who lived in the district. The M'beti tribe were an agricultural, docile and somewhat friendly tribe.

The goals of the church at this time were to convert the natives from whatever pagan beliefs they held, give them medical treatment which they did not have at all except for witch-doctors, and teach them the bare rudiments of sanitation. The children would be the future of Africa, and the Catholic Church would do everything in its power to see that they were educated at least to the level of being able to read and write.

The previous priest had, with difficulty, convinced the wary chief that it was important that all of the children be allowed to attend school. At first, he only allowed girls to take classes, but after much discussion, Father Dupree had been able to convince the chief to allow the boys to attend school also. Since the children respected their teachers, it was easy for the nuns to maintain discipline, allowing them to learn. They were taught religious studies, reading, writing and simple mathematics. They were allowed to be in school for four hours a day, then they had chores to do for their parents.

Both of the nuns were middle-aged women and had been living in this part of Africa for over ten years. They resented having a priest in charge who was so much younger. Also, they missed their beloved priest, Father Dupree, who had died from a snake bite six months ago. He had been a kind man loved by children and their parents.

Neither Martin or the nuns had any conversation during the one-hour walk to his final destination. Everyone seemed to be absorbed in the changes that were occurring around them, and none seemed very comfortable with anyone else.

It was up to Martin to break the ice and take charge of this bastion of the church and to investigate how things worked.

He told the older nun, Sister Mary Veronica, he would like to speak with her and Sister Mary Clare the next day. He wanted details of the operation of the church, school and hospital. Sister Mary Veronica looked at him with disdain and did not answer directly, but merely nodded her head once, turned on her heel and walked back to her quarters.

After an uneasy three-week period, the church, the school and a makeshift hospital seemed to be functioning in a somewhat normal manner. Martin concentrated on saying daily Mass early in the morning. The nuns would attend the dawn service, and surprisingly, a few of the M'beti people would also attend and seemed comfortable. Martin made the correct assumption that Father Dupree had made several converts among the people.

Finally, Martin began to make appearances at the daily school sessions and was introduced by Sister Mary Veronica. Classes were normally taught in French, and it was surprising to see the children had picked up the language quickly. They were bright and enthused with the learning process.

It was Martin's three-month anniversary in French Equatorial Africa.

He looked up, and in the fading light of evening, he watched a man walking toward the small bungalow that was his residence. Since the sun was behind the man, Martin was not able to see who his visitor was until he stopped to face him.

"Good Evening Father Ober. Paul D'Arnot told me you had relocated here a few months ago and I wanted to look in on you." Until Martin heard Tarzan's voice, he did not immediately recognize him to be D'Arnot's companion, whom he had met in Paris.

"Hello, John. You are the last person I expected to walk into my parish, for what it is," Martin said with a laugh. "Please have a seat and tell me how you located me. I feel as if I had fallen off the face of the earth, and no one would be able to find me,"

Lord Greystoke told Martin that he had received a letter from D'Arnot, asking him to stop by and be sure Martin was all right.

"And," Lord Greystoke said, "I had some business in this area, so I decided on the way home I would stop to visit you. How are you getting on here? I know this is not the countryside of France, but hopefully, you are getting settled in, and you will be recalled to France shortly."

Martin scoffed, "I will be stationed here for the rest of my life, I am afraid. You know what is said, 'out of sight, out of mind.' Anyway, I am doing okay.   It is not where I want to be, but I will make the best of it. May I offer you some supper or a cup of coffee?" Tarzan replied that he needed to keep traveling, as his family would be worried about him.

"If you ever need anything, I will give you directions to my farm. You can send one of the M'beti men with a message. It is a many week journey if the messenger is fast."

"Before I leave Martin, it was very good to see you again, and I wish you the best of luck here. Oh, by the way, there is a gift for you on the right side of the trail, about a hundred yards from where I entered. Use it to provide for the M'beti people, you and your assistants. You can consider this as a gift with no strings, but I may require some help from you in the future."

Lord Greystoke stayed for a few more minutes, speaking about D'Arnot and the few other things they had in common.

After Lord Greystoke left Martin, his curiosity got the better of him, and he asked one of the M'beti to accompany him down the path with a torch. There laying on the ground where Tarzan had placed them were two gold ingots about seventy-five pounds each. Martin examined them and could not understand the symbols that were stamped upon them. Later that night, Martin began to wonder further as to what Lord Greystoke had meant about 'a favor.'

CHAPTER FORTY-ONE — RETURN TO OPAR

Lieutenant Albert Werper had a checkered past from the Belgian Army. He had been punished in Brussels and sent to the Belgian Congo and a remote jungle outpost. In a fit of anger and depression, he had murdered his superior officer and fled the military station.

Werper's flight eventually brought him into contact with Achmet Zek, a notorious brigand. Zek befriended him and convinced him to assist in a plot to seek revenge against Tarzan for his interference in his 'trading operations.' The Arab had a plan to kidnap Tarzan's wife, Jane, and sell her to the highest bidder in the middle east. Or perhaps he could blackmail Tarzan into allowing him to act with impunity, in return for his beloved wife.

Werper adopted the alias of Jules Frecoult. After disguising himself as a wealthy European on a hunting trip, he came to Tarzan's estate asking for assistance with directions. He led a small safari of men who were in actuality several of Achmet Zek's gang of cutthroats. The plan was to wait for an opportune time and kidnap Jane.

One evening Werper overheard Tarzan speak of a financial disaster that had befallen them. He further heard Tarzan's plans to visit a place called Opar and take some gold. Werper saw this as a perfect opportunity to change his plans. Though he was a murderous villain, he had reservations about selling a white woman to an Arab Sultan. He thought he might be able to follow Tarzan, steal some gold, flee from Zek, whom he did not trust, and escape to Europe to live like a king.

A few days later, with travel instructions in hand from Tarzan, he left the estate and camped waiting to be led to Opar. Within a few days, he spied Tarzan and a band of men traveling at a fast pace. Werper followed, with twelve men. He had dispatched a messenger, and the rest of the safari, back to Zek telling him of the change in plans.

The party led by Werper stayed well back from Tarzan and his men, so Tarzan was unaware he was being followed.

The jungle lord sat high in the mountains that surrounded the ancient city of Opar. The early evening air was very chilly at this altitude and felt good to the ape-man; quite a refreshing treat from the steaming heat of the jungle.

It was the second night Tarzan had climbed the mountain. He wanted to be sure of his welcome before he exposed himself by coming into the city. As the light faded, he looked out and took in the scope of Opar. Whoever had designed the city had done everything in their power to make it self-sufficient.

Almost straight in front of him was the Temple of the Flaming God and the street that paralleled the high wall. The road went north to the small private oasis and pool that was exclusively used by the High Priestess. That area also contained a small chapel to the Flaming God.

Directly below him were the houses of the upper-class residents, and to the west was the large dormitory surrounded by some huts used by the common workers who lived as families. Further north was the livestock area, which furnished the meat used by the working class. The Neteru lived in these less desirably located huts because they did not mind the smell that came from the animals who were enclosed there.

The largest area, the central-most portion of land, was used for agriculture. It contained at least ten different kinds of fruits and vegetables. Another area for growing grain for flour and beer was located outside the enclosure. A large amount of land was required for these crops. The Neteru, the upper class, and the working class all shared the responsibility of farming. The animal husbandry was the responsibility of the Neteru and the working class.

As the sunlight faded to an afterglow, Tarzan saw that most of the foot traffic inside the wall was ending. Everyone was moving toward their shelters and their evening meals. Tarzan could smell their cooking fires. In the twilight, the only human movement was the slow pacing of the sentries. They had started wood fires in pots for illumination around the temple and one or two along the main avenue behind the wall. There was one sentry who slowly walked along the wall-side perimeter of the temple. Tarzan was looking for some human activity besides the guard on the temple roof.

The journey back to Opar had been easier than the first time. Tarzan had been able to make better time, with only Busuli as his companion. Since he did not know what kind of reception he was going to meet up with, he suggested to Busuli that he stay a few miles away, and to await his exit from Opar. Busuli was instructed, he was only to wait for two weeks then he was to return home.

As Tarzan sat for the second night in a row, he thought about the reason for his return trip to Opar. Several months ago he was going through the monthly batch of mail that had come from England and was surprised to have a thick letter from the manager of his estate. Tarzan's eyes quickly scanned the pleasantries of the first paragraph. The second paragraph had caused his stomach to knot and the scar on his forehead to redden with anger. The letter stated that there had been legal action taken against the financial advisor whom Tarzan had employed on his last trip to Great Britain. The man had been found guilty of embezzling the investments of several clients, and Tarzan had been one of them.[4]

A bit further down, the letter stated the chances of fund recovery were nearly impossible, as the man had fled the country supposedly for the continent. There had been several restless days before Tarzan broke the bad news to Jane. Tarzan said he was going back to Opar and bring more of the gold from the underground storage to cover the loss.

Jane was quite livid, "Oh John, please don't go back there. You barely got out with your life, and I don't want you to risk another contact with those crazy sun worshippers."

"Don't worry, Jane. I left on good terms with their leader at the end of the last trip. All I have to do is convince them that my promise of protection is worth some more of their precious gold. They have no idea of its value. There are several other charitable endeavors I want to get into, so it will help finance those as well as replenish our losses."

"Jane, if you will just take care of Monsieur Frecoult, I am sure everything will be fine. I will get ready and depart in a few days. I would

---

[4] The location of Lord Greystoke's farm has recently come to light. It is located about one hundred miles north and east of beautiful Lake Victoria in British East Africa. The Greystoke estate is quite huge, and Lord Greystoke is one of the largest landowners in British East Africa. British East Africa will later be referred to as Kenya.

The nearest town to the farm is Eldoret, which is a principal city in western Kenya. The town lies south of the Cherangani Hills. At the time Lord Greystoke established the farm, there were only about a hundred families scattered through the area. The town grew to a quarter of a million people by 2009. The town name is based on a Masai word which means "stony river" — a reference to the Sosiani River.

When the Waziri migrated south, they settled in this area, prior to Lord Greystoke's land ownership. The Waziri Nation has grown greatly over the years, and loosely circles Tarzan's estate, providing a buffer of security.

like to be back before the rains begin." The truth was that Tarzan had never quite trusted Frecoult, and had asked several of his Waziri to stay close to his wife.

The journey back to Opar had been like a vacation to Tarzan. He had not been deep into the jungle in a while, and this was where he thought he belonged.

After arriving, the jungle lord had set out to survey the lands around Opar, looking for anything that might be threatening to the city. All seemed normal and peaceful within a hundred mile circle. There were no apparent threats. The only tribe of native people he observed was located more than fifty miles to the north. Tarzan had spent several hours watching the village which consisted of about two hundred inhabitants. They appeared to be nothing more dangerous than farmers, who like the Oparians, just wanted to be left alone.

Tarzan was having a twinge of conscience about taking more gold from Opar. Something in his mind told him it was wrong to take the gold and give nothing in return. He could not use La's obvious affection for him to take advantage of her. He hoped he could find some way to give Opar something back, to help ease his guilt. The more Tarzan thought about La's situation, the more tenuous it seemed to him. Perhaps he was only feeling overly protective of someone for whom he felt some responsibility.

Tarzan was sure that something in coming years would require the money that the gold of Opar represented.

Several hours after sunset, the ape-man was about to depart the uncomfortable perch on the side of the steep mountain and retire for the night, when he saw a person climbing the steps to reach the top of the temple. In the very dim light, Tarzan was sure he recognized the figure as La. He began his descent down the mountain, and he then found enough hand-holds in the temple wall to scale to the roof. It was easy for Tarzan, as he had climbed many surfaces with a lesser amount of room for his hands. When he reached the top, he cautiously looked around to see, up close, who was there. He was delighted to see La alone, with her back turned toward him. He easily gained a foothold and hoisted himself onto the roof.

With the stealth of a cat, Tarzan walked up behind La, spoke in a low-voice, "What is the matter, can't sleep tonight?"

La could not believe her ears. She whirled around and came face to face with Tarzan. Tears of joy filled her eyes, and she threw her arms around him and whispered in his ear, "Thanks to the Flaming God you have come!"

La knew at this hour that no one would be awake in her part of the temple. She led Tarzan down the darkened steps to the main level and her suite of rooms. La bade him sit in one of the chairs across a small table from her, and she went to awaken May-at. Tarzan heard La address the handmaiden in Waziri.

May-at, her eyes still filled with sleep, saw a large man sitting in La's reception area. She smiled when she recognized the great shock of black hair, that turned and revealed a face she knew from the past. Tarzan greeted May-at with a large smile and told her, "How nice to see you May-at, and I am glad that you can now understand the Waziri language."

May-at grinning said, "I have not seen my mistress so happy in a long time. I, too, am glad that you are visiting us. I have been ordered to get you some food and drink. I will return shortly with refreshments."

Tarzan and La sat and talked for most of the night. Toward dawn, La summoned May-at and told her to prepare a room for Tarzan. "Already done, Mistress," was May-at's answer.

The next morning over breakfast La expressed her feelings about Cadj and Oah. She said both had served their year in the mines and had expressed their regret for what they had done. Now after a few months back, there were hints that perhaps they were not as repentant as they initially appeared.

Tarzan's answer was clear and definitive, "If you think they are trying to take over, do not hesitate to kill them, or at the very least exile them." Tarzan added with a grim smile, "I can follow and see that some animal does a job that you do not want to undertake."

La wrinkled her forehead and replied, "I know what you are saying, but I just cannot do that to Nedjam's granddaughter. I owe Nedjam so much."

After this the discussion ended on a very unresolved note. La asked Tarzan, "Can you please take me out into the jungle. There is no one I will feel safer with than you. I want to see the animals, especially the elephants."

Oah had been standing and listening to Tarzan and La's conversation. When she heard about the two of them leaving Opar, she turned and ran into the male priest area of the temple.

Oah found Cadj and told him the good news, "Let us put our plan into effect. If Tarzan and La separate, we will capture and sacrifice Tarzan and then La. He will be the hardest, so we will start with him. Go and find Maj, the priest."

Maj appeared, and Cadj said it was time to put their plan into action. He was to take four Neteru guards—the biggest ones—three priests and the sacrificial knife. Maj would be in charge of this sacrifice. They were to follow at a discrete distance from Tarzan and La.

Tarzan and La began their walk to the south, where he knew from experience grassland began, containing enough water and trees to attract and feed Tantor, the elephant. For an hour or two they went quietly, with La enjoying the sunshine. It reminded her of when she and her father, Ware, had left Opar and the one time they had seen the elephant. Her memories of Ware were bittersweet; she still missed him terribly.

"Tarzan do you think we will see elephants hiding in the trees ahead? You know that since I was a child, I took the elephant as my totem," said La.

The ape-man smiled and responded, "I will take to the trees, where I can scout ahead more quickly." After a short run, Tarzan was scampering up a large tree and into the middle terraces, where he would begin his search.

Tarzan was quickly a half mile ahead, and he had begun to circle looking for elephants. He should have glanced over his shoulder, for there was a large bull standing under a solitary tree, close to where Tarzan and La had just passed. The breeze had brought their scent to Tantor and had prevented Tarzan from smelling the great beast.

Tantor was under the influence of musth, a condition that male elephants endure periodically. Testosterone levels in an elephant in musth are as much as sixty times that of a non-suffering elephant, and with it comes extreme aggression. This creature was at his peak of suffering. La heard the elephant's stomach growl and heard the characteristic sigh that an elephant emits. She turned and saw, about thirty yards away, the great beast just standing looking at her. La raised her arms and began slowly walking toward him. The elephant was her totem, and she believed that the creature would not harm her. Tantor raised his trunk and let out a piercing trumpet of anger and rage – directed at La.

Tarzan was circling back toward where he left La when he saw the elephant move from cover beneath the tree. He knew there was a problem when the animal dragged the end of his trunk in the dust before him and then began to raise it to warn he was attacking. Tarzan saw this while he was racing through the trees in an attempt to get La to safety. He was horrified when he saw La slowly walking toward the charging elephant.

Tarzan was approaching the impending tragedy from a forty-five-degree angle and he was twenty yards away. The saving fact was that Tantor had just begun his charge and was not up to his full speed. Tarzan hit the ground running and crossed in front of the madly trumpeting elephant and scooped La into his arms.

An elephant, despite being a massive beast, can turn very quickly to chase a target. This elephant was no exception. He saw the man flash across his vision and grab the woman he was about to trample. He voiced an even louder and more frustrated trumpet. Tarzan glanced down at La, and he saw she was in a swoon, with her eyes wide open and obviously not seeing.

Tarzan returned his concentration to reaching the nearest stand of trees. This would interrupt the elephant's mad charge. He tried changing direction to disrupt the elephant, to no avail. Tantor was so focused on the running man that he saw nothing else. Tarzan thought he might be able to reach the trees before he felt the prehensile trunk grab him by the head or neck.

Tarzan's speed on foot had allowed him to reach a small forest. As soon as he cleared the first tree, he turned sharply to his left and went between two larger trees. Tarzan heard from behind him the elephant crash head first into a large limb then the trunk of a tree. Tantor felt the world go dark around him for a few seconds and dropped to his knees. When his senses returned, the elephant began to search for his quarry. He did not see them, and the breeze was not bringing him any scents. The elephant had a massive scrape on his forehead which was bleeding profusely. He was dazed from the encounter with the tree, and most of the fight had gone out of him.

Tarzan now knew that he could elude the maddened elephant, so he rested with his back against a tree and caught his breath. He glanced back and saw the great beast was down on its front knees with its rump still at normal height. Tarzan had heard the collision of elephant and tree, and he was amazed to see the great tree was only listing slightly.

Tarzan gave La a shake and tried to get her to respond to him. After several seconds La's eyes closed and reopened with a look of intelligence in them. She asked, "Tarzan, what happened, and where is the elephant?"

"I was able to save you from Tantor. He would have ground you into pulp if he could have gotten ahold of you. What happened to you back there? I shouted a warning, and you did not respond. You were in a swoon when I grabbed you, and I do not understand why."

La could give no answer, but in her mind, she remembered a message the elephant, her totem, had sent to her. The message had simply said, "Beware of Cadj." She thought perhaps she should re-evaluate her relationship with Cadj and Oah. La, obviously upset, placed her arms around Tarzan, and said simply, "I should have listened to you."

CHAPTER FORTY-TWO — BETRAYAL

Tarzan propped La against the tree trunk and told her he was leaving to get water. He had seen a stream while in the middle terraces looking for elephants. It was close by, and the water looked clean.

Tarzan's mind was on La as he sought to find the stream and so he was distracted. The party of priests and Neteru had staked out the water as a place that he was likely to visit, and so they waited there.

Their patience was rewarded, as Tarzan began to walk toward them. They silently melted back into the foliage and waited for him to pass. Tarzan should have seen the movement with his peripheral vision, but he did not. A Neteru came out of concealment and hit him in the back of the head with a cudgel. Tarzan dropped face down in the grass. The Neteru were on him immediately, and as he was regaining consciousness, he was aware of being roughly handled by several large men. He heard one of the men shout, "Someone get the rope! Hurry! He is going to awaken shortly."

Too late, the jungle lord was awake and livid. The scar on his forehead was glowing bright red, and he was like a snarling, savage beast. He broke the grip of one of the Neteru, and as luck would have it, the man dropped his cudgel. Tarzan reached down, grabbed the club and brained the Neteru. He kicked out with his mighty leg and put another of the burly Neteru on his back where he promptly received a full strength blow in his chest, breaking several ribs and puncturing a lung. Tarzan whirled around for momentum with his weapon and brained the third Neteru and then one of the priests. Unfortunately, the priest was Maj, Cadj's henchman, and so Tarzan was not going to hear from Maj that Cadj had ordered the assault on him.

The other priests fell upon their knees and with terrified eyes and high-pitched voices begged for their lives. Tarzan grabbed one and lifted him off his feet. He hissed his question to the man, while the remaining Neteru escaped deeper into the forest, "Who ordered you to kill me? Speak now, and you may live to see tomorrow."

The terrified priest answered in one word, "Maj."

Tarzan brought his face closer and asked, "Who is Maj?"

The priest turned his head and with his left hand pointed to the man laying on the ground in an ever-growing pool of blood from a fatal head wound. Tarzan with a feeling of disgust flung the priest from his grip and scowled. "Go find your cowardly companion, and may the lions feed well upon you both tonight." Without looking back, the priests ran as fast as he could from Tarzan.

Tarzan was feeling woozy from the head blow and the blood he had lost. He walked back to where he had left La and collapsed several feet from her reclining form. As he lost consciousness, he heard her scream his name.

Tarzan awakened an hour later, and La was attending him. She had somehow found the stream and had carried water back to Tarzan in the cloth that had been her skirt.

"How long have I been out?" Tarzan asked.

"A finger width movement of the Flaming God."

La asked, "Who were you fighting with?"

"Several Neteru and several priests. I let two of the priests go. Let's hope the lions find them tonight. I doubt they can find their way back to Opar, and if they do, I will cut their throats tomorrow. They had a sacrificial knife and were obviously going to offer me up to the Flaming God."

"By whose orders?"

"The coward I held by his throat said it was one of the priests I killed – Maj. He had no reason to lie."

"Tarzan, that can't be right. Maj is one of the stupidest men in Opar. There had to be someone else behind it. Let's get back to Opar. I had May-at following Oah, and Mitry had one of his best men follow Cadj. Let's see what they learned."

The day that had started out so well had turned into a disaster of intrigue. Both Tarzan and La were silent through most of the several hour trip back to Opar. They arrived in late afternoon and went directly to La's reception area. She was winded from the exertion of the long and rapid walk. She sent for a handmaiden, told her to bring May-at and send for Mitry.

Tarzan sat in a chair on the side in the reception room as Mitry arrived first, saying, "I heard you were back, Mistress, how was your outing?"

"Not good. What did your man report that Cadj was doing while we were gone?"

"He reported Cadj worked on cleaning up a storage room and spent some time in the company of one of the other minor priests."

"Any contact with Oah?"

"No, Mistress."

"That is disappointing. I would have thought they would be plotting the whole time we were gone." La then told Mitry of the events of the afternoon.

May-at entered the room as Mitry was leaving. "Sorry it took me so long to get back. I was out near the private chapel. I followed Oah, and she spent all her time alone in the chapel. There was no contact with anyone."

La glanced over to Tarzan with a look of disappointment on her face. "Clever, aren't they, Tarzan? My thought is, with their plans made all they had to do was establish an alibi for the afternoon. Both undoubtedly knew they were being watched."

"La, my thoughts on those two are the same. Kill them now. They will never stop trying to take over ruling Opar. It is plain to me that Cadj's goal is to be High Priest and have Oah as his High Priestess."

La answered, "I know you are right. I have known it all along, and I allowed my love for Nedjam to cloud my judgment. I will not kill them, but I will banish them from Opar. Immediately."

An hour later, two of Mitry's most trusted men brought Cadj and Oah before La in the throne room. Their hands had been bound behind their backs. La's face showed no emotion as she addressed the few council members, older priests and handmaidens who were present.

La began, "As most of you know there was an attempt on my friend Tarzan's life. Undoubtedly my life was the next in danger. I believe that the two people who stand in front of me were the instigators of these treasonous acts."

Cadj, with a look of righteous indignation on his face, opened his mouth to speak. La cut him off immediately, "Not a sound, you snake, or I will have you gagged as well." Cadj's head dropped, and he was heard to say, "We are unjustly accused."

La resumed after the interruption, "This is the second treasonous act by you two, and it is the last. Armed guards are to escort the prisoners five miles from Opar, and in two different directions. They will then be left in the dark, bound as they are now."

La's stare went from one stunned face to another as she said, "If you attempt to return to Opar, you are to be killed on sight." Tears began to flow down Oah's face, and in a faltering voice she screamed, "We are innocent!"

"We will see if the roaming and hungry cats in the jungle think so."

"Guards, take your arms and torches and lead these traitors into the jungle. May the Flaming God guide our guards back safely to Opar." La flicked her left hand at the prisoners to signify the judgment was over.

The next morning La and May-at came into the room where Tarzan was sleeping. He awakened as soon as he heard their soft sandals scrape on the stone floor. "How are you feeling this morning, Tarzan?" asked La.

"My head has stopped bleeding, so I am sure I will live. Bolgani did much worse to me, and I survived that." The meaning of this was lost on La and May-at.

"Mitry told me yesterday that another white man was found in the storage areas below the temple. Is he a friend of yours?" La asked.

"I will have a look at him, but I know of no one who is aware of the location of Opar, or has a reason to be here."

Tarzan continued, "La, we need to talk shortly. I have been in Opar for nearly a moon, and I need to be heading to my home."

La's lip curled back, and she hissed, with a face as red as blood, "And back to your woman?"

"Yes, and back to my woman." was Tarzan's response, as he looked calmly into La's face. He was somewhat surprised at her words, and the emotion behind them. Tarzan felt he should let the conversation die at that point and move on to another subject. La turned on her heel, her face still an angry crimson, and hurried out of the room, with a bewildered May-at trailing behind her.

Tarzan moved to a chair, sat and began to plan his next step. He thought he would leave in the morning and travel slowly home. He would forget about the gold of Opar. He would bedevil the Arabs who had large caches of ivory hidden in the jungle. He would take it from them and transport it to the west coast ports to be sold for cash.

May-at entered the reception and said, "My mistress wants to see you immediately."

Tarzan walked slowly down the temple's central corridor, and into the throne room. La was seated on the throne, with a scowl of hatred on her face. She and Tarzan were alone.

"So, once again you reject the affection of La. The last time you were here I saved you from being sacrificed to the Flaming God. Now, after a brief visit, you are going to leave me again—and go back to your cow of a woman." At this point, tears were streaming down La's face, and her voice had risen to a shriek.

"I offer you more riches than you have ever seen. I offer you rule of this great city with me. I offered myself to you. Am I so repulsive to your eyes that you cannot wait to get away from me? Why am I not enough for you? What am I lacking?" The hysterical shouting ended with La placing her face in her hands and bending over her knees, sobbing quietly.

There was nothing Tarzan could say, so he waited a few minutes, and when it became apparent that La's fury was spent, he turned and walked back to his room.

Tarzan was sitting quietly in his chair. He had decided to leave Opar immediately. He felt sorry that his visit had upset La so badly. He vowed this would be his last trip here. La would be better off not seeing him again. She should forget him and mate with one of the men of Opar. Perhaps she would find a man like her father.

As he rose from the chair, Tarzan turned to view a silent La. He noted that her face was puffy and her eyes were bloodshot and swollen. She hesitated, her head dropping onto her chest and her body shaking. He felt a twinge of remorse for having caused such an extreme reaction in someone he cared about. Tarzan was not sure what to expect or what to say, so he did not move.

In a barely audible voice, La said, "I am sorry. Can you forgive me? I did not mean the things I said, please let us not part in this way."

Tarzan did not move or make any response. La raised her arms and thrust her body against Tarzan, holding him close in an embrace. Again she said, "Tarzan, I did not mean the things I said." She whispered, "Please don't leave yet. Please talk to me."

La felt Tarzan nod his acceptance. She released her hold, and without looking back at him, she turned and walked out of the room into the hallway.

The next morning May-at appeared in Tarzan's room and said, "My Mistress asked if you would like to have breakfast with her. She is waiting at her private swimming area."

"Yes," was Tarzan's response. They walked together in a northerly direction along the stone path that began at the Temple of the Flaming God. The route would continue past the houses of the workers and then towards the homes of the upper class.

It was early, and there was still fog in the air, which dampened sounds. Tarzan turned to May-at and asked, "And how is your mistress today?"

May-at smiled at Tarzan and said, "She is much calmed down from yesterday. You should have seen the maidens scatter out of the temple when she was screaming at you! No one wanted to get caught up in her wrath." Tarzan smiled back at May-at. He liked the handmaiden. She was intelligent and had a good sense of humor.

May-at pointed to La, turned and began walking back to the temple. La was seated at a small table on which had been placed fruits and fresh bread for breakfast. La had obviously been swimming or bathing.

La looked up and saw that Tarzan had noticed her wet hair, and said, "Since you do not care for me, I thought I would not have to bother my handmaidens grooming my hair for your visit." He thought to himself, here we go again. La smiled at Tarzan and bade him sit down.

She began, "Again, I am sorry for my outburst last night. The events of yesterday brought back a lot of memories. It was very upsetting, the attempt on your life and having to exile Oah — too much drama for one day."

Tarzan thought the less said about yesterday's events, the better. He just returned La's smile. The tension that surrounded them seemed to have disappeared, and normal conversation began.

"When we finish here, I would like you to look at the prisoner. I also want to hear what you were going to tell me yesterday afternoon." Tarzan agreed and told La what a lovely spot this was for her relaxation. The water coming from a spring high in the mountain kept the lagoon pleasantly cool.

Tarzan began the postponed conversation, "La, I am concerned about your safety here in Opar. I have been here twice, and luckily I was because there were two attempts on your life."

La responded sarcastically, "Why, Tarzan, are you afraid something is going to happen to me? I have to be careful, or I will begin believing that you care for me." A smile crossed La's face.

Tarzan continued, "If you think it would help, I will send a squad of Waziri warriors to guard you. While I believe Mitry genuinely likes you, he can't be everywhere at once. I think Cadj has sown the seeds of hatred for you among the male priests, and it will only be a matter of time before you have another problem and I will not be anywhere near to assist you."

Clearly, La had not thought along those lines, and she asked if she could consider his offer. Tarzan replied, "Yes, but remember I will be leaving in the next few days." He thought he saw a shadow of disappointment come across her face but said nothing.

"La, regarding security, I believe it would be good if you had two or three of your messenger monkeys trained to find me at my farm."

"That is an excellent thought," replied La. "I will have the monkey trainer visit with you, and teach you the method that the monkeys can find you."

Tarzan thoughtfully replied, "You never know, La. There may come a time when you need to summon me quickly. The monkeys can make the trip from Opar to my home in two or three weeks. A man on foot will take over a month."

La thought to herself, 'I wonder what his woman will say if I send for him?' But she did not vocalize the thought.

With a pause in the conversation, La asked Tarzan if she could show him the prisoner. Tarzan nodded, and they walked back to the temple.

This time in the temple La led Tarzan down a set of narrow stone stairs. They both carried candles that pushed back the darkness a bit. "This is the third level of the temple," La stated. "It is still being built so be careful. Do not walk here without light. There is a wide gap in the floor that is meant to kill intruders who come in from the outside."

"This is where we found the thief that you may know. Obviously, he knew about the gold stored here and was going to steal from us. He broke into several rooms and had a bag of the pretty stones in his possession when we captured him. He had lost his candle and his sense of direction.

He was screaming and sobbing like a child when one of the temple guards discovered him."

"The priests are calling for him to be sacrificed," La said, "What do you think we should do?"

"Do what you want with him, he is of no concern of mine," was Tarzan's response.

"Where is this man being held? I can find out his intentions."

La had summoned Mitry, and after he joined them, they continued to where the prisoner was being held. Mitry opened the door and voiced his dismay. The soldier who had been guarding the man lay dead on the floor. He had somehow slipped his ropes and used them to strangle the guard.

Tarzan asked Mitry to describe the man they had found. Mitry brought one of the men who had found the hysterical captive and repeated Tarzan's request for a description. After further questioning of the man, Tarzan came to a rapid conclusion — the man was Frecoult. He must have followed Tarzan and found the city.

"Don't worry," said Tarzan "I believe I know who he is and I know where he is headed. I will deal with him on my way home."

On the morning Tarzan departed, he spoke with La at her swimming area again. When they had finished breakfast, Tarzan said, "I will have a group of the finest Waziri come here to be your bodyguards. Expect them in six weeks. I will be anxious to see if the monkeys can truly find me."

La smiled and said, "Farewell again, Tarzan. May the Flaming God keep you safe. The gold I promised will be buried at the foot of the escarpment. You can have your men pick it up in a few weeks. And here is the bag of pretty pebbles that the escaped prisoner was trying to steal. Perhaps your woman would like them."

Tarzan smiled as he left the shady area and walked back to the entrance to Opar in the front of the temple.

Tarzan left Opar for the second time. La did not give him a tearful send-off. She saved that for the privacy of her sleeping room.

Press clipping from London Daily Gazette dated January 8, 1915.

Wife of Lord Greystoke Injured

Lady Jane Clayton, wife of Lord Greystoke was injured yesterday while apparently attempting to cross Mount Street to reach the Connaught Hotel for High Tea.

Apparently she did not look in the correct direction, and stepped directly into the path of a public bus.

Extent of Lady Clayton's injuries is not available.

Lord Greystoke, a member of the House of Lords, is not available for comment. He is enroute to London from the family farm in East Africa.

Lady Greystoke is resting in the Wekbeck Hospital.

No visitors are being Permitted.

Jim Malachowski

CHAPTER FORTY-THREE — THE STORY OF KIYA

Tarzan was making his leisurely way back to his home near the east coast of Africa. Some of the time he was in the middle terraces traveling at a fast speed, other times he was walking through the jungle. The walking gave him time to think about La and what he perceived as her precarious position in Opar.

Tarzan sensed or heard a man traveling in his direction at a rapid speed. He immediately took to the lower branches of the trees and waited to see what this person was doing.

As the warrior approached, Tarzan recognized him as one of the Waziri tribe.

The Waziri war chief dropped to the ground ten yards in front of the sweating man. "I do not know your name, but you are Waziri, are you not?"

The man nodded, and replied, "Yes, my chief, I am Embobway. I bring you a message. It was brought to your home, and Msizi read it, and ordered me to find you as soon as possible."

Embobway handed Tarzan a slightly wrinkled and folded piece of paper, a telegram. It had been sent by his chief of staff at Greystoke Castle, near Cumbria.

As Tarzan read the brief note, the color left his face. Jane had been injured in a motoring accident in London. She had been hospitalized, and he was urged to come at once.

He turned to Embobway, "Thank you for finding me. The mistress has been injured, and I need to get to the farm as quickly as I can. I will leave you now and take to the trees, where I can travel much faster than on foot."

Embobway bowed his head accepting the compliment, and watched as Tarzan took to the trees and was out of sight in seconds. He turned and began the march back to the Waziri Village.

After Tarzan reached his farm, he quickly prepared for a trip to Nairobi to charter an airplane back to England. But first, he called for Msizi and told him to take ten men and travel quickly to Opar. He gave him detailed instructions on who and how he wanted the warriors to guard. Msizi silently listened and nodded his understanding, and left Tarzan to his packing.

La's sister, Kiya, was now fifteen years old. She had changed very much from being a palace child to the beginnings of being a woman. The transition was still not complete, and Kiya still fluctuated from child to woman very quickly and easily.

Kiya would not be as tall as La, nor would she be as slender. These were the observations of both La and May-at. The women were keenly interested in the growth and maturation process in Kiya. They were anxious for her to join the close-knit group that La and May-at had become.

Kiya was still very much a tomboy. Because she was physically more mature than the few boys her age, she could dominate and bully them easily. She was quite proficient with bow and arrow, and had the ability to fight with her fists.

Of late, she had shown interest in the sexual nature of being a woman. She had asked May-at and particularly La about her relationship with Tarzan. She had seen her older sister look at Tarzan with affection, so she knew La was interested in him. La angrily answered Kiya's questions about her relationship with Tarzan by emphatically saying there never was anything physical. Kiya was astounded at that answer and demanded to know why. More anger appeared and Kiya was told this was none of her business, and to change the subject.

May-at was present during this conversation and somewhat enjoyed watching La be interrogated by her younger sister and being badgered into admitting something she would rather have kept to herself. May-at left the room with a slight smile on her face. She would gently tease La about the questions just asked, and the answers she had given. But not right now.

May-at had, in the past several years, grown comfortably into the position of chief handmaiden to La. She knew when to offer advice, and when to keep her opinions to herself. Slowly La began to see her in the same light that Nedjam had been seen by La, her mother and grandmother. The thought of Kiya becoming chief handmaiden had been pushed aside by La, and May-at was firmly entrenched there.

La would soon begin the process of grooming Kiya to be her successor in the position of High Priestess, despite the fact that La was only ten years older than Kiya. Both La and May-at had accepted, at least for the foreseeable future, they would be maidens without mates. The prospect of La producing a daughter to succeed her was not a realistic goal. La, in her heart, was still hoping Tarzan would come around to be being her mate. May-at was so engrossed in being La's handmaiden and friend that she did not want a male companion, at least not on a long-term basis.

The city of Opar had changed very little in millennia. Once La had some experience in governing, it became a boring routine for her. Meetings with the council had become less frequent. Either the council had gained respect for La as High Priestess, or as men, they had lost even more interest in governing the city.

World War I was raging in Europe. There have been many analyses of the causes of the Great War, but one of the most forgotten facts is that three of the great countries' monarchs were cousins: Emperor Wilhelm II of Germany, King George V of Great Britain and Czar Nicholas II of Russia. Three men who should never have allowed the conflict to begin.

The countless alliances between major and minor countries would eventually drag almost all of Europe into the fighting. World War I was a conflict that would never settle any of the issues fought over. Ancient hatreds between countries and their inhabitants existed before the war and were not resolved with its cessation. The continuing problems were instrumental in inciting another World War twenty years later — continuing to trouble us today.

The war was bankrupting most of the European powers, with the possible exception of Germany. Industrialization had risen quicker in Germany than in the other European countries. The mechanization brought huge profits, especially in the areas of war machinery.

The British aristocracy beginning with the twentieth century had been on a path of slow decline. The aristocrats were used to providing low paying jobs to the people who lived in their area. The lower classes were now moving to the cities to find higher paying jobs that did not require working day and night for the lord of the manor. As a result, the great houses were falling into ruin, because the owners did not have the capital to maintain them. Likewise, many of the great families were mere shells of their former selves. In many cases, the title was the only item of prestige, as the property was falling apart, and there was no hard cash left in the family coffers.

Lord Greystoke was aware of the financial condition of Great Britain and France as a result of World War I. Over the course of the war he donated the majority of his resources to keep England and France afloat.

Lord Greystoke had returned to Africa many times during World War I. One of his greatest fears was that Germany would stumble upon Opar. He was afraid if that happened the Hun would kill all the inhabitants and would empty Opar of it's fabulous riches. This alone could tip the war in Germany's favor a prospect Tarzan would give his life to prevent.

Lord Greystoke had sent confidential instructions to the Waziri warrior leader, Msizi, stationed in Opar. He was to send regular patrols to search for German troops or scouting parties, in addition to providing La with personal protection.

Lord Greystoke also knew his financial situation would lead to another trip to the treasure vaults of Opar—and La.

Jim Malachowski

CHAPTER FORTY-FOUR — THE THIRD TRIP TO OPAR

Tarzan selected fifty Waziri warriors and began the long march to Opar. It had been over four years since he had last visited, although he was kept abreast by Msizi, who once a month wrote him a report. While not a secret, Msizi had never mentioned to La that he was sending Tarzan messages.

The first World War had ended with an armistice over a year ago, but the Waziri were still on guard around a hundred mile perimeter of the city looking for soldiers or spies left behind by the warring nations. So far there were no indications that Germany had any inkling of the presence of Opar. The Waziri had sometimes seen or just heard primitive aircraft flying overhead. Tarzan knew it was a matter of time before planes with cameras capable of photographing the ground were in use.

After a long march, the large group that Tarzan was heading came to the foot of the escarpment. This time Tarzan had brought some sophisticated European climbing equipment for scaling the sheer rock face. It would increase safety, preventing any of his men from falling to their deaths. The gold ingots could be lowered more quickly and safely than on the other trips.

Tarzan instructed his men to camp at the foot of the great barrier of stone, and wait for him to return in about a month. The next morning Tarzan began the long climb up the rock face, carrying with him some of the mountaineer paraphernalia so he could anchor ropes and pulleys at the end of the climb.

All through the ascent, Tarzan wondered what kind of reception he would get from La. La's younger sister would be close to twenty years old. It hardly seemed possible. Tarzan reached the top and began the several mile journey through the desolate land. He traveled far to the left in the valley to prevent being seen by the sharp-eyed sentries.

In the late afternoon, he climbed the mountain that was behind the Temple of the Flaming God and waited to see if La would make an appearance on the roof that night. An hour before midnight, a tall figure dressed in ghostly white, thin material appeared on the steps and began walking to her bench. Tarzan quickly descended the mountain and climbed the temple wall in a few minutes.

He silently walked across the temple roof perimeter and moved toward La, who was standing gazing at the myriad of stars in the night sky. Tarzan stopped about six feet behind La, and in a low voice asked, "A penny for your thoughts?" La turned, and with a smile on her face, said, "You again! Whatever could you want here?" The smile quickly left her face and tears began to flow down as she wrapped herself around Tarzan. He put his arms around her and held her close.

La released him and said, "Your Waziri are terrible at keeping secrets. I knew a month ago that you were on your way, and I have been coming up on this roof for a week waiting for you." They both enjoyed a laugh and sat together.

"Well Tarzan," La began, "do I look more unattractive to you than I did on your last visit? It has been several years."

Tarzan smiled and replied, "You know better than to say that La. You are one of the most beautiful women in the world."

La produced a smile that discounted Tarzan's words.

"La promise me that during this trip if you get angry with me you will not hold it in until you explode. I desperately do not want another visit like last time."

La sheepishly nodded her head in affirmation and said, "Me either."

"How are the Waziri bodyguards working for you?"

"They are wonderful. There are two of them around me at all times. I have assigned one of them, his name is Msizi, to May-at." La lowered her voice and said, "I believe they are quite taken with each other. I sense they may be closer than friends."

La continued, "Two of the men are out in the jungle most of the time, and I have no idea what they are doing. They all have rooms at this end of the temple. While three are sleeping, the others are guarding May-at and me."

"I will let you in on another secret, Tarzan. The women of Opar are quite taken by these muscular giants. I fear that we will have several more new babies in the city a few months from now," La laughed.

"As long as these men know they are here to guard you and not make babies. I will talk with Msizi and let him know my feelings."

"Don't take this too seriously, Tarzan, since we can use some new babies in Opar with different fathers, rather than by the regular fools."

Tarzan smiled and nodded because he knew La was right.

Then he asked, "Do you have a place where a traveler from the road can get some sleep? It has been a long day."

"Of course, May-at has been anxious for your arrival, and she has had a room ready for you for weeks. Plus she will be glad to see you again."

Tarzan said, "We need to talk. There are several important items that we have to discuss."

The next morning May-at arrived at Tarzan's room and greeted him cheerfully, "Good morning Tarzan, Mistress La is waiting for you by her private swimming area. Would you like to follow me?"

La greeted Tarzan and dismissed the several handmaidens who had been helping her dress and prepare breakfast. La motioned for Tarzan to be seated beside her.

"I spoke with Msizi this morning, and he gave me some disheartening news. He said there have been some sightings of priests leaving Opar in the middle of the night and not returning until the next night. Could either Cadj or Oah still be in the area of Opar?"

La's face paled, and her stunned look clearly said she had not been aware of this questionable behavior.

"Do you want me to send some Waziri out to try to find if they are still hanging around?"

"Yes," came the one-word response from La. "There has been some surly behavior from some of the younger priests lately. They are complaining about the lack of sacrifices and conditions in the quarters of the priests."

"What do you want me to do about it?" Tarzan asked.

La's response was, "Nothing. I will have Mitry deal with them if they are truly nearby."

La changed the subject, saying, "The Waziri warriors you sent have eased my mind about someone trying to take over. They are all wonderful men, and I feel very secure with them around. But do you really think I need them around me all the time?"

"La, I did not want to bring this up to you now, but since you asked, I will. The world outside of Opar has become very violent. And even though you cannot see the danger, I can assure you that Opar and your people are in danger, and it will only get worse. Can you not trust me on this, because I cannot explain it in a way that you will understand."

"What would you have me do?" La asked.

"The time may come when you have to lead your people out of Opar, never to return. Or you alone must leave."

La had a look of disbelief on her face, and she asked, "Where would we go? And never to return, I do not understand why we would have to abandon all this work of our ancestors. Tarzan, I could never abandon my people just to save myself."

"These may be your choices, and you do need to think on them. The danger to you and your people may be closer than you think. One of the reasons I sent Msizi and his warriors here was to guard you, and also to be lookouts for invaders from the outside world. La, please trust me on this, I know I am right."

La thought a moment and answered, "Tarzan, I trust you with my life, but I do not see any danger, and I cannot imagine any threat so great that we should abandon Opar."

"I hope you are right, La."

Jim Malachowski

CHAPTER FORTY-FIVE — SOLD

One of the Opar hunters had requested a meeting with Tarzan. He arrived at La's reception area and introduced himself as Eri to Tarzan. Before he sat down, he handed Tarzan a large quiver of arrows. There were three dozen arrows, each fletched with beautiful and ornate feathers. Eri, a proud look on his face, said, "Tarzan take an arrow out and look at it." Tarzan removed an arrow, and to his surprise, the arrow was tipped with an ornate golden blade. The arrowhead was incredibly sharp and Eri said with pride, "The arrowhead is not pure gold, it would be too soft, so our artisan blends other metal to make it as hard as we need it to be effective."

"Thank you; this is a fine gift, I will be anxious to try them out," Tarzan answered, still admiring the arrow's workmanship.

"There is something else I want to talk to you about," Eri said and motioned for Tarzan to be seated. "I have spoken with the High Priestess, and she likes this idea. I am inviting you to join us for a hunt. Once a year our hunters go on a long trek, searching for animals that we find tasty, and ones we do not normally find close to the city."

"I will be glad to join the hunt. How long will we be gone, and are some of my Waziri warriors welcome to join us? I think we can all learn some new techniques from each other."

"Your warriors are more than welcome. I will inform La of your decision. We will leave in two mornings." Eri was pleased that Tarzan had accepted.

That night, two hours after midnight, a priest dressed in dark clothing left the city by way of the main entrance. His departure was not noticed by the snoozing sentry. He turned south and walked past the short section of the city wall, and into the mountains. An hour's walk brought him high into the mountain, where he strained his eyes to find the feeble light of a small fire.

At last, he saw the tiny flame and seated himself across from another man and a woman. Even though they were miles from Opar, they spoke in very low tones. The woman spoke first, "We hope the preparations are complete. Are our Arab brothers and their black troops in position? Since the hunting trip is on, we will have our choice of what evening to complete our plans. Is that not so?"

"Yes, Mistress. Everything is in readiness. All we need is for the hunters to leave and be far away."

The trio went through the plans for another few hours and concluded the meeting before dawn. As the priest rose to make his way back to the city, he heard, "My brother priest, you have done well and will be most generously rewarded in a few days." He left with a look of satisfaction and began the long walk back to Opar, uttering a prayer to the Flaming God asking his protection from hunting leopards.

In the past weeks, a man who entertained his sultan by being able to climb the steepest wall had been scaling the north end of the wall around Opar. He carried with him iron spikes which had been fabricated to have a loop for rope on one end, the other end being pointed. He spent every night for a week almost soundlessly drilling holes in front of the oasis, into the stone. The spikes had been driven into the cliff and had been tested to hold the weight of several large men. This night he descended by a rope, and announced to his Arab leader, "The rope is ready to be used, Effendi." The climber gave the line a sharp tug, and it fell down the wall and ended up in a heap at their feet. The climber smiled as did the Arab leader, Abdul. He turned to the cannibal chief Maaka, and said two words, "tomorrow night."

The relationship between the Manyuema tribe and their Arab partners went back over a century. The Manyuema people originated in central Africa near the west coast. They may have been one of the many splinters of the Bantu tribe and were more nomadic than most of the other central African tribes. They could have been associated with or even recruited by the notorious slave trader Hamad bin Muhammad bin Juma bin Rajab el Murjebi who was better known as Tippu Tip. Somehow the Manyuema learned how to make money from selling their brothers for use as slaves on the Arabian Peninsula.

The next night La, May-at and Kiya were enjoying the oasis, as they had been doing every evening since the hunting group had left. Tonight they had taken a cooling swim in the pond and were now eating a light dinner.

Outside, a climber had scaled the wall, threaded the rope into the spikes and signaled silently that all was set. The sentry on the north wall turned his back, as he had been doing all week. Six young cannibal warriors began climbing the line, with never more than two on it at a time.

The men silently threaded a different rope into different spikes for the descent behind the trees that screened the wall from the oasis. One at a time the men climbed down until all six were on the ground. Around their necks were gags and shorter lengths of rope.

Boldly, three men approached the table from two sides where the women were chatting. May-at was the first to see the invaders. She had time for one screamed word, "Mistress!" before a filthy black hand clamped over her mouth. May-at watched in wide-eyed horror as La and Kiya were likewise grabbed from behind. It took less than a minute for the warriors to subdue each screaming woman. They were quickly gaged and bound.

La was struggling mightily. The warrior raised his left hand to strike her across the face. His companion grabbed his arm and hissed, "We will be killed if they are marked." The women were carried behind the oasis, and there the three strongest warriors climbed the ropes with a woman slung over his shoulder. When they reached the standing area on the crest, more restraints were placed around the women's waist and arms, and they were lowered down the wall into the waiting arms of muscular men.

The warriors on top of the wall removed the now excess lines, and the six men descended the long rope to the base of the north wall. A tug was given, it was released and was hastily removed. The climbers looked around for anything left behind and hurried to catch up with the main body, which was by now a hundred yards ahead.

The camp of Arabs and cannibals was twenty-five miles from Opar and was reached after fifteen hours of walking. The three women had been thrown into one of the filthy huts. A few hours later, almost at dawn, a figure bent down and entered. La looked up, and her eyes went wide when she recognized the man who had just entered the hut. He reached over and roughly removed the gag from her mouth and jerked her by her hair to her feet. La's mouth was so dry that she was barely able to utter anymore than a croak that sounded like, "Cadj."

"Yes," was the reply. "Now you pompous cow, you will be repaid for the disgrace you have heaped upon me. My suffering has ended, but yours is just beginning." Cadj's voice was rising to a shrill scream, "Now you will pay for what you have done to Oah and me. It is too bad that I will not be able to witness your humbling and indignation when you arrive in the land of the Arabs. Oah and I will be busy ruling Opar. But we will have the satisfaction of knowing you will be used as a courtesan until you are no longer pretty, then you will be thrown to the dogs of the street."

Despite her inner feelings, La thrust her chin up at Cadj, and screamed as best she could, "No Cadj, my life is just beginning. Yours will end very shortly, as will that spawn of my best friend. I will be there when you both breath your last."

244

Cadj had regained some of his composure, saying, "You still think that outsider will save you? Think again. Not only is he many marches away, but he also will not live to see the end of the hunt."

La went cold again inside, but she said nothing and kept the defiant look on her face. A smile came to Cadj's face as he spoke again, "Just so you have something to look forward to, here are your traveling plans. In the morning, which is very close, you will begin a walk of several weeks to where the Flaming God rises every morning. There you will join with Abdul's main party of men and slaves. A few days further and you will come to a large body of water. You will be taken across into the land of the Arabs where you and these other scheming women will be sold. You will then begin your brief career in the seraglio of one of Abdul's friends."[5]

With a smile, Cadj looked at May-at and Kiya and said, "I fear your other two companions will not meet the Arab's specifications for beautiful women, but surely their new owners will find some degrading work for them. Just so you do not worry about Oah and me, here are our plans. We will receive a hero's welcome from the priests and people of Opar. We will bring back the true religion and worship of the Flaming God. We will again seek the Flaming God's approval with more sacrifices, which have been sorely lacking under your sloppy rule."

The smile on Cadj's face grew as he said, "It is almost time for your big adventure to begin. Enjoy your nice walk and the boat trip across the big water. Contemplate your new lives, even though they will be short." With that, Cadj turned and walked out of the hut. Cadj was enjoying the feelings of revenge, and he did not even mind the thoughts of the long walk back to Opar. Seeing the look of despair on La's face had been worth the time away from Oah.

La sat back down, her sister Kiya with wide eyes and a look of disbelief asked, "Do you think what Cadj said is true?"

La's head dropped slightly, when she answered, "Yes." Her thoughts went back to Tarzan. She could only imagine what dangers he was facing. She wondered if he would ever know what had happened to her. Would

---

[5] One of the most used slave routes. Across southern Ethiopia, depart Tadjourah by boat to the port of Aden on the Arabian Peninsula.

he just go back to his woman and forget her? La turned her head to begin to weep quietly.

The hunt was going very well for Tarzan and his companions. They had walked for several days south of Opar. The path was taking them further from Opar and the slave party, leading to a great plain dotted with millions of animals. They had killed several large and different species of antelope and had sent two messenger monkeys back to Opar for helpers to smoke the meat and carry it back to the city. The next goal was to find and kill a yearling of Cape Buffalo.

Eri had told Tarzan, "We have tried to kill one of these beasts before, but have never accomplished it. Their tough hides prevent our arrows from penetrating. The last time we went after the great beast, we lost two hunters who were gored and trampled by the ill-tempered brutes."

The lord of the jungle replied, "I rarely hunt them. There is so much meat it will feed the entire city of Opar." Here is how we will kill one. Have your men carefully herd the buffalo amongst that stand of trees over there. I will be up in the branches waiting to select a young bull and shoot him."

It took several tries to guide the skittish animals between the trees. As a small herd was worked through Tarzan's hiding place, he selected an animal and fired his arrow directly down between the great beast's shoulder blades. Tarzan's bow was much stronger than his fellow hunters. None of them could draw an arrow completely on his bow. The arrow flew the short distance quickly and disappeared totally into the buffalo's back. A few steps later the animal staggered, snorted blood from its nostrils and went to its knees. The hunters watched cautiously from a distance, as the animal died quickly.

It took all the men working together to hoist the one-half ton buffalo so that it could be dressed and cut for smoking. That night the group of hunters enjoyed roast buffalo loin and spoke happily about the success of the hunt. Tarzan would have preferred his meat raw but compromised by finding a chunk of meat that had been cooked very little.

That night Tarzan decided to sleep on the ground, distancing himself from the warriors who would be talking for several hours. A few hours into the night, Tarzan came fully awake but did not open his eyes or move. His keen hearing had detected movement in the grass around him. One eye opened slightly, and he saw a figure coming toward him slowly. Then Tarzan saw the skinning knife in the man's hand.

Tarzan made a sleeping snore and rolled on his side toward the man, so he could better defend himself. The man hesitated slightly and waited until Tarzan seemed to settle back to sleep. He approached, knelt beside the ape-man and raised the knife. In the blink of an eye, Tarzan drove his left fist, with all his might, into the man's stomach just below the rib cage. All the ability to breath left the man immediately and the knife was dropped. Tarzan was on his feet in a heartbeat grabbing the man by the throat and calling for Eri.

"Eri, who is this man," Tarzan demanded.

"I do not know him. He is one of the peasants brought along to help skin the game."

By now the entire camp was awake, and one of the hunters spoke to Eri, "Let me have him, and I will have his story by breakfast."

Eri nodded his approval and moved with Tarzan away from the group of men. "Tarzan, I have a bad feeling about this. Why would anyone want to kill you?"

"A better question is who put him up to this …" replied Tarzan, looking Eri straight in the eye.

Jim Malachowski

CHAPTER FORTY-SIX — THE RACE AGAINST TIME

An ancient infantry could march, with full gear, about fifteen miles a day. The Zulu army of the 19th century, fully armed, could run thirty miles a day to fight a battle. Tarzan in the fully forested jungle of his home territory could do a bit better than thirty miles a day in the middle terraces.

By first light, the would-be assassin had told his story. He had been contacted by a minor priest and told he was to make a sacrifice to the Flaming God. He had been promised a private home for him and his family and choice foods for a year. Tarzan was present at the end of the interrogation. The hunter was pressured for the name of the person who had ordered the attack on Tarzan. The man answered with one word, "Cadj."

Tarzan took Eri aside and told him, "There is something more to this than meets the eye. I don't know what is happening, but I believe we should start for Opar today. Put the meat behind a thorn boma, where the cooks can find it. They should be here this afternoon. Bring that worthless butcher back with you. He may have more information to tell us."

As this conversation was taking place, a messenger monkey ran to Eri, scurried up to his shoulder and sat exhausted. Eri looked and told Tarzan, "This ribbon on this arm means the sender is Mitry, the two ribbons on the other arm are saying great danger and come immediately."

Tarzan told Eri he was going ahead to Opar and he would meet him there. Eri shouted to the men to break camp; they were leaving. Tarzan ran and was in the trees and out of sight in a minute. He wished it was solid forest all the way to Opar, but it was not. He would have to travel a large amount of way on foot, slowing him down.

Two days later Tarzan arrived back in Opar, sent one of the sentries to summon Mitry, and he demanded food and water. Mitry arrived shortly, led Tarzan to a room in the temple. Mitry began, "About seven days ago La, Kiya and May-at disappeared. I have been searching the area ever since, and I can find no trail. But, of course, you have the best trackers, in the hunters, with you."

Tarzan asked where they were last seen, and Mitry told him, "Almost every evening since the hunting party left, they had been spending the evening at La's bathing area."

"Mitry, I have some ideas and want to do some scouting on my own. I need to warn you; I believe Cadj is behind this abduction, and he and Oah will be arriving here to try to take over Opar. Why La did not kill them years ago, is beyond me. I am afraid she has paid the price for this omission. Gather the troops that you know are loyal to you and be ready for Cadj.

Tarzan ran to the oasis, looking for clues. He scampered up the wall behind the trees and discovered a left-behind rope and many climbing spikes driven into the rocks. It did not take him long to figure how the kidnapping had taken place. The answer to who had taken La sent a long stone-cold chill down Tarzan's spine; slavers, who would be headed east along routes established hundreds of years ago.

Tarzan went back to Mitry, told him what he had found, and informed him he had traitors in the sentries. He again warned him to take great care since Opar was surely infiltrated with turncoats. He told Mitry to send half his Waziri warriors after him; he would leave a trail for them to follow.

Tarzan wished him good luck and left immediately to follow the now long cold trail of La.

After their week of captivity La, May-at and Kiya were exhausted. Each morning they had begun their journey an hour after the Flaming God appeared and marched at a good pace until late afternoon. Each night after a meager dinner La or one of the other girls had to fight off the unwanted advances of Abdul. None of the women was interested in Abdul's promises of more food or better treatment.

The forced march was taking its toll on all of the prisoners. La had lost over ten pounds, as had her companions. Their ankles and necks were chaffed and irritated to the point of bleeding from the leather or metal restraints they were forced to suffer. Their feet, even though they were used to walking barefoot most of the time, were cut, scraped and extremely raw from the rough terrain. The pain of the first hour of marching was excruciating until the onset of blessed numbness.

After five more endless days of marching, La lay exhausted on the ground of the filthy tent. She had been suffering from despair, and tonight it came out. "Oh, Tarzan are you still alive? Why have you not come for me? Perhaps you do not even like me enough to try to rescue me. I am terrified of what lies ahead of me. I will not live the life the filthy slaver, and Cadj have threatened me with. I will kill myself first, and I will do it before we reach the great water."

May-at was desperately trying to sleep, but she was fighting her own demons. She heard La mumbling and was able to understand some words. She knew what La was questioning. May-at began to sob silently, "La has Tarzan, but there is no one to come and rescue me." May-at cried quietly while La's sobs grew louder. Exhausted, they finally fell asleep.

By his calculations, Tarzan believed the slavers had a long head start on him. He also knew that he only had seven or eight days to overcome the deficit and catch up with La's kidnappers. He had little hope of having his Waziri catch up with him for a potential battle with the slavers. He needed another idea for help. Tarzan thought about trying to find a tribe of Mangani this far east. He decided it was worth a half a day, and began circling the heavy forest he was now traveling. His luck was holding; he began to see signs of feeding and nesting by the great apes. Tarzan was watching the ground for signs of an amphitheater used for the celebration known as the Dum Dum. When he looked up, he was staring at a large Mangani, who was six feet away and had heard him coming.

The ape-man greeted him by saying, "I am Tarzan, mighty hunter from the tribe who live where the sun disappears. I was raised by the Mangani who live there." He signaled to the far west. "What is my brother's name?"

The deep voice of the Mangani responded, "I am not your brother. Why are you searching for my tribe?"

"I am your brother, do I not speak the language of the Mangani? I am seeking assistance from the most powerful people on earth. Men have stolen my woman, and I need the assistance of several males in getting her back."

"Why should I help you, if you are so stupid as to lose your woman?"

"She was taken while I was away hunting. If you and your fighters are so afraid of the hairless men, then I will leave you in peace."

The huge male bristled with anger and defensively answered, "We are not afraid. What will you give us in return for our help?"

"I can bring you, after you help, the most tender meat, from the animals that you are too slow and clumsy to catch."

The Mangani did not like the word clumsy and snarled again at Tarzan. The ape-man held his ground, and four more great apes materialized from the shadows.

The first Mangani said, "My name is Tubok, mighty hunter and, this is my tribe. We will help you, for a few risings of the sun. You will owe us the meat whether we find your woman or not."

The ape-man agreed. The six great creatures began a rapid pursuit following the trail that was becoming fresher with every hour traveled. It had been eight days since La was kidnapped, and only a few more days until the rapidly moving caravan reached the coast of the Red Sea and the waiting boats.

The next day led to open savannah with almost no trees. The six wild creatures ran quickly through the waist-high grass. The ape-man found evidence of a camp. He believed it to be one or two nights old, he hoped. By the ape-man's thinking, they were getting close to the Red Sea.

The following two days found Tarzan back in an area of heavy forest. The pace of the pursuit quickened, and Tarzan believed they had gained a bit of ground. The recent travel had been mostly on foot, and the pace was too slow for him. He believed he covered about fifty miles in the last two days.

As the early morning mist lifted Tarzan, standing high in the treetops, could make out the Red Sea and a ramshackle village sitting close to the water. He observed a harbor with many empty boats. There were also pens used to hold slaves. By the looks of the pen's sizes, they would easily hold a thousand prisoners. By the time the captives had been marched to this point, from as far away as central Africa, at least a third of them had already died. Many committed suicide by eating mud at the filthy water holes where they were allowed to drink. What Tarzan was looking at was the slave city of Tadjourah in French Somaliland. This crude town and harbor were one of the two most popular slave routes and the shortest trip to the port of Aden on the Arabian peninsula.

The ape-man knew time had run out. Today had to be the rescue day. The Mangani were beginning to lose interest. He had to keep reminding them of their reward. Tarzan knew if the slavers holding La reached the town and the women were placed in boats, they would be beyond any hope of rescue.

In late afternoon the ape-man found the slow-moving caravan from high in the trees. They were getting a camp ready for their last night of heavy travel. He whispered to Tubok, "These are the men who stole my she. Have the Mangani rest and we will attack tonight."

Throughout the early evening, the ape-man watched the activity in the camp. The slavers were also tired from the long trek. Tarzan watched as the Arabs brought the three women, now shackled in irons, into a small tent in the center of the encampment. The Arabs and cannibals made a very simple resting place. They knew they were close to being at their destination if they could endure hardship for one more night. They busied themselves with a cold meal of smoked meat and vegetables. No fires were allowed. Their muskets were stacked in triangles in open areas close to the sleeping areas.

Tubok appeared behind Tarzan soundlessly and asked, "When do we attack these white men?"

"We will wait until they have been sleeping for a while. Tubok, tell our brothers to be wary of those sticks standing there and there," Tarzan pointed to the stacked guns. "Those sticks can kill at a great distance. Have our brothers get those first before the men can get to them. Kill all the men, and be careful not to harm the shes."

"Have the Mangani silently surround the camp and wait for my signal to attack." Time passed as the jungle lord watched the Mangani slowly descend the trees and surround the camp. He watched with great interest as Abdul rose from his blanket and moved toward the women's tent. Tarzan watched as the Arab opened the flap and entered. A moment later he heard a female voice shouting and watched Abdul exit, pushing aside the tent flap. Turning back he shouted, "Last chance to gain my favor; tomorrow I will be rid of you."

The ape-man's anger rose, and he lifted his bow and carefully delivered an arrow. The arrow's path was true, and he watched the unbelief that appeared in the Arab's eyes as the arrow sank deep into his chest. In seconds the body fell face down back into the tent.

From within the tent, La looked down at the Arab body. She saw the arrow, dripping blood, pointing up. She watched in fascination as a drop of blood slowly fell off the protruding arrowhead. To her amazement, she saw the arrow point was gold. She knew. She gasped, her eyes flew open wide, and she screamed as loud as she was able, "TARZAN !"

The ape-man shouted back in Waziri, "Get down!" Then he gave the signal to attack. The Mangani struck with a pent-up fury that had built in them from the long chase. The fight was over in less than a minute. Six of the cannibals had been brained by Mangani with clubs, four dead from arrows from his bow, and the remaining Arabs killed by their muskets beating them to death. The cannibal leader Maaka had taken an arrow in his side but managed to escape into the heavy underbrush.

Tarzan dropped quickly to the ground and ran to the tent. He pulled the tent flap open and saw three women laying on their stomachs. "You may get up now," Tarzan said. One look at the faces that turned up to him said they were too exhausted to rise. Tarzan helped May-at, then Kiya and finally La to their feet. All were crying hysterically and grabbed onto Tarzan, clinging tightly to him. It had been a brutal ordeal.

La pulled her head back and looked Tarzan in the face saying, "I feared you were dead, or worse, did not want to rescue me." The release of her fears triggered another spasm of hysterical tears. It took more than an hour for the women to release Tarzan, then hobble to view the carnage outside the tents. Tarzan had warned them about the presence of the Mangani, but they were still shocked by the huge, fierce beasts. May-at, upon viewing the dead bodies said, "These were bad men, and I am not sorry they are all dead." There was no disagreement from anyone.

The ape-man said they should move inland as quickly as possible. He convinced May-at and Kiya to be placed on two of the Mangani's backs. Tarzan put La on his back, and they took to the trees and quickly moved west. The weakened women could barely hold on to their transport. Tarzan called a halt so they could rest. He found places where the branches were tight enough for the women to lie down. He asked, " Tubok, will you ask two of our brothers to guard the women, while the rest of us hunt?"

Tubok answered, "Yes, this is good. We have not eaten in days. Find us meat!"

Within a short distance the ape-man was able to find antelope which he dispatched with arrows, and two small bushbabies soon after. This amount of meat would be a good meal for everyone. Tarzan cut the loin from one of the antelope, ate a generous portion raw, and saved the rest to be roasted for the women. As the women slept, Tarzan gathered fresh fruit and roasted some vegetables. The Mangani, like Tarzan, preferred their meat raw, and within a short period had eaten all the antelope meat. The Mangani, except for Tubok, stuffed with the meat, sought a soft pile of grass and went to sleep.

Tubok spoke to the ape-man, "The Mangani will be leaving you in the morning. We want to get back to our shes and balus. Tarzan, you are a good leader and a fierce warrior. I am glad you found us. You and your women are welcome to travel with our tribe."

Tarzan smiled and nodded to Tubok and said, "The tribe of Tubok are great warriors, and you are a wise leader. As Tarzan and his women travel back, we will search for you. I still need to hunt for more meat for you."

It was late afternoon as Tarzan brought the women to the ground and tried to feed them roasted meat and vegetables. The women were very quiet and were able to eat only a few bites of food; Tarzan made sure they drank water. All the women wanted to go back to sleep. Tarzan reclined on a branch six feet above the women and slept his usual light sleep. He was grateful the rescue had gone well, and none of his friends were injured.

Chapter Forty-Seven — La's Revenge

Three days later the women felt more like themselves. Appetites had returned, and they were able to walk short distances. Tarzan had fashioned boots from antelope hide he had cured. They contained several layers of the soft leather and would make walking more comfortable.

The third evening after their rescue Tarzan and La sat around the evening cook fire, that was slowly burning down. "We should start back to Opar, Tarzan," La stated.

"As soon as you and May-at and Kiya are up to it, we will walk a few miles a day, gradually building up the distance. It is going to take us three weeks at a slow pace." Tarzan knew that the longer Cadj and Oah became entrenched in Opar, the harder it would be to deal with them

La replied, "We need to be back quicker than our current pace. I fear what Cadj and Oah are doing in Opar. We need to deal with them as soon as possible.

"I agree," Tarzan replied. "We'll start two days from now."

The next morning Tarzan received a pleasant surprise. His group of Waziri bodyguards from the hunt arrived an hour after sunrise. Tarzan greeted them warmly and offered to bring fresh meat for them. They gladly accepted, and Msizi was glad to be reunited with May-at.

While the Waziri were grilling the antelope steaks, Msizi said, "Nkosi, we have not eaten in several days. We stopped for only a few hours each night and took no time for hunting. We only ate the fruit or vegetables we found along the way. We followed your trail as best we could. It is hard to track you when you are in the trees," he said smiling.

Tarzan took Msizi aside and asked what had happened when the Waziri and the hunters got back to Opar. "We were met at the entrance by Mitry he was very upset. He had come back early from the search for the women, to be present when we got back. He said the soldiers were still searching, but he did not have faith in finding anyone. He did not seem aware of the slave routes. Since Cadj and Oah had not yet returned, he thought it safe to send us to find you, Nkosi and hopefully, the women."

After carefully listening, Tarzan answered, "Mitry is an excellent and loyal leader, and I believe his decision was a good one. You men will make our return to Opar much easier and faster."

"My brothers you have done well," Tarzan praised with a great smile. "We will rest today and tomorrow, the following day we start back. The only thing I want you to do is to make litters to carry the women. We can get to Opar much quicker if the women do not slow us down. I am sure there will be a fight when we get back."

"Our spears and knives are hungry for a good fight," was the answer.

Cadj and Oah entered Opar with four cannibal warriors. They believed Tarzan was dead and La was on her way to being the plaything of some Arab potentate. The pair thought the only threat to them was from Mitry, and they had plans for him. Mitry and most of the troops loyal to La were searching eastward. They did not appear to have a clear plan.

They knew if La and Tarzan and his Waziris were alive, they would be somewhere in this direction. And far away.

Cadj and Oah were joined by the male priests loyal to them. They summoned everyone in Opar to meet in the altar room. Here Cadj announced that La was dead, and he was taking over the position of High Priest, and Oah was to be his High Priestess.

Cadj announced, "There will be an offering to celebrate our ascendancy to the throne. My High Priestess, Oah, will be performing the ritual. With Mitry's troops out on some fool's errand, I will be assuming his duties as head of the military. He is relieved of any further duty." Cadj promised conditions for the military would be better, and he asked them to swear their fealty to him, which they did, with great reservation.

Meanwhile, their war chief was leading the Waziri at a rapid pace back to Opar. Six of the warriors were carrying makeshift litters, where the exhausted women rested while being carried.

By the end of the second day, Tarzan had his plan for getting back into Opar or at least finding out what was happening. That night Tarzan asked La to give him some quick language lessons in Oparian. He would need to be able to speak with common guards and sentinels, in their native language. Mitry was the only non-royal person that understood the Waziri language of the rulers of Opar.

After five days of being carried, the women told Tarzan they were ready to march again. The pace naturally slowed, but gradually the women were able to walk more and at a greater speed.

Several days later they came within view of the great wall of Opar. Tarzan told the Waziri to hide everyone in a cluster of trees and to guard the women, while he went to the city to observe what was happening.

Tarzan waited until after midnight and stealthily approached the end of the city wall, where La's bathing area was located. As the acrobat had done, he climbed the wall and looked over the walkway that ran the length of the wall. Tarzan spied a sentry sitting and snoozing twenty feet away. He silently approached the man from behind and quickly encircled the sentry's neck with his mighty left arm, hissing into the man's ear, "If you want to live to see the sunrise, do not make a sound." The man nodded his head quickly and turned to face Tarzan, "Thank the Flaming God you are here, Cadj has taken over Opar." Tarzan told the man, "Follow me. We are going out of the city; we want to hear what has been going on since La has been gone."

"La is alive?"

"Very much alive, as you will see." The two men, under a brilliant African moon, reached the temporary camp in a short time.

The sentry was in awe of being in the presence of the High Priestess. Tarzan saw this and told La, "No matter what he tells you, show no emotion. He will think you are upset with him, and stop talking. We need all the details he can give us." La nodded her acceptance after a moment's thought.

La sat across from the sentinel and asked him, "When did Cadj and Oah return to Opar?"

"Just a few days ago."

"Was he accepted by all the male priests?"

"No." was the answer.

"How about my handmaidens and priestesses?"

The guard thought a bit, "I am not sure. I have not seen any females following him around the city."

That is a good sign La thought to herself.

"Tell me what he said at his meetings." La smiled at the man, and said, "Do not be afraid of me, no harm will come to you. I need details unless you do not want me to regain rule of Opar."

The man's eyes went wide, and he said, "Oh no, Mistress. All the people want you back. Cadj is a bad man and a liar. Everyone is fearful of him."

La continued the questioning for another two hours. The subject of Cadj's plans came up again, and this time the guard remembered some important details. "Mistress, Cadj said there would be a sacrifice to celebrate his return to Opar. He wants to thank the Flaming God."

261

"When is this sacrifice?"

"Tomorrow as the Flaming God travels over the mountains behind Opar."

"Do we know who the sacrifice is to be?" asked La.

"Oh yes, I almost forgot. It will be Mitry. That is too bad; he is a good man."

La gasped and turned toward Tarzan, and with pleading eyes said, "We must save Mitry." La looked back to the sentinel, telling him to go to get something to eat and rest. "We will need your services tomorrow." She turned to Tarzan and said, "Now, I will tell you all this man told me."

La and Tarzan sat alone across the fire which was dying slowly. Tarzan saw that La had deep feelings and respect for Mitry. He hoped he would be able to save him tomorrow.

La and Tarzan sat talking and planning for many hours after the fire finally died. By the first hint of dawn, they had agreed on a plan. But only after hours of disagreement. Tarzan had made his position clear, kill Cadj and Oah immediately and the problem would be solved. La was so adamant in what she wanted that she told Tarzan with or without his help she needed to mete out final judgment and punishment to the two usurpers. La wanted the satisfaction of watching them suffer and die by her hand, not a quick knife or arrow from Tarzan.

After a brief period of rest, Tarzan gathered his Waziri and told them his plan.

He, along with two Waziri warriors, armed with bows and assegai short jabbing spears, would scale the mountain in the afternoon, beginning the ascent from behind the mountain where they would scale the foothill rocks. This path would be out of sight of the temple where Cadj would doubtless have sentries posted. They would not become visible to the guards until they climbed to the top and began their descent to the mountain front. This position would put Tarzan and his two companions in danger of being discovered.

The plan was for Tarzan and the two warriors to eliminate any cannibal guards, clearing their path into the city—regardless of where they were located. This task would be the most difficult, Tarzan knew.

He would have his four best Waziri bowmen climb the great city wall and lay on their stomachs, remaining hidden from eyes about the temple and ground. The sentry would be taken with them in case they needed someone to speak for them. The other Waziri were ordered to guard the women with their lives. Upon a pre-arranged signal, if all went well, they were to bring La, her sister Kiya and May-at for a triumphant return to Opar.

About two hours before sunset, Tarzan and his companions began their ascent of the mountain. They quickly reached the summit, and Tarzan looked down into the city and saw a surprisingly small number of people moving about. He could see fires burning inside the temple, with the flickering light reflecting off walls and making strange patterns seen through the dome opening.

Tarzan saw below him a single sentry on the mountain. His mistake was he was watching the wrong way, into the city. Tarzan silently began to move to the man, his father's hunting knife in hand. Tarzan planted his left foot, and as he shifted his weight to it, the rock suddenly gave way, causing him to fall, and he began sliding toward the patrol on his back. The cannibal raised his spear to impale Tarzan but as he was pulling his arm back for the strike into Tarzan's unprotected chest, an arrow flew over Tarzan's body and struck the cannibal between his eyes, killing him instantly.

Tarzan scrambled to his feet and grabbed the dead man, preventing him from falling into the temple grounds. He secured him behind a shrub and looked back at his companions. It was easy to see who had saved his life. The smile on the Waziri's face was a mile wide. Tarzan nodded to the warrior and turned back to the task at hand.

He fastened his rope on a stunted tree that he judged would hold his weight and was satisfied when he gave it a hard pull. Tarzan quickly rappelled the fifty feet to the ground behind the temple. He signaled to one of the bowmen, the rescuer M'titi, to follow him. The other Waziri untied the rope and let it fall to the ground. Tarzan grabbed an end of the line and scampered up the almost smooth wall of the temple. He then signaled M'titi to climb up.

On their hands and knees, to avoid being seen by the sentries, the two men scampered to the raised round dome. The opening on the dome was about ten feet across. Tarzan raised up and peered into the sacrifice area below him. The ceremony was just beginning. The invited were still finishing the drink prepared by the daughters of Soma. Neither Oah or Cadj were in the immediate area. As one of the female priestesses began the opening prayer to the Flaming God, the sacrifice, Mitry, was carried into the room and trussed to the altar. The Neteru began their part in the ceremony by rushing in, pretending to capture the prisoner. The priestess, with a golden club, drove them back. The sacrifice would be made by Oah the High Priestess.

The second prayer was begun by a priest. As this long chant was being spoken by the priest and the people Cadj and Oah began their slow, dignified entrance into the altar area. Tarzan saw Mitry watch the two enter and turn his face away from them. Tarzan adjusted his position to align with where Oah would be standing, and he signaled M'titi to join him at the opening, but to his right.

As he saw the pair were slowing their entrance, he signaled M'titi to fire an arrow over the wall, which would signal the rest of the Waziri on the wall the rescue was beginning. Tarzan changed his position to a crouch; he looked at M'titi and signaled 'me first' then 'you.' M'titi assumed a similar crouch and nocked an arrow to his bow.

Oah had stretched herself high on her toes, with her hands upraised, the sacrificial knife in her right hand, eyes closed, her head back to accept the final rays of the sun. She was ready to begin taking the last few steps to Mitry. As she was looking up, her eyes opened, and she saw the figure in the dome opening. She barely had time to recognize the danger when a gold-tipped arrow pierced her thigh. The arrow stuck the femur, changed course, and began to exit the back of her leg. She was thrown down by the arrow's force, crumpled in agony, screaming loudly.

Cadj saw Oah fall and looked up in time to see M'titi send a shaft, tipped with a razor-sharp gold arrowhead. The bolt struck him in the left leg, with almost the identical result that Tarzan had inflicted on Oah. He went down in a heap next to her. Both the usurpers were bleeding profusely, emitting high-pitched wails of pain. Neither was able to regain their footing.

By this time Tarzan had nocked another arrow and sent it into the heart of one of the cannibal guests of Cadj. A moment later, M'titi sent another messenger of death into the heart of a second cannibal. The four arrows had taken fifteen seconds to dispatch because the crowd was moving as the targets were hit.

The drug-satiated crowd at first did nothing, but by the time Cadj fell to the floor, they had begun to rush the exit, screaming in fear. By this time the Waziri had come down the stairs from the wall and were waiting on either side of the temple exit. They paused until the two remaining cannibals were outside and then they attacked. The cannibals were as surprised as everyone else in the temple. They appeared to be in shock and were easy targets for the assegai short spears which entered their chests bringing a quick death.

Within minutes the temple was empty, except for Mitry who was still bound to the altar. The Waziri were under orders not to kill any of the attendees of the ceremony.

Tarzan nodded to M'titi to send the messenger arrow, with a white ribbon attached. It would fall short of La's hiding place, but the Waziri would understand the meaning and inform her. The Waziri lead guard ran into La's presence, where she sat with a very nervous and unsure look on her face. "Mistress, Tarzan has sent the signal it is time for you to enter your city."

La covered her face with her hands and wept with joy. She had not believed the operation would go this smoothly and quickly. With her Waziri bodyguards surrounding her, she walked the quarter mile to the city gate. Two Waziri entered before her and looked for trouble. M'titi greeted them, with a great grin on his face. He teased, "Where have you been? You missed what little fight there was." The other Waziri enjoyed the joke and began laughing with him.

As soon as La entered the city, she was transformed into the steely-eyed ruler of Opar. She grabbed one of the minor priests who was milling about aimlessly dragging him into the annular sacrifice chamber. She picked up the sacrificial knife and moved to Mitry, cutting the ropes restraining him to the altar.

La turned when her task was complete and viewed the writhing traitors lying in pools of blood. She grabbed the hapless priest and screamed at him, "Bind up those wounds, you fool, before these two traitors bleed to death."

"I have no cloth, Highness."

La answered with a hissing tone, "Use your priestly garment. You will not need it again." The man scrambled to do her bidding.

By this time Tarzan and M'titi had descended from the temple roof and joined La and Mitry. Mitry did not seem much worse for his experience. He was delighted to see Tarzan and La and made his feeling known by his enthusiasm. Two of his soldiers appeared and assisted Mitry into the reception hall, still recovering from the nectar. La called for her handmaidens, and after a tearful reunion, they were asked to bring chairs, and she ascended her throne.

She told the soldiers to bring in Oah and Cadj. The pair could not stand so they were forced to lie in agony in front of La. La made eye-contact with both of them, and leaned forward with a scowl that froze them speechless.

Retaining his control, Cadj gasped, "We thought you dead, how did you escape the Arabs?"

"Do not concern yourself with that," La replied. "I made a mistake by trusting your words, not once but twice. I will not make that mistake again. The punishment for both of you with be from the tools of treachery you left behind on the wall behind my private area. Since you both saw fit to kidnap me that way, with ropes attached to metal spikes driven into the stones, I will return the favor. You are both to be hung from your spikes until you are dead. We will properly bind up your legs so you may enjoy a leisurely death. You two will serve as examples of how I will deal with anyone who dares to challenge my authority. Carry out my wishes for these two treacherous dogs immediately."

"Cadj, I told you when you entered my slave tent a few weeks ago, I would not die, but I would watch you suffer a slow death by my hand. So it shall be."

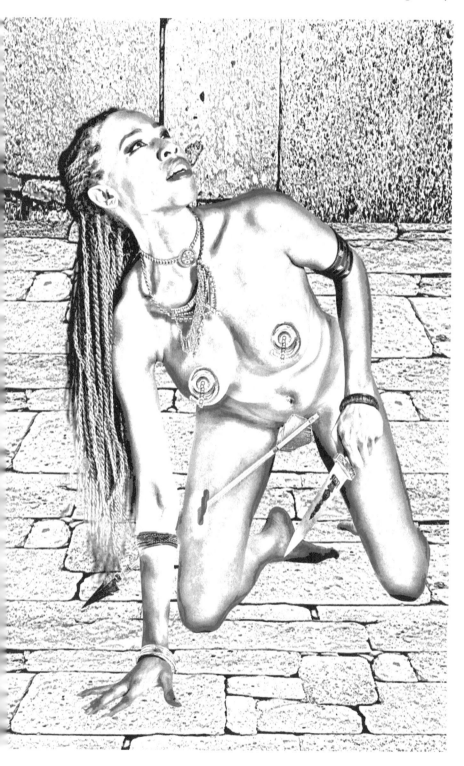

CHAPTER FORTY-EIGHT — THE PREPARATIONS

The three Daughters of Soma were on their semi-annual forage to find herbs to replenish their stock. Many of their medicines would lose their efficacy after being stored for a long period. Through the countless generations since the founding of Opar, the Daughters of Soma had perfected their healing crafts to an extremely high level. They had remedies for most of the common ailments of the day.

They had been foraging for several weeks and were now within a three-day march of Opar. They had been combing the forests for two months, and the results had been well worth the time. The two Neteru guards they had with them were carrying thirty pounds of their discoveries.

Late in the afternoon, the group came upon the body of a leopard that had been recently killed. The female had obviously been in a fight with another animal and had taken the worst of it. One of the women noticed the cat had recently given birth and was probably desperately trying to get home to her offspring.

The women decided they would try to locate the litter, which was probably in close proximity. They would give a couple of hours to the task before resuming their travels back home.

There in the bole of a rotting tree was a leopard kitten. It was about ten pounds and appeared to be almost three months old. She was just beginning to shed her gray coat, and the typical spotted coat would soon appear. The leopard had no fear of the women and allowed itself to be picked-up with only a small amount of hissing and scratching. A few bites of the offered meat from last night's dinner were rapidly eaten by the kitten. The women took turns carrying the cub until they reached the city.

One of the Daughters was an acquaintance of La's younger sister Kiya and decided she would show her the find. She sat in the reception area, with the fidgety cub on her lap, and waited until Kiya returned.

When Kiya appeared, her heart melted when she spied the leopard kitten. She squealed with delight, and asked, "Can I hold it? Where did you ever find this little beauty." An hour of play with the tiny cat passed quickly, and Kiya cautiously asked, "I love her, what would you take for me to purchase her?"

The Daughter thought for a moment and answered, "The yellow metal necklace you wore the last time we saw each other."

Kiya was not sure which it was and called for her handmaiden. She instructed her to bring the jewelry box immediately. The woman scurried away quickly and returned. Kiya offered the box to the daughter and said, "Take your pick, any one of them."

The woman reluctantly handed Kiya the cub, and asked, "I have gotten so attached to this baby, may I visit her? I want very much to continue seeing her."

Kiya answered absently; her full attention was now on the squirming kitten on her lap, "Oh yes, whenever you wish. I may need some advice as she grows a bit larger."

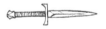

Maaka ran for a short distance after he escaped from the massacre in the slave camp. The apes and the white man had ruined the opportunity for him to get a large amount of gold from the Arabs. The three women had represented a great deal of money. They would have increased his importance in the eyes of the Manyuema's partners. He noticed the arrow wound was bleeding profusely, and he knew he had to stop the flow soon.

He made the decision, feeling he was far enough from the camp, that the white man would not come after him since he now had nothing of value.

Maaka found a place where he thought it was relatively safe to lie down for a few hours rest. The pain in his side was getting worse as was the flow of blood. He knew he had to stop the bleeding or he would die. There was only one solution; he had to remove the arrow and pack some moss into the wound.

Fortunately, Tarzan's arrow had missed his kidney and the arteries. He had to remove the arrow himself. The sole choice was to break the shaft, remove the arrowhead and pull the shaft out – the way it went in. Pulling it the other way risked more damage from the feather fletching. When he broke the shaft and arrowhead, his head began to swim, and he lost consciousness for a few moments. Removing the arrow was now complicated by the fact that the pull area was located behind him and covered with blood, making gripping the arrow difficult.

Maaka dried his hand from blood as best he could, reached behind and pulled the arrow out on the third attempt. He screamed with pain and mercifully lost consciousness again for several minutes.

Two days later, Maaka had succeeded in stopping the flow of blood and felt he might be able to begin traveling, slowly and for short periods of time. He was fifteen miles from where he and his men had left their women and children in a temporary camp. His only hope was that the few old warriors he had left there in charge had not decided to move the camp to where he could not find it. In his condition, he knew he could not last on his own for very long.

The gods of Maaka must have been watching out for him. He was spotted by a Manyuema warrior who was a member of the search party that was looking for him and the other kidnappers. The leaders he left in charge had become worried and began to send out searchers.

M'Keeta was a man of about forty. He, like most of the men in camp, was considered to be too old to be included in war parties. However, he was an experienced warrior and was a good man to guard the women and children. M'Keeta's eyes were very sharp for a man of his age, and he spotted slow movement in the waist-high grass coming toward him, a great distance away. He concealed himself, readied his bow, and waited. He was delighted to see his chief stumbling, badly wounded, toward him. If he could get Maaka back to the village alive, his rewards would be great.

As Maaka saw one of his warriors walking toward him, he greeted M'Keeta warmly and was grateful to have been found. M'Keeta gave him water and some berries he had been saving for his dinner. M'Keeta decided to make a small camp and allow his chief to rest until morning, then start out for the village.

On his way back to his farm, Tarzan's thoughts went to preparing the Waziri to aid in the next defense of Opar. He knew that if world affairs did not improve in the next several years, they could be facing German soldiers again, in this part of Africa. The ten bodyguards he had left in Opar would be no match for a large force of Manyuema warriors or a German military squad of any size.

Tarzan planned to have his troops trained and armed and back to Opar as soon as possible. His thoughts were that they would defend Opar against an all-out assault by the cannibals. He hoped there would be enough time.

Tarzan had a confidential discussion with Msizi before he left Opar. Msizi was to ensure the safety of La, Kiya and May-at. In case of an all-out attack on Opar, they must use the shelter deep underground where La and her companions would be safe. As a backup warning plan, several runners could make the long trip from Opar to the Waziri village. He emphasized to Msizi that, if necessary, he would need to — carefully — go directly against La's wishes to accomplish these tasks. Tarzan emphasized that La did not truly believe the dangers that Opar was facing. "The Manyuema are not going to take the loss of the four men brought to Opar by Cadj. The other men were killed during the rescue of La at the slaver's camp. This was a large loss of men—the cannibals will demand revenge.

If I am not mistaken, a warrior who I wounded with an arrow, escaped from the slavers' last camp. He may have died, or he may have made it back to the cannibal village with quite a story."

"Msizi, just to make this clear," Tarzan said, "you and the other Waziri are not expendable. You are as important to me as are the three women. You have my authority to do anything in your power to save everyone here in Opar. Do not sacrifice yourself or any of your squad."

The leopard cub had become civilized under Kiya's care. She was comfortable living in the temple apartment with her mistress. The other handmaidens, however, were terrified of her, and none would dare come into Kiya's apartment. Her snarling and spitting, although still juvenile, was conveying a message.

Due to her superior diet which Kiya hand fed her, the cub was growing rapidly, and within several months she weighed sixty pounds. She was twenty inches high at the shoulder, tall for her age. She was going to be a large and powerful animal. She was losing more of her woolly tan coat, and the promise of the traditional pattern of spots was already on display.

One of the speech patterns that had come down from the dark past was the use of onomatopoeia in the Egyptian Language. Kiya had named her baby leopard Miu which meant cat or kitten and was a play on the sounds the young leopard made.

The only attempt Kiya made to civilize Miu was by having one of the leather workers make a collar and leash. The fact that she found the young leatherworker attractive was a secondary benefit.

The next to last meeting was with the trainer of the messenger monkeys and Soma. Tarzan had wondered how the monkeys knew where to go when they were sent out to find the recipient of their message. Tarzan and the other two Oparians sat down, with May-at doing the translating.

Tarzan began what he hoped would be a short meeting, "Will you share with me how the monkeys will know where to find me?"

The trainer chuckled and replied, "So simple. The monkeys have the best sense of smell of animal we know of." He produced a small packet about the size of an orange and handed it to Tarzan. "The monkey can smell this for nearly twenty miles. If he loses the scent because the wind is blowing the wrong way, he is trained to travel back and forth until he picks up the scent again."

Tarzan was impressed, and asked, "How does the monkey know when he has reached his destination?"

"By hanging two of the scent packages about ten feet apart in the trees he will begin to shriek a distinctive call until someone comes for him. That person must be carrying a scent bag."

Tarzan had wondered on his trip with the hunters, how the monkeys could find them so quickly. He had seen their trainers reaching up in the trees, but did not realize what they were doing.

The trainer brought Tarzan's attention back into the conversation by saying, "I have prepared for you thirty-five of the scent packages. I understand your home is many days march from here."

Tarzan did some quick math and knew this would be enough scent packets.

On his way out of the meeting, Tarzan stopped into La's apartment to bid her goodbye. "La, I am going to my home, and will not be back for several moons, probably six or eight. I will return with many men who will have weapons that are more superior to any owned by the Manyuema. Try to hold the peace until I can get back. You do not have the manpower to confront the cannibals. Remember to hide in the lowest tunnel, the one with the man trap that falls into the underground river, in case you are attacked."

After World War I, the English kept a military presence in British East Africa. The British government wanted to protect their interests, and the British citizens who owned farms. Plus there was the fear of invasion from the growing number of German troops and the threat of Italian forces invading from Italian East Africa.

Tarzan diverted his path and headed for the British army base to see his friend Captain Chard. He had been Lieutenant Albert Chard when Tarzan first met him in the early days of a return to peace at the end of World War I. When Tarzan entered Chard's office, he was not immediately recognized. But after a few seconds, Chard remembered who he was and greeted him warmly.

"Sorry, I did not recognize you. It has been several years since we last talked. To what do I owe the privilege of a visit from a member of the House of Lords?" Chard asked with a smile.

"Since you are the closest telegraph station, would you please send a telegram for me? I also need to talk to you about another matter."

"Of course, my Lord."

"Not my Lord," Lord Greystoke replied with a smile, "just Tarzan. That is who I am in this part of the world."

Chard asked Lord Greystoke if he would like refreshments, which Tarzan accepted. He wrote his message and handed it to Captain Chard.

"You may read it if you like."

Chard read the short message addressed to Lord Greystoke's estate manager in England: Purchase 100 Winchester (latest model) five shot pump ten-gauge shotguns. Purchase 100 Winchester Model 94 lever action 30-30 rifles. Purchase five thousand shells and cartridges. Purchase all appropriate cleaning kits and lubricants. Advise expected arrival time in the Port of Mombasa. Rush the order.

Chard face somewhat dropped, and he looked at Tarzan and asked, "Are you expecting some trouble I am not aware of?"

Lord Greystoke smiled and said, "The trouble will be in the east, in an area of Ethiopia. This situation is not a concern for you or the garrison. Please send a runner to the farm with details of my order."

Chard nodded acceptance as he handed the message to his wireless operator. "Anything else?"

"As a matter of fact, yes," Lord Greystoke replied, "I need a man who can instruct my Waziri to be a disciplined English fighting unit. He will need to turn men who have never handled modern weapons into experts.

He will have a month to do this training. He may have to travel with us to advise on tactics, once he sees the fighting terrain."

The Captain smiled and responded, "I may have just the man for you. Would you like to meet him?"

"He is temporarily residing in the camp lockup. It seems he got into an altercation with several of the local stevedores in a saloon last week. He is currently sitting in the detention barracks for a couple of days. I hope he has sobered up by now."

"Is he reliable? I don't want someone who is a drinker."

"He is one of my best men. On their weekend leave, the men get rid of a lot of steam. It seems he got into a disagreement with several of the locals, and the fight was on. He is a large man, and he cracked a couple of heads before the local law enforcement arrested him, and turned him over to us. We had no choice but to give him some punishment, after all, he did break up a good bit of the saloon." Chard's smile told Tarzan that he was somewhat amused by the soldier's antics.

"Yes, I would be interested in meeting him, since it appears I am going to be here for a while. I will take you up on the offer of tea."

As Lord Greystoke and Captain Chard were finishing their tea, they heard a knock, and a very large man filled the door frame. "Come in please." The man advanced and stood at attention to his superior officer.

"Lord Greystoke, let me introduce Sergeant Major Robert Hopkins. At ease, Sergeant." Chard motioned to Tarzan, "Lord Greystoke needs a military advisor and a man who can whip native troops into a fighting unit. Do you know anyone who would be able to do that?"

Lord Greystoke looked at the Sergeant Major and saw a man four inches over six feet, slightly overweight at about two hundred fifty pounds. His somewhat disheveled hair was beginning to be streaked with gray, and his mutton chop sideburns were almost completely gray. He had the air of someone who was used to being in charge. He looked straight at the Captain and to Tarzan without looking away or dropping his eyes.

Still standing somewhat in a military stance, he answered in a loud and booming voice, "Sir. Yes, I can do that."

"Lord Greystoke, would you like to speak with Hopkins here about your requirements? I have a few matters to attend to, and I will be back in about a half hour."

Lord Greystoke motioned for Hopkins to be seated across from him. "The information that Captain Chard has told you is about all that is known at this time. The training will take place in the Waziri village near my farm here in British East Africa. Captain Chard is familiar and can give you directions on how to find the village. The job could be for as short as a month or as long as several years. Are you familiar with Winchester rifles and shotguns? These are my weapons of choice."

Without thinking, Hopkins blurted out, "Are these the guns you use on your estate in England to kill pheasants and an occasional deer?"

"If you don't think these will work, I had better find someone else who has more faith in my decision. My feeling is that the current Winchester rifles are superior to what the British army is using. If there is close fighting, the shotguns with buckshot cannot be bettered."

"Sorry, my Lord. I did not mean for that to sound like I am sure it did to you. I am quite sure the weapons you have selected will be adequate. It will be good to have a job that is more than just hanging around the post with make-work projects. I am used to training young men and getting them prepared for battle. I am familiar with the latest military strategies, and I am confident I can produce an army you will be proud of."

"Sergeant Major, I will be talking with your Captain, when he returns, about having you join us. I believe the weapon shipment will take about three months to reach us here. You will probably join us one month before the weapons arrive so that you can meet the troops. There may even be some information that will make all this clearer – to both of us." With that Lord Greystoke stood signifying the meeting was concluded.

The Sergeant Major thanked Lord Greystoke for the information and said he was looking forward to seeing him soon.

CHAPTER FORTY-NINE — THE FIRST DOMINO

Maaka sat in front of his hut in the temporary village. It had been several months since his rescue. The first week he spent in a fever-ridden delirium. As he was thinking, Cyprian the witch-doctor sat down across from him and began, "How is my chief today?"

Maaka answered with a scowl, "No better than yesterday. Are you sure of the potions you are giving me?"

"Yes, they are correct and working. You are lucky to be alive. When M'Keeta brought you, you were more in the land of your ancestors than here."

Cyprian was an old and wizened witch-doctor. Maaka feared Cyprian as much as anyone in the village and remembered Cyprian had looked the same when he was a boy. No one in the village could remember Cyprian as being young. The women hated him the most, fearing the evil eye. They protected their children from his gaze. No one in the village even knew if Cyprian was a man or woman The name was not a Bantu name, and itself did a lot to enhance Cyprian's mystique.

"May I offer some advice? " Cyprian asked.

"I will always entertain your wise counsel," Maaka replied.

"The tribe and the gods do not understand why you have not heaped your vengeance upon the people of the cloud city. They are beginning to wonder if their chief is turning into a fat old woman afraid of her shadow. I have thrown the bones several times, and they say a raid will be successful."

Maaka scowled again but did not show his contempt for the witch-doctors words. Finally, he replied, "I have been planning a raid. When it is complete, we will march."

Father Martin received a telegram, containing bad news. His father had passed away. His mother had petitioned the bishop to allow Martin to visit her, and permission had been granted for a month's visit. Since Sister Mary Veronica had also died, Martin was also going to seek a replacement for her and perhaps have her return with him.

John Clayton walked up the steps from the Russell Square tube station. Upon reaching street level, he turned left and crossed through Russell Square and rapidly walked toward Great Russell Street, where he turned right and walked to the entrance to the British Museum. His appointment was at 9:00 AM with Sir Frederic Kenyon.

Sir Frederic was a paleographer and biblical scholar. He had been associated with the British Museum since 1889, and he had held his current position as museum director since 1909. He was a specialist in ancient manuscripts including Egyptian hieroglyphics and papyrus.

The young lady at reception took Lord Greystoke to Sir Frederic's office and seated him before a great and empty desk. Her offer of coffee or tea was declined.

Sir Frederic entered the office by a private door behind the desk. "Welcome Lord Greystoke. It is not often I find myself addressing a member of the House of Lords. How may I help you this morning?"

Sir Frederic was on his very best behavior. He wanted to have this meeting go well, as he would need a friend in the House of Lords because funding for this years operation had been cut. Sir Frederic would need assistance getting the museum through the year without detrimental cost cuts to staff and projects.

"Sir Frederic, this is somewhat of a long story. I hope you have time for me."

Sir Frederic smiled, "Always have time for a peer of the realm."

After a somewhat sanitized version of his trips to Opar, in which he conveniently forgot to say that Opar was still inhabited, Tarzan handed over a large manilla envelope.

Sir Frederic opened and removed several grainy eight by ten photographs. Lord Greystoke explained, "These photos are of tablets mounted on the walls. Perhaps you can make out enough to tell me what the symbols mean."

Sir Frederic picked up a large magnifying glass and began to scan the top image. Lord Greystoke watched as the man's jaw dropped and a look of intense interest came on his face.

"I need to get a reference book from my private library. Please excuse me."

After a short wait, Sir Frederic returned and placed a large well-used volume on the desk near the photos. He began a search of a section marked King's Names. Another look of astonishment and Sir Frederic Said, "Are you familiar with the throne name Neferkare? Of course not. Perhaps you have heard the name of an Old Kingdom pharaoh— Pepi II?"

Lord Greystoke shook his head to indicate he was not familiar with the pharaoh.

Sir Frederic in an animated voice said, "Pepi II ruled Egypt more than forty centuries ago. Think of that over four thousand years ago! Extraordinary. Lord Greystoke, are you sure these photos are genuine?"

Lord Greystoke smiled and replied, "Quite sure. I took them myself this year."

After several hours Lord Greystoke heard what he wanted to hear, and he stood to indicate the meeting was ending. He asked Sir Frederic the following, "Would the museum be interested in an expedition to this location? Everything we can carry out of the city will be donated, with some stipulations and exceptions."

"I demand total silence about this discovery, for reasons that will become evident as we go along. The relics for the exhibition will not be made public for one hundred years. Nothing can or will be exhibited. No one will ever know the location of this ruin."

"I will be back with you in a few months for your answer."

As he walked toward the door, Lord Greystoke turned and astonished Sir Frederic once more, "Oh yes, Sir Frederic, I will be personally financing all costs for this expedition, but I will need a preliminary budget."

Lord Greystoke put his upraised index finger across his lips and walked out of Sir Frederic's office. Fifteen minutes later, Lord Greystoke was heading down the steps of the Russell Square tube station.

Two weeks later Tarzan was on his way back to Africa. The shipment of guns was on its way and would arrive within weeks. He had cabled Captain Chard to have the Sergeant Major ready to begin training in the Waziri village. He also requested Captain Chard to find and obtain many flat barges that would carry the troops and their armaments East. The British Museum archaeological crew would be arriving soon and would also need to be transported to the city of Opar. Waterways would be used to get men, munitions and supplies close to Opar. Making overland transport much shorter.

La stood at the entrance of the female suite of rooms that were the bedrooms of La's handmaidens and her sister's apartment. She watched a very disheveled version of her sister, along with her leopard, Miu, walk toward her. The anger on La's face was evident and spewed out quickly, "Kiya, how dare you disobey a direct order from me?"

"Stop it please, La. I am an adult now, and you need to quit ordering me around. Besides I am with all these brave and handsome hunters. Do you think they will let anything happen to me?" Kiya said with a sincere smile on her face.

La's anger was slowly ebbing away, but she hated how Kiya could manipulate her. "Kiya, it is not okay. You are my only sister, and I love you. I would never forgive myself if anything happened to you."

"Besides, I have this ferocious leopard to protect me," said Kiya as she was walking away from La, and toward a bath.

Before he left Opar, Tarzan had instructed the men on some strategies, in case the Manyuema decided to attack. Those ideas became very useful when Maaka decided to send a squad of raiders to the cloud city.

It was a moonless night when twelve of Maaka's best troops walked up to the entrance into the temple area. They thought they had approached with no one seeing them, but they would find out differently.

Two Neteru warriors were positioned inside the wall and were waiting for the first Manyuema warrior to try to exit the maze and enter the city. As soon as one appeared, he was given a short spear in his stomach. He fell in agony through the entrance, blocking the other six warriors who were between the two portals. They did not think to look up and did not see the boiling oil until it coated them. Their screams were heard throughout the city. The grinning guards atop the wall then threw torches down on the men, and they all were aflame, trying to get out the way they had come, but unable to keep their feet under them from the slippery oil. One finally got back out, grabbing two of his brother warriors who were also quickly aflame from the burning oil. They would have severe wounds but probably would not die.

The scene was chaos. Burning men were screaming in their pain and two from broken bones after slipping on burning oil in the entrance-trap. The chief sentry signaled to his men to allow several wounded men to escape. The other men who were still upright, completely stunned, soon felt arrows slam into their chests. Seven Manyuema warriors were dead from burns, three from arrows, and two men holding badly injured arms ran back to their village.

"Another humiliating defeat at the hands of the cloud people." The Witch-doctor, Cyprian, screamed at Maaka.

Maaka replied weakly, "But, you said you saw victory in the forecast bones."

"Only with effective leadership, not that dead fool you put in charge. You were supposed to lead your troops, like a real king, not the fat lazy woman you have become."

"This time send your son, Kasagama, and let him lead us to victory."

Maaka was too tired to fight because he knew he could no longer lead his people, due to the devastating wound from which he had never fully recovered. Maaka's face was looking in the fire as he said, "Tomorrow I will name Kasagama chief. I am still too ill from my wounds to lead the tribe." He added to Cyprian with an accusatory stare, "No thanks to your worthless remedies."

La called Mitry to the throne room and bade him sit. She looked at the worried military commander and began, "I want a raid on the Manyuema village. I want those people destroyed, every last one of them."

"Easier said than done," Mitry replied. "The cannibals still have a fighting force of several hundred soldiers. We have less than a hundred, even if you count the hunters."

La stood and glared at her old friend and screamed, "We cannot allow them to attack our city any time they wish. We must inflict vengeance upon them, and quickly."

"Take fifty soldiers and attempt to surround their village. Inflict much damage with fire and kill as many of them as you can. Then get back here as soon as possible. Attack at night so they will not be expecting it."

Mitry wanted to tell La the foolishness of her plan, but he dared not while she was in this frame of mind.

As Mitry left the room, he heard, "Make the attack soon."

On the fateful day that Kiya had gone into battle with the warriors she was armed with a knife at her side, a quiver of arrows across her shoulder, a bow in her hand and Miu on the leather lead at her side.

When the Manyuema launched their surprise attack, as they approached the cannibal village, Kiya had attempted to save herself, and Miu, by leaving the battlefield. From a distance, Kiya could view the troops with whom she had been laughing and joking a short time ago. They were all lying dead, peppered with arrows or severely wounded. Some had escaped like her by scattering. Kiya knew she was in deep trouble; she knew the Manyuema had seen her run away, and she was sure they would attempt to hunt her down, and worse yet they would kill Miu. She reached down and freed Miu from the lead, leaving her collar intact.

In a shaken voice she ordered Miu to run with her. Hopefully, they could outdistance their tormentors and get back to Opar safely. Less than a mile from the battle scene, Kiya came face to face with a Manyuema who stepped out abruptly from a tree in the forest. He raised his bow and fired an arrow which struck her in the thigh with a great and painful force. The impact of the arrow knocked her to the ground, on her back. As she fell and shortly lost consciousness, she screamed for Miu to run home. She never knew what had become of her beloved pet.

Two other warriors stepped from behind trees and helped the first warrior pick up Kiya, carrying her back to the main group. One of the men smiled and voiced his thoughts, "I believe this woman is a sister to the bitch queen of the cloud city."

Miu went unnoticed by the Manyuema warriors as they lifted the unconscious Kiya. Miu did not understand what had just happened, but she realized her mistress had been injured. She could smell her blood as leopards can do so well. She followed at a distance until she came to a large village filled with the hated odor of man.

La was exhausted physically and mentally. She had walked the many miles from Opar to the site of the Manyuema village. The last few miles, she and her two Waziri guards were being as careful as possible to avoid being detected by sentries. La did not know if her sister Kiya was alive or dead. A search after the massacre had yielded bodies, but they were all members of La's raiding party. Kiya's body had not been found.

La could not believe Kiya had been so foolish as to sneak out with the raiders last week. The Oparian war party had been ambushed by a cross-fire of arrows. The majority of the men had been killed before they could raise their bows, or shields to defend themselves. The Manyuema had been waiting for them, within a few miles of their camp. No one suspected an attack this close to their village.

The few surviving members who had come back to Opar told La what had happened. They believed that Kiya had survived the battle and may have been wounded and fled into the jungle. A careful search of the surrounding area by a search party had yielded no evidence of Kiya's flight, which left only the terrible option that she had been captured.

La was not sure what she could do to aid Kiya if she had been caught. Perhaps nothing. The concept of ransom was unknown to the Manyuema, but revenge was not.

La and her two Waziri guards stood high on a bluff and looked down into the village. They had waited for several hours, and were preparing to leave, hoping against hope that Kiya was still hiding in the jungle. La watched her sister dragged from a filthy hut. She appeared to be only semi-conscious. Her feet were dangling loosely in the dirt, and she did not seem to be aware that there was an arrow protruding from her leg.

Kasagama said, "This makes up for all the men we lost in the attack my father ordered." Cyprian nodded his acceptance.

La had watched in horror as Kiya was tied to a stake in the village center. The fire in the middle of the village was being fed a large number of medium-sized tree limbs. As the flames began to die down to glowing embers, a large iron grate was put into place.

Cyprian, the witch-doctor, danced around the figure of Kiya bound to the stake. He shook his rattles in her face, and spoke to her in some language she did not understand. Kiya had seen enough sacrifices in her young life to know what was going to happen. She said a silent prayer to the Flaming God that her life would end quickly.

Kiya, as if on cue looked up the hill to where she hoped La was watching. She had only been looking for a moment when Cyprian delivered a crushing blow to her head with a heavy stone club, killing her.

For several days Miu sat high in a tall tree near the village, as high as the branches would support her weight. Late on the third day, she saw her mistress being dragged to a post in the middle of the village. A shift in the breeze brought her the hint of another smell she recognized. Her eyes, sharper than an eagle, found the source of the familiar scent. Far up on a distant hill, she saw the woman her mistress had frequently visited and talked with in the temple. The scent told her the distant woman was distressed.

Miu brought her eyes back to her mistress in time to see Cyprian deliver the death blow. Copious amounts of blood flew from Kiya's head, and her mistress went limp. Miu's mouth opened; her lips pulled back showing all her pure white teeth, but no sound came from her mouth. In her way, she knew her mistress was dead, and she swore her vengeance upon the people that had killed her.

Tears of disbelief and anguish poured down La's face. In her heart, she knew she was placing herself in great danger by staying, but there nothing she could do to help. Being numbed in body and spirit, she began the long and painful walk back to Opar.

Perhaps it was a blessing that La did not remain to view the final savage horror inflicted by new King Kasagama, who turned and cast his gaze for a second time onto the now vacated hill. He turned his face back to his wives and gave them the signal that Kiya's body was to be placed on the iron rack over the fire for the second part of the victory celebration.

Jim Malachowski

CHAPTER FIFTY — THE FALL OF OPAR

La, Mitry and Msizi were meeting to try to work out a strategy for dealing with an attack that they all knew was coming shortly. La was in shock and mourning for her sister, Kiya. Mitry was still livid with La for having ordered the attack on the Manyuema village that had decimated the army. About twenty men came back from the ill-fated attack, with wounds of varying degrees of severity. Mitry knew some would not be fit to fight.

Msizi gave Mitry a sign to excuse himself from the room, and he quietly spoke with La about he and Mitry taking over the defense of the city. La agreed and quietly walked to her apartment.

With the defense issues taken care of, Msizi called for May-at and asked for her assistance.

"May-at, I need you to take care of the following, can I rely on you?"

"Yes, Msizi, you may depend on me," she said with a brave smile.

"Good, now here is what has to be done and quickly. We need enough food in the lowest tunnel for two months. We need the black oil and all the torches you can find. We need tinder, and implements to make fire. We need whatever weapons that are available. These are for you La, May-at and Soma, as we may require you three to fight also. Be sure the wooden planks that lock the doors are ready and in place for the ground-level entrance, and the entrance at the lowest level."

"Msizi, there is something you must know. For the past several months La has had several workmen at the far end of the tunnel working. She wants the gap enlarged from side to side of the man-trap. Do you know what that is?"

"No I don't, please tell me."

May-at began, "La's mother began in earnest the completion of the lowest tunnel. There was an exit to the outside of Opar through a man-made cave at the end of the tunnel. To keep invaders from just entering, there was an opening cut from wall to wall and about four feet wide. La wants it enlarged to create a seven-foot opening where invaders would fall into the river below and drown. The floor was cut in such a way that it was not apparent in dim light that there was a drop-off. Supposedly, some man came in there a few years ago and got out with some pretty stones."

Msizi answered, "Don't tell La this, but I am stopping work on that project. We need all the manpower we can find to defend the city."

Msizi had two Waziri scouts watching the Manyuema camp for a sign of the expected invasion. One foggy morning the scouts watched as three hundred heavily armed warriors marched out and began to move on Opar. The men hurried to get back with a warning.

When they arrived, they went directly to Mitry and told him they had only a few hours to prepare. He called for his lieutenants and told them the news.

Mitry had all men able to bear arms assemble. The count included hunters, the Waziri, and every able-bodied man in the city. Twenty of the men would be deployed atop the wall with bows and arrows. Four would be manning the hot oil by the entrance maze. The rest of the armed men were located inside the wall because they were not sure where they would be needed.

The cannibal battle leader had six men on each end of the wall climbing the steep rocky hill. At his signal, the men began firing arrows at the Opar warriors on the wall. Three men had died and fallen off the wall before they realized the arrows were coming from behind them. Men from the ground level hurried to return arrows against the invaders.

The Manyuema brought lines which they anchored to the battlements and dropped to their fellows on the ground. In groups of three and four, they climbed the ropes and began to overpower the remaining defenders on the wall top.

No one was trying to come through the entrance maze, so the hot oil was useless. Mitry signaled to his crew to soak the torches thoroughly in oil, light them and try to hit a group of invaders, hoping the burning oil would splash.

The Manyuema who were climbing the lines were beginning to outnumber the Opar troops on the wall and take control. In a last-ditch effort, the hot oil was used in an attempt to light the ropes, at least on one end of the wall.

The tide of battle was turning by the sheer number of casualties. The Oparian troops on the ground were holding their own, but the number of invaders each man had to deal with was growing rapidly.

As the defenders continued to fall, Msizi, knew the battle was lost. He tried to signal his charges to join him, but none were able to hear him over the din of battle.

With a heavy heart, Msizi began to close the access door. As he did he saw Mitry, one of the last defenders, go down to a black warrior with a spear. Msizi watched until all the defenders were killed. He closed and locked the door which led down to the tunnels. The door was constructed to look like the building stones, difficult to see. A great sadness had come over him as he had watched his Waziri brothers, the Oparian soldiers, and hunters killed. The slaughter seemed worse because it happened at the hands of the greatest enemy his people had ever faced.

He thought about his ancestors who had been driven from the north and relentlessly hunted down by the Manyuema for years, killing many men women and children who were his forebearers. Msizi took out his knife, after locking the door behind him, and cut into the palm of his left hand. He swore he would avenge the Waziri who died today and those Waziri people who had died so many years ago.

He walked down the many steps where La, May-at and Soma were standing. They did not have to ask what happened, they knew by the look on his face.

For what seemed like forever, the four-remaining people of Opar ate, slept and talked very little. After two weeks La asked Msizi when he thought it would be safe to venture out. Msizi told her he felt the Manyuema knew they were hiding somewhere, they just did not know where. They must be patient as the invaders would grow weary of being here, and would leave. That is what he hoped.

Two more weeks passed. The survivors were tired of living in the dark and eating very little provisions. Their torches were not used very often since the invaders would probably smell the burning oil, and it would give their location away.

As a group, they decided to try to see if they perhaps could sneak out and begin an escape. Msizi knew the way back to the Waziri village if they could only make it outside the wall.

They had no idea if it was day or night outside their barricaded shelter. Msizi decided to take a chance, light a torch and place it in a holder at the bottom of the steps. The four made their way up the steps, the torch throwing weirdly shaped shadows on the wall beside them. Finally, they made the top of the stairs at the small exit landing. Holding his assegai in front of him, Msizi quietly lifted the thick wooden block that secured the door. He stepped out and immediately saw he was facing two Manyuema warriors. He struck one a glancing blow to the head with his short spear, which stunned the man. The second Manyuema dealt Msizi a glancing blow to the head, and he dropped his spear and fell to his knees stunned. May-at saw what happened and was able to grab the fallen short spear and drive the point into the enemy's unprotected stomach.

The first Manyuema man down had gotten to his feet and slipped into the entry door, and rapidly walked down the stairs. The second man was doubled over with pain from his stomach wound. May-at and Soma grabbed him and threw him down the long flight of stone stairs. La stood in shock at what had just happened and was pulled quickly into the secure area by the girls, and the door relocked. The three women helped the still stunned Msizi down the stairs.

At the bottom of the stairs, La caught a bit of movement out of the corner of her eye. The Manyuema warrior who had snuck in with them was about to strike a blow to her head with a stone-ended club. La ducked the blow and grabbed the torch from the wall and began running for the man-trap in the floor.

La could feel the man gaining on her with each step. Just as he was about to grab her by her long hair, La threw the torch over her shoulder, and it hit him in the arm and chest – burning him. The torch fell to the ground and was now only throwing a feeble amount of light, not enough for La to see where she was going.

La knew she was close to the edge of the gaping hole and she also knew the man had regained his stride and was closing in. She could not see the hole now that the torch was no longer burning brightly.

It was now or never. She was not going to run off the end and into the river and its boulders so far below.

La leaped!

Far behind Msizi had regained his faculties enough to see La throw the torch over her shoulder. All went black very quickly. There was a long shrill shriek, which lasted for a few seconds, and everything went totally silent.

CHAPTER FIFTY-ONE — THE LONG WAIT

Tarzan stood on the edge of the training area where Sergeant Major Hopkins was putting his charges through their paces. The Waziri warriors were acquainted with guns but none of this power. The Sergeant Major knew from experience that some would not be able to deal with the deafening noise of the guns that would be coming. So instead of starting with the number of men. Tarzan needed he added twenty more, hedging that some would not pass the tests that lay ahead.

The plan was to drill the Waziri until they were competent with the shotguns and rifles. The difficult part of this was the development of several well-practiced sharpshooters. As it worked out, the notice of the attack on Opar came two days before they were scheduled to depart for the cloud city.

The Sergeant Major was surprised that many of the Waziri men spoke at least a bit of English. Tarzan had brought in educators to teach reading and writing skills to the tribe years ago.

Hopkins began with the Winchester carbines. Each man was taught how to disassemble the rifle and re-assemble it quickly. Rewards in various forms were awarded to the most nimble troops. The Sergeant Major began to screen them, trying to find the ones whom he could develop into sharpshooters, men who would be accurate at two hundred yards. The Sergeant Major had brought with him a drill sergeant who was instructing men on how to march and various military offensive and defensive maneuvers. Great emphasis was placed on the formation known as a shooting block, which had been used effectively by the defenders of Rorke's Drift (South Africa) in 1879, during the Zulu wars with the British. The two military advisors knew these warriors would need to be well versed in dealing with an overwhelmingly large force of enemy troops.

Two nights before the invasion of the Manyuema sentry, Soma and Msizi had prepared a messenger monkey to send to Tarzan. They cautiously climbed the steps, opened the upper door and crept out into the moonless night. They had been lucky. They saw two figures asleep twenty-five feet from the door. They signaled the monkey to be silent and released her. They watched as the speedy creature scampered up the mountain face near the south end of the temple. They lost sight of her as she climbed nimbly into the rough shrubbery high on the mountain. Quickly they went back inside, locked the door and descended the stone steps.

At best they could expect Tarzan to arrive in a month.

When Father Martin arrived in Paris, he was surprised to find a message waiting for him at the diocese office – the bishop wanted a word with him. Martin found his way to the bishop's office and gave his name to the secretary. He was asked to sit in the waiting room, and await a summons.

Within an hour Martin was escorted into a room decorated in gold with beautiful religious oil paintings. The bishop entered and approached Martin with an extended right hand, ring up, for Father Martin to kiss. After this formal beginning, the bishop sat in a chair opposite Martin.

"Father Martin," began the bishop, "I have received a glowing letter about you and your work in Africa …" He fumbled with his glasses then produced a folded letter which he opened and displayed. "Seems you have a friend and patron, by the name of …" the bishop scanned the letter for the name and announced "John Clayton, Lord Greystoke."

A somewhat bewildered Father Martin acknowledged that he knew him saying, "I am honored that he has contacted you, Your Excellency."

"The man has made an offer to fund a staff increase for your mission in … Where are you again?"

Father Martin answered "French Equatorial Africa. This is a surprise to me. What did John want for the mission?"

"It seems he wants three additional teachers, two more nurses and a surgical doctor. He has offered to fund expenses for not only the staff, but he has also sent a bank draft for hospital supplies and equipment to supply a good sized medical center, which he has offered to build. Martin, it seems that with the help of Lord Greystoke, you are carving out quite a nice empire in …. Where are you again?"

"French Equatorial Africa, Your Excellency."

"I understand you lost one of your parents, is that correct? My condolences."

"Yes, Your Excellency, and thank you, Your Excellency."

"I want you to supervise the shipment of material and your new personnel back to …"

"Yes, Your Excellency."

"I am afraid you will need to extend your stay here to two months while the shopping list from Lord …. is assembled. Enjoy your visit with your relatives. We will have someone contact them when everything has been assembled. Please be sure to give that information to my secretary."

Martin thought he would try pushing his luck when he approached the secretary. The young priest looked up from his desk at him and smiled.

Marin began, "For my return trip to Africa, could you get me a better cabin than one in steerage?"

"Yes, Monsignor. I will take care of that personally."

The secretary saw the surprised look on Father Martin's face, and said "He forgot to tell you, didn't he? He is such a busy man; I'm sure it just slipped his mind. "

"Yes, I can see that," Martin replied.

He left the reception area and walked out the front door, down the marble steps onto the sidewalk. Martin could hide it no longer and burst out into a loud laugh. He thought about his good fortune, as he lit an English Oval cigarette, and walked with a great smile on his face to the train station.

Father Martin thought he would have to do something for Tarzan. He just didn't know how nice and how soon this would take place.

The messenger monkey was traveling at breakneck speed through the small branches of the great trees that stretched from Opar toward the west coast where the scent packages were leading her. She was three years old and an experienced messenger. This was her longest mission, and she had been traveling at full speed for over a week. The monkey had barely stopped for food and a few hour's rest in the late afternoon. She liked to travel at night when there was a nearly full moon, and the air was much cooler. However, there were the leopards to be wary of, so she traveled high in the slender branches that would not support a hundred pounds of cat.

On the tenth day of her journey, she came to a location that smelled especially strong to her of the scent she was trained to follow. As she had been taught, the monkey slowed and approached where her keen nose told her to go. As she got to within a hundred yards of the scent packages, she noted a rather large village of people. She carefully located one of the scent packages, then the second. She chose a tree that was between them and sat down to catch her breath. The monkey let out her verbal signal she had arrived, loudly. She was exhausted and probably could not have gone much further without a full night's sleep.

The monkey watched as a young woman approached the tree, and she could smell the third scent package being offered up to her. The tiny monkey slowly climbed down and jumped on the girl's shoulder. She was grateful when she was given a half coconut shell filled with cool water.

The monkey rode the woman's shoulder until they reached a large building, which looked different from the straw huts nearby. A large man approached and said to her in her native language, "Hello, my little sister. Welcome. Please stay here until you are rested. Have you brought me a gift of pretty ribbons?"

The tiny monkey answered, "Yes, I have. I do not believe it is a good message. There were many people I knew. They are now dead."

Tarzan saw the three ribbons but did not have to see them to know the message. The ribbons were: white, meaning it was from La, red meant blood spilled from an attack, black was the message of death and destruction.

Tarzan said to the young lady, "Provide the monkey with food, water, and shelter. She will leave when she is ready. Do not let any of the village children bother her."

He turned on his heel and ran to Sergeant Major Hopkins and the Waziri and explained what had happened in Opar. "Hopkins, get these men ready to travel; we leave at dawn. We are probably too late to protect Opar, but we need to avenge our friends and provide security for the museum staff that is coming soon."

The jungle lord grabbed the great bow and arrow a young man was rapidly carrying to him. He turned his eyes east, ran to the nearest great tree and was out of sight in thirty seconds. Tarzan's mind was deeply troubled as he raced through the middle terraces. He had hoped this obvious attack by the Manyuema could have been delayed until his military force was trained more and on location in Opar.

Most of all he worried about someone he cared for very deeply — La.

The single thought that went through La's mind was that she had jumped too soon. And she was right. The leap that La made was more of a dive than a jump. With a jumper, the expectation is to land on their feet.

La's only thought was getting to the other side. This dive probably saved her life.

In the split second that remained of her consciousness, La first felt her left knee hit the rock floor. Instinctively her hands went palms down and extended to break her fall. They felt the rough stones; then her left cheek hit the flooring, followed by her left forehead. She lost consciousness immediately and lay motionless.

May-at screamed for Soma or Msizi to fetch a torch and implements to make fire. Both Soma and Msizi were feeling for what they needed in the stygian darkness.

Soma shouted, "I have found it. Give me a little time to get the torch lit."

Mat-at yelled back, "Hurry we may be able to save her. Msizi go fetch some rope."

Soma's eyes were on May-at and the chasm in front of them, both looking down. The flickering light was showing seventy-five feet below them, lying in the water upon a boulder, the corpse of the Manyuema warrior who had entered the cavern.

Soma looked down and asked, "Where is she? Did they fall together, and she is underneath him?"

"No," Msizi said with some authority. "She is over there," he said holding the torch high over his head. As he did so, the women could make out a body lying on the stone floor, close to the edge, but not moving.

Msizi looked to his right, then left and spotted some rough boards leaning against the wall. He called May-at and Soma to help him carry the long boards to the chasm where they pushed them over the gaping hole. When the planking was safely secure on the far side, Msizi tested the bridge found it supported his weight, and walked across.

He called back to May-at and Soma that they should stay on the other side. He would get La awake and carry her back. May-at brought a wet cloth and threw it to Msizi. He bathed La's arms and face. The skin on her cheekbone was scraped and bleeding heavily, as were her knees and left temple. There was a large amount of blood, but it did not appear to be gushing from an artery. Msizi had seen many friends injured in battle or by lions, so he was able to tell the difference and severity of wounds.

He lay the wet cloth across her forehead, and he began to talk with her in a low voice.

May-at called across, "Is she okay? She does not appear to be moving."

"She is unconscious, I believe from hitting her head. I see bad scrapes, and cuts; but no broken bones," he replied. "I do not want to shake her; it's best if she awakens by herself, then I will bring her across the trap."

Within an hour La was sitting up, and although still stunned, she seemed to be recovering on her own.

"As soon as you are up to it, I will carry you to the other side," Msizi said.

La nodded weakly in agreement. After another hour La indicated she was ready to go back over. Msizi picked her up and carried her effortlessly across the wood plank bridge.

When La was placed on her feet at the other side of the chasm, she asked Soma and May-at to help her to lie down. They made her as comfortable as possible, and she immediately went back to sleep.

On the twenty-fourth day, the jungle lord had climbed the escarpment and was getting closer to Opar. He would approach the city at night, when it was moonless. He would climb the south wall behind the temple where he would have a good vantage point to observe what had happened.

Tarzan saw two figures in the deep shade of the temple. They appeared to be sleeping in blankets. There was no other sign of life inside the city wall.

Even in the dim light, Tarzan had been able to tell what had happened. The attackers had climbed over the city wall and killed the defending force. The scavengers had done their job. There was no one identifiable, just piles of clothing that the winds had gathered.

The remaining bones were not enough to account for the whole population of Opar, so some must have escaped or been taken as slaves.

As soon as it became light, Tarzan began to scout the area surrounding Opar. After four hours of looking for any more warriors, he concluded the two guards inside were all the men left behind.

Tarzan surmised some people were hiding, and the sentries could not get to them. He would dispatch men to begin looking for those who were hopefully concealed.

Eliminating the remaining invaders was easy. As soon as one left his post, Tarzan sent an arrow into his heart. The second man was not aware he was alone. Tarzan crept behind him wrapping his arm around his throat .

"Let me go; my companion will kill you when he returns."

"I think not," replied Tarzan.

"Where are the people hiding? Tell me now, or your death will be long, slow and painful."

The frightened man pointed to the ground level door that Tarzan knew led down into the bowels of the temple. Tarzan squeezed the man's throat until he passed out from lack of oxygen. He then bound him, thinking he may need him later, hiding the trussed and gagged body in a room on the ground floor of the temple.

Tarzan picked up a large stone and began beating on the door. After a half hour of repeated banging and waiting, he stopped.

Perhaps whoever was here had escaped without the guards knowing it. Tarzan also knew that Werper had escaped from the third level of the tunnels. It was worth a look. If no one were there, he would try to pick up a trail. Perhaps they were in the cannibal village.

Tarzan walked down the path to La's bathing area. He began climbing down outside the city wall looking for the hidden cave. An hour later he found a small opening big enough to get his broad shoulders in with some difficulty. Lighting a torch, he forced his way in and was greeted by a long black tunnel, with the sound of running water faintly ahead.

As he moved quietly along the stone floor, the sound of the water grew louder. Shortly Tarzan came to the edge. He had to know the truth, so he stood and shouted for Msizi, in a very loud voice.

His call was weakly answered. He noticed the tunnel became a bit brighter, dimly lit by a flickering torch. Tarzan watched, and approaching from the hazy darkness he saw three figures carrying a dim light.

"Tarzan, we thought you would never come. We were so worried the messenger monkey had not gotten to you." The relief in the words was evident.

Tarzan gauged the distance across, took a few steps back and effortlessly jumped, landing in front of the small group of people. By their smiles he was able to see they were relieved to see him.

The people moved quickly to him. Tarzan knew immediately whose arms encircled his neck, when she whispered in his ear, "Tarzan, I knew you would come back to me." La then broke into tears of relief.

Jim Malachowski

CHAPTER FIFTY-TWO — THE 100 WAZIRI

L a was still feeling the effects of the concussion she sustained while eluding the Manyuema warrior. When Tarzan got a good look at her, he was shocked at the lump on her forehead, the black eye, large facial scrapes and many body contusions.

For several weeks after the fall, La exhibited the classic symptoms of a concussion: a headache, nausea, temporary loss of memory, and sleeplessness.

As soon as Tarzan was certain La was having everything done for her that was possible, he turned his attention to Msizi.

"What happened that the Manyuema attacked again?"

"The only reason I can think of," answered Msizi, "is that they knew we were weakened when we lost a lot of troops in the ambush. We did nothing to provoke them."

Tarzan then asked, "When did this attack happen?"

"Sorry, but I have lost track of time in this perpetual darkness. I believe it was about thirty days ago. I tried to keep track of the days, but my count may be off."

Tarzan asked, "What happened to all the inhabitants of Opar? I have counted the bodies of the people and it seems many are missing. Did they get away, or are they hiding somewhere else?"

"My Chief, " Msizi spoke, "I watched as I was getting the women to the safety of the temple and the Manyuema killed all the old, sick and infants. I am sorry to say that the young and healthy were collected and herded out of the city. I am sure by now they have been sold as slaves, and are across the big water."

"You have done well Msizi. You did exactly what I wanted you to do, and that was to save the women. I guessed it was you who sent the messenger monkey with the attack news."

"Yes, it was I. Tarzan, I worried greatly the monkey would not reach you. I was beginning to plan to take my chances with the guards outside and make a break with the women for Waziri country. Will we be returning to our village as soon as La is better?"

"No," Tarzan replied, "there are old scores to settle. There is much that will be removed from Opar and sent to England. There are heavily armed Waziri warriors coming to defend the city. We will be attacked again. There are scholarly men who are coming from across the sea to study the city. It is essential we provide both support and protection for these men.

Three weeks later the one hundred Waziri warriors arrived along with two hundred porters who were carrying many heavy boxes. Sergeant Major Hopkins was very glad to see Lord Greystoke again after his rapid exit from the training area in the Waziri village.

"How was the trip from the west?"

Hopkins replied, "Very uneventful. The flat barges saved a lot of the porters' strength. Not having to carry those boxes and the rest of our supplies for well over three-quarters of the journey, was a God-send. Given the block and tackle, we were able to raise the heavy boxes, in stages, up the escarpment in fairly short order. This was much faster than a single porter carrying one box up at a time."

"Since you left so suddenly, we will need to do our planning soon. I expect another attack by the cannibals. I did remember your wishes that I would be the only one who would be seen with modern weapons. All the Waziri troops have shown is their traditional weapons."

"Thanks, Hopkins, you have done an exceptional job. The other part of the expedition will be arriving in a few weeks and we need to be prepared to defend them and ourselves. After dinner tonight, you and I will sit down and make our plans.

Hopkins asked, "What of the people who lived here? Were you able to locate the leaders?"

Lord Greystoke answered, "The inhabitants not killed have been enslaved, and are most probably beyond our help. The city ruler, La, her handmaiden, and shaman are secure in the tunnels below the temple. La was injured during the escape and is recovering. She should be fit to travel in a few weeks."

"Now Hopkins, let me show you probably the oldest Egyptian colony ever discovered. Normally Egyptians did not colonize, but they did in this instance." So Tarzan and Hopkins began walking and looking at the city they would need to defend.

Later that night Lord Greystoke, Hopkins, and three Waziri lieutenants sat by the fire and discussed strategy. Hopkins spoke first, "We need to control where the enemy will enter the city. We are too small a group to defend invaders entering from multiple entry points. The Manyuema were working on opening a breach in the city wall and they nearly had succeeded. I say, let's give them an opening to come in so that we can control them. We can handle how many they bring—between five hundred and a thousand warriors in this manner. We have the element of surprise in our weapons. We must keep that surprise. No Waziri is allowed to be seen having the guns we brought with us —bows and arrows only."

Tarzan nodded his head in agreement and added, "Beginning tomorrow, we will be placing sentries all around the city and in the mountains behind. Later in the week, we will be organizing scouting parties to spy on the Manyuema village and give us a heads up when they are moving against us.

"Tomorrow we will be selecting defensive positions and organize squads of men who will force the enemy to enter in a way we can control them."

Tarzan looked in on La, May-at and Soma late in the evening. Soma greeted him, "Tarzan, it's good to see you. Thank goodness, La is resting. She has been sleeping fitfully, and endured many nightmares."

"In your experience with head injuries, is La getting better?"

"Yes," she replied, "head injuries take time and patience. Hopefully, in a few weeks, she will be well. Tarzan, I must ask, is there anyone alive from the city?"

"You three women are the sole survivors. You must come to grips with leaving the city, never to return. I will provide a place for you where you will be safe."

Tarzan saw a look of fear come across Soma's face. "Leaving is between you and me. La will be told when she is improved. I will tell La and May-at together. Do not be afraid. Your life will be better than it ever could be here in Opar. There are good things, over the far mountains, that you cannot even dream of that will change your life for the better." This seemed to placate Soma, and she managed a smile.

"One more thing," Tarzan cautioned, "the cannibals will be back. There will be guards with you, but you and May-at must watch La and keep her in this tunnel. I promise it will be the Manyuema's last visit."

Within one day, Lord Greystoke and Sergeant Major Hopkins had assigned scouts to all necessary positions. There was virtually no way that a war party of any size could make their way to Opar without being detected. Inside the city walls, a group of the porters and Waziri warriors were working on widening the opening in the middle of the city wall. When finished, the opening would be fifteen feet wide and about five feet high, just enough so the invading warriors would have to stoop to get through. The displaced stones were broken up and scattered along the path inside. There was no sense making the path too easy for the cannibals.

In the Manyuema camp, Cyprian was once more in the face of the new leader, Kasagama. "Those pitiful Waziri are back again my spies tell me. It is time for you to wipe them out so the earth can be free of those cowards. I have sent a message to your cousin in the north and he has promised all his warriors for this honorable cause. They should be here in a week and ready for battle."

Kasagama's face contorted into a snarl, and he snapped, "How dare you usurp the King's authority? It is my word that rules the Manyuema people. Do not ever do that again, or you will find yourself over a hot bed of coals."

"Majesty," Cyprian responded, "I did not mean to take your authority, I was merely relating what I know you wanted to tell him." Cyprian dropped his eyes and smiled inwardly. 'I will be king of these people yet,' he said to himself.

"Your cousin in the north has pledged eight hundred warriors. Here we have over six hundred. It will surely be enough to wipe the Waziri people from the face of the earth."

In the next week, Waziri scouts in the north of Opar began to see a movement of a great many troops headed for the local Manyuema kraal. They immediately went back and told the sergeant major and Tarzan the news.

Kasagama's village was about thirty miles from Opar. When the troops from the north arrived, they rested for one day. Then the combined force of about fourteen hundred warriors began the trek to Opar.

Kasagama had said to Cyprian, "Are you sure we need every warrior in the Manyuema empire to kill the Waziri who have taken up in the cloud city?"

"This victory must be complete and overwhelming. Not a Waziri must be allowed to survive. It is my opinion that it is better to have too many men in the battle than too few. Kasagama, do you not remember your father sending in too small of a war party against the cloud people?

Our troops were defeated and the survivors were sent back to us in shame. That can never happen again. You must show your people you are the strongest and best possible leader for the Manyuema people," Cyprian answered. "You need to appoint Danbuze as a battle leader and let him choose two assistants. They can take charge of the attack and you and I can be comfortable here in the village awaiting news of victory."

The trip to Opar would take four days. The Manyuema could travel between twelve and fifteen miles per day, and would rest on the third day for the battle. Early on the fourth day, they would walk the last few miles and attack about noon.

Work had begun immediately upon the Waziri arrival into Opar. After a day's rest, the soldiers and porters began digging a ditch which would roughly parallel the north end of the wall. The trench would be four feet deep and three hundred feet long. The dirt had been removed, carried back and spread evenly in the forest.

A considerable amount of rubble from the opening created in the city wall had been dumped at the edge of the northern edge of the trench. This was to encourage the Manyuema approaching from the east to condense their group closer to the wall, rather than walking through sharp and rough stones and rubble. As soon as the digging was complete, work began on the weaving of branches, leaves and palm fronds into rectangular shapes that would cover the trench.

Two days before the Manyuema were expected to attack, Tarzan gathered the Waziri warriors into a group in the shade of the Temple of the Flaming God. He looked into the faces of every man who stood before him. The warriors were quiet, and Tarzan did not say a word until he had made eye contact with each one.

Their war chief began in a quiet voice that could barely be heard, "It is always good to remember why and for whom you are fighting. Tomorrow we will be protecting the honor of the Waziri people. The Manyuema have been our enemies for hundreds of years. May I remind you that in most cases they have gotten the best of you in battles?"

"These are the men who chased your ancestors from your traditional lands and made you settle where you live now. Their raids on your villages killed your relatives, enslaved many of your women."

"If you want, tomorrow can be a day of retribution. It can be a time when all the Manyuema pays for the grief and heartache they have caused your parents and grandparents. Is this what you want?" In one loud voice, the gathered men gave their answer, "Yes!"

The war chief continued, "You one hundred men have new training and new weapons. If you follow what you have been shown, you can have revenge tomorrow. Tell me again, is this what you want?"

Again, in one loud voice, the gathered men gave their answer, "Yes."

On the march to Opar, the Manyuema moved at a rapid and steady pace. They failed to see along the way, high in the trees, camouflaged stands where Waziri sentries watched their progress. After they had passed, the sentinels flashed, with pieces of glass mirrors, signals that were relayed back to Opar. They knew the attack would come that afternoon, and as soon as it was safe, they left their posts and ran back to Opar by another route.

Jim Malachowski

CHAPTER FIFTY-THREE — THE BATTLE

I f you take a short brisk walk, in London, north from Temple Underground station, you will come to the London Silver Vaults, an imposing structure on the right side of the street.

A closer tube station is Chancery Lane, which is less than a quarter mile north of the Silver Vaults. Rumor has it that during the years leading up to World War II, there was a rail spur going from the tube stop to the London Silver Vaults. Rumor also has it that construction was financed by a private individual, and the purpose of the tunnel has never become known. Construction supposedly involved a small narrow tunnel which utilized a narrow-gauge rail system, similar to those used in mining operations. Obviously, something very heavy was being moved.

A small version of these vaults had occupied this area for many years. The Silver Vaults opened for business in May of 1885. Spaces in the vaulted structure were rented to whoever had valuable goods to store or sell. Silver dealers became the principal tenants during the passing years.

With nearly four-foot-thick, steel reinforced walls, the vaults have never been broken into or burgled. The ground level building above the vaults was hit directly by a German bomb during World War II. This building was destroyed, but the vaults remained undamaged. The replacement building, Chancery House, was constructed in the early 1950's.

The shops, located two stories below street level are a discerning buyer's delight, offering silver, old Sheffield Plate and silver gilt tableware, cutlery, decorative pieces, gifts, jewelry and watches, as well as collectors' items such as stamps and coins. There are about thirty fine merchants who do business in the underground vaults.

However, there is one business not listed on the marquee. This merchant does business by appointment, made by calling a phone number listed as being in Mayfair. Upon arriving at the main elevator at the appointed time, a young lady confirms name and appointment and escorts the buyer to a floor not listed on the elevator's floor lights.

Rumor has it, the anonymous vendor sells gold.

The Manyuema warriors, despite being covered with a light sweat, were not the least bit tired. They were anxious to engage and destroy the Waziri. The early morning sun was burning off the haze, and the cloud city was just becoming visible in the distance.

In less than an hour, the Manyuema would be at the breach in the wall and ready to pour into Opar.

Sergeant Major Hopkins formed his troops into the now familiar shooting formation. The steely-eyed Hopkins looked at the faces of his men lined before him, and he saw courage and determination. He was sure these warriors would fight as one, and they would protect him from all harm. He had no weapon—not even a handgun, and he knew he would not need one today.

The fourteen hundred Manyuema warriors were three abreast, close to the wall. They had stopped short of the opening in the wall. Danbuze, the battle leader, was wearing the traditional white feathers around his biceps and mid-thigh indicating his leadership role in the battle. He stepped into the opening and looked inside.

He saw what appeared to be ten sentries, with no bow and arrows, shields or spears. They were standing in a straight line with a four-foot gap between each of them. They were in the open, about forty to fifty yards away from him. He also saw a white man in a bright red shirt standing to the Waziri's right.

Danbuze ducked back out of sight and told his squad of men, on his order, they were to pass through the wall opening and form a line of eight men across. All were to charge, upon his order, and kill this obviously small party of defenders.

The Manyuema with wrath in their war cries and murder in their hearts ran through the opening. When two hundred men were through, the command to attack came, and they charged. More warriors kept entering the gap to fill where the others had been. Danbuze put his head in and watched what he believed would be the slaughter.

When the running warriors reached thirty yards from the shooters, the front ten Waziri raised their shotguns to their shoulders, and at Hopkin's command fired. Ten guns exploded as one. The shells contained buckshot; each cartridge contained a dozen steel balls. When the guns fired, a wall of steel balls six feet in diameter, at fourteen hundred feet per second, ripped into the approaching war party. Even at this distance some of the shot passed through the bodies of the first wave of men and went into those behind them. Thirty men immediately fell.

The soldiers who had just fired immediately dropped to their knees and pumped their shotguns, moving a fresh shell into the firing chamber. The second ten, behind them and out of sight moved into the opening, fired another volley in perfect unison, and dropped to their knees, reloading. The third rank stepped into the gap and followed with another volley, dropped and loaded a fresh shell. By this time there were one hundred Manyuema warriors dead or severely wounded on the ground.

Danbuze could not believe what he was seeing. He ordered the rest of his men to run faster to get to the men with guns. He had never seen guns that did not need reloading between shots. The usual Manyuema tactic, when fighting men with guns, was to overwhelm them with new bodies. It would not work this time.

Despite the commands from Danbuze, the attacking warriors were slowed by the dead and dying bodies they were trying to run through.

Hopkins screamed again, "First squad!" The first ten men rose again, fired and dropped to their knees, replacing the spent cartridge in their guns. The second line rose, fired and dropped to their knees and added fresh cartridges. The third rose and fired. This tactic was repeated five more times. In less than a few minutes, five hundred of the invaders were dead or dying. They had been dispatched by slightly more than two hundred shotgun blasts.

By now very few of the hundreds of Manyuema who had come through the wall still standing. The ones who were vertical saw, from their right and left, three new Waziri warriors each with shotguns approaching and shooting any stragglers who were attempting to escape. None did.

All went quiet for a minute. The only sounds were the moaning of the critically wounded Manyuema. The stack of bodies had reached three feet. The Manyuema had ignored their dead and wounded, running over them in a desperate and futile attempt to get to the Waziri guns.

The silence was broken by a single shot from a Winchester Model 94 30-30. This was the signal for the second stage of the Waziri revenge. The bullet struck Danbuze in the back of his head. His blood sprayed the men who were standing in front of him waiting for his orders. He fell lifeless at their feet, creating panic. All fight and confidence left the invaders. They had just heard and watched five hundred of their fellows die in less than two minutes. They wanted to run into the safety of the forest and make their way home. One or two men noticed movement in the field behind them and realized too late what was happening.

The ground appeared to be moving as the sixty Waziri who had been kneeling in the trench, shoved their camouflaged covering behind them. They stood and fired a volley into the Manyuema who were stunned, just standing along the wall waiting for orders that never came.

The shot from atop the wall had been the signal and the sixty shotguns fired. A solid bank of steel buckshot ripped into the invaders. At this range, the shotguns were producing a circle of death eight feet high and wide. The Waziri gunmen had been placed so the spray from their weapons would overlap with the shooters on the other side, leaving no gaps for Manyuema warriors to hide. It was a solid wall of death. With military precision, sixty spent cartridges were ejected and sixty guns fired again as one. The Manyuema did not know which way to run. Some went to their left, some to their right, and the outcome was the same – they kept running into steel balls that either wounded or killed them. They fell over the bodies of their dead or dying companions or ran into each other.

After nine volleys there was not a Manyuema invader standing. Three Waziri warriors at the far right end of the trench looked at each other and grinned. They were watching their wounded enemies running as fast as their wounds would allow, north back to their village. Within a minute three shots rang out followed by silence. The two sharpshooters in the tree stands had killed the only survivors. No Manyuema would be returning home that day.

An hour after the battle, Tarzan came down from the roof of the Temple of the Flaming God where he had watched the most glorious day in Waziri history. He walked out into the field of battle, inside the wall, and was swamped by the thirty-some deliriously happy warriors. It was hard to tell who was more pleased with the results, the Waziri or Sergeant Major Hopkins. The Waziri soldiers had swamped Hopkins after the battle, thanking him for teaching them how to win.

Tarzan continued through the opening in the wall to view up close the battle that had just concluded fifteen minutes ago. The same Waziri delirium was taking place outside the walls.

Nearly fourteen hundred Manyuema warriors were dead, and not one Waziri had even been wounded. The day would be spoken of forever in Waziri history. The annihilation would also crush the slave trade in central Africa. The Arabs would not have their henchmen who would do anything for money to their black brothers. No other tribe would even consider an alliance with the Arabs. They all had been victimized and were happy to hear of the terrible end of their enemies.

Tarzan walked back through the wall breach, there he turned to his left and quickly headed down the stone path to the temple. He stood in the entrance area to the stairs that led to the three lower levels. With a stone, he tapped his code on the door for Msizi to open.

A cautious Msizi, assegai in hand, looked out and was relieved to see Tarzan's smiling face. "Safe for everyone to come out, the battle is over."

Msizi looked puzzled, "All ready over? I thought the fight would last all day."

"No," replied Tarzan, "the heart went out of the Manyuema when they saw and heard how quickly one-third of their army was destroyed in less than two minutes. The rest of the battle was no more than slaughter."

La's eyes, as well as May-at's and Soma's, went wide when they saw the carnage of five hundred bodies lying on the ground that had once produced food for the people of Opar.

They walked out into the open space where the main Manyuema army had been destroyed. La could not believe what she was seeing. The Waziri's greatest enemies and hers lay dead at her feet. Tarzan knew what she was thinking and said, "Only two more to deal with, and the revenge will be complete."

She told Tarzan she needed to sit down. The astonishment at the sight in front of her faded from her face, she turned to Tarzan and whispered, "All my people, Mitry, and my beloved sister Kiya are now avenged. I thought I would feel better, but I do not. Even this does not make up for the people I loved so much."

La placed her hands over her eyes, lowered her head to her knees and sobbed, her body shaking. Tarzan looked at Soma and May-at and saw they had the same reaction.

CHAPTER FIFTY-FOUR — CHOICES

A week after the decisive battle against the Manyuema Tarzan told La he wished to talk with her. After that conversation, he wanted to speak with all the three women – La, May-at and Soma.

Sergeant Major Hopkins and Tarzan had sent five groups of heavily armed Waziri warriors on scouting expeditions. Both men wanted to know what was within a fifty-mile radius of the city. The sentry groups were sent to the four major compass points. The fifth was sent to keep an eye on the Manyuema village. Tarzan particularly wanted to know the location of the chief and the witch-doctor Cyprian. By now they must have figured out that their army was not coming home, and he wanted to know their plans.

Tarzan and La spent the rest of the morning hours viewing the desolate city of Opar. The invaders had ravaged the city on their successful assault. Both knew the loot had been taken to their village and would be easy to recover. All crops were destroyed, the livestock taken away, and most of the houses that would burn were destroyed.

The Temple of the Flaming God, being built of stone, was intact and had sustained no significant damage. The invaders had not been able to get below ground level, so nothing was disturbed. La noted that the sacrificial knife was missing and she appeared to be quite upset by the fact. "That knife is my only link to my mother and grandmother. Why would those cannibals steal it?"

Tarzan made a mental note to recover it when the Manyuema village was "visited." After the inspection, Tarzan and La sat in her oasis area. Following the battle of a few days ago, Tarzan had moved La, May-at and Soma to the buildings surrounding the oasis area. Tarzan began, "La, what do you want me to do about the chief and witch-doctor?"

La's face reddened with anger, "Those two fools have killed my people, the ones I loved, and have changed my life forever. Tarzan, I cannot think of anything heinous enough to inflict upon them. Can you?"

"Nothing in the world will bring back the ones you loved. There is no vengeance that will not prove to be hollow. Killing them is too good. I have another idea. Will you leave this to me?"

"Of course, will you at least let me know what it is?" Tarzan nodded yes.

"I wanted to have this conversation in private with you before May-at and Soma are told. If you have some violent disagreement, I want it to be discussed between us. Some things have been put into motion, that will affect all of you and I want to explain why I did them."

"Let me start with a question. Do you believe I know more about the outside world than you? Do you believe I have your best interests in my actions?"

"Of course, I do. Now you have me extremely curious, and the suspense is killing me." La had a very confused look on her face and seemed to be fearful of what she was about to hear.

Tarzan smiled and began, "La, since the first time I came to Opar, there have been many changes in the world you know, and the world I know. They are two different things. More people have become aware of the existence of Opar, and it is only a matter of time before the extent of the city's wealth becomes known."

"I told you years ago to consider leaving Opar because of the impending threat. Those dangers have become even larger and closer. Now that you have almost no people requiring your rule, I now insist you leave Opar. It is too far for me to be able to support and protect you here."

Surprisingly to Tarzan, La answered, "Yes, I agree. May I bring Mayat and Soma with me? Do you have a place for the three of us to go? You know, Tarzan, since I was a child I wondered what was beyond the jungles Ware took me to as a child."

"That was the big issue to be discussed, so the rest of the topics will probably come easily. But there are decisions to be made that I should be making. You simply do not know enough about the outside world to make them. Will you trust me?"

"Yes, I will trust your judgment. But I want you to tell me what you are doing, and how it will affect me. I know I will not always understand, but please try."

"Here is the 'shortlist' of my plans for Opar, and you:

"One, all the gold and treasure will be removed from Opar,

"Two, a group of scholars will be arriving here soon to study Opar,

"Three, what is left of Opar will be destroyed, hidden, or removed.

"I am going to take you to my friend, Martin. If you choose, he will educate you. This will permit you to decide on what you want to do next."

La felt that her whole world was being destroyed, and her face showed her dismay. "Is the gold all going to you? Am I to be a poor woman?"

Tarzan laughed, "No La, the gold will be split three ways. You will have a share that will be enough for you to be one of the wealthiest women in the world. I will take some. The rest will be used for a very good cause. Next year, you will be told about that great cause. Please trust me."

"What do these 'scholars' want?"

"One day in the future, the world will be told about Opar and the women who made it great. You don't know the origins of your ancestors; you told me as much the first night we talked in the storage room below the sacrifice room in the temple. You cannot read the marks on the temple walls. These learned men can. They can tell you your people's history and achievements. Does this interest you?"

"Tarzan, who is this person Martin?"

"He is a priest and very learned man."

"You mean like a witch-doctor?"

"No," Tarzan answered smiling. "He is in charge of a place of worship, education and healing. He has several female assistants who work with him."

La fished, "Is your Jane one of them?"

"No." Tarzan showed a bit of a frown; La seemed to have lost track of the subject.

"What will this witch-doctor do to me?" La asked with a bit of sarcasm.

"You will be taught the knowledge you will need to survive in the world outside the jungle. Take what I am offering you very seriously, La. You must decide where you will live. You may remain in a more civilized part of the jungle, or move to where you can become an important woman, in a world you cannot even imagine—your choice."

La looked at Tarzan with pleading eyes. Shortly she could hold her composure no more. She threw her hands in front of her face, dropped her head to her knees and cried hysterically.

Tarzan sat and observed. What he was watching occur with La, took him back to his youth, when he had faced similar circumstances. He had voiced, silently to himself, the same questions about his future. He had been much younger when he faced similar choices. He had not been a king, but he had experienced the loss of Kala, the only mother he had ever known. He believed leaving the jungle would mean a further separation from her memory. So he knew what was happening inside La.

He waited until she slowly regained control of her emotions and heard her muffled words spoken into her hands, "Tarzan, I am so afraid."

Tarzan told Msizi and La he would be gone for at least a moon. The next morning he left before either of them woke. There was one unfinished piece of business that begged his attention.

Tarzan needed his solitude. It had been several months of intense activity. As it happened, it all worked out the way he had hoped. He knew La, May-at and Soma needed time to think about all he had explained to them. They all had decisions to make that would shape the rest of their lives.

Three weeks into his journey, the ape-man, in the middle terraces, began to make great circles in his travel. He was searching for something. He came upon a dozen dirty tents in proximity—the camp of one of his most hated enemies – the Arabs. Tarzan watched the site for two days; he was looking for the dwelling of their leader. In the late afternoon, as he was finishing his evening meal of loin of warthog, he had made his choice. He wiped the blood from his hands on some handy leaves, settled back into a branch of the great tree and was asleep in minutes.

Tarzan awakened several hours later. Looking down into the camp, he saw almost no activity. The lone sentry was sitting asleep in front of a rapidly dying fire in the center. Tarzan silently climbed down the tree and was standing on the ground twenty feet from his tent selection. In his teeth, he had three pieces of rope and a foot square piece of cotton cloth.

The ape-man silently crept to the back of the tent, removed his father's hunting knife from its sheath, and slit the canvas from top to bottom. He stuck his head in, and as his eyes adjusted to the darkness, located his objective. He silently moved to the man. Tarzan clasped one hand over the man's mouth while the other gripped his throat cutting off his air. The man struggled but was unable to break free, and within less than a minute he had lost consciousness. Tarzan gagged him and bound his hands and feet. He picked him up as though he were a child, threw him over his shoulder and exited the tent, moving silently into the jungle.

Abbas Salam became aware the motion he had sensed had ceased. He felt himself being lowered onto a hard, rough surface. As his gag was removed, he rolled his head and looked down into the darkness. He could make out that he seemed to be high in a large tree. He turned the other way and found himself looking into a white man's face a few feet from him. Abbas Salam jerked in surprise and heard the man's voice say to him in Arabic, "Better lie still. If you fall, I will not save you. You are nearly at the top of this tree, miles from your camp."

With wildly frightened eyes the Arab answered, "Who are you and what do you want from me?"

The ape-man answered, "I am your worst nightmare. Here is what you need to know if you want to survive this night." He leaned closer to the Arab placing the knife on the left side of the man's neck, and said, "I require a favor. In return, you will not die, if I have your oath to Allah that you will do what I want."

Abbas Salam's eyes narrowed, "What is it you want?"

"You will send a written message to the camp. You will send them instructions. If they comply, and if everything is accomplished as I demand you will be released."

"Do I have a choice?"

"Yes, you have a choice. I can kill you right now — if that is your choice."

The Arab smiled weakly and said, "Give me writing tools and tell me what to write." The ape-man reached behind the man and untied the rope holding the prisoner's hands.

He smiled warmly, handed him the gag-cloth and a stub of a pencil. "Oh, I forgot to tell you, I can read Arabic."

The sun had just risen when Tarzan threw the message, tied around a rock into the middle of a group of men sitting around a fire eating their morning meal. He watched as one of them read it, rose and walked rapidly to the leader's tent. After a quick look inside, he shouted an order for everyone to assemble. He gave orders which Tarzan could clearly hear fifty feet above the man's head.

The ape-man went back to where his prisoner was bound. He looked at Abbas Salam and said, "You and your men will be followed to the port that you use to send slaves to your Arab brothers. Any treachery or lies will be dealt with severely and personally."

"There will be none," replied Abbas Salam. "The business with the Manyuema has not been good since the witch-doctor and the new king took over. The prices we are getting for slaves back home is falling to the point where there is no profit. The Manyuema are demanding too much money for their help. The slave business is getting to be too difficult, and we will be discontinuing it shortly."

The ape-man answered, "As soon as I see the chief and witch-doctor, and I have your word they will be sold in Arabia for the lowliest of jobs, you will be released. Remember what I told you about having many well-armed soldiers watching you."

The next morning, as promised, four Arabs approached fifty yards from the tree. They held between them a wizened old figure and a man of thirty who looked like he was sixty.

"Stop right there," Tarzan shouted. "Strip them both of their clothes." Tarzan looked at the wizened figure, and thought to himself, 'Msizi was right, the witch-doctor is a woman.' Tarzan looked at Abbas Salam, and he saw the same reaction. "By Allah, we have been working for a woman, an old woman, all these years. No one must ever learn of this."

The ape-man repeated, "Do you swear on the holy Koran, that you will uphold the terms of our agreement. Both of these people must be sold as slaves for the lowliest jobs."

Abbas Salam said "I so swear. You must promise me something also."

"What is it?"

"You will never tell anyone that Abbas Salam and his men were ordered about by a woman."

Tarzan gave a half smile, "You have my word. Go in peace."

Abbas Salam looked from the ape-man to the six people and shouted, "My sons, come and get me. I am free." He turned his head back, and he was sitting alone in the tree.

Msizi was notified the war chief was approaching, and he sprinted out to meet with him. "Greetings Tarzan. It is good to have you back in Opar with us. The men from the museum arrived, as you said they would, several days ago. They were given your written instructions and have rested after their long trek. Early this morning I saw they were unloading their equipment. I have done as you asked and kept La, May-at and Soma away from them. This was not an easy task since La is most curious."

"Msizi, you have done well. What of the cleanup after the battle?"

"There were no survivors among the Manyuema. All the bodies have been buried in the trench which had to be deepened to accommodate all of the dead. They were treated with respect and given fallen warriors services."

"Several of our scouts watching the Manyuema village came back this morning telling of a great commotion."

Tarzan said, "I will share the reason for that with you, La and Hopkins. Have the other scouting parties returned?"

Msizi answered, "Yes the other four parties returned, and there was no evidence of any more hostile tribes. They found some pygmies in the mountains, some farmers, but not much else."

"Good news," Tarzan replied, "I still want sentries posted on top of the mountains in back of Opar, and sentries around the clock on the wall. I also want patrols continually scanning the jungle. The number of men patrolling near the Manyuema village is to be doubled, with messenger monkeys ready to return if anything is threatening to us in Opar."

"Please take me to the men from the museum, and Msizi, introduce me not as Tarzan, but by my English name and title. Do you remember it?" Tarzan asked with a smile.

"Yes, I do remember. I worked in your home in England, while I was being educated," Msizi answered with a wide smile.

The two men walked along the stone pavings that led to the temple. The noise of generators and bright electric lights greeted them as they entered the main corridor. They walked up to a group of four men and one woman who were using soft brushes to clean the hieroglyphics on the walls. One of them stopped, set down his brush and advanced toward Tarzan and Msizi.

Msizi spoke, "Lord Greystoke, may I introduce you to Mr. Phillip Baker. Mr. Baker your host John Clayton, Lord Greystoke. Mr. Baker is in charge of the Opar expedition and recently arrived from Luxor, by order of Sir Frederic Kenyon."

"My Lord, it is a pleasure to meet you. I am looking forward to talking with you." Handing Tarzan a manilla envelope, he said, "A message from Sir Frederic. Good news, I hope."

Lord Greystoke smiled saying, "Baker, welcome to you and your team. I am just returning from a trip. I trust you have been made comfortable. If there is anything you need, please contact Msizi as he will be my liaison. I have several other matters that are pressing this morning, so I will see you and your staff tonight at dinner. Please excuse me until later." Lord Greystoke and Msizi turned, allowing the archaeologists to resume their work.

CHAPTER FIFTY-FIVE — FAREWELL MANYUEMA

The Waziri hunters had returned in mid-afternoon with several yearling antelopes, which were now grilling slowly over a hardwood fire. The warriors had asked Tarzan if he minded if they ate by themselves. This was their celebration of the tribe's greatest victory. He had, of course, granted their wish.

Tarzan sat in the afternoon with La and told her what had happened with the Manyuema leaders, Kasagama and Cyprian. La was pleased with how Tarzan had handled their punishment. After a few minutes, she said, "I could not have inflicted a better punishment, than turning the slavers into slaves. Are you sure the Arabs will hold their end of the bargain?"

"I am quite certain when an Arab swears on his holy book, he will not dishonor that promise. Besides, I have Waziri warriors watching to be sure the punishment happens."

"La," Tarzan began, "what do you want me to do with the women and children and old men of the Manyuema tribe still left in the village? They are no threat to us anymore, and they will have horrible deaths without the protection of their men."

"I don't care what happens to them" La answered.

"I will permit my warriors to take them back to the Waziri village. They will not be slaves, but they will have to earn their acceptance in the Waziri tribe. All will be required never to eat human flesh again. The young Waziri warriors showed great valor in the fight last week and should be given some reward for their deeds."

Tarzan asked La, "Have you spoken to May-at and Soma about the part of our conversation that pertains to them?"

"Yes, I talked to them both together and briefly to each one privately. Since I am no longer High Priestess or Queen of anything, do I really have any authority over them?

"Yes, you do La, but as their friend and mentor, no longer as a royal person."

"I agree." La began, "There is a hole in my heart for my dead sister, and I believe if I let it happen, May-at could fill that void. Soma has much experience with medicine. She can be very useful to your witch-doctor friend Martin. They both have the same apprehension that I have about the unknown, and fear for our safety."

"La, have I not protected you for all the years I have known you? Why would I have saved you so many times to harm you, or May-at and Soma, now? Your fears are groundless. You all are afraid because the future ahead of you is unknown. Believe me, it will be better for all of us than you ever could imagine."

La smiled at Tarzan when she realized what he was telling her about her safety. She knew it was true, she was able to keep from falling into the pit of despair again. They both sat in silence, each absorbed in their private thoughts. They remained this way for several minutes.

Tarzan began the conversation again, "You and I, May-at and Soma will be leaving Opar in the next several days. The trip will take over two moons. There will be twenty warriors traveling with us as bodyguards. These are the older men who have families and responsibilities in the village. Msizi will be accompanying us – you may tell May-at," Tarzan said with a smile on his face.

"The scholars studying Opar will conclude their work in the next several weeks. What happens next to Opar depends on what they find and how they want to remove it. One possibility is to flood the valley and protect the city by placing it at the bottom of a lake. Several of the Waziri and Hopkins are familiar with explosives."

This was beyond La's understanding, but she nodded her affirmation just the same.

Tarzan continued, "Since the battle ended, some of the warriors and porters have been locating gold from all the temple storerooms, preparing it for transport to the Waziri village. The scouting parties have found the easiest way to carry the gold from the temple to boats. The best water route has been identified. The gold will be floated to very near the Waziri village. I don't want the men to carry gold on their backs any further than is necessary. There is more gold than I ever imagined, and it will take many trips to transport all of it to the village. A few of the Waziri soldiers will guard the men studying the temple. The rest will protect the porters and the treasure."

He continued, "The gold will stay in the Waziri village until it is moved, by barges, to Libreville where it will be put on ships to England. The Waziri are working out river routes from their village to the west coast. The gold will be sent on several different ships for security reasons."

"Tomorrow I will send a message to Martin to expect us in a few months. He does not know anything about you. I have told him nothing, but I believe he is curious about what I want from him."

"I have not forgotten my promise to get your sacrificial knife, and anything else stolen from Opar. Tomorrow you will not see much of me. I will be spending the day working with the people who are studying the temple and the words on the wall."

La was losing interest in the planning. She was very eager to meet the learned men and woman who were studying her city. The meal tonight would be her first contact with them, and she wanted very much to impress them. La wondered how the people studying the temple would judge her. She did not want them to perceive her as a savage. "Tarzan, I need to prepare myself for the feast tonight. I will see you at dusk for the celebration." Tarzan smiled, rose and watched La as she walked from him.

I hope this dinner goes well, he thought. La can be somewhat unpredictable at times.

As it turned out, many of the Waziri warriors were good cooks also. Several of them had foraged the jungle for edible vegetables and greens for the evening meal. There were the five archaeologists, Sergeant Major Hopkins, La, May-at, and Soma, Msizi and of course, Tarzan They were served dinner in the area where La had her bathing pool, located at the north end of the Opar complex.

As everyone appeared for the dinner, it became evident that La, May-at and Soma were going to be at a disadvantage. They did not speak or understand the English that was being spoken by all the other guests. The three Oparians were dressed in their very best linen skirts and sandals. Their hair and make-up had been carefully crafted by May-at. The female archaeologist, named Nicola, obviously felt out of place and upstaged by the beauty of the three Opar women. La looked at her and saw a frumpy middle-aged woman who was no competition for her, or any of the other ladies.

At the beginning of the evening, La, May-at and Soma did their best to look interested in the table chat but were becoming more uncomfortable as the meal went on. Tarzan and Msizi tried to keep the Opar ladies informed of the conversation that was taking place.

This all changed, at least for La, after Baker had discussed his findings today with Tarzan. He turned his attention to La, and somewhat to May-at and Soma. The archaeologists had a great many questions for La. They were interested in how women had taken over governance of Opar. They were all quite curious that she did not have a mate. La was showing them her best side, lots of smiles and individual attention, to at least the men. For a first meeting, the archaeologists came away with an understanding of La and the way she had governed Opar.

Close to midnight, Tarzan announced to his guests that they should continue this another evening. He also told the Waziri to end their celebration and be sure the sentries on the walls were both sober and awake.

Lord Greystoke had read the report of Sir Frederic's translation of the inscriptions on the walls which Phillip Baker had delivered that afternoon. It was not a surprise that the city of Opar had been founded by Pharaoh Pepi II in roughly 2215 BCE. Tarzan did some quick mental math and realized that Opar was over forty-one hundred years old. No wonder there was so much gold and precious gems. He skimmed the rest of the long document and had little interest in any of the other translation information.

Lord Greystoke met early in the morning with the head archaeologist, Baker, and gave his written instructions to him. The main question on Tarzan's agenda was: Should the temple be left standing, hidden, or destroyed? Tarzan wanted to know if it was feasible to dismantle the temple and move it to London. He informed Baker he wanted a full report of his findings sent to him in West Africa. He and his team were then free to leave. Any items they wished to take back to the museum would be taken by his porters or warriors to boats for transport back to Luxor.

Msizi had been given a few last jobs. He and twenty-five warriors had arrived in the Manyuema village. They were met with side-glances and outright hostility by the women who watched them arrive. Msizi addressed the adults, consisting of the tribe's women, and the men who were too old to be warriors.

"I have two purposes for coming here today," he began, "one is to recover anything taken from the cloud city when the warriors invaded a short while ago. Two, do you women, men and your children wish to move from here and become part of the Waziri nation? Three people will be selected to speak for the rest of the people here. You will not be coming as slaves, but you will have to earn your place as members of the tribe. Anyone who elects to come to our village and commits an act of treason, in either word or deed will be killed immediately. No one will ever eat human flesh again."

Late in the afternoon two women and one man arrived for a discussion. The man spoke first, "We accept your offer and will move to the Waziri land. We feel that we have some use left in us, and pledge our loyalty to the Waziri tribe and its leaders." The women both gave an almost identical address. There was clear relief showing now in the facial expressions of the people. Their fears had ranged from everyone being slaughtered to sold as slaves, as had been the case with Kasagama and Cyprian.

From the looks on the people's faces, they were hungry. The old men had not been good hunters and food was in short supply. Msizi immediately dispatched five hunters to find game and bring it back to the people.

There were about four hundred women and one hundred children. The count of old or disabled men was about twenty-five. Many of the younger girls of marriage age, twelve to seventeen, would find a position as a second or third wife, and would have a strong warrior to defend them.

That evening after the meal of zebra, the people began to bring booty from the raid and placed it near the fire. Msizi went to the pile and found the sacrificial knife and put it in his arrow quiver. La would be so happy.

The next morning the camp was broken down and the people began a several-day walk to the cloud city. There the warriors would choose the women and the children they wished to adopt.

One warrior stayed behind, and when the group of people was a mile on the way to their new life, he made a fire and set everything in the camp ablaze.

That was the end of the Manyuema people.

CHAPTER FIFTY-SIX — EDUCATION

Tarzan, La, May-at and Soma had left Opar two days ago. As they had neared the escarpment, Tarzan stopped and looked back for the last time. It was a bitter-sweet moment, and every one of the women had tears in their eyes. By now they were somewhat looking forward to beginning their new lives, but it was still difficult to let go of the only home they had ever known.

So, as Waziri had done almost a hundred years ago, they turned their back on Opar and began their long walk to the west.

The women had been unusually quiet. They were all absorbed in their apprehensions and projections of what was to come. Tarzan felt he had to get them focused on the future before one or all lost their nerve about leaving.

Miu had witnessed the final battle as it occurred outside the city walls. She had left the safe shelter of her tree, to pursue a Manyuema warrior, who had been wounded and had blood streaming down his chest and arm. She somehow knew the man was one of the hated killers of her mistress, and she launched herself from a low-hanging branch. She landed on the wounded man's back, where she immediately dug her four-inch rear claws into his flesh. This brought a scream from his mouth. It would not last long, for Miu seized his throat with her powerful jaws and bit with all her might. With the jugular pierced blood spewed from his neck in great red jets. Miu shook him as easily as a terrier would shake a rat. He was dead before she finished.

Miu retreated to the safety of a tree and began to clean herself of the blood of the hated man.

The next day, Miu saw the woman whom she remembered from being with her mistress. She was walking with several other people, two of whom she thought she might have seen before. Miu thought it best to see if the woman would be alone, where she could approach her.

Tarzan and Msizi, as they were sitting around the evening campfire, told the ladies it was important for them to learn to speak English. It was the language everyone spoke where they would be going. Plus no one there would understand their words. Tarzan narrated to them how he had taught himself to read and write in his parent's cabin, so many years ago. He said he would begin teaching them some English during their long walk.

Tarzan had brought ten heavily armed soldiers for security during the long trip. Two of them had traveled a mile ahead scouting for problems, leaving two soldiers each a mile from the group to their right and left. The others followed behind.

Tarzan estimated the journey would take between sixty and ninety days, assuming no accidents or illnesses. The women were allowed to set the pace, and they seemed to be traveling a bit faster than Tarzan had estimated. When Tarzan thought they were about a week away from Father Martin's mission, he sent one of the Waziri ahead with a message. Tarzan smiled as the messenger left camp and watched him set a trotting pace that he could easily maintain to reach the mission in a day and a half.

The note read:

Martin,
Calling in all the favors. Will be arriving with ten Waziri and three female companions within a week. The women will be staying with you. Will explain when we get there.

John

That night May-at and Soma had retired to their blankets early, leaving La and Tarzan alone in front of the fire.

"Tarzan," La began, "we are all dying of curiosity as to what is going to happen when we reach the camp of the witch-doctor." La had gone back to speaking Waziri, after almost an entire day of attempting to speak English.

"I have asked you and the other ladies to have faith in me and my judgment for you. I will tell you my plans when we reach Father Martin's mission. He has two or three women assistants who will be in charge of educating all of you. They will teach you to read, write and speak English and French. They will teach you about clothing. You cannot continue to dress as you do.

La's face reddened, she started to rise, and said, "So, you are ashamed of us. We are an embarrassment to you, and you want to change us into people we are not."

Tarzan's face became serious. He shouted, "Sit down! Get that temper of yours under control! Look down the road to the future. You will be expected to blend in with the other women of the world of whom there are more than the leaves on the trees. If you do not 'fit in' you will be an outcast. You will not be accepted by anyone who comes into contact with you. Is that what you want for a future?"

La sat back down, and glared at Tarzan, but said nothing.

"After you are educated, you will be given a choice of where to live and what to do with your life. You can stay here in Africa, or you can relocate and go into business with me. This choice is not to be taken lightly, but it is your choice. La, you can throw away all I am offering, or you can control your temper and change— your choice."

Without another word, Tarzan rose, walked to a nearby tree, climbed up until he chose a branch and went to sleep. La sat with her hands and chin resting on her knees. She stared into the fire. After a few minutes, she got up and walked to her blanket for another sleepless night.

The next days passed uneventfully and quickly. Several days ago the party had passed out of the mountainous terrain and the rolling green hills, and into the long flat grass savannah. The number of animals and seemingly endless stream of different species was a constant source of conversation for the women. Every experience was new to them. As their world expanded greatly at times, it seemed overwhelming.

As they finished setting up camp, Tarzan said, "Tomorrow we should reach Father Martin. I hope all of you are excited about being over with the walking and starting new lives." The nervous looks on their faces told Tarzan there were other thoughts there also.

Tarzan turned to Msizi and said, "Would you tell of your experience with your education?"

May-at had already been told of his time in school. She listened to him as though it were all new. "When I was in my fifth summer, Tarzan and my parents sent several other children and me to school. I spent the next several years being taught a few days a week. I was then sent on a long boat trip where I continued my education. I lived and worked at Tarzan's house in England. I came back here several years ago, and when we return from this trip, I will be using my education to improve farming on the tribal land and Tarzan's farm."

It was good to see someone besides Tarzan being asked a seemingly endless barrage of questions. The women were able to speak more comfortably with Msizi.

The next day, about noon, they arrived just outside their destination. Tarzan had gone ahead of the rest of the party and was greeted warmly by Father Martin.

"I thought it best if we had a few minutes alone before I bring in the rest of the people." Martin's curiosity was over the top, but he let Tarzan guide the conversation. "The three women you will meet shortly are all that is left of a people who lived in the mountains of Abyssinia. Fierce cannibals killed everyone and destroyed their city. They have been isolated for thousands of years, and in most ways are quite primitive. The gold I gave to you came from their city."

"I am asking that you educate and care for them for one year. Your work will be generously compensated."

"Martin, the woman La, she has few inhibitions. She has a volatile and violent temper and is a violent person, used to getting her way. She was the ruler of the city. So please tread lightly and slowly with them, especially La. Don't judge her by her outward appearance."

Martin responded with a smile, "Wow, this sounds like some favor. We will discuss this in detail later. I know you have been planning this for some time, and I am grateful to be able to repay your generosity. Are my staff in any danger from these women?"

"They should not be,' Tarzan replied, "as I said, just tread slowly and carefully."

Tarzan did not want the women to be left alone for too long. "Everyone is very anxious to meet you," He said as he returned to the party. They rose and walked beside Tarzan as he led them the short distance to a small pavilion where the staff ate their communal meals.

Martin was standing alone by the table and benches, as the group approached.

In English, Tarzan introduced the women. Martin stepped forward smiled at each woman and lightly shook her hand. Tarzan had practiced this greeting with them several times. So far, so good.

He could tell something was amiss but listened as Martin said, "I don't want to overwhelm our guests so we will introduce their teachers later today." Martin indicated everyone to be seated and motioned for one of his cooks to bring out snacks and cool drinks. Tarzan translated, as he would continue to do for several days to come. Msizi would take over that duty after that.

Martin, with his best smile, said, "There have been rooms prepared for you in the guest cottage. I hope you will be comfortable during your stay. I am so glad Tarzan has included us, here at the mission, to help you in any way we can.

The ladies were shown their sleeping arrangements, leaving Tarzan and Martin alone. Martin said to Tarzan, "we will need to do something about those nearly naked women. I was not expecting to have three very beautiful women walking around that way. It may be a bit too much."

"Why Martin, I thought you were a man of the world?"

"I am. I am thinking about poor Dr. DuPont," he said with obvious tongue in cheek. Both men laughed and settled back for some discussion of Tarzan's expectations.

Two weeks later, Tarzan announced during dinner he would be leaving the group and returning to England. He had some shipping interests to take care of, and there were some matters in his home that he needed to address.

That night Martin and Tarzan spent their last evening together. Tarzan began, "Everything seems to be going reasonably well with the schooling. If you need to contact me, send a messenger to the commander, Captain Albert Chard, at the British military base in British East Africa, and he can cable it to me. I did not want to tell the group, but I will probably be gone for six to nine months. Do you need anything from me while I am in England?"

Martin hesitatingly said, "Before you go, I need to ask you about a sore subject. How is Jane? I have not heard anything about her condition for many years, and I am curious. I hope you don't mind my questions."

"There has been no change in her health; sometimes I lose faith there will ever be any improvement."

Martin nodded. By his return to silence, it became obvious Tarzan would say nothing more on the subject.

"I am going to venture some observations. The woman La is infatuated with you. Are you aware of that fact? "

"Yes, I have known this for years. Martin, do you have any idea how difficult seeing her has been for me? When I first met her, Jane and I were not wed, and I was torn in my feelings. Then Jane and I married, and that was that. I was coming home from Opar when a messenger met me with the news of the accident."

"Obviously, I care for La, or I would not have visited her several times; risking my life and the lives of my Waziri to defend and rescue her. What other feelings are there, I am afraid to acknowledge or even admit."

"Martin, you are the only person I can ask, and I do not guarantee I will heed your advice, but I am asking. What if Jane does not recover? Where does that leave me? Is my life to be tied to a person who does not even know I am in the room with her? "

Martin answered, "John, I can only tell you what the Church has taught me. Till death do us part. It sounds harsh and cruel, to watch you living your life this way. There is always a big difference in what we are taught and the actual living of it."

"As your advisor, I am bound to tell you what I have been taught as Church doctrine. However, I am a man like you. You know that despite my vow of chastity, I had an affair with a woman. I am still fighting the same battle as you about my relationship with women in general and that woman in particular."

"All can say is, if Jane were able to be asked, do you think she would want you to live your life alone? John, you must do what is in your best interests, and what is in your heart. Jane, I believe, is beyond feeling and caring for you."

La had found it difficult to sleep. She had seen Father Martin and Tarzan sitting at the dining table. She had approached, hidden by darkness. While she was still in the shadows she saw the serious nature of their discussion, she stood quietly and listened. While she did not understand every word, she understood enough.

Chapter Fifty-Seven — A Snake In The Nest

Tarzan was quite anxious to get out of the city of Libreville. The British ship, the S. S. Fazilka, was a steamship which would frequently carry freight and cargo, bound for Dover. Occasionally the vessel would take passengers if they were not too choosy about accommodations. The boat had docked early which would give Tarzan a chance to exit the city before the heat of the day set in when the town would rapidly smell much worse than it currently did.

The two-week sailing trip had given Lord Greystoke time to plan for his next steps in moving the gold and La to London – if that is what she decided. He checked his baggage with the staff at the cruise passenger office, saying someone would pick them up in a few weeks. He quickly made his way to the edge of town where he discarded his inexpensive shirt, shoes, and trousers; and took to the trees.

Miu had recognized her mistress's companion within the group of women and men who exited the city. She watched as they began to walk toward the escarpment. The great leopard shadowed them through the entire trip, not once giving up on the idea of presenting herself to the woman she knew.

Miu had suffered greatly on the long walk. Her pads were rubbed raw from first the rock climbing and then the sharp grasses. She had not eaten properly, drunk, or slept enough to remain healthy. She had lost much weight until she was able to get back into somewhat of a normal routine when the party reached the mission.

Finally, the travelers arrived at a fairly large village that Miu hoped would be where her mistresses' friend was going to stay. After several days Miu decided she should look for some decent food, rest and wait for an opportunity to present herself.

Miu watched the camp from a tree, as was her habit, only leaving to get water or kill some small animal for food. Her patience was finally rewarded, and she followed La for several miles. She was about to present herself when a woman came up behind her striking her mistress' friend in the head with a wooden club.

Miu watched as the woman tied La to a tree, and began pacing back and forth, talking to herself in a loud and angry voice. Miu climbed through the branches until she was nearly on top of the tableau that was playing out below her. She could tell there was much anger and bad blood between the women. Miu decided she had seen enough.

Most of the Manyuema women had volunteered or had been assigned jobs to pay for their room and board. Work, and becoming another wife to a Waziri warrior, were the two paths to become assimilated into the community. Batia has no interest in becoming a wife of one of the Waziri men. She had a smoldering contempt for all things 'Waziri.'

Batia was not a very social woman, but she knew how to be friendly enough to get what she wanted. She was still mourning the loss of her brother Kasagama. She wanted to know what had happened to the bitch who was the chief of the cloud city. She feigned a good nature and began to ask any of the former Manyuema women if they knew what had happened to the cloud city woman.

Finally, one her former acquaintances, who had become a third or fourth wife to one of the Waziri warriors returned from Opar shared a bit of information with her. She had overheard the man bragging to his primary wife that he knew information that none of the other warriors knew. That was wrong. Batia was told the following: Tarzan and the women who had left Opar were traveling west to a village where there stood a church and school. It was run by a priest who had visited the Waziri village several years ago. They were being escorted by many Waziri warriors. It was a very long journey to where the Opar women would live. The woman thought the M'beti village was almost a two-month trek.

Batia smiled and thanked the woman for the gossip. She quickly changed the subject to anything else since she did not want to make the woman suspicious. When they parted company later that evening, Batia began to formulate a plan to find the women of Opar.

Batia did not care what happened to her. She hated being here in the village of these inferior people, who her brother and his warriors should have been able to destroy. Somehow they had been tricked and all killed. Her brother, Kasagama, and the witch-doctor, Cyprian, had disappeared. The gossip was that they were probably dead.

She began to store non-perishable food and empty containers for water a few miles from the village. She needed some weapons, but here she would need to be careful. Many of the Waziri wives were assigned to watch for any suspicious behavior and report it to the tribe council. Then it was dealt with quickly and mercilessly.

Batia knew this was going to be a one-way trip. There would be almost no possibility of coming back to the village after a four-month absence. Her revenge would most likely cost her life. She loved her brother and desperately wanted to avenge his death no matter the cost. She was not a hunter or tracker so there was a strong possibility she would become hopelessly lost, or killed by some wild animal or starve to death. Despite these realities, she made up her mind to try.

A week of further preparation and storing food brought her the opportunity to steal some weapons. There had been a party in the village, and most of the warriors and younger people were up late celebrating. She rose early and was able to find an assegai and a long knife unattended, so she took them. She wrapped them in her blanket and exited the village for the last time just as the sun was beginning to drive the darkness away.

The first several weeks were the most difficult. She was able to find some small animals, berries and fruits for meals. She learned to watch what the monkeys ate and assumed correctly that it would be good for her also. It took her almost a month to be able to walk all day. She just hoped she was heading in the right direction. In the mornings she kept the sun directly behind her, and in the afternoon she walked directly into the sun as it set before her.

Because she had no idea where the village was, once a week, she would seek the highest point of land and look for signs of cookfire smoke, especially in the evenings. She was determined to persevere no matter how discouraged she became. Finally, after almost two months, she saw signs of smoke to the south. She rested that night well and began a detour the next morning. This was her third attempt. The other two signs of hope had proven to be just small groups of farmers, not the destination for which she was looking.

Early in the day she began her detour and was immediately encouraged by the fact that there was much smoke from fires. Passing a large garbage dump, she carefully observed a fairly large village. There were several white buildings. One had a cross attached to a peak on the thatch roof. She would take her time circling the village for observation and rest a few days.

The village appeared to contain about a hundred and fifty adults, plus a large number of children. The people seemed to be farmers and everyone she observed had a well-fed and healthy appearance. A week after she began her surveillance, she saw three white women appear from a small building in the back of the village. They ate some food at a community table, and went into another building. They did not leave there until the sun was low in the sky.

After observing the women for several days, she noted that one of the women, the taller one, seemed to be the one the others looked to for answers and direction. Batia of course, could not hear their conversations; but rather relied on body language.

Several days of watching the three women's movements cemented in her mind that she was fairly sure which woman was the target of her rage. Batia had to continually fight down the fury that constantly rose in her breast. She stayed carefully hidden in the trees, and thought with satisfaction, 'I believe I know which of them is the bitch queen of the cloud city. She ordered my brother, Kasagama, killed. She will die for that. I don't care what happens to me. I will gladly sacrifice my life to avenge his disgrace.'

One day Batia noticed that her target walked out of the village and into the grassland. There was a path that made a several mile loop, ending back at the village. She had an idea the woman made a walk a part of her routine, and Batia saw the opportunity to execute her reprisal. Sometimes planning revenge is as sweet as the actual act itself.

Batia finally decided it was time to act.

As La was taking an afternoon walk after school had been dismissed, she thought she heard rustling in the grass behind her. That was the last she remembered until she awakened and found herself tied to a tree with extremely rough bark. She shook her head to try to regain control of her senses. The pain from moving her throbbing head was excruciating. La realized she was in the forest a long way from the path. She turned her head and found herself looking into the face of a very large black woman.

"Who are you?" La asked in a drunken sounding voice.

"I will ask the questions," came the response. "Are you the woman who ruled the cloud city?"

La felt her stomach clench in a cold knot, "Yes."

Batia had been working herself into a frenzy while La hung unconscious and defenseless against the tree. Batia was proud of her work, and the way her plan was working. Her blood-shot eyes were wide, her body was quivering with pent-up anger, and her speech was slurred. She was pacing with a small assegai spear, that she was waving in front of La's face. As her fury built, she hit parts of La's body with the blunt wooden end of the spear, raising welts and creating looks of anguish on La's face.

Batia turned the short spear with its deadly sharp pointed blade an inch from La's nose. She took it and cut into La's shoulder, just deep enough to cause pain and bleeding.

"You shall die gradually, bitch. Yours will be the death of a thousand cuts. Slowly you will bleed to death, and in the end, you will beg me to hasten an end to your miserable life."

"I do not know you, why are you doing this to me?" La asked in as calm a voice as she could conjure up.

"I should have introduced myself. I am Batia, sister of Kasagama, daughter of Maaka. I am the one who assisted in the revenge we heaped on your slut of a sister." Batia laughed a shrill piercing laugh and began shaking faster.

La stopped being afraid and struggled with the ropes that were securing her hands behind the tree. "Let me free you fat cow, and let's settle this as two warriors."

"No chance," was Batia's response "I tire of playing with you already. Your death will not be quick but will be faster than the thousand cuts. I will cut out your wicked heart as you did with so many of our people."

Her anger had reached a crescendo and Batia was rapidly losing self-control. She screamed, "You have killed all our young men and destroyed our tribe. You will not live to enjoy that for one more minute."

She drew back the assegai, pointing it at La's chest. As she moved her arm to thrust the spear with all her might, her ears heard the sound of intense rustling in the tree above her, and she turned.

Miu could control herself no longer. With all claws fully extended she lept out of the tree. She let out an angry leopard scream that was so loud it froze both women as they looked up.

The great animal's front feet landed on Batia's shoulders and embedded themselves. The powerful back paws began below Batia's breasts and dug in ripping like many surgical blades from her rib cage to the pelvis. She was immediately disemboweled, screaming and writhing in intolerable pain. Batia had dropped the spear and was lying on her back looking into the face of one hundred pounds of spotted fury.

As if to make sure Batia knew who had killed her, the leopard screamed in her face, and with her powerful jaws and teeth, she pulled Batia's face from her skull. Batia had been in shock from the disembowelment. The last sight her eyes saw was the fury in Miu's expression.

La was likewise in shock and did not recognize the cat until she saw the wide leather collar on Miu's neck. Many streams of emotion and thought went through La's mind. Upon recognition, she yelled, "Miu! Miu, you have saved me!" La's eyes went wide and rolled into her head as she slumped against the tree. As she was losing consciousness, she thought, "Is this my Kiya come back to save me?"

The search party, carrying torches, did not find La for several hours. Even then Miu paced in front of La and would not let anyone near her. Finally, La remembered Kiya's commands to instruct Miu to sit.

Once she was set free, La sent the searchers ahead and sat with her arm around Miu. She looked into the cat's great face and said, "I will never leave you, Miu, you are Kiya's spirit returned to me."

CHAPTER FIFTY-EIGHT — THE CORD IS CUT

Tarzan had greatly enjoyed his conversations with Father Martin's choices of teachers. The two nuns were vastly different from what he had expected. They were younger and did not wear the traditional black and white clothing. They wore skirts and blouses, and a small cloth that covered most of their hair.

Sister Mary Catherine grew up in the countryside of France. She was intelligent and soft-spoken, very caring and could easily gain the trust of anyone. She gave advice when asked, never before. She had a way of being everyone's best friend.

Sister Mary Clare was a street-smart woman who had been raised in the slums of Paris. Although she never spoke of her childhood, it was difficult being the only female child in a household with four brothers. Her father had been a laborer, who had died when she was a teenager. There had never been an excess of money in the house. The brothers were close to their mother and were able to help her with living expenses.

Both women were seeking adventure, and the religious life offered that because of the foreign travel to missions in primitive, and exciting, parts of the world.

When the women arrived, Tarzan made several requests of Father Martin. There would be no other students in the school at the time. All the nuns' efforts, he felt, would be needed to educate their charges. There would be no attempt to convert the women to Christianity. However, they would be taught what the major religions of the world offered and could choose, or not choose. Lastly, the teachers were to be given nine months to complete their work.

After ten months, the nuns were still cramming knowledge into their students. Lord Greystoke spoke individually with both teachers and told them he was impressed with the progress they had made. He told them they had one month to complete their work. They both told him the women had been good students, eager to learn. Their education had accelerated once their command of the English language had strengthened. The teachers said they wished they had more time to work with them. Both nuns were convinced the women could exist in the world of England or France with little difficulty, once the shock of relocation had relaxed its grip.

Lord Greystoke said again, "I am very grateful for all your hard work with the ladies. There has been a very great change since I dropped them here many months ago. I want addresses for your mother Clare, and your parents Cathy. Occasionally I get to France, and I would like to look them up." This brought smiles from the two nuns. "One last thing, the very existence of these three women must remain a secret among us."

"Soma, please come in and sit down," requested Tarzan. "I hope your visit here has been enjoyable. I understand you have absorbed the education like a sponge. I am sure some of what you have learned has been beyond your imagination."

"Tarzan, I am very grateful for all you have done for me. I love it here, and with your permission, I want to stay here. I know my knowledge of the plants of the forest is more than either Doctor DuPont or the Waziri healers. I can make a difference in the medical area."

"I thought this might be your decision. I think it is a good one. You will always have my support, and I want to hear from you often."

When Soma had left, he sought out La and asked her to join him. "La, I'm sorry we have not had much time to talk since I have been back. But there is much to do and little time. I hope your experiences with school have been positive."

La was somewhat hurt that Tarzan had spent almost no time with her, and her feelings showed. She had been the most resistive to the lessons. She struggled with the vast changes made and seemed not to be able to see the purpose of all the education. But she had done the work, and done it well, out of her respect for her close friendship with Sister Clare. They had an underlying bond that drew them together. Both were strong-willed women, and the good thing was that Clare was able to mold La's temper and will into positive channels.

Tarzan asked, "La, what is it you want to do with the rest of your life? As you know, you could stay here and live in a familiar environment. Or, you can come to England with me."

La dropped her eyes, "Come as what?"

"I can only answer for today. You will come as my friend and business partner. I can provide you with a life you could never have here. It will be nothing like you could ever live here in Africa even in one of the big cities."

"Tarzan, you know what I want. But if 'friendship and business' are all you can offer, I will take them. I want to be with you very much."

Tarzan knew where this conversation was going, and he wanted to change the direction.

"What of May-at?" he asked.

"Since she no longer is my servant, so to speak, I can only tell you what I would like. I look upon her as my sister. Perhaps she is filling a need from the loss of Kiya. I want to have her close to me. However, she is infatuated with Msizi and will probably ask your permission to marry him."

Tarzan smiled, "You have not told me anything I did not already surmise. We may be able to accomplish something that will please everyone – including Msizi."

"One last thing," Tarzan smiled, "be ready to leave within thirty days."

"What of Miu? I promised ..."

"That leopard will be the biggest headache of all, but, I believe it can be done. Please ask May-at to come here."

May-at entered, sat down, and promptly broke down in tears. "Oh Tarzan, I want so much to please you. You have done so much for me, and I am so grateful. But I don't know what I want to do. I love Msizi and want to marry him, but I love you and La, and I want to be with you too."

"Do you think you can be happy in the great city of London? You can't begin to comprehend how different it is from Opar."

May-at smiled and said, "If I can be with the people I love, I will be happy anywhere."

Tarzan stood and said, "We leave for London within thirty days. And tell Msizi I want to speak with him."

A month later, four people were standing on the deck of the S.S. Fazilka as it slowly edged away from the pier and began its two-week trip to Dover, in the south-east corner of England. They were all absorbed in their own thoughts about what was transpiring.

La looked at May-at saying, "I will be glad to leave this place. It smells worse than the garbage dumps of Opar." May-at nodded her head in agreement and gripped Msizi's arm a bit tighter.

"Two weeks on this bucket seems like a lot of time, but we four have lots to discuss and plan for when we get to London. Don't forget La you are in charge of taking care of Miu. She did not seem to like the compartment where she and her cage were placed."

"This ship primarily carries freight with not too many passengers, and certainly not young ladies like you two. The accommodations are rather primitive, but we will make the best of it."

La's eyes were wide, and she asked, "Are we sure this thing will float? I don't understand how something this big, made of heavy metal can float."

"Yes, it will float and get us to England. I have made this trip plenty of times, and it always seems to make it through."

"We need to all get to our cabins. You ladies are not to go on deck without either Msizi or me with you. There are some tough men working on this ship, and I don't want any problems. There is a small private dining room on our deck where we will meet in one hour for lunch."

After a meal of soup and sandwiches, Tarzan produced two passports and placed them in front of the women.

La looked at the brown cover of the small booklet and saw:

Nom: Dubois

Prenom: Lareina

May-at looked at hers, and saw, next to prenom the word May.

Tarzan smiled and began, "It was easier to give you ladies a background that cannot be traced. The story is that you were the daughters of French diplomats who died in a colony of France in Africa. You were raised there by an older aunt who passed away last year. You both then requested to be able to return to Europe. I had a French friend create these identities, and get passports for you. This process of making up identities must never be traced back to me. You are now returning from Africa for a sightseeing trip to England. Guard these passports carefully. They will be very difficult to replace."

"These documents will get you into England, and eventually we will be able to obtain English passports. I have all the necessary paperwork which detail you and your parents' lives, should it ever be requested. You will have to read and memorize this information as you will need it when we get into customs in Dover."

"Msizi, there are ten heavily armed men guarding cargo crates in the hold. Please be sure they are well taken care of, with plenty to eat and drink. When we arrive in London, you will be in charge of getting the cargo moved to its new location. I will show you how I want it done. There are several more shipments to come, and you will be in charge of security."

Upon arrival in Dover, La asked Tarzan to buy her a newspaper. She had never really had one in her hands, but she wanted to keep it to remember what had happened the first day she arrived in England, December 15, 1928.

Several nights later, Tarzan, Msizi and the Waziri guards jointed a group of burly men at the port. The boxes marked 'Farm Machinery' had been loaded onto trucks. The convoy took many hours that night to reach a maintenance station for the London Underground. This was not a regular stop for customers. It was an above-ground station which would send repair crews into the tunnels. The trucks were unloaded by cranes smaller than the ones used at the docks. They were loaded onto flatbed cars used for transport and sent into the tunnel.

The cargo arrived an hour later at a spur close to the tube station near Chancery Lane. From there, a cart was waiting on the narrow gauge track. The wooden boxes were moved from the flatbed car onto the cart. The distance from where they were unloaded in the Silver Vault was less than a quarter mile. There were three flatbed cars to unload, and it took several hours, and many trips, to move the goods inside the vault. This was accomplished by twenty very large men who were used to heavy work. This was the third of five projected cargo transfers. When the five shipments from Africa were safely in the vault, the metal door would be welded shut, surrounded by a brick wall built and filled with concrete. Another brick wall would be built where the spur began off the tube tunnel, concealing that there ever had been an entrance.

Nearly eight hundred tons of gold were stored in the vault. This represented nearly three thousand five hundred years of mining activity.

Tarzan and La were sitting alone in a small restaurant. May-at and Msizi were out walking in a nearby park. Tarzan produced a manila envelope and slid it over on the table top to La. With a quizzical look on her face, she asked, "What is this?"

Jim Malachowski

Tarzan replied, "Years ago, on one of my trips I brought a camera into Opar and took images of the walls of the Flaming God Temple. I took them to the director of the British Museum for him to translate. I wanted to wait until your reading skills were up to it before I showed it to you. They reveal what I thought. You and your people are descended from the ancient Egyptians. The walls name a king Pepi II. He ruled Egypt about forty-one hundred years ago."

La dropped her eyes to the document and read it in its entirety. "I can remember my mother always wondering what the temple walls said. It is amazing that I now know. Those names, 'Nebra', 'Menkhaf', 'Thutie'[6] None of these names are known to me. As for the events that occurred, they also are unknown to me, because the people of Opar had almost no writing and did not keep track of history. It is an interesting story, that is believable and could be the history of our origins."

"When we get to London, if you would wish, I will take you to the British Museum, and introduce you to the director. He is the one who translated the writing. He was unaware any people were living in Opar when I took the pictures. It will be quite a shock to him to meet one of the inhabitants."

La asked with a smile, "Am I to be put on display in this man's museum?"

"Of course not."

---

[6] Transliteration of images to words is not a precise science, differences in spelling and interpretation can occur.

CHAPTER FIFTY-NINE — THE LONDON LIFE

The Nineteen-Twenties were drawing to a close, and right after those years were the beginning rumblings of political unrest in Europe. La and Lord Greystoke were quite probably the wealthiest people in England and possibly in all of Europe. Lord Greystoke did nothing that would bring attention to himself. He preferred to work through agents in both Great Britan and on the continent.

Six months after the migration to London, Tarzan asked La if she would like to accompany him on a trip to France. She immediately said yes.

"Why are we going to France? The only person we know is D'Arnot, and you told me he is in America."

"The parents of your teachers at Father Martin's mission are getting on in years. I would like to show my appreciation for their efforts with the three of you. One of the families is quite poor. I feel I need to share some of our wealth with them,"

"I agree, " La replied, "I owe those women more than I can ever repay."

La enjoyed the one-month train trip which covered most of France and ended up with a seven-day stay in Paris. Both nuns' relatives were surprised to receive visitors from London. Neither knew their daughters had educated La, and she wanted it kept that way. When they left both families homes, Tarzan handed them a small elegantly wrapped box, containing a bank book with the equivalent of fifty thousand dollars. He had asked them not to open the package until the next day. His only explanation for the gift was that their daughter had done Lord Greystoke a great favor, and this was his way of repaying it. Since the nuns only knew him as Tarzan, not Lord Greystoke, the secret of La's identity remained safe.

During the last night on the train, Tarzan told La he wanted to take her to Egypt, to see where her ancestors had originated. She was delighted, as she had always been about travel. Tarzan wanted to get this trip in before any hostilities began in Europe.

"I hope you remember Phil Baker, the archaeologist. Well, I have asked him to join us in Cairo, and I am sure he can answer all your questions about your heritage."

"Just tell me this does not involve a long boat trip," La asked with a smile.

"Much shorter and a lot more elegant. South Hampton to Port Said is about eight days and not aboard a freight vessel."

In Cairo, La and Tarzan were met by Phillip Baker at the Egyptian Museum. Baker was in his element and spent the entire day enlightening La, and sometimes Tarzan, on the history of the oldest civilization on the earth. La was particularly interested in seeing anything that related to the sixth dynasty of Pepi II, as written on the walls of the Temple of the Flaming God. After a very long day in the museum, the three retired to the Mena House hotel, where they enjoyed a dinner on the terrace, watching the pyramids as the sunset.

La said, "I love it here in Egypt. There are almost no mosquitos. Sitting outside in Opar, one would be eaten alive."

"Today is something new, which I hope you enjoy," Baker began as Tarzan and La got into the Jeep. "We are going into one of the oldest sections of Cario. Several churches have been built together in a tight cluster. We will be visiting one in particular, and the other ones if you would like. This church is over fifteen hundred years old." He parked the Jeep along Meri Gerges, which was less than a quarter of a mile from the River Nile. La entered the Saint Virgin Mary's Coptic Orthodox Church, sometimes called the Hanging Church. He and Baker followed La inside. Tarzan quietly asked when the service would begin

"We have about ten minutes to look around inside," added Baker.

Tarzan could tell La was impressed with the ornate wood carvings around the altar. The interior was extremely dark. The few windows there were located near the top of the walls. The wooden seats looked as though they had been in place for centuries, and they probably had. The scent of incense was very noticeable when the three of them sat down. The pleasant smell could have been from that day, or left-over from a thousand years ago. There were only a few residents attending the services, and they were already seated. The three visitors found pews near the front of the church and watched as a priest entered the altar area with one server.

He greeted the people and began reading from a large and obviously old book of prayers. After a few minutes, La turned toward Tarzan, with tears in her eyes and said, "I don't know how this is possible, but I can understand what he is saying. How can this Christian man be speaking the language of Opar?"

Tarzan smiled and said nothing. La's eyes opened wider and wider as she grasped what was happening around her.

When they left the church at the end of the service, Baker gave her the explanation of what she had just experienced.

"As the Egyptian civilization was ending, the Greeks who were ruling at the time wanted the Egyptian language written in Greek. They were unable to read the hieroglyphic, hieratic and demotic scripts. The Coptic church followed the Grecian Ptolemy Pharaohs and used the Greek alphabet but kept and spoke them in their Egyptian words. Therefore, the Copts preserved the ancient Egyptian language for almost two thousand years."

Late that evening, La told Tarzan how much she had enjoyed the day and the visit to the Coptic Church. "Are there any Coptic churches in London? Think I would like to attend one since they speak my language."

"We will check when we get back. In two days we are booked to sail the Nile from here in Cairo south to the bottom of Egypt."

"This cruise sounds very pleasant," La responded.

The paddle wheeler left Cairo on the morning of a beautiful day. Being the end of the year, most of the intense heat was gone, and cloudless blue skies were the order of the day. Even in late afternoon, it was still quite pleasant to sit on the top deck, in a comfortable chair, and watch the people, animals, and farms quietly slip past.

"La, this is the route that your ancestors would have followed on their way south to search for gold and set up your city of Opar. The river and the people who live on its shores look the same as they did thousands of years ago."

La was fascinated by the river. She had never seen so much water activity before. People were farming and irrigating their land, animals grazing and drinking, women washing their clothing. There was also an incredible amount of animal life. The most fascinating to her was the Nile crocodile, some of which were fifteen feet long. It was easy for her to imagine the trip her ancestors had made. She was sure they had not traveled in this amount of luxury, with a clean bed each night and three meals every day.

Almost every evening she thanked Tarzan for bringing her on this trip. She had been fascinated by what she had seen, by so many new things. Often as they walked the streets of Cairo, she saw finely dressed ladies who looked like women she had known in Opar.

"Tarzan, please promise to bring me back here again someday."

This had been Tarzan's first trip to Egypt. He enjoyed the country, the people and the history that seemed to be everywhere. He had made his promise to La, and he sincerely hoped he would be able to come back someday.

The train ride back to Cairo had been pleasant, taking two days. The station was packed with people arriving from other cities. The people of the city were beginning their workday. The railroad was the main means of travel, and it served all classes of travelers twenty-four hours per day. They reached Ramses Square train station and had the remainder of the day to rest before their boat trip back to England.

Jim Malachowski

CHAPTER SIXTY — THE WAR YEARS

The 1930s seemed to pass in a blur.

May-at and Msizi had married and currently were expecting their second child. Twice Msizi had accompanied Tarzan back to Africa, but he was always anxious to return to London. On their last trip, Tarzan had booked passage for him and Msizi on the Imperial Airlines. Msizi was somewhat anxious about flying like a bird, but once underway, it was difficult to get his attention away from the window

Msizi oversaw the changes that were taking place in the Waziri village. It was now looking more like a town than an African village. They had all the advantages of any other medium-sized town. In addition to a large selection of goods to buy, there was a modern medical facility which Tarzan aided in setting up. New homes were built with indoor plumbing and electricity. There were enough Waziri men and women with college degrees that they represented just about every advanced skill needed to make a modern town.

La and May-at had made the transition from boss and employee to being equals. La was fascinated with May-at's first child. She was godmother to the baby, and it would never want for anything as long as

La lived. Now there was a second child on the way, and it was had to tell who was more excited May-at or La.

The two women had abandoned their earlier beliefs about clothing. Upon discovering large department stores like Harrods and Selfridges, they spent a lot of time and money shopping. Tarzan never seemed to mind. He just had the bills paid regardless of the amount.

The storage in the Silver Vault was used for the safekeeping of the large quantity of gold and gemstones from Opar. Occasionally, by word of mouth, someone would call the Mayfair telephone number and would want to purchase the precious metal by the forty to fifty pound bar. There were men and women in the world who wanted the safety of owning gold. After all, it was the standard on which all currencies in the world were backed. Either La or May-at would attend to the transaction in an office at the Silver Vault.

Tarzan's love of Africa and its people and animals never left him. He often returned several times a year. He yearned for the adventures of his youth, and without much effort, he was able to find exploits that kept him entertained. Over the course of years, La only went back to Africa with Tarzan twice. She did not share his love of the vast jungle. She spent a lot of time with Father Martin and Soma, and in both cases had returned to England alone.

On one of the flights to Africa, La asked again, "Why are we storing so much gold in a hole in the ground. This is what we did in Opar."

Tarzan smiled and said, "Everyone in government believes another huge war is coming. England and France are still recovering from the war twenty years ago and will be hard-pressed to support a large army. The madman in Germany wants to control the entire world. That just cannot be allowed to happen. During the first World War Germany had troops in many places in Africa. Were they allowed to steal the wealth of Opar, there would have been no way to stop them. La, the money that the gold represents is the best chance we have to remain a free people."

"Some of the things you explain to me I know the words but do not know how they apply. I will just as always put my faith in you."

"I have never let you down yet. Have I?"

The war did come and was a long and terrifying event for La and May-at. The constant shortages and the bombing of London made both women ready to leave, except there was nowhere to go. The war raged on all continents. At the height of the bombings of London, Tarzan moved everyone he could into the gold storage area. It was one hundred feet below the street and provided a great level of safety.

As the fighting dragged on, the money the gold represented was desperately needed by Britain. France was under control of the Nazis, and any monetary assistance was given to underground groups who were fighting the Germans as best they could. Tarzan was propping up the Churchill government with large infusions of gold. He was very concerned that the wealth would be exhausted before Germany could be defeated.

After Hitler was dead and the war ended, Britain still desperately needed assistance obtaining food and consumer goods from the United States. Tarzan assisted as best he could. The supply of Opar's gold was nearly gone.

When La and Miu had arrived in London, La found an animal veterinarian who had large enough caged space for the leopard. After a few months, La purchased a house in Mayfair which had a spacious semi-finished basement. She tried to keep Miu there, but the experiment failed. There was not enough light and space for Miu to be happy and she could not roam at all. The great cat stopped eating and became lethargic, and La feared for her life.

La began a concerted campaign to find Miu a new home. Her search led to a small animal rescue farm located halfway between London and Oxford. After a half day of negotiations, Miu had found a new home. La had always had a soft spot in her heart for animals and was glad to make a very large contribution and the promise of monthly "boarding fees" for Miu.

La had also paid for all the fencing and housing that would keep Miu safe and warm in the chilly England winters. She had an acre of enclosed land to roam with several trees for her to climb. Throughout the years La visited Miu almost every week and would spend the majority of the day playing with her. It was about an hours train trip from the Knightsbridge underground, then a short car ride to Miu's new home.

The farm owners were always amazed that La was able to enter Miu's area without being attacked, something that no one else had been able to accomplish. When La went into the pen, Miu would greet her and immediately begin acting like a very large house cat.

Miu lived happily until the 1950's when she passed away quietly in her sleep. La never vocalized her belief that Miu was the spirit of her sister Kiya after she had been killed.

The relative peace of the fifties and sixties was a godsend. A new queen brought hope for the United Kingdom. However, the British Empire was living its final days, since more and more colonies were demanding their independence. The African continent, in particular, was a powder-keg of hatred for the British and whites in general.

Tarzan was forced to enlarge their armaments and arm all of the Waziri men. It was commonly known that the Waziri were friends with the white Tarzan, and were looked upon with disdain by their neighbors.

Since the late 1960's, La had become physically inactive. She had lost interest in travel, or any other the things she had enjoyed in previous years. She only showed interest in May-at's children and grandchildren. She loved to have them visit her.

About 1970 Tarzan decided he had had enough politics, and gave up being active in the House of Lords. He resigned from all committees and began to spend more time with La.

A year later La's health had begun to fail. She was often in hospital and never was able to regain her vigor. After a particularly difficult illness, more tests were performed, and it was discovered she had cancer and had a short time to live. Tarzan did not leave her side from the moment he learned of her illness.

La was aware she was dying but did not seem upset by the fact. She and Tarzan spent many hours reliving their lives together, and an unspoken conclusion was neither would have changed anything. They were as happy as they could have been.

"John, you still look like a man of fifty. When I am gone you will, I am sure, be able to find a much younger woman to take my place."

"I will never be able to find another woman like you, so there is no point in even looking."

"What will you do after I am gone?" La asked.

"The majority of the vast fortune from Opar was gone saving Britain in the war. I don't care; I don't need money anymore. I will go back to the farm in Africa. I have always believed I would die there."

He added with a smile, "perhaps after another adventure or two."

La's private nurse, Mary Davies, came into her room and to her delight found that La was not only lucid from the painkillers but was in a good mood. "Mary please close the door, and sit with me for a while." Mary had been on private duty with La, hired by Lord Greystoke, for the past six months. Early in their association La, Lareina Dubois as she was introduced to the nurse, had told her a sanitized version of her early life. She spoke of having lived with people who valued their privacy and camouflaged themselves from any contact with their neighbors. She told Mary that her early life had been quite adventuresome. There had been many times when her existence was in peril and she had survived by her wits.

La's stories of dangerous people and animals fascinated her. At some time, La had traveled to several mysterious locales in central Africa. She had spoken of a wild man who had been born in the jungle, with whom she had been acquainted for many years. The extent of that relationship was never elaborated upon. When asked whatever happened to the wild-man, La only smiled and said, "He just seemed to disappear."

Mary seated herself as instructed, smiling as she sat down in one of the two straight-back chairs that were in the private room. Lord Greystoke had insisted La have a private room. He did not want her placed in one of the more numerous wards. She knew that La wanted to talk with her, so she merely sat and waited until La had collected her thoughts.

"Mary, I have given considerable thought to what I am going to ask you, and I want two promises from you. One is that Lord Greystoke will not be told what I am about to ask you to do for me. Secondly, you will swear that my wishes will be carried out." Mary smiled and voiced her assent. "You are to contact my niece, May-at, and tell her to open my letter and comply with the wishes it outlines."

"My second task is you will bring the valise in that clothespress to me, and I will explain what I want." La pointed to a small closet in the room. Mary lifted the heavy valise onto a table near La, unlocking it with the key given to her. Inside she saw several rather ordinary looking journals. They were large thick leather-bound books made up of tough but thin sheets of unlined paper. She looked at La for further instructions. "These diaries contain the story of my life. I have been keeping these since I learned to write. They are the story of my ancestors and details of my life before I moved to England." Mary opened the top journal and saw a small neat script that filled the pages from top to bottom. She could not understand the script, La saw this and said, "The journals were kept in French since it was the first language I learned to read and write."

La handed Mary a note and told her to open it. Mary read a name and address, outside Great Britain, and looked quizzically at La. "You are to box those journals securely and send them to the address in the note. There is a letter in the suitcase. Be sure it is on top of the contents, so when they are received, it will be seen immediately." She handed Mary a one-hundred-pound banknote and instructed her to send this package the most secure manner possible right away.

"Keep the excess monies, and hopefully I will be lucid enough for you to tell me the jobs were completed. Now go and do as I ask." Mary carefully put the journal back in the suitcase, left the hospital and set out for the most secure packaging and shipping company she could find.

That afternoon, when she returned to the hospital, to tell La her wishes had been filled, she found that once again La was in a deep sleep from the painkillers. La would never know that Mary had fulfilled her wishes.

Mary had telephoned May-at and told her that her aunt seemed temporarily better. She conveyed La's instructions for the note which May-at had stored in her desk since La's illness became acute.

May-at, having read La's note, was standing in the bedroom of La's Mayfair home. In the spare room was the large briefcase La had described. She picked it up and walked to the front door that she now knew would be hers shortly. Locking the front door, she seated herself in the back of the limo and returned home to her husband and children. While being driven home, she opened the briefcase and read the note. Her left hand felt the familiar items that were beneath the velvet cloth. A tear came to her eye, as she thought, "The tradition is being passed on."

The note read: "Opar is gone. The High Priestesses of Opar are all dead, but the tradition must continue to live. Teach your line of granddaughters, our story, and the old ways, and see they know the meaning of the items in the bag. Ask that, in their hearts, they carry on as High Priestesses for generations to come." In the bag were the sacrificial knife and the headdress made from gold disks that May-at had seen La wear so many times.

May-at's daughters at this time were middle-aged, and had no interest in the ways of Opar. The granddaughters were a different story. They were always asking about Opar and the beliefs that La and their grandmother still held sacred. One of these girls would pick up the responsibility of being a High Priestess of a kingdom that no longer existed.

May-at had wondered over the years what had become of the items; she had assumed they had been lost or perhaps donated to the British Museum. She felt a sense of pride that La considered her daughters to be worthy candidates for High Priestess.

Chapter Sixty-One — The End

Tarzan left a sleeping La in the hospital. He knew that the end for her would come soon. Walking to a nearby green commons, he found a bench, where he could be alone. He was a frequent visitor to this park bench. He sat and gathered his thoughts wondering what life would be like without La.

As he settled in, a nurses aide rapidly walked up to him and handed him a folded paper. He opened the note and read: 'Sorry to inform you that Lareina Dubois died a few minutes after your visit. Our condolences. Please stop at the Nurses' Station when you return. She left a letter for you.'

Even though Tarzan had been expecting her death for the past several days, the reality came as a shock to him. He began to think about the passing of the people who had been close to him: D'Arnot, Father Martin, Alice the mother he never knew, and Kala, the mother who raised him.

In his dealings with females, Tarzan only ever had room in his heart for one. In his youth, he became aware that the woman in the locket was his birth mother. But, when asked, as a grown man, he denied Alice and said his mother was an ape.

In his adult life, Jane was the first woman with whom he fell in love. On the surface, she seemed not to be a great match for Tarzan. Her outward appearance was of being a weak person. But, that was not the case. She had the inner makeup of a woman who was both physically and mentally strong.

La presented the exact opposite. She exhibited a tough outer appearance, a woman who could take care of herself, a woman who was physically and mentally strong. Once again appearances were deceiving. La was unsure on the inside, always seeking someone to take care of her. She seemed to make decisions without regard to the consequences.

These two women dominated and shaped Tarzan's entire adult life. Even though they were as different as possible, they filled the same need in him. They were companions who not only adored him but cared about all the people and places around him. They shared his interests, and never tired of being in his company.

Now, for the first time in his life, Tarzan felt terribly alone. He thought back to his youth when he had rescued the witch-doctor. The grateful man had, in a lengthy procedure, given Tarzan an extended, if not immortal life. The way Tarzan felt now, we wondered if it the gift was perhaps really a curse.

A tear dropped from his eye onto his cheek. He did not mourn the people he had lost; they had all lead full lives. He wept for what might have been.

A few days later, Tarzan stopped by the hospital to pick up the few belongings La had left. Several of the nurses who had taken care of her came up to Tarzan and expressed their sorrow at her passing. He entered the room where La had been for several months. When he saw the empty bed – perfectly prepared, the fact that La was gone came back strongly. Tarzan left the hospital and walked to the green common where he had learned the news of La's death recently.

He found the same bench and sat down. The weather was changing. It had been sunny and bright on the way to the hospital, but now the sky had clouded over, and a cold wind was blowing from the north. He looked at the white hospital stationery envelope. It had 'John' written on the front. He opened, and unfolded the single sheet of paper, and read the small neat script that he recognized as being written by La.

The note said: 'I want to go home.'

Two months later Tarzan had returned to Africa. He retraced his usual path once he arrived in Libreville. He dreaded what needed to happen in the next several days, the first of which was a trip to the Waziri village.

When Tarzan arrived, he was taken aback by how much had changed. It was now a town. Many of the residents were dressed in European style clothing. The people could have been transported anywhere in Europe or America and fit right in with the residents.

Tarzan was greeted by the chief and the council of elders. He was asked if it was convenient to hold a ceremony that evening. There were many people still alive in the village who remembered the sharp-tongued, naked woman who had appeared one day. That same woman left, one year later, as a serene educated lady.

Tarzan was sorry Soma was not there to be part of the ceremony. She had died ten years ago. She had throughout the years sent Tarzan a quarterly correspondence telling what was going on in her life. She always ended her writings with a thank-you in appreciation of all Tarzan had done for her.

At dusk a large number of the people assembled at an area a quarter mile outside the village. All grass and shrubbery had been cleared in a hundred yard circle. In the middle was a twenty-foot arrangement of logs that would be the focal point of the evening's ceremony.

As darkness approached, the priest who had taken Father Martin's parish began the service with a very brief prayer. He spoke eloquently about La for a few minutes, and how much she had done for the Waziri people and their village over the years. The current chief spoke a bit about his remembrances of La.

Tarzan thanked everyone for coming. He concluded his brief comments by saying he was glad that La's suffering was at an end. He told what a special person La was to him, and what a void her absence would leave in his life.

Everyone stood quietly as Tarzan lit the funeral pyre. The people stayed until the great logs had been consumed by fire and were collapsing. Tarzan signaled to the chief that the celebration was over, and he began the walk back to his farm.

Tarzan had written, asking Busuli, and several young Waziri of his choice, to accompany him on his last trip to Opar. Tarzan was shocked when he saw Busuli; he was now an elder warrior. Tarzan had forgotten how long it had been since he saw his oldest friend in the tribe. He asked politely if he was up to the trip, and Busuli insisted he was perfectly able to take on the month's walk.

Tarzan could not remember how long it had been since the two men had seen each other. They spent many hours talking about common experiences in their lives and events unknown to the other.

The small group reached the foot of the escarpment in the late afternoon, and at Tarzan's request made camp. He told them he would go on alone from here and would rejoin them in a few days.

The hidden mountain climbing equipment, replaced over the decades, was in perfect condition and made Tarzan's steep ascent almost easy. He began scaling the escarpment an hour or two before daylight, and after a steady climb stood atop a small hill and looked out where the desolate valley was once located. Instead of being a place of great bleakness, he was looking at a beautiful man-made lake.

As he gazed at the water for the first time since the lake had been created, it was difficult for him to recognize the area. The surface was like a mirror, and from this distance, it almost appeared to be a mirage. It reflected the cobalt blue of the sky, and the high mountains behind. Not a ripple was showing.

A short walk brought Tarzan to the water's edge. He knelt and removed the knapsack he had been carrying since he left the farm. The small one-man boat inflated itself when the can of air was emptied into the nozzle. He pushed it out and climbed in, along with his knapsack. Tarzan knew his location as soon as he was able to locate the several columns that looked as if they had been part of a wall. He paddled to his left and began to look for another structure. He found it easily. The remains of the temple dome were only six feet below the surface.

Tarzan looked into what remained of the dome. The disturbance of the water made by the movement of his boat subsided and became still.

As he stared into the temple, a strange effect began to happen. The light around Tarzan began to change. The bright clear day around him began to fade into semi-darkness. It was as though he were in a motion picture theater, and the film had started.

Looking down into the water, the interior of the temple began to change, becoming lighter and brighter. The dome and the entire roof of the temple began to dissolve away. Now Tarzan could see the entire circular sacrifice room without a roof.

People began to materialize from the shadows of the scene. There were no sounds of any kind, as though it were a silent movie. A stone altar materialized, and he could make out a muscular youth of eighteen or nineteen tied to the stone altar. The young man glanced up, and Tarzan found himself looking into his own face. He saw himself as he had appeared so many years ago.

He could see the tops of many heads turn to face the direction of the struggling man. From the left side of the chamber, he saw a tall scantily-clad woman enter the scene with very slow graceful strides. A large wicked-looking knife was in her right hand. Tarzan could not see her face, only the top of her head which featured long black hair that contained a bit of a red cast.

She stopped and stood statue-still for a minute, as though she were collecting her thoughts. The scene and all the people seemed to freeze again. The only change was the slow-motion movements of the woman.

The woman slowly raised to an extended height and stood on tip-toes. She drew her shoulders back, dropped her head until it could not go back any further, raised her arms and faced him with closed eyes. After a few seconds, her eyes sprang open, and she seemed to be looking into his face as he leaned from the boat. It was the beautiful face of a youthful La. There was a slight smile on her face as though she had just been thinking about something very pleasant.

Her smile dissolved and the look of self-confidence faded.

She had totally lost the appearance of self-assurance. Tarzan watched the expression change as he had so many times over the years. Again, she appeared to be looking directly into his eyes. Her lips parted, and he heard, clearly, once more the four words —

"I'll always love you."

Now it all made sense. The memory from sixty years ago came flooding back. The words were like an echo. First from the present, then back to so many years ago. He had heard La's words years before, but they had made no sense to him at the time, but now they did.

How did La know, all those years ago, what was going to happen between them, and their feelings for each other, after only having seen him for a minute?

The scene did not slowly fade away; it just disappeared.

La's message had been delivered.

Everything reverted to being the empty ruined temple, as it now existed. The images Tarzan had just witnessed had turned him cold inside, and he was in shock. He was glad he had come alone, as he would not wanted anyone else to have seen his reactions.

Tarzan sat very still in the small rubber boat for almost an hour, before he was able to compose himself enough and finish his last duty here.

Tarzan shook his head, clearing his thoughts back to the task at hand. He glanced around, and there was nothing near him, just the clear and beautiful lake. Looking down into the water again, he saw the Temple of the Flaming God standing in ruins. There was very little light penetrating the water. Now visible was just the opening on top of the dome and dark shadows within.

Tarzan reached inside his knapsack, removed the urn, and gently poured the contents into the water. The particles traveled the short distance into the dome opening.

He watched the stream of powder sparkling in the sunlight as it slowly descended. Then the particles began to disappear as they reached the level where the light could not penetrate.

The contents of the urn were now part of the temple.

La was home.

Dramatis Personae

The Ancients

		Chapter
Nomes	Name for a geographic political area .. such as state or territory	2
Nomarch	Administrative leader, such as governor. Appt. by Pharaoh but her	2
Apries	Architect for Pharaoh	4
Henenu	Advisor to Pharaoh friend of Menkhaf's Father	2
Melit	Concubine of Menkhaf later becomes wife	2
Menkhaf	Son of Governor of Southern Egypt Nomarch /1st governor of Opar	2
Nebre	Son of Apries, travels to establish cities and the new Opar	4
Neith	Son of Thuthy. High Priest Opar Governor after death of Menkhaf	4
Neteru	Small pocket of Neanderthals surviving in Africa	6
Pepi II (Pharaoh)	Last Pharaoh before First Intermediate Period	2
Piye	Military advisor for trip south	4
Soma (name taken by healers)	Healer, expert in medicine and drugs	4
Thuthy	First Prophet of Ptah Religious Leader	4

Ancient Opar

Opar, Akh and Ra-Mat	Original three gold mining colonies consolidated into new Opar	5
Amose and Ako	Brothers/Hunters in early period. Important in building of new Opar	12
Muvo	Superintendent of Mines in colony	11

The Waziri

Waziri	The tribe who will become associated with Tarzan	18
Waziri (the man)	Many men who are chief take tribe name for their own name	18
Murvo	Accompanies Waziri to Opar	20
Dingane	Accompanies Waziri to Opar	20
Busili	Waziri leader accompanies Tarzan to Opar	41
Msizi	Leader of the squad of Waziri bodyguards for La	43
Nedjam and Waziri's Children	B/G/G youngest girl dead Oah is daughter of first Girl	
M'titi	Waziri archer who saves Tarzan's life	47

Queens and Attendants

Mery	High Priestess of Opar Grandmother of La	19
Set	Life Partner with Mery	19
Nedjam	Handmaiden to Mery, Ayesah, and La	19
Ayesha	High Priestess of Opar Mother of La	23
Ware	Partner with Ayesha, father of La hunter defacto High Priest	23
La	Last High Priestess of Opar	30
May-at	Handmaiden takes over when Nedjam dies	36
Kiya	La's younger sister	31
Miu	Kiya's pet Leopard	48
Cadj	Priest in Opar-wants to marry La plots with Oah	36
Oah	Handmaiden-granddaughter of Nedjam	33
Lareina Dubois	Lareina-Fr for Queen Dubois-Fr for From The Forest	60

Dramatis Personae

Modern Opar

Cha	Hunter and Ware's best friend	24
Eri	Lead hunter	45
M Frecoult aka Albert Werper	Chief villain in Jewels of Opar	38
Jub	Friend of Set leave Opar and die in jungle	27
Ho	Neteru used by Set to leave Opar and die in jungle	26
Maj	Lesser priest	41
Mitry	Chief military leader in Opar	37
Saba	Chief Sentry in Opar	37
Tha	Berserk Neteru	38
Tur	Hunter during reign of Mery	19

The Manyuema

Manyuema Tribe	Henchmen for Arab slavers/Greatest enemy of the Waziri	45
MBonga	Manyuema Cannibal chief *(Killed in Tarzan of the Apes)*	32
Maaka	Manyuema Chief badly wounded-gives kingship to Kasagama	45
Kasagama	MBonga's Son Last Chief of Manyuema	55
Cyprian	Cannibal witch doctor	49
Batia	Sister of Kasagama	57

Missionaries

Fr Martin Ober	Jesuit exiled to Africa leads church.school.hospital Friend of D'Arnot	32
Mary Veronica	Sister / Teacher dies of Malaria	32
Mary Catherine	Sister / Teacher	56
Mary Clare	Sister / Teacher / La's Favorite	56
Mary Clarise	Sister / Nurse	56
Dr DuPont	Doctor	56

Military / Museum / London

Colonel Albert Chard	British Base Commander on West Coast	48
Sir Frederic Kenyon	Director of British Museum	49
Tubok	Leader of Eastern Mangani tribe	46
Sergeant Major Robert Hopkins	Trains Waziri in modern warfare	48
Phillip Baker	Archaeologist assigned to document Opar for British Museum	54
Mary Davies	La's last nurse	60

Arab Characters

Abdul	Arab leader who kidnapped La	45
Abbas Salam	Arab leader who sells Cyprian and Kasagama into slavery	54

Supplementary

Intermediate Periods	Two in Egyptian History Total collapse Like European Dark Ages
	2181-2055 BCE at end of Old Kingdom 6th Dynasty
	1650-1550 BCE at end of Middle Kingdom 12th Dynasty

Time Line for Song of Opar

Character	Dates
Tarzan born	1888
Wazin born	1815
Wazin visits Opar	1840—1845
Set (Ayesha Father) born	1829
Mery (Ayesha Mom) born	1820
Ware born	1855
Ayesha born	1860 — 1900 — 1906
La born	1891 — 1970
La becomes High Priestess	1906
Kiya La's Sister born	1900 — 1925
Nedjam born	1825 — 1907
Oah (grand d of Wazin) born	1900 — 1925
May-at born	1890 — 1975
Fr Martin Ober born	1880 — 1940
Fr Martin African Mission	1908 — 1940
Events of Return	1908 1910
Events of Jewels	1913 1915
Events of Golden Lion	1921
Mery High Priestess	1837 — 1870
Ayesha High Priestess	1870 — 1906
La High Priestess	1906 — 1970
Dates for World War I	1914-1918
Dates for World War II	1939 1945

Timeline scale: 1800 1810 1820 1830 1840 1850 1860 1870 1880 1890 1900 1910 1920 1930 1940 1950 1960 1970 1980 1990 2000 2010 2020

Bibliography

Brueckel, Frank manand Harwood, John edited by Hanson, Alan and Winger, Michael. *Heritage of the Flaming God*. Spokane, WA: Waziri Publications, 1999.

Burroughs, Edgar Rice. *The Return of Tarzan*. Chicago, Illinois: McClurg, 1915.

Burroughs, Edgar Rice. *Tarzan and the Jewels of Opar*. Chicago, Illinois: McClurg, 1918.

Burroughs, Edgar Rice. *Tarzan and the Golden Lion*. Chicago, Illinois: McClurg, 1923.

Clayton, Peter A. *Chronicle of the Pharaohs*. London: Thames & Hudson, 1994.

Dodson, Aiden and Hilton, Dyan. *The Complete Royal Families of Ancient Egypt*. London: Thames & Hudson, 2004.

Farmer, Philip Jose. *Tarzan Alive*. Garden City, New York: Doubleday and Co, Inc., 1972.

Heins, Henry Hardy. *A Golden Anniversary Bibliography of Edgar Rice Burroughs*. West Kingston, Rhode Island: Donald M. Grant, 1964.

Mertz, Barbara. *Red Land, Black Land*. New York: Harper, 1978.